MW00955161

Passage of Vines: Clara

Patricia G. Kay

(Copyright 2019)

Passage of Vines: Clara

Passage of Vines: Clara

Cover Photo: Tero Estates *52015 Seven Hills Rd*

Milton-Freewater, OR 97862

Title Page Photo: Pioneer Park, Walla Walla, WA.

Photos by Patricia G. Kay

Dedicated to my adult children, who through their own lives have taught me, one must follow their passion. To my husband who has supported me through this journey with the clinking of wine glasses reminding me to never stop writing. And to the hummingbirds who feed outside my office windows, their busy tiny wings urging me to recognize a moment.

Patricia 2019

Passage of Vines: Clara

Passage of Vines

An Inheritance

I looked down at the specks of pedestrians, visitors, cars, taxis, shuttles, challenging each other's movements like a game board. Start, stop, slide to the left, move ahead of the shuttle bus, and allow the messenger biker to squeeze through, and watch the traffic lights robotically move from yellow, red, green. I love New York, and my job as Chief Financial Officer at the prestigious financial firm that offered me this landscape- windowed office, a six-figure income, a company car that waits outside my twenty-story condominium building each morning, and returns me after my twelve-hour day ends. I could see the Hudson River with commuter ferries between the steel fortifications of towering buildings, daring the sun to telescope a beam of light onto the shadowed cement blanket of mechanical and human journeys.

I followed the tiny drops of raindrops sliding down the outside pane as if they were on a playground slide. With my speakerphone blaring from my desk, I motioned to my secretary to come in as I finally responded to my family's attorney.

"Yes, Bruce, I am listening, listening like I do every week, and my answer is the same. I do not want the family Long House Winery. I do not want to move to Walla Walla. I know my mother would be disappointed, but I want only to sell it. Not only do I want to sell it, but I want to sell it quickly. If I must go to Washington I will, but only for a very limited time."

"No, Bruce, there is nothing I wish to keep from the house. I do have memories, but they do not need to be materialistic. Nothing can replace Mother, not one painting, piece of clothing, or glassware."

Later, I listened to Mom's cell phone message, a daily ritual replacing our past hour-long phone calls; a silent meditative moment to remember her, remember us, and push the guilt away from my heart knowing I was not there that final night, the night she died. For the past three years, I have flown from Newark Airport to Spokane, Washington, over 2100 miles each way. I took a small passenger plane that transported me 158 miles to the family winery in Walla Walla, Washington.

Mom's chemotherapy had been in Spokane, blood tests were at the local hospital in Walla Walla, and I was there with her every time except her last night when her Native American wolf spirit guided her away from me. I still feel the slight shiver in my chest when I speak her name; I think my heart continues to splinter with emotional shards of grief.

I will be returning within the week. Our family attorney had begun the lengthy process of selling the generation-old Long House Winery. He told me it was a simple paper process; he would handle the sale, and keep me updated with offers. He repeated several times that it should be a quick sale. The Seattle Corporation was eager to purchase the smaller wineries to merge them into a mega-production facility that could not only produce large quantities of bottled wine but also reduce the price of each wine.

Glancing at my calendar for the week after I returned, I smiled at my busy social events: two Happy Hours with my best friends from college, one employee retirement breakfast at Mazi's, shopping for a New Year's Eve dress, stopping by the shoe repair shop to pick-up my silver stilettos, and ordering my weekly food delivery from Lee's Asian delicatessen.

My assistant waited by my office door, telling someone in the hallway I was unavailable, as I had a plane to catch. Motioning to me, she handed me my briefcase and I walked through my private door down the back hall to the executive elevators where a company car was waiting in the secure underground parking garage.

After the flight, I stood on the dust-blown driveway of the Long House winery in my navy blue silk suit with matching stiletto heels. Brushing the fan-shaped dust circles from my skirt, I had no idea it would be weeks before I dressed again as a chief financial officer. I looked at the house where I grew up. The sprawling front porch, the upstairs windows aligned liked two eyes, the flowering arbor welcoming guests to walk through to the front door. The winery was opposite the house, solid brick red with a cement parking lot for guests. I gazed at the vineyards cushioning the house and winery with their purple and green shades of overflowing grapes bouncing in the afternoon wind.

As I began to walk, I remembered one of my visits when I saw the shadow of an Appaloosa walk slowly past the end of our vineyard, its head passing the Syrah grapes, its tail swishing against the Chardonnay leaves as the sun began to rise. No one was riding the horse. White circular body spots turned into shades of gold with each sunray. Slowly, the horse disappeared down the gravel slope leading to the Snake River. I often wondered why this horse appeared at the winery, at a time when I was unaware that I would have inherited the winery.

The horse appeared another morning after I saw a night bonfire pointing a thin finger of smoke to the cloudless sky.I remembered the horse appearing after Mr. Crenshaw Mildsgate, the corporate investor, had visited the winery. Crenshaw introduced himself as a wine magazine reporter as he stood in the Long House tasting room during an afternoon wine tasting. Crenshaw stood with his back to me, looking at the photographs of Great-grandmother, Grandmother, and Mother. Then he leaned closer to each frame, reading their history, my heritage. He picked up the flier inviting the community to the 125th anniversary of my family's winery, an event Mom had planned before she became ill. I remember the shudder I felt when he turned, looked at me as he folded the flier into a fan, waved it in front of his reddened cheeks, and lifted his glass to me.

The second time I saw him his black SUV had wedged itself up the dirt road that divided the twenty acres of vineyards, red grapes to the west, and white grapes to the east. From behind the arched doors of my winery, I watched him walk under the morning glory trellis to the house front door. He knocked softly at first, and then pounded his fists, rattling the stained-glass window, forcing the hummingbird feeder to swing in lazy circles. He brushed his red lathered hair away from his face, took off his sunglasses, held one hand over his eyes, and searched the horizon looking for me. Hitting the hood of the car with his sunglasses, he returned to his car, slamming the door shut, picking up his cell phone, and maneuvering the SUV away from the fence.

At first, he angled the car between the fenced front yard and the winery, turning the wheel sharply to avoid the lifelike, carved wolf holding the customer parking sign, and finally aiming the car directly at the winery. He looked surprised. He mistakenly hit the gas pedal, and the front bumper slammed into the wood-frame door of the Long House Winery. The impact caused a tremor in the winery walls and a slight swaying of the roof, and I can still hear the sharp slam of the winery door against the concrete floor. The oak barrels shook on their shelves and slowly ricocheted down toward my head.

I jumped from behind the door, leaped to the path leading to the tasting room, watching him pull away nonchalantly, unaware of the empty oak barrels he caused to fall and splinter on the floor. I was tempted to run after him and thought I should call the state patrol. I shrugged, resigned to the fact I may never see him again. I turned to look at the oak staves heaped like a pile of wooden rigatoni pasta under the domed skylight. Fortunately, they had missed the furniture, windows, and the boxed wine stacked on the wall separating the tasting room from the production room.

Today, I rubbed my hand along the winery door looking for any tell-tail signs of damage. The door was smooth, the cement underneath smeared in two shades of gray that covered the deep black marks from when the door had slid open.

Leaning on the doorframe, I realized once again, my struggle to accept my inheritance of this old winery overlooking a rolling valley of vineyards, the Snake River, and the Columbia River.

The Long House Home

I walked through the front door of the house after stepping over a newspaper. The house smelled of aged wood, the furniture covered with worn blankets, and the window shades pulled tight. I listened to a message on my cell phone, a sales call from a Seattle-based corporate wine company offering condolences regarding mother's death and in the same breath asking if I am considering selling the winery. The headlines of the local newspaper featured an article listing the most recently sold vineyards absorbed by a Seattle cooperative promising to return a profit to each winery by increasing production and distribution of the wines.

Exhausted, I looked up the stairwell and cautiously stepped up the wooden, concaved stairs to my bedroom. After reaching the top of the stairwell, I looked down announcing, "If I stay or leave you, dear stairs, you will need to be repaired, before someone is hurt."

I watched the pink skies ducking behind the jagged barriers of rocks to the sound of the coyotes. Falling into a deep sleep, I was jarred awake by the first howl, followed by the second howl and finally a chorus of sounds that bounced off the canyon walls. I heard their paws on the front porch after leaping up the four log steps. They shuffled back and forth, scraping the floor under the porch swing with their claws and pushing pots holding garden herbs with their snouts. After that, I made it a habit to sweep the porch every evening

Early in the morning, I stood in front of the mirror of my mother's armoire that had been my grandmother's standing hope chest. I slipped my feet into thermal socks that would buffer the inside of Mom's old, rubber boots. I placed my stilettos onto a shelf, grateful to hide my toes with their chipped nail polish. Standing in front of the mirror, I laughed as I stood in my cotton T-shirt, Mom's shoes partially hidden by the denim jeans coated in mud, probably leftover from her digging around in the soil of a vine.

I unpacked a crimson sequined dress I had worn at last year's Christmas party. I made a gap in the back of the closet for the dress and zipped the dress in a garment bag. My winery calendar was empty, with no plans for any parties, gatherings, or events to acknowledge a birthday, a holiday, or friendship. I realized quickly that I was the city girl who knew nothing about wine, who had season tickets to the Metropolitan Opera and front row seats at Broadway plays, with miles separating me from my former life.

It was only months ago I came to my mother's memorial. One hundred and fifty strangers, who had morphed into crumpled, wrinkled faces, weathered by years of the sun's thermostat came. I recognized a few who would come to the house when I was visiting mother, offering meals, taking her laundry to wash and hang outside on their clotheslines, infusing it with the smell of the evening breeze.

Each offered me warm support and whispered their sadness in my ears while hugging me, their finest bottle of wine held in their hands grasping crumpled tissues. I remember standing next to Mother's picture, accepting bouquets, watching people sign the guest book, and listening to their memories when the minister invited the guests to speak. I heard familiar words, "kind, helpful, generous, great laugh, made the best bread in town, grew a Cabernet Sauvignon grape that tasted like the inside of dark cherry."

One man stood up, took off his floppy straw hat, his pink bowtie clashing with his burgundy and green-checked shirt. "My name is Benjamin Thomas. Most of my friends and family call me Ben. I loved your mother. Oh, do not worry, Clara," he glanced at the crowd listening to their murmurs, "We never even slept in the same room, but I wished I could have just once unclipped her long black hair and watched it fall onto her shoulders. You mother was striking, Clara, and looking at you I think of her, I remember the times we would sit on the porch swing and watch sunsets."

"We had a simple love, but I wanted her to marry me and asked her five times. Why did I only ask five times? Well, when it came to be the sixth time and I started with my question she held up her hand and put her fingers over my mouth. Clara, she told me that night she was dying of metastatic breast cancer. It was the night my soul wept." He placed his fingers on his lips perhaps feeling her last touch.

"We sat on the porch not speaking but she never let go of my hand. When she did talk, she talked about you, Clara, and asked me to take care of you. She asked that our community extend ourselves to you from our valley homes. She just knew that with your education, your contacts in New Jersey that you would not die of breast cancer. She knew that you would find only the best medical care and you would be cured."

I listened to the sniffles and sobs of some women who sat in the front row fanning themselves with pieces of cardboard. No one paid attention to the chickens scattered through the vines, or the distant sound of the sightseeing helicopter that crossed the valley. I remember the sharp pinch I felt under my left breast, thinking it was my heart cracking in fragmented shards of sadness; surely not breast cancer.

I did promise Mom when she was having chemotherapy that I would see a physician in New Jersey, I would have annual mammograms. I realized all too quickly that muscles were straining from spending the mornings before the memorial bending, pulling, and cutting throughout the vines. Funny, how even with my daily visits to the gym, and hiring a personal trainer no weight I had lifted prepared my muscles for the tasks of hard-core labor.

Meeting My Mentor Benjamin Thomas

I can still remember Ben stopping by my winery days after I arrived. He wandered through the vineyard dipping his face into the green leaves and smelling the grapes. Once, he pulled out a small magnifying glass, examined a cluster of grapes, and put several on his tongue. He closed his eyes, chewed slowly on the grape, and nodded his head with a smile.

I stood under the trellis covered in ivory morning glory and greeted him. The heart-shaped leaves hugged the white funnel-shaped flowers that I had nicknamed angel faces with their wide opening blossoms. I noticed a slight limp in his left leg and his left arm tucked into his pocket. I knew at Mother's memorial that he held a small folder with both of his hands, standing secure on both of his legs as he spoke of mother. He gave me a lasting, compassionate hug when he left the memorial, grabbed the steering wheel of his truck with both hands, and waved good-bye with his left hand. What I saw this morning was not the same image of Ben at the memorial service.

I opened the gate for him. He followed behind, grasping the stairway rail with his right hand. I heard a small groan as he stepped up with his right foot first and slowly brought his left foot up with a sharp thump. "Odd, Clara. I woke a few days ago with my left foot feeling like it still

20

wanted to sleep for a few more hours. It has gone from a tingling feeling to no feeling. I was warned by my son to buy bigger boots. I think I cut off my circulation." I waited for him to sit in one of the rockers, cautiously sensitive to his physical changes. I watched him pause, focusing on his feet, hesitating for a moment before twisting his body around to sit with a subdued sigh.

Before disappearing into the house for two cups of freshly brewed coffee, I moved the wicker table to the right side of his chair to assure he could easily reach his mug. After the screen door banged against my shoulder, I yelled to him, "I just can't fix everything in this house, Ben. I do not even know how to hold a hammer or screwdriver. I just figured out how to unlatch the shears for the garden vines. I almost fractured a finger when they sprang open. I just do not know how I can keep this vineyard. I am a city girl."

When I returned with the coffee, I felt the need to expand on my statement. "Do you know what a city girl is, Ben? First, we hire people to fix broken pipes, we have a door attendant who welcomes us to our condominium building, and if I need my car, I only need to call the valet. I have a kitchen but I do not cook. I usually hire a catering company when I have small events at my home and," while peering over my coffee mug for emphasis, "I have home delivery of all my meals."

Ben listened, staring at my eyes. I found myself brushing the swath of black hair that had fallen over my forehead, the two braids hanging lazily over the front of my T-shirt. I fingered the ribbons that I placed at the end of each braid. I saved strands of ribbons from the wrapped flower bouquets at the memorial and cut them into three-inch pieces. I kept the ribbons in a wide canning jar next to Mother's picture and each day would pick two, assuring that the ribbon's color did not match. Shaking the jar, I would pick from the palette of shades of purple, light rose, pale whites, deep lipstick reds, and blushing pinks.

I inherited Mother's habit of saving braid ties. She had saved pieces of thin leather rope from my grandmother, who had saved leather from my great-grandmother. Mother would tie her hair in a loose ponytail with a tie, wear braids, or pull her hair back with a comb carved from elk bone. Ben placed his hand on my knee, saying the vineyard belonged in my family and he would make sure it stayed in my family. He winked and took the opportunity to emphasize family, several times. He spoke of his son who decided later in his life to attend Walla Walla Community College to study viticulture.

"Vindicult?" I asked.

"No, no, viticulture. He is a viticulturist, trained, and educated in understanding everything about growing grapes, making wine, and managing a vineyard."

22

I looked out at the vineyard, then back at Ben. "Really? Running this place requires an education. If so, I certainly am educated. Finance, statistics, project management all led me to my MBA. Sounds as if I just might be the perfect candidate: new graduate, mid-twenties."

Ben coughed, swallowed loudly, and put his coffee mug on the table. "Yes, you have credentials but not quite the same as my son. Let me just give you an idea of what he has learned: the anatomy of a grape, photosynthesis, grape growing, and the soils of the vineyard, chemical analysis of grapes, grape diseases, and expert wine tasting. His first year of college was a fine balance between a choice of beer bashes and wine."

"I would be flattered if you thought I had a twenty-two-year-old son, but my guess is he is closer to your age, early thirties. He owned a German restaurant along the Columbia River, well known for its Wiener schnitzel, and was a collector of beer steins. The rumor was that people traveled to his place to see his beer steins and take pictures in the room that held shelves of them. I think he had more than one thousand steins, often gifts from his customers."

"He told me he dressed in German lederhosen, short pants, and posed for pictures. I am embarrassed to say that he hired an accordion player for portraits. He is my creative spirit and like me, he has a love of wine. He grew up in a vineyard but I suppose his childhood memories are stomping in the grapes, drinking the grape juice in a wineglass, and dressing up as a bunch of grapes for Halloween. He took first place in the kids' division of the AVA."

I stared at the coffee grounds at the bottom of my coffee mug, missing the morning Latte Caramel Macchiato my assistant would place next to my office phone. "Wait, Ben. First, how was your son transformed into a grape costume, and second, what is AVA?"

"Ah, my student, I will give you your first lesson in grapes. We are in AVA or an American Viticulture Area or appellation community of grapes. Here in Eastern Washington over eleven AVA wineries grow and produce more than 85% of Washington grapes. Multiple state and federal laws must be met to qualify to be an AVA."

"I will give you a general idea of the basic concept. The challenge that some vineyards are facing is that if they are smaller, they could never produce enough grapes. I am sure you know of the corporate limousine filled with," he emphasized, "THE SUIT around in town. He is trying to buy and merge the vineyards into one single proprietor.

"However, none of us are entirely convinced this is true. We think he is creating a wine warehouse in Seattle where he will produce all of the wines cheaply. He is not welcome, but he keeps trying to become one of us. It is not going to happen in my lifetime."

"Now close your eyes, Clara, and imagine everything that you can think of that might be purple that was used to design my son's childhood costume. This is a test; I want to see how creative your mind might be."

I leaned back in the rocker, covering my eyes as if we were going to begin a game of hide-n-seek. "The first thing I see is an eggplant, a plum, a head of purple cabbage, grape juice in a carton, my purple knit winter hat, my crocheted afghan from Auntie Mary, the logo of my company in amethyst swirling triangles and the decorated cakes in my favorite Hoboken, New Jersey bakery, Carlo's Bakery. Am I getting closer?"

"Looks like I will need to give you a hint: party decoration." Trying not to focus on where my social events were or what they were about I answered, "I went to so many parties with hats, paper cups, tablecloths, napkins, and fancy drink stirrers." Pausing, I tickled Ben on the knee, "Of course, he was wrapped in a purple tablecloth. That still does not sound like a grape to me."

He began to interrupt and I stood up announcing, "No, I know, I know exactly; it was balloons. He blew up purple balloons and pinned them to himself or glued them or taped them?"

"Yes, it was purple balloons that we tied together and then pinned the string on his sweatshirt and pants. However, he refused to buy purple clothing. You will need to learn that

25

east of the mountains is red college football colors and west of the mountains is purple college football colors. Just make sure, when you are coming to a community event that there is not a rivalry game that day. I want you to be liked by our neighbors but I am afraid a purple knit cap or wrapping yourself in a purple afghan could set you back a few weeks."

Nodding, pretending to act as if I knew or in truth cared what teams played in Washington State, I asked him who participated in the masquerade costume extravaganza.

"I wish I could say it was my wife, but she died soon after Ben was born. I had an amazing crew of workers, migrant workers whose wives embraced my son. Ben is bilingual and attempts a little German sometimes. However, he is fluent in Spanish. With all his adopted mothers, he easily could have opened a Mexican restaurant. Their influence alone brought him closer and closer to his love of cooking. I never quite knew how tequila shots became part of his cooking classes but somehow he always found his way home after leaving their cabins"

"I am very fortunate to have the crew I have had for all these years. I now have fourth generation workers. I did not know their great-grandparents, but they certainly have stories to tell about this land in the mid-nineteenth century." "Clara, you are the curator of this vineyard passing through time, or should I say the passage of vines? These vines started with your great-grandmother and now have passed on to you. You hold your family in your hands now, their hands are now your hands, their feet walk with you, their eyes will help you see your grapes and their mouths will taste your successful wines."

I thought of my mother and grandmother, and my childhood in this house. My face flushed, my lips began to tremble, and Ben quickly changed the topic. He began to laugh, "I don't know what you drank in New Jersey, Clara, but I am guessing it was not beer and I am sure if you drank wine it was only for an occasion. Am I right?"

I smiled thinking of the wet bar I had custom-built to hold my vodka, whiskey, port, and brandy. The glass cabinet doors held drink glasses that I had discovered in neighborhood antique stores, all in different color rims trimmed in gold, etched glass, and solid bottoms bubbled in chunks of glass. "Well, you got me, Ben, I only drank wine when I had a business meeting, or I would buy wine to take to dinner parties. I must confess that when I stood in one of the corner delis in Times Square, I would stare at the shelves of wine and usually pick something that did not cost too much. I never liked red wine. I thought champagne was tolerable if I added orange juice, but I did like the sweetness. Tell me about your son, is he working for you now or is he still in school?"

Ben looked over the vineyards and chuckled, "He never married because his work took up too much of his

27

time. I am sure it sounds similar to your life. I would bet that you had long hours in New Jersey with work, commuting, and spending hours trying to buy a good bottle of wine. Tell me what you left behind, and who will be your first visitor from home."

I rolled my eyes not quite prepared to share all my life with my new friend. "I suppose there were several acquaintances. Several mistakes including the office romance, the married online fan, and the worst; falling in love with my best friend's boyfriend."

"I think most disasters came when Mom became ill and I was torn between work and returning to the winery. I felt like emotional predators were taking full advantage of me in a weak time of my life. I hope you did not have the same experience when your wife died."

I became silent for a moment while Ben lifted his cup to his mouth, caught a few caffeine drops with his tongue, and closed his eyes. I watched his chest rise and fall, and closed my eyes, remembering the night I fell in love with my best friend Jilly's boyfriend in the hot tub, how I attempted to blame my behavior on the whiskey, on my recent breakup with an office lover, and the stress of my job.

I listened to Ben's light snoring, closed my eyes, and returned to the memory of longtime friends sitting in the hot tub, drinking whiskey, and my friendship with Jilly. She and I always tested each other's recall, our first dance, the first time we kissed a boy, and showing each other our first menstrual blood-tinged pad. I remember Jilly asking, "Remember, Clara, how we had saved those pads, wrapping them in waxed paper and compared who had bled more? I forget who had more blood but I do remember we were gagging from the smell. I guess we should have had another comparison when we lost our virginity. You were first but I was not far behind you. Alex was pretty lucky to have laid two best friends a week apart."

As the three of us soaked in the hot tub, Jilly began to kiss her boyfriend's neck, dipping her finger in her drink and rubbing it on his lips. Leaning her back against the edge of the hot tub, she giggled as her boyfriend ran his tongue under her neck, slurping loudly. In a slurry voice, she said to me, "Things change, Clara; no more sharing."

Jilly asked me about my office lover. When I told her the romance had ended she gave me a sympathetic hug. With her bikini top tossed three drinks ago, Jilly pressed herself against my arm running her palm across my cheeks streaming with tears, "My Clara has a broken heart. My best friend is sad, and I am sad, too."

She jumped out of the tub giggling, "Me got to pee and not in front of thee." I remember her boyfriend Stephen moving toward me, his lips pushing on mine, hugging me and running his hands through my hair. We both knew we had emotional foreplay since the evening began, but I had no intention of anything else happening.

Jilly returned finding us embracing. Looking at us she whispered, "Well, I was wrong, Clara. I guess my Stephen was lucky too. Get out of my life, both of you; out of my life, now!" She grabbed the empty whiskey bottle, aimed at Stephen but threw it into the hot tub. I never saw her again, even after repeated emails, texts, and written letters to apologize, begging for her friendship.

I mumbled, "I am so sorry, I am so sorry. Do not be mad at me, Jilly." I opened my eyes wide hearing Ben's voice loudly saying my name; I wondered how often he had tried to get my attention. "Ben, I am sorry. I think I must have taken a quick nap. Please tell me about your wife."

"I will tell you my story after my wife died when I became the grieving widower. Probably not quite as exciting as life from New Jersey but it is a true story. I suppose what we are all about today is truth and tell. Just like one of those adolescent childhood games."

He repeated my name one more time, for reassurance that I was listening. Then he spoke. "Clara, it was the after-death vultures. The women who would stop by with their home-cooked meals and pies wearing perfume that lingered in my house, low cut dresses showing bosoms, tanned by our desert sun, and fingers that would attempt to entwine in mine."

"I can probably count on four hands, two toes, and one earlobe how many times I was invited to a dinner or when one would approach me at a wine tasting to explain something about my wine. Oh, sure, I went to some dinners, yes, I did ask some to dance with me at the valley wine-crushing event, but it never went further. First, I was mourning my wife, second, I was raising a young son, and finally, I was committed to my wines."

"I soon realized how quickly my responsibilities changed when I had to divide my time between my son and my work. Oh, he was never a problem, not even when he became a teenager. He did want me to take him to the cemetery weekly before he was driving."

"He would always place a bouquet of grapevines wrapped in a rubber band on his mother's grave. Once he started driving, he would head up to the mountains and gather wildflowers. With German in his blood, he would climb the boulders and cut yellow buckwheat that grew in the crevice of the rocks and pick the purple lupines at the bottom of the trail."

"I hardly had the time to hike with him but something always drew him to those plateaus especially at sunset. Sometimes he would tell me that he thought he heard his mother talking to him. I know you two have not met but you do have one thing in common with the loss of your mothers. Our community is changing. As the younger vintners emerge, those of us who own the vineyards are getting older and it becomes time to, how did I say it? Pass the vines on to the next generation, like you."

"I said it once, Clara, and I will say it repeatedly. The woman I wanted to marry, your mother, is now an angel, but I have a feeling when I do meet her again she will say yes to my proposal. I do have a bit of a social challenge. When I do meet her in heaven I think we are going to need to elope. I worry about the circumstance of running into my former wife."

"I suppose it does not happen, I mean how many angels do you think are wandering around up there? Sound like a silly old man, don't I? I will have to figure this all out before I head up there."

I responded quickly to his comment, "Ben, it scares me when you say something like meeting my mother. Do you feel ill? Have you talked with your doctor about your lack of feeling in your leg? I did notice that you do not use your left hand. Is that numb, too?"

Ben banged his coffee cup on the table, "Besides drinking cold coffee and teaching you about wine, why do I now have to listen to you analyze me? That will never do, Miss Clara. I can take care of myself. I do not need anyone to take care of me." He began to stand, shaking his coffee cup.

I fumbled for an apology saying, "I am sorry, please do not be angry. I think my mother's love for you just fell into my mouth; it was as if I was her voice. I will not bring it up again but you must know that I will worry about you. If you do wish to talk fine, however, if there is anything I can do for you just ask."

Grabbing the coffee mugs, I threw the cold coffee over the railing and moved quickly into my house for refills. When I returned, Ben stood at the end of the walkway. I balanced the mugs on the rail and walked to him. Standing near him, I spoke in humble tones, "I want to meet your son. Can we set a time or date for the two of you to come back to my home? I do not wish for our day to end like this. I am very sorry."

Ben turned slowly around, leaning against the trellis, "I do not want it to end this way either. I suppose now you have two things in common with my son; he nags me about my health, too. I say the same thing to him I just said to you but my words are not quite as female-appropriate."

"Yes, we will meet for dinner but not at your house, at our house. We will have another wine class so be sure and bring paper and pencil or use your New Jersey laptop. You will be quizzed this time by me and my son." He gave a weak laugh, took his right hand, and tucked his left hand in his pocket. Quickly I asked, "His name, what is your son's.

33

name? And I must bring something. I cannot just come empty-handed; we don't do that in New Jersey."

I could hear Ben's voice as he walked away. "We are just a generation of two, Clara, my generation, and his generation. When he was born, we decided he should take his mother's name, and my name is his middle name. His mother's name was Stephanie. His name is Stephen."

Waving his right hand, he finished his introduction of Stephen with a final direction, "One of my crew will pick you up at 7 pm. and bring some homemade bread. I seem to remember your mother baking bread; perhaps you inherited the baking genes? I must warn you, Clara, daughter of Clarish, I will be pouring red wine."

I shuddered when I heard the name Stephen again. I never knew much about Jilly's boyfriend except the rewards of his physical self in the hot tub. I remembered Jilly's boyfriend Steven's hands were smooth and manicured, not callused with dirty jagged fingernails like a vintner's hands. I stood on my porch, held the mugs, and stared at the Columbia River. I could see the smooth river rippling slightly when an occasional barge would ease past its shores or a pleasure boat would speed by, startling the white pelicans. I watched the pelicans along the plateaus, squatting, balancing on their orange legs.

Waddling they dipped their beaks into the shallow water for fish. Their legs and orange beaks were beacons that caught the eye of the local tourist or excited the bird watchers who, with binoculars to their eyes and pointing fingers, would shout their finding. I always wondered why their wings had black feathers brushing against their pure white body. Nature may have left them a tattoo, or perhaps it was a shield protecting them if they hid in trees or bushes.

Walking into my house the screen door slammed on my elbow, I told myself that I would ask Ben whom I could hire to begin to make repairs. I knew if I were to live in this fourth-generation house, someone would need to help me with the repairs. I glanced around the living room and with pen and paper began a list: priority, urgent, and necessary. I wrote on the top of the list in bold letters, FIND MOTHER's RECIPE FOR BREAD. Yes, she and I had made bread together when I was much younger.

House Filled With Memories

The living room was spacious, the hardwood floors shiny with occasional stains from wine or a lazy pet. The stone fireplace dominated the room by standing over more than six feet tall with small irregular rocks shaping its mantel. Several cracks were along the top where a nail had left its mark. The mantelshelf was pieced with different shapes of polished mahogany wood and animal bone. The tile-like pieces were sawed into thin slices and placed together like a jigsaw puzzle that spelled out the name of the winery: L-O-N-G-H-O-U-S-E.

Running my fingers across the lettered tiles, I remembered how Mother never put anything directly onto the letters. Candleholders were placed to the side, picture frames stood before the letters, and decorations sat behind or at the ends of the mantle. The hearth of the fireplace was pieces of multi-color marble resembling the head of a wolf. I grew up knowing that the wolf was one of the spirits belonging to my great-grandmother's tribe.

The corners of the hearth were broken and either dirt or the smoke from the fireplace smudged the face of the wolf. The fireplace was open with a grate to hold the twigs and logs. I sniffed the scent of swept ashes remembering how I sat inside the fireplace in the summer months after the winter shoveling of charred wood and ashes. I played pretend-cooking at a campfire. Mother would bring me a thick-breaded sandwich, lean against the side of the fireplace and hold the sandwich on a stick. I remember even with the summer months our home had a lingering scent of smoke and cedarwood.

Above the fireplace was a four-foot-high framed mirror, bordered in animal skins braided into ropes. When I was younger, the mirror, bolted tightly and leaning slightly to its side, was beyond my reach. Now I could run my fingers from the top corners, and across the bottom edge of the furry frame. Pictures of great-grandmother MaMinny and my grandmother Margaret stood like visual bookends on the mirror's sides. Both of my grandmothers had inkwell black hair, braided hair, and wore the familiar necklace, a cluster of wolf claws bound by a net of blue string. Smiling, I looked at the table next to the couch where my picture and my mother's picture still stood.

I remember facing the pictures together to kiss or placing my mother's picture in my doll buggy to take along for walks. Single-pane windows lined the front of the house, coated now with the aftermath of a windstorm: flower petals, twigs, and smashed bugs. Before the weather warmed, I knew I would replace the screens that looked like wire jack-o-lanterns with holes poked through from birds. I loved it when the evening breeze twirled around the house and the chatter of birds throughout the house. I was surprised to see that only one window opened in the living room, one in the dining room, and one opened partway in the kitchen after someone had lacquered all of the windows shut.

Closing the front door, I admired once again its stained-glass window shaped like an L with clusters of grapes pouring a stream of red wine into a wide-mouthed wineglass. I remember standing on my toes and running my fingers along the leaded beveled edges and announcing to my mother that I could read the letter L on my stained-glass primer. When I wished to annoy Mother, I would shout a different letter, call the grapes cherries, or even ask for a glass of milk just like the ones in the door.

The polished stained-glass window had no trace of dust or scratches from the turmoil of a windstorm that pelted dirt against the house. The entire window was made of one-way glass so I could stand and look out without anyone knowing I was on the other side. One grape cluster had a hidden peephole for me to look into the face that belonged to the knock.

I do miss the condominium butler calling me on my intercom with his slightly Scottish drawl asking Miss Clara if she were expecting her guest. My intercom sounded like a harp that preceded the butler's voice. I also had a camera where I could see who waited for me in the lobby. No one could randomly knock on my condominium door without my knowing who they were, which added to my sense of security in the city. Now I tap my fingers along the top of the L, feeling safe within this vineyard, this home, and this valley.

The dining room was to the right of the living room, part of the large open space. The table, made of planks of mahogany, easily seats twelve people, with two wooden carved chairs on each end and two long benches made of polished, halved logs.

The table shone from the sun coming through the windows giving a polished glow. I remember my mother explaining to me that the wood had been prepared especially for this table and it would never lose its shine. Now there was nothing on the table: no centerpiece, no flowers, and no leftover dishes. It stood stark. For now, I could not sit at the table because the last time I sat at the table it was with Mother. I sat on the porch with its wicker chairs or the couch, temporary dining spaces.

A saloon door parted in the middle of the doorframe leading to a contained kitchen. White cupboards lined the walls, a cutting board counter stood in the middle of the room, and a four-burner gas stove with a vent was opposite the door. The enameled basins of the kitchen sink were two feet deep and the water came from two faucets, hot and cold. I reminded myself to check the water heater and explore another location for a dishwasher. The thought of considering washing dishes or dirty pans was absolutely out of the question. My condominium had a top-of-the-line dishwasher that I rarely used because most of my meals were at local restaurants or delis. I do remember a few catered events where I entertained; I placed unclean dishes in the dishwasher and often forgot to turn it on. I tried to picture where a dishwasher could fit within the limited kitchen space.

I had to talk to Mom briefly. I looked up at the kitchen ceiling, "Mom, I am not domestic and I will try to not change the kitchen too drastically. If you remember, I rarely did chores, hardly ever cleaned my room, but I did love to hang sheets on the line with you. I would appreciate it if you would help me find your bread recipe."

Grease smears formed irregular patterns on the stove, the vent smelled like bacon fat and stains covered the butcher-block counter. Cast iron pans hung above the counter, large soup pots nestled beneath the counter, and thirty different knives rested in a block.

All the white cupboards had doors, but one row of shelves held all of the dinnerware, cups, glasses, and bowls. Under the lowest shelf, wineglasses slid into brackets, red wine glasses, white wine glasses, champagne glasses, and tiny port glasses. Each wineglass had a rim of green and purple, representing my mother's colors, the house colors, and the winery's colors.

The pantry off the kitchen had a washer/dryer apartment size unit. I remember washing a load of towels with my sheets and hearing the grinding sound as the washer shook. I learned that I could easily throw in a half basket of clothing but anything larger would require multiple loads. I quickly added a washer and dryer under the listed dishwasher. The floor tile in the pantry room was broken or missing. I noticed several holes around the laundry unit that may have been entrances for rats. I listened to recommendations of my office mates and brought several rat traps, a wasp catcher, and a dozen cans of bug spray.

Mother's bedroom was at the top of the stairs at the end of the hall, I climbed the stairwell stepping over stairs with caved-in boards and a railing that swayed when I gripped it. The second bedroom had a large walk-in closet, windows facing the river and vineyards, with a door leading to the bathroom shared by the third bedroom.

The bathroom had a clawfoot tub, which stood on a marbled pedestal overlooking the vineyard. It was elevated so that any curious binoculars would only see a head. I spent many evenings lighting candles, filling the tub with bath salts, and drinking glasses filled with whiskey. I placed my stereo speakers facing the bathroom door to assure I could hear the classical music, music that took me back to New Jersey and away from the valley. Occasionally, the howl of a coyote woke me, or the night rumble of farmer's aircraft crossing over the land. I would sit on the porch and stare at the stars for hours, recalling that when I worked late nights at my window-lined office, I never saw stars. I saw the evening skies dress into a nighttime ritualistic dark drape, the streets, the Christmas lights, the ferries never the stars.

The bedroom that shared the bathroom had been my childhood room. After college, when I moved to New Jersey, I left a single bed, dresser, lamp, and bookshelf; now a space for a future guest. The room had a window seat that rested in front of a floor- to- ceiling window, a favorite childhood spot where I watched Mother in the vineyard, or the school bus approaching from a mile down the highway, and counted the semi-trucks, writing down each of their names in a tablet. As I got older I would change my counting game to include farm equipment, and trailers hauling horses or motorcycles.

A small armoire held all of my clothes. The drawers that lined the bottom were filled with my craft supplies, coloring books, and my treasures tucked inside a coffee can. I recall shelves lined with books, baskets overflowing with outdated newspapers and magazines, and drawers holding boxes of puzzles, playing cards, and games. A hanging lamp made from a snakeskin hung over the bed its bulb shattered and the pull cord broke. One padded armchair with its pillow seat sinking had become a fort with stacked pillows, and ship's crows-nest to observe the valley with binoculars.

I noticed hanging calendars behind the bedroom door of Mother's room where a visual diary of harvesting days, irrigation days, and soil testing transitioning gradually to doctor appointments. Handwritten in January were the ingredients for weekly bread. I wrote each item on my pad, satisfied that I would be capable of making a loaf of bread later in the day.

Leafing through the calendars, I saw the appointments: the day of Mother's diagnosis, the day of surgery, and the first day of chemotherapy and the day her radiation started. Each week, each month, Mother's handwriting went from the sharp exact letters of the marker tip to scrawls or words that drifted from one calendar date to the next. On her last chemotherapy date, there was a giant smile, the head of the character looked like a cluster of grapes.

On her first hospital admission only a dark cloud with drops of rain. I looked closer at the smeared ink, blurred by human tears, mother's tears. I ran my fingers across the ink; touching a piece of a crinkled calendar page, knowing I had touched her tears throughout the years assuring her she would survive. Mother had always marked past calendar dates never forgetting to circle my first day of school, school open house, Christmas bazaar, Christmas vacation, Valentine's Day party, my birthday, her birthday, spring break, last day of school, summer camp, school clothes shopping, and registration for school.

I circled the dates labeled "chemotherapy" with my fingertip, remembering how Mother described her treatment plan from her oncology team as "big guns chemotherapy," trained to kill all the cancer cells invading her breast, her liver, bones, and lungs. Mother would call the little bombs her "fighters," equipped at blowing up anything in their path.

She wore a C on her shirt, a shirt I had custom made for her to wear during the cold months. A rose-pink thermal top with lace on the cuffs and the neck. The letter C was gripped in the mouth of a wolf with gnashing teeth challenging the world Mother had entered. Whenever she wore the shirt to the hospital, she would smile at the approving comments, return the high fives, or stoop for the children in the therapy suite to touch the wolf. "Oh no, he won't bite you; he is our friend. He is here to protect us."

I felt helpless while Mother battled cancer, and found a gift store in Lower Manhattan that sold sequined ribbons in shades of pink. The store never sold yards, only the entire roll. Leaving the store with two rolls of thin ribbon for $50.00, I had planned to tie them on the ends of my mother's braids.

After her first treatment, mounds of her hair floated in the bathtub, mother sobbed looking at her bald head. "I should have been a man, Clara." she had spoken between

44

sobs. "A man would not lose this much hair, he could wear a baseball cap, and no would care if his eyelashes were gone." I watched mother struggle with her appearance and ordered a wig catalog from The Hair Lair, an exclusive New Jersey boutique where all of the stars set up private appointments to purchase a wig made from human hair. I remember meeting secretly with the owner, Jessica, one night after work, offering to buy her dinner at a small Italian New Jersey restaurant to discuss Mother's needs. When Jessica suggested I bring Mother I clarified where Mother lived, why she had lost her hair, and the urgency of the wig purchase.

The New Jersey Italian oasis offered the best fettuccini, Alfredo, in town. While I waited for Jessica to join me, I sipped a Manhattan and watched an older couple at the next table holding hands, laughing, and giving each other tastes of their meals from their forks. At one point the older man picked up the woman's hand, kissed it with his marinara lips, which she returned by blowing him a kiss through meatball crumbs from her mouth. I wondered what it would be like to have a life where kisses still mattered, where a night out brought out the suit, tie, and a feathered net hat tipped haphazardly on a woman's head.

Mother never talked about her relationship with my father. Mother would just say he had left, her grandmother would say that he was worthless. I wondered if my life

45

would have been different if she had had another person to run the wine business, another person to face life's bumps, another person to stay at her side while she went through cancer treatment. I was the lucky one; I had two amazing women, my mother and my grandmother who protected, supported and loved me unconditionally. How I wish they were with me now.

I smiled at the woman whose chatter and giggle reminded me of my grandmother, Margaret, whose laugh encompassed an entire room, bouncing off the fireplace, circling the kitchen, and forcing me to fall over the back of the couch screaming with equal laughter.

I reflected on the last days my grandmother spent in our winery home, the home where she died. I remember Grandmother mumbling and tossing in bed when she could no longer walk when her eyes began to look like foggy marbles, and when her lips would no longer absorb the sips of water or cold washcloth pressed to them. My grandmother died of breast cancer, hiding it from my mother, yet unknowingly giving Mother the cancer gene that would end her life.

Mother told me how she screamed when she saw the first glimpse of her mother's condition, the black charred half-moon circle peeking over her peasant blouse; a reaction she later regretted for it forced her mother to retreat to her room and lock the door.

Mother and I would listen to Grandmother singing loudly for hours, banging the walls with her hands, and telling Mother to leave her alone to die in the vineyards. Mother sat outside her room and talked to her through the door, drew pictures of hearts with tiny messages, and finally slid a slice of home-baked bread with butter. Grandmother slowly opened the door, her face reddened by tears, her skin wrinkled from sunshine's pinches.

Mother held her, did not say another word, and spoke to her quietly. Grandmother refused medical care, refused to let any medical doctor touch her, and wished to stay home to die. I remember the day Mother announced that Grandmother ate three pieces of bread, and drank a half glass of warm milk.

I will never forget the day Mother forgot me, forgot to sit next to me while I ate a peanut butter sandwich cut into four little squares, or listen to me describe the new baby chicks that were running through the vineyard, or offer me hot cocoa to drink with a warm baked molasses cookie. I waited for the bedtime kiss that never came, held my pillow over my ears to muffle Grandmother's screams, and felt the wood floors vibrate as Mother walked past my room into Grandmother's room throughout the night.

As my grandmother's illness consumed her body, it left Mother exhausted. I remember her forgetting to call me for supper, and I depended on the coyote's howl to send me racing up the hill from the river to the front door before darkness. I waved to Mother hanging Grandmother's sheets and blankets on the clothesline. This was a time when Mother would not hide behind the sheets. She chanted my name, a game we played before Grandmother became ill. I understand now how emotions drown your thoughts and why I had become the forgotten child. With my heart still exploding with grief over Mother's death, I know what she felt as she anticipated the inevitable loss of her mother.

I wiped my eyes on the burgundy napkin, looking one last time at the couple as they prepared to leave the table. He pulled out her chair; she blotted her bright red lipstick on the cloth napkin. Odd, I do not remember Grandmother wearing makeup. I remember watching her morph into an unrecognizable figure, lying on her side with her cheeks hung loosely, her tongue moving back and forth over her lips, her eyes staring, glassy and immobile like the salmon that died along the river's edge.

The couple nodded at me and the woman touched my hair, smiling. I looked up at her, realizing that the woman's face was covered in layers of powder, her lipstick streaked slightly past the corner of her mouth. Her thick glasses were tucked into a tight cinnamon-roll whorl of hair, clasped in a seashell barrette.

Watching them leave, I thought of grandmother's braided long black hair. Tucked under the covers and laying behind her head, her hair glistened with little drops of moisture that slid down her forehead. Mother had asked me help and dab Grandmother's forehead very gently to take away the little drops. I asked if the drops meant that Grandmother's hair was crying. Mother nodded and hugged me, as I felt her tears sliding down my forehead.

Grandmother Margaret never talked about my grandfather. I knew Mother was an only child, originally growing up on a farm that was a two-hour truck ride away from the vineyard. She lived there with Grandmother, surrounded by a small orchard of apples. One day, Grandmother discovered that the vineyard was for sale from an auction notice posted at the local farmer's market.

After researching, she discovered it was the family property owned by her mother, MaMinny. No one wanted to tend the overgrown vineyard, or reenergize the soil, establish an irrigating system, or build a home. Smiling, I realized my Grandmother did, once she realized it belonged in the family heritage, and she was not going to let anyone take it away or destroy the vines.

I often wondered about the generations before my grandmother, single women who held individual inborn strengths and belief in their family traditions. I never knew if I inherited strength if self-worth was a gene that found itself in one's DNA if perseverance came from the mother or father's side. I was the product of three other generations. I also realized that I was different and did not inherit the desire to get my hands dirty, preferring to wear only designer clothes and drink hard liquor rather than wine.

I glanced down at my watch; the owner of the Hair Lair was late. I ordered another Manhattan and left my mind to wander to my childhood remembering when Grandmother died.

At my grandmother's memorial, my mother's house was filled with people from the wine community: the migrant workers, a priest from a local church, and families from the school I would be attending in the fall. I smiled, pretending to read the menu when I thought of the few indigents that lived along the river walking up the driveway holding a string of wiggling salmon. Grandmother's memorial was one of laughter, Mexican food, wine, and beer.

No one seemed to notice when I wandered away from the front porch sipping the last liquid left in the wine bottle. Sticking my tongue inside the bottle, I tasted the sweetness of a cherry, and spit out the few fragments of cork clustered around the neck of the bottle. I dipped my tongue into the Manhattan, pushing the ice cubes into the alcohol when I heard a strong voice; my guest had arrived.

"Hello, are you Clara?" I looked up to find a tall African-American woman standing, holding her briefcase in front of her sleek red dress. I stood, reaching out to her hand,

and invited her to sit at the table. I was startled by her appearance. She appeared as if she had just stepped out of the pages of a fashion magazine. Everything she wore matched her red dress: her earrings, her blush, her lipstick, her nails, the two bracelets she wore on her right hand, the tiny ruby ring she wore on the finger of her left hand, the single drop ruby necklace. When she smiled, her lips parted to show sparkling white teeth, with one tiny silver tooth on the lower left side.

Her voice softened, words bouncing gently as if to not disturb a sleeping child, "I am Jessica, the owner of Hair Lair, and I thank you for inviting me to dinner. I know this might sound unusual to you but I have never had a client meet me for food. Typically, I am the one offering champagne to my rich and famous divas. You told me briefly about your mother. I am very sorry for the journey she is on, but I must tell you that with your support and progressive medical treatment hopefully, her struggles will end in a saving triumphant." I watched her brush her hair away from her face, noticing the large-red globes that hung from her ears. "Thank you. I just could not come to your store now. I was just not ready to face what my mother is facing."

"Clara, it's fine; I understand. So, what are we drinking?" I lifted my Manhattan glass to her and winked, saying, "This is number two." Jessica ordered a glass of

Cabernet Sauvignon and I shook my head, covering my half-filled glass.

"Let me tell you about myself. I have been in business for fifteen years. I started as a hungry actor getting small parts in commercials, a few off-Broadway plays. That is when I realized, based on the audiences that came to shows, that women needed something for those hairdos. I mean, I might have been on the stage with those bright lights shining in our faces, but goodness I saw some ugly, and I mean ugly hair." She lifted her wineglass to me. I found myself giggling from both nervousness and the whiskey.

"I began by just practicing on some of the cast. We had plenty of time between rehearsals and slowly I gained a reputation as the Comb Queen. Following unlimited hair fluffs, twists, curls, buns, and locks one of the leading Broadway divas fronted me a loan. Here I am today, a very successful entrepreneur. How did you hear about me?" I moved my fingers across an imaginary keyboard. "What would life be like without the Internet? I mean, how did they research anything years ago? I am the descendent of a Native American great-grandmother and how did she figure out where the local store was where she could buy flour?"

"Out of all the choices for wig salons, and," I emphasized, "Jessica, there are many, I chose you because of your business name. Tasteful but cute, a smidge naughty, but specific in purpose, and the photographs covered with every gender model was truly the selling feature."

"Clara, they always say the cover sells or, in my case, the Web design. Your hair is stunning. I would have guessed you were Spanish or Jewish with your thick layers of black hair. I do see your type of hair here within the Jewish communities that have the gift of hair, hair that is luscious. Often they will come to see me for a shorter wig, or a shorter style that will not tangle or catch in some of their evening dresses that are rows and rows of rhinestones. Your hair must be similar to your mother's hair?"

We both ordered from the menu and I continued, "Yes, and I truly do enjoy my genes, the Native American gene. I constantly receive compliments about my hair and have to keep it a sensible length because my travel makes my second home an airplane. Flying is not too kind for kept hair, especially when I fall into a dead sleep leaning, drooling, and snoring on someone next to me."

"Jessica, your hair is amazing, equally dark like mine and may I add smooth without the frizz. You must spend hours looking like you do, and after a long day you are a perfect picture." Patting her hair, she took a glance at her face in the reflection of her dinner knife and continued. "If I remember correctly, you told me your mother lost all her hair after her first chemotherapy treatment, and that you live at a winery. Your mother travels to Spakan, Washington, for her treatments. Correct?"

I burst out laughing, almost spitting out my drink on Jessica's hands. "Yes, you have it almost right. My mother owns the winery. She is the third generation. Yes, she has treatment far from our community in Spokane. It's pronounced "spoke," like the spoke of a bike. I am paying her to fly quick trips and minimize stress for her. Some of it we use as a write-off; allegedly that she is on a marketing trip, which is a white lie but it will help in the end. I mean my business is numbers so I am always looking for some loophole.

"Well, my dear although I am still a little confused I assume that you live and work here?"

"I live in New Jersey and work in Manhattan for the finance firm of Brogshaw and Associates where I am one of the senior vice presidents. I have been traveling back and forth to Washington since Mom's diagnosis. We are all we have as far as a family. My grandmother died about twenty-five years ago of metastatic breast cancer. The Cabernet Sauvignon you are drinking is one of the grapes we grow in our vineyard. I doubt if our wine made it this far, but perhaps someday you will be drinking one of my mother's wines."

Jessica pointed her fork at me, "Well, had I known, my dear, what your occupation was and who you worked for I might have charged you more for your wig. Your firm has quite a reputation within the finance world and I do have several clients from there. Do you wish to purchase a wig tonight as a surprise for your mother or wait for her decision? Do you have a photograph of her that may help me make some recommendations?"

I leafed through my purse to find the picture that I carried with me everywhere. I handed the small circular framed photo to Jessica. "Here she is; Clarish, my amazing mother."

Jessica touched the glass frame, moving her finger down across the glass. "She is beautiful and she could be your twin. Do you ever wear your hair in braids?" I shook my head, no. "Not sure braids would work in my world, but Mother wears her hair pulled back and clasps it on her head. She has several elkhorn hairpieces that hold her thick hair easily. I took the picture with braids to give you an idea of the original length of her hair."

"What is she wearing now?"

"She alternates among silly cowboy scarfs that you see in every Western movie and, I must add, everywhere around where she lives. Somehow, the scarves will slide off her head unless she wears a hat, so she has been alternating between a baseball hat, a cowboy hat, a gift from a friend, and a little chic beanie I bought her from down the street. She is truly struggling with her image right now, and why I think a wig just might boost her morale."

She unlatched her briefcase with one long enameled nail after quickly punching in a code. She brought out two catalogs bound in soft leather covers and began to leaf through the pages while holding Clarish's picture. "No, this one is too long; this one is too curly, this one is way too short but would require hardly any care. Well, this one is a possibility." She handed the catalog to me, reaching to the side of the candle, the sugar bowl, and the salt grinder.

I looked at the model wearing a thick black wig that hung to her shoulder, a sweep of bangs across her forehead, and a hairband holding the hair away from her face. I shrugged, "I don't know. The headband is not my mother. She does like to tie her hair in leather bows handed down from her great-grandmother. Would this wig work if she wanted to pull her hair back?"

"Absolutely, and with a wig cap, it would be secure if she chose to style it similar to how she normally does. I think it would be perfect for her, especially now that I can see what she looks like. Now, I know you know this decision must be hers but you certainly can lead her to this page. I am assuming she does not want to change the color or the length; she is perfect the way she looks. A completely new look is my daily mantra in my shop."

I leafed through pages, the catalog divided into hair color, hair length, shapes of faces, and there were actual diagrams of eye positions and size of ears. For a moment, I felt like I was looking at a catalog of most wanted villains.

"Jessica, how could anyone resist your wig selection? I am curious to know how many people come in with a family situation like ours."

After blowing a kiss at Mother's picture, she handed the frame to me, holding my hand for a moment. "In truth, not many women clients are on journeys. So many cancer treatment centers have free wigs that women will choose, or they will wear designer scarves, or the bravest of the brave will go bald."

I nodded, "I have seen a few women throughout the city bald, but so amazingly beautiful. Even without the hair their makeup and jewelry are the focus after you get past their beautiful smiles. My mother's skin has taken on a gray hue and I think I will need to find what I can do to give her some color without the makeup she dreads. It seems as though chemo just sucks the skin dry."

I noticed she had grown quiet and ended her story quickly for fear that she had shared too much sadness. She put her hands on the table, spreading the fingers across the linen tablecloth and tapping the bottom of her wineglass. "I have something I should share with you, Clara. Just give me a moment. "She put her fingers to her forehead and slowly pushed at her hair. Nudging it discreetly, she exposed part of the top of her head that was completely bald. She watched my mouth drop slowly as she glanced back and forth at the diners who had long ended their meals and were prepared to leave.

Jessica took a deep breath and, returning to her deeper voice, said, "I am bald, and I am a man. I have been a cross-dresser for as long as I have owned my business. My success is the other men, my true divas, who come to my shop and pick my wigs. My wigs are for those clients who want to be exquisite, who want to live in the world they hide from others and who walk proud, with confidence." I was speechless as I listened to Jessica's voice deepening into a fluid baritone. "My world, my client's worlds are all the same. We are on a different journey and wish to be accepted, not noticed, not islands in a crowd saturated only with false normalcy."

"Your mother is like me. We are of the same cloth, wishing to hide our secret identity. Clara, I need you to say something and if I am not who you thought I was, I will shake your hand and leave. Please do not fear me. I am still Jessica."

I put my hand on hers. "I loved you from the moment I saw you. I loved every sensitive, kind word that you have said during dinner. You are not only the owner of a wig shop you are a soul, a sip of a late harvest wine that offers sweetness to all you meet. I am now honored that you will have a small part of our life, my mother's life. I would have never known but there was a part of me wondering how a woman like you could be as compassionate as you were. You were not selling to me; you were grasping my pain and slowly transforming it into a solution that would work for my mother. Jessica, I thank you for being here tonight and for being part of my mother's new path."

She slowly pulled her wig down, checking that her bangs fell slightly above her eyebrows. "Keep the catalog until you pick the wig with your mother. Send it back or come to my shop and return it in person. You are a charming woman, Miss Clara. Whenever you get tired of that amazing Native American hair you can sell it to me to make a wig."

"I have to confess that when I saw you, my little lace undies found themselves pushing up because you just excited my tucked in self. Darling, I was worried I just might jiggle the table and cause our glassware to slide off."

I turned crimson, imagining her lace panty. Laughing, I tossed my head back. "All right, Miss Jessica, I now have an image that will stay with me for a day or two. Again, thank you, and if I ever decide to trim this hair, I will certainly consider your offer."

Jessica stood, reaching out for my hand, I remember noticing immediately that the grip was stronger, firmer, and the same strength my male clients offered on initial introductions. "Until I hear from you; take care of yourself, your mother and, goodness girl, take care of that hair. "I watched her leave trailed by glances from the wait staff.

Clarish, My Mother

When I returned to the winery the following weekend, I did not tell Mother about Jessica's life, only that our meeting was full of laughter and that I had promised to send Jessica a bottle of Cabernet Sauvignon. I sat with Mother, watching her open the catalog cautiously, peaking at the first photograph, closing it, and sighing. Finally, she stopped at each photograph of shorter hair. I reminded her of how she enjoyed putting her head on top of her head with the leather twists. Whenever she shook her head and mumbled about the cost, I would scratch out the price with a thick, dark squeaky marker.

I would gently try to sway her thoughts. "Please, ignore the price, Mom. This is about you temporarily wearing a wig so you do not have to worry about people looking at you. And if I see you wearing that cowboy hat again, I just might have to throw it down the slope and into the Columbia River. That hat does nothing for you, nothing."

Mother touched her bald head and reached behind her to put the hat on. "Clara, it is not just any cowboy hat, my friend Ben gave it to me. You will need to meet him someday. He owns a winery about five miles down the road. He has been my friend for a while but I just have had to push him away now. I mean, what he saw in a bald woman who had a missing breast, a scar darker than some of our grapes, and a future that remains unknown, I will never know."

"Do you understand, Clara that I cannot give up this hat; that it would like giving him up? Well, I am giving him up, but the hat is like a little promise ring. That is exactly what he said to me, "Promise me you will wear this hat and I promise you that I will stand right next to you now and tomorrow." She began to cry, crumpling the hat against her, its straw edges rubbing against her skin, now tender from her radiation.

I put my arms around her, let her cry, and felt her face burrowing in my long hair. She ran her fingers through my hair and pulled on the ends, repeating, "I miss my hair, I want my hair back. I don't want someone else's hair."

After a cup of tea and a short nap, Mother found me sitting at the dining-room table tapping the keyboard quickly on my laptop. Approaching me quietly from behind, she hugged me around the shoulders gently. "Sweet daughter, I am through having my tantrum, my feel-sorry-for-Clarish time is over, and my selfish words like, I am the only person who has been diagnosed with breast cancer, is silent. What happened to the strong me? What happened to the me that fought with that awful district office land surveyor, who tried to tell me that the lower acres of the vineyard did not belong to me?"

"Do you remember, Clara, how I brought out the records from your great-grandmother and put them on that obnoxious surveyor's big oak desk? I did it, Clara, remember, without an attorney, just me," and, she paused, "Well, Ben came with me and brought one of his workers whose grandfather knew more about this land that I ever knew. I can still fight, can't I, Clara?"

I watched her slip into the chair across from me and crumpling her head on the table, sobbing. I sat and listened without trying to stop the tears. The oncologist had told me to expect this emotional reality when treatment started, after surgery had ended and when the physical changes began. I found myself swallowing gulps of shock watching Mother's appearance dwindle into a stark figure. I tried to tempt her with some of the street corner hot dogs from Manhattan, or bagels seeping with cream cheese that I had stuffed into my carry-on bag, but Mother would only nibble.

Mother finally pushed the catalog across the table and pointed at the wig she wanted, the same wig that Jessica had thought would work for her. I grabbed my cell phone and quickly dialed Jessica's shop. She picked up and said she missed her little lace panty tease, and I burst out laughing.

"Jessica, I am sitting across from my mother in her dining room. She has had a very tough afternoon picking a wig and we are both so excited that she picked one."

Jessica's voice became subdued and she responded in a baritone whisper. "I am so sorry Clara, for being a total horse bottom; I mean, what I was thinking. I am sure this afternoon has been equally hell for both of you. Please accept my apologies. May I talk to her, please?" I hesitated for a moment listening to Jessica assure me that she was there to offer support. I handed the phone to Mother who shook her head, no.

"Mom, just talk to her for a minute, please. Just one minute."

Mother took the phone, holding it in her palm that had wadded, wet strands of tissue. "Hello, this is Clarish, Clara's mother." She grew quiet, nodded her head several times, mumbled yes, yes, and finally broke out laughing. "Oh, you are kidding me! You are bald, too. You were born that way. You have worn a wig for fifteen years and no one knows you are bald. Your wigs are magnificent."

She became quiet again and began to cry. She dipped her nose on one of the tissues hanging from her fingers. "Oh, Jessica, how kind of you to worry about me, but please don't. I just know once I get through this chemo and radiation that I will have more strength. Hey, I understand you were enjoying some Cabernet Sauvignon with my daughter."

"That is one of our grapes growing for over one hundred years. Do you believe it, Jessica? We have a vineyard older than your age, Clara's age, and my age."

"No, I will not take a trade for a case of our wine for one of your wigs. I saw the prices on your wigs and one case of wine will not even come close to the one I have picked." Pausing again, she winked at me. "Oh, a trade and a monthly case of wine for one year? I think it might work if my daughter agrees. She would need to be the one delivering the wine to you, or we could easily ship a case monthly. I have some very special 2000 Cabernet Sauvignon that I only keep for special occasions, but I think this would qualify for a special occasion. You are what made it a celebration."

"You and Clara make the final arrangement and we will send the case first thing tomorrow. When do I get my wig?" Pausing again, she laughed harder, "Yes, we have roads in Eastern Washington, and yes we have highways not dirt roads for horses. Just ship it to our postbox and we will pick it up at the end of the week." Smiling, she looked at me, "Sure I will take a before-and-after picture and send it to you." Nodding her head she finished the call by saying, "Thank you, Jessica, whoever you are, you have made my day. Thank you."

Mother handed the phone to me, stood up, and pretended she was tossing her imaginary hair back. Raising her arms to the ceiling, she walked toward the photograph of her mother on the fireplace mantle. "Mother, I am getting a wig by the end of the week. Walking up the stairs, she looked back at me, "Clara, I am going to check out my leather ties."

I knew that Jessica had heard the announcing voice. "Are you there Jessica? I guess you were a hit!" I repeated her name but the phone line was silent. In tiny hiccup sobs, Jessica began to talk. "I do not need a case of wine every month, send me empty bottles, but I must make this wig for your mother. You bought my dinner the other night, so let us just call it even. Hug her for me when you get a chance. She is a jewel, Clara. Love her, love her every day."

I put my head down on the table, perpendicular to where mother had been minutes before. Placing the phone to my mouth I said to Jessica, "I do every moment, and thank you for being my girlfriend aka boyfriend."

I hung up when Mother reappeared wearing her cowboy hat and carrying her mason jar filled with the leather ties. Spreading the ties on the table she asked, "Which should I wear first, second, next week, next month, next Christmas?"

She looked at me and wrapped her arms around me again. She brushed her hands across my wet face, "We will get through this, Clara, we will. We are the strong women, the third and fourth generation of strong women. I love you, sweet daughter."

Mother only wore the wig for two months when her weakened immune system could not fight pneumonia. She died in a Spokane hospital, alone. I had talked to her earlier in the day. She was laughing, joking, and telling me the staff wanted to know who her hairdresser was. "The wig is such a big hit. Jessica did such a good job. I spend my whole day talking about Jessica, about how I am trading our estate Cabernet Sauvignon as monthly payments for the wig, and where the leather ties came from. I am fine, Clara, I just have a cough; a little rough for the moment. Call me tomorrow and we will make plans for when you come home next week."

"Oh, Clara, I found the sequined ribbons that you left me. Clever you." She began to cough and wheeze and I could hear her gulp a liquid. "Yes, I found them hiding under the leather ties."

"I have my hair in braids tonight because I keep sweating so I do not want my new wig to get all soaked. I have a pink, sequined ribbon tie in each of my braids, my dear daughter, Clara." She began to cough loudly and I could hear someone tell her to end the call so she could take a nebulizer treatment for her lungs.

"Sorry, I need to run, Clara. I have a date with oxygen. My friend Ben is going to visit in the morning. I think he is planning to sneak up a bottle of Pinot Noir. Maybe I will share it with the nurses or just maybe he and I

will drink the entire bottle. Call me tomorrow. Love you."
Clarish, my mother, hung up, and I never heard her voice
again.

I realized my frequent travels to Mother had left me
in an emotional desert, thinking, remembering, and wishing I
were not in this house by myself. I spoke to the empty house.
"Enough. Who is watching my every move, Mother and
Grandmother?" I shouted up to the long beams that held the
triangular roof. "I am doing just fine, thank you, and I will
let you know if I am going to keep this winery or sell it. You
two will be the first to know."

I began to climb the steps to my bedroom and saw the
chandelier sway slightly. Odd, I thought, no windows are
open, the front door closed tight because of the dust storm.
Smiling, I blew a kiss at the chandelier, waved at the picture
frames on the mantel, and whispered a soft, "Love you all;
stay close."

I stood in front of Mother's armoire trying to pick
something to wear for dinner, not a date, I said, just a wine
class and friendship. I had grown so weary of wearing jeans
and cotton sweatshirts that quickly saturated with sweat even
with the best deodorant. I looked forward to dressing up.

I found my long, suede green skirt with the matching
patchwork vest filled with quivering, square and half-circle
shapes, resembling a starlight sky. Looking at my hair, I
remembered how Jessica had wanted to buy it, wanted to

make a wig from it. I slowly unraveled each braid, watching my hair strands frizzle, forming a mound of curly strands on each side of my head.

Brushing my hair, I watched it touch my shoulders, an even cut from my hairstylist. I moved my head from side to side, pulled it behind my ears, crumpled it in my hand, and placed it at the top of my head. Finally, I let it fall and smiled content with my dinner look. The smell of baking bread wafted up from the kitchen, along with the sounds of Dvorak playing on the radio.

Starting to relax for the first time in days, I stepped into the claw-foot tub, feeling the running water soothe my tired body. I looked out the window next to the tub and watched the waves of a dust storm fan across the valley, sweeping the tops of the grapevines, sprinkling particles on the top of my car, and pushing against the house. Slowly, the dust began to lift, raising itself like a blanket shaken from a bed.

I saw that four cars that had stopped in the middle of the highway, each a geometric angle to the next, each barely visible through the cape of dust. People jumped out from the cars, running to each other, looking back at the storm that had departed like an unwanted guest. No one had been hurt; no cars were touching, only two horses stood in the middle of the road covered with a veil of dust.

Through my binoculars I saw one horse begin to run away, the other horse stood still, its harnessed head moving back and forth swinging its rope. One of the drivers approached the horse slowly, reached it with his extended hand, and gently grasped the rope. I saw the horse nuzzle the man, an appreciative gesture, or an assumption that through its dust-covered eyelids; it had found its owner.

I watched more cars enter the highway, moving slowly, rolling down windows, and calling to the isolated cars. The drivers and passengers gave a thankful wave and continued to brush off their windows, headlights, taillights, and tires. A truck pulling a horse trailer drove up and ran to the horse. The driver hugged the horse, patted the man holding the rope on the back, and slowly led his horse to the trailer. I cannot imagine that politeness or kindness in a traffic jam in the streets of Manhattan.

The Columbia River was silent. No boats, no barges, and I focused my binoculars on the shore where pelicans gathered. Only one stood on a boulder, statuesque, without moving its head. I waited, and finally, the bird slowly pulled up its wings, once, twice but did not elevate. I worried that it had broken a wing or leg and told myself I would check on it tomorrow on my weekly hike.

The warmth of the bathwater and the silence of the day after the dust storm helped relax my body. I closed my eyes until I heard the timer buzzing from the oven. Grabbing a towel, I ran down the stairs, hopping over the broken stairs and placed the golden bread covered with sesame seeds on the tiled hot plate. I lifted it to my nose for one reassuring whiff, opened the window, and placed the hot plate on the nearby counter.

I heard the cuckoo clock and knew it was time to get ready. I grabbed my purse and cell phone, running back up the stairs. My luck in navigating the steps was gone, as I did not miss the sunken step. I caught my foot in one of the fractured boards and was thrown against the rail. I could feel the ripping of my skin on my toes and my left ankle twist slightly.

I turned, eased myself on the next step, released my clutch from the rail that wiggled slightly, and slowly lifted my foot from between the two boards. My foot looked as if an animal with a giant claw had grabbed it, peeling the skin from my toes to the end of my foot. Surprisingly, there was no blood, but the bruising forced the skin to begin to bubble in red streaks.

I held the wall, limped down the steps, and filled a towel with ice. I bumped my foot up the steps, sat on a small stool in front of Mother's armoire, and began to put on my makeup. Talking to myself, "I do not have time for this. I have work to do tomorrow, I have a dinner date, and I have a first impression with my future winery manager. Do not be stupid, Clara, just take your time. You are not in New Jersey, no need to rush, no meetings to attend, nothing you must do." Correcting my self-admonishment I said, "Yes, there is something you need to do; you need to fix the stairs."

I stood to dress, feeling the ache in my foot and held onto the bedpost to keep my balance. When I looked down, my foot had swollen to the size of a small balloon inflating slowly. I tried to fit my foot into my rhinestone sandals, then suede flats but felt like a failed Cinderella. Not one shoe could slide easily over the swelling.

Tossing shoes over my head, I pulled out the chenille yellow slippers that Mother wore when I was a little girl. My foot slid easily into the open toe covering, my suede skirt covered the yellow fluff. I buttoned up my vest, brushed my hair back to expose my two silver circular earrings.

I heard the honking truck and slowly edged down the steps, limped to the kitchen, and wrapped the bread in a brown paper bag, tying it with ribbon. I stood on the porch looking at the truck that waited for me at the end of the walkway. The hood leaned toward the front fender. The truck looked like a bad Easter egg dipping with blues smeared into yellows, greens streaked across orange, and purples dotted with splotches of red. The enormous tires lifted the body of the truck three feet off the ground. The truck's sides pushed out as if an enormous load squeezed itself into the bed of the truck; however, the truck was empty. Waiting by the passenger door was a boy around sixteen who waved eagerly, calling my name. "Miss Clara, I am your driver this afternoon. I look forward to taking you to Mr. Ben's and Mr. Stephen's home."

I began to descend the steps and felt the sharp pain in my left foot. I waved and called, "Please, come and help me."

The driver waited, leaned against the truck, sipped a drink from a glass soft drink bottle, and waited. My cell phone rang and I heard Ben's voice. "Everything OK, Clara? Did Thomas the Fifth arrive to pick you up?"

Smiling I repeated the name, "Thomas the Fifth?"

Ben laughed, "When you get here you will meet all of the Thomas men. Thomas One and Maria liked my middle name and adopted it for the first child, including the final fifth child. But where is he and where are you?"

I explained where I was standing, and how I could not get down to the car without help. Within moments, I heard a ringing phone from the truck, and Thomas running toward me.

"Sorry, Miss Clara." Thomas the Fifth jumped up the three steps. Taking my arm, he walked slowly down the steps with me. The walk from my porch to the truck seemed to have taken more than five minutes as I slid my chenille slippers through the thin layer of dust. Arriving at the truck, the sweat dripped down my face offering a trail for my carefully applied mascara to streak down my chest.

Thomas reached up to the elevated truck door, let out a moan, and stood back trying to decide how I was going to climb into the truck. He jumped into the truck, dialed the phone, and spoke Spanish in a rapid, nervous, pre-adolescent voice.

He started to run around the truck, look down at the driveway, speaking on his phone, to the repeating, "No, No, No." He hung up, looked at me, and mimicked with his hands a driving car, pointing down the road.

I repeated a gracious thank you and motioned to the porch. He helped me up the porch and I sat in one of the rocking chairs. I pointed to the house and mimed a glass of water. Thomas immediately understood, left to go to the kitchen only to have the screen door hit him on his backside. He looked at the door, winked at me and I could hear him opening the refrigerator, cupboards, and finally returning with a glass of water.

"Thomas, please, you too." I pointed to the empty soft drink bottle he had in his back pocket and waved to the house. "Please."

He returned with two bottles of soda, a leftover piece of bread crust, and a handful of cherries. Smiling, he sat on the top step when again I said, "Thomas, please," and pointed to the chair next to me.

He looked taller standing in front of me, his hands filled with bread and cherries as if he had had a successful trick or treat night. He bowed and sat in the chair. I wanted to sit, not think of my foot, and would have considered a pain medication but feared that I would not have been able to take a wine class, and drink wine with the effects of a codeine tablet floating in my head.

Twenty minutes later, Ben pulled up in a convertible BMW, deep red with no resemblance to a dented, worn truck. He approached me using his cane. "Hey, I have one good foot and you have one bad foot so we should make a perfect team this evening. I left Stephen at home cooking and searching our first-aid kit for an icepack for you."

"Come to my home, Miss Clara, daughter of Clarish," Ben spoke to Thomas who had returned after leaving the empty soda bottles in the kitchen, tucked another slice of bread in his shirt pocket, and wiped his chin streaked with cherry juice. He smiled at me and took my arm and they walked me slowly down to the car.

I noticed that my bright-yellow slippers were slipping and the ribbon from the loaf of bread had unraveled. Ben held the door open for me after pushing the front seat against the backseat edge. I slowly eased my left leg, sat, and brought my right leg in. Ben noticed the yellow slippers and he blushed.

"I remember those slippers, Clara. Your mother wore them outside in the evening when we would sit on the porch waiting for the sunset. Sometimes she would rest her feet in my lap, and I would take one slipper off at a time and massage her weary feet."

"This was before she became ill when she would walk up and down these vines checking on her precious grapes. Her grapes will become your grapes too, Clara, I just know they will."

Ben easily turned the car around, waved to Thomas, who followed. "Short, twenty-minute ride, Clara. Our winery is located near Bennington Lake. Younger days of life allowed me to hike every one of those trails for years. Stephen and I hiked every chance we had to explore this amazing valley. Are you a hiker, Clara?"

"Are you asking before I tore my foot up today or just for today?" I laughed, rubbing my arm on Ben's driving arm. "I think the first time I tried it, one of my stilettos broke and I rode piggyback on one of my coworkers back. Also, before you ask yes, it was the married one. I do plan to check out an injured pelican perched on a bluff by the river. I saw it with my binoculars today after the dust storm. If you know of a trail I will check it out tomorrow."

"Perhaps Stephen can help you with some trails, or he could recommend a valley contact that might head out and check out the bird before tomorrow."

We both were silent, Ben enjoying what was familiar, and I absorbed the valley that spilled into the Columbia River. The pain had increased and I closed my eyes, feeling the wind against my face while keeping my foot immobile. Occasionally, Ben would describe a river, or a historical offering of the boulders, the Native-American fishing, and a promise to show me where the first vine planted by my great-grandmother stood. He began humming along to the big-band sounds that came from the radio while the Blue Mountains offered a blanket of orange, pink, and goldenrod by the sunset.

Startled, I opened my eyes when Ben shouted, "Damn it, I almost hit a coyote. Why do they think they can just jump in front of cars? I mean, I remember years ago when I hit a deer up by Snoqualmie Pass. It was an innocent baby fawn following its mother, sadly ignorant of cars. I think Stephen was in elementary school and he stood next to the doe in shock."

"He kept telling me to pick it up and take it to the doctor to make it better. He was throwing paper towels on the cement to sop up the blood and he was yelling at the police officer to call someone quick, and he did not stop crying until we reached home.

"When he and I talked about the fawn after his mother died, I remember something he said." Ben paused and shook his head. "I remember these words although it was so very long ago. He said, "I guess you could not just pick up mother either, and take her to the doctor to make her better.""

"You must have some coyotes or wolves around your place, Clara because your mother and I would hear them. I do think they keep their distance. Sometimes I think the noise of the windmills frightens them. Stay alert and constantly aware. I would suggest that you not consider any poultry. Unfortunately, chickens adopt us all the time. I think they favor the dirt around our vine roots. Please understand I am not trying to tell you what to do, I just wish to be your guru for the short term."

It was my turn to get angry. "There you go again, Ben, throwing out random statements about the length of your life. Well, I just might be the most stupid student you have ever had and it might take me twenty years to learn this business. So what are you going to do if I don't graduate?"

Ben grew silent. "Clara, I meant short term because you will eventually be learning from Stephen if you chose to hire him as your winery manager. I will change my role to become the official taster and of your wines."

I wondered how I ended up in this BMW, with a throbbing foot, a loaf of bread wrapped in a crinkled brown paper bag, and mascara that had now formed perpendicular lines from my neck to the top of my vest. Makeup, I thought, my makeup. I pulled down the visor and was pleased to discover that except for my lipstick that had paled from the glass of water, the mascara had dissolved on my face. Even my hair looked as good as it had earlier in the day.

I relaxed in the car seat and watched the mounds of hills slowly hide in the clouds evening shadows. Tufts of tumbleweeds and grass dotted the landscape as if nature had left pimples to pop into desert flowers in the spring. Nothing here resembled New Jersey. I strained my eyes, searching for anything taller than the windmills lining the hills, resting, unmoving silhouettes quieted by minimal evening wind, but no giant structures appeared.

I was curious about the windmills if they grew weary trying to keep up with the dust storms afraid to spin their two arms right off. I looked at roads that disappeared into the hills, dirt roads often lined with shrubs, some with a hanging sign announcing a ranch.

Fences provided the framed border to define the land that belonged to the farmers and wineries. I wondered how my great-grandmother survived in this vastness, how she knew east or west, and why she decided to plant those first seeds not far from the river. Cows started their nightly ritual lining up single file, like children returning to their classroom, and lumbered toward their stalls.

Ben finally put on his turn signal, announcing our arrival at his winery. I noticed the tiny lights threaded through the bushes, followed by torchlights that lit the snaking road climbing the hillside. Occasional pickup trucks were scattered among the hedges. I wondered where Thomas the Fifth parked his truck.

He pointed to several houses behind the hedges. "That's where part of my crew lives, the official bachelor pad. Several crews have children and I have provided them with bigger homes behind these homes. We just had another baby born. It is quite a celebration here when another family member comes into the community."

"Our women do not perform hard labor in the vineyards. I always find plenty for them to do around the house. Now I must remind you that the smaller houses out front are for bachelors, and I do not want you wandering around there alone. They would not dare touch a guest of mine but they can embarrass you. Promise me that if anyone offers you a donkey ride you will say no. Why you may ask? Well, we don't have any donkeys."

Ben began to slow the car. I noticed the reflective sign that said "raccoon crossing." The next sign read, "beware of running children," and the final sign warned that the road belonged to serious sippers. He turned the car sharply and I faced the estate, shaped like a moon, divided into two horizontal halves.

Lanterns lined the brick flower boxes that acted as a natural barrier between the driveway and the house. The lights lined the arch and two flags hung limp in the breezeless nights. Ben commented, "United States flag, Mexican flag, and I suppose we could put up a New Jersey flag if it would make you feel more at home."

The gap between the two halves allowed him to pull the car through large, secure gates and into a courtyard. Feeling the bumping in the tires, Ben explained that we had left the cement and were on cobblestones. "We imported them from a demolished villa in Italy. You will see them better in the morning."

Morning, I thought, why morning. I needed to go back home tonight. Two great Danes ran up to the car barking, whining, and running in front of the car. "They won't bite. The white is Chardonnay and the black one is Pinot. Reach into the glove compartment and grab a couple of treats to give them before you step out of the car. I emphasize "before you step out" because if you wait until you stand, well, they will most likely put their paws on your shoulders and lick your face until you give them a treat." Ben pulled the car into an expansive garage where three other sports cars rested.

Pointing to the back door he said, "You only need to walk through those doors and a tunnel will take you to our winery and tasting room. The driveway we came up will take guests to the winery when they follow the signs. Before, you and I came through the house gate, a secured gate. I asked Stephen to leave it open until we arrived."

"We do worry about unwanted animals, unwanted guests and, occasionally but rarely, my crew like to bring their parties closer to the house, which means that someone does something stupid like throw glass bottles at the pillars, or worse, use the flowers for their bathroom."

With a big sigh, Ben continued. "I have to call a meeting. The crew boss has to present the mistake and defend the crewmember who is likely related. I have never had to fire anyone, but I have punished crew."

I asked, "Punishment from you must be by stoning with corks or being dragged by the imaginary donkey down the hill?" I became aware of the brightness of the lights, almost as if we had driven into a white balloon. Ben stared at me with a weary but patient look. "I simply withhold their wages for one day. No one here wants to lose wages that are not just for themselves. The money they make is sent back to their families in Mexico."

"I know that you will hear stories about the immigrant population in the valley but every rancher and winery created their rules and regulations for their staff. I truly have never had a problem but I am sure you understand that because you have a human soul, like your mother. They know I am the boss. They know they can come to me with questions, and they know I will try to help."

"They live here rent-free but are responsible for their food and personal needs. Most women are amazing, talented tailors. If you ever find the need for any of their talented work, I will introduce you to our housekeeper who will be happy to help you. You will see their work throughout the house from embroidered table clothes to lampshades and carpets woven by their ancestors.

"Perhaps their biggest challenge is health care. Multiple clinics and city medical schools have started mandating rural health practice as part of physician training. For anyone to come here and live, to learn a new language, and treat basic health issues--it's no moneymaker for the new, eager doctor. We have several nurse practitioners, one whom I am sure you will meet shortly."

I did not say anything, assuming Stephen's girlfriend was one of the practitioners.

I opened the car door slowly, hoping that Ben would help me out of the car. He sat staring at the white walls and he nodded slightly. "Ben, Ben, are you all right?" He smiled and mumbled into his shirt, "I am fine Clara, daughter of Clarish, I am just weary. I missed my afternoon nap to be your limousine driver. Wait; let me help you out of the car."

He stood, leaned against the car and patted Chardonnay and Pinot. The garage light flickered on and off for a moment, and a side door opened with a figure of a man standing dark against the backlight of the house. "Stephen, I need your help, and our guest needs your help. Take your pick. I promise you she is much prettier than I am."

Meeting Stephen

I watched the shadowed form move closer to the car into the light. My eyes locked on him; curly blond hair, clean-shaven face, wearing a white T-shirt, jeans, and a waist apron. He had flung a towel over his shoulder, and a smudge of sauce was resting on his chin chiseled with a small indentation. I smelled his cologne when he opened the door and reached for my hand. Neither of us said a word, neither noticed that Ben was on the other side of the car shoving dog biscuits into the dogs' mouths so their barking would not ruin the moment.

Stephen lifted me slowly from the car, standing close to offer balance. I felt the hair on his arms rub my bare arms and felt his hands grip my waist, "I suppose I should introduce myself, or do you allow all strange men to help you out of my father's car?"

I looked up at him, at his white teeth with one tiny silver cap, his green eyes that glowed in the light and his long eyelashes. "No, I only let men help me out of BMWs; I can normally get myself easily out of a pickup truck, except for today."

"Well, I am Stephen, Ben's baby boy, cook, winery manager, and the proud owner of the cars you see in the garage, which I must add Dad took without my permission.

The other cars, known as "the collector cars," appear rarely except during wine events. However, please do not let our cars impress you; please let my cooking impress you. Lean on me. Let me help you."

Stephen looked over at Ben who was grinning so widely he was acting as if he had just drunk two bottles of Pinot. Winking alternating from eye to eye, he clearly was showing Stephen his approval of me. I began to walk and realized that my legs had cramped from the ride and my foot had swollen to the point that my yellow slipper was balancing at the end of my toes.

My slipper fell off and Stephen smiled. "Looks like our princess has lost her slipper, Dad." With those words, he took my arms and placed them around his neck, and slowly lifted me. His hands were smooth; his fingers that took my arms were slightly calloused. My head rested on his shoulder, my lips rested on his neck. "Not now," I said to myself, "not now. You cannot nuzzle, you cannot lick, you cannot even taste." There was no doubt; I wished I could have done all three.

Stephen walked to his father. "Come on, Dad, I have room for you to lean on me. Let's just take it slow." He gave a quick command to the Great Danes to lie, and they walked slowly to the doorway. His father walked in first, hitting his cane on the floor. He disappeared beyond the kitchen and landed in a recliner chair near the fireplace.

Stephen stood at the edge of the kitchen looking through the fireplace shared by both rooms. "Clara, you need to lie down and elevate that foot. Do you wish to go elsewhere before I put you down?"

I nodded and whispered the bathroom in his ear, his perfect ear. Stephen carried me through the living room, through a tiled arch and through a painted door with irregularly shaped letters that spelled baño. "Now just be patient for a moment, let me get you inside and I will wait here for you."

When Stephen put me down on the marbled floor, he kept his hand on my waist for a moment, brushed my hair from my face, and I wished he would never move. He looked down at me one last time, pointed to the door, and repeated, "I am right outside. One flush plus your voice and I will return."

I sat on the toilet, my bladder bursting and competing with the size of my foot but I could not force anything from my body. I cannot pee with someone standing outside the door in a regular situation but now I have this amazing man waiting to scoop me up when I flush. I reached to the sink to start the water in the sink and heard his voice, "Clara, I need to step away from the door for a moment; I think my sauce is burning. I will be right back. Just wait. Don't move."

I waited to hear his sandaled feet move away from the door and finally filled the toilet with hours of urine, one hidden gasp of gas, and flushed the toilet. I stood, took one glance in the mirror, and called his name, "Stephen, I am done." Hearing no response, I slid my hands along the painted walls decorated in bright oranges, blues, and greens. Giant flowers in terracotta vases lined the walkway to a house with a red-tiled roof.

Opening the door slowly, I heard Stephen laughing with his Dad and a female voice. I thought she was probably his girlfriend, the nurse Ben said they were planning on calling for my ankle. I have no doubt she is probably a dazzling blonde-haired woman like him, has breasts falling out of her halter-top, with a tan, a glowing desert tan. I called again, and when he did not respond I began to hop between walls, pressing my hands on their cool tile, until I reached the living room.

I saw Stephen in the light, his back to me. I noticed a tiny tattoo on the back of his neck, letters, a heart maybe, or perhaps it is just a familiar wineglass. The nurse was half the size of Stephen, cropped short gray hair and she wore a long black dress similar to a religious group.

Ben immediately saw me. "Stephen, you have left her stranded." Stephen turned around moving quickly to me, lifted me, and laid me gently on the leather couch. "Clara, this is Estavia, our community nurse, family friend, and lover of wine. Estavia, please meet Clara, someone I just met someone Dad has fallen in love with and she greets you with a banged-up left foot, maybe a twisted ankle."

I felt the softness of the lambskin pillow under my head, felt Stephen slowly lift my foot onto two pillows, and cover me with a soft throw that felt like cashmere. Facing Ben, I listened to his conversation with Estavia sharing, with an excited voice, the birth of the latest baby in the community. Ben defined me as Clara the daughter of Clarish. Estavia immediately came to my side.

"Your mother, your beautiful mother was loved by all. Everyone knew her and everyone wanted her to know them. She was involved with our clinic in so many ways. I cannot even count the number of times she would send baskets of bread and jam to give away to the patients."

"Once she drove down to the clinic with a box of blankets she had sewn for the babies. Now they were not fancy, just two pieces of fabric with a lining of quilting sandwiched between, but she had made them in the colors of their culture. They were so bright in shades of yellow, red, and green. The families would come into the clinic and sit in the waiting room that resembled a still painting, with mothers holding babies, sitting in a circle of chairs, and patiently waiting for us."

"Sadly, some of their waits lasted two hours due to our limited medical team. Some brought lunches; many brought other siblings, transforming the waiting room into another oil painting of picnicking mothers and children. However, there was no stillness with so many children's voices and cries."

"Occasionally, your mother would just come and play with the children. There was the time; I believe it was around the Day of the Dead celebrations when she came dressed as a clown. I suppose she could have even worn the more familiar skeleton costume and the children would have had the same giggles and smiles when she appeared. Oh yes, I cannot forget that she kept our candy bowl filled with suckers. That bowl never went empty."

"Perhaps one of the first calls we got from her when her illness began to weaken her was her apology that she could not bring suckers that week. However, by the miracle of websites, she had a box shipped."

I interrupted briefly, "I must ask the current status of the candy bowl today."

Estavia's hands had begun to move slowly over my foot. "Well, it could use a little refill. Now, tell me as I squeeze the toes what hurts, what aches, what makes you want to kick my hand." She slowly moved the toes back and forth, twisted the foot to the left and right, and pushed the foot down, and using her palm pushed the foot up. Her hand was half the size of my foot and felt silky.

"Nothing is broken, but this swelling is impressive and you do have quite a puncture hole here from either the

89

wood or a nail. I do have to ask when your last tetanus shot was. The floorboards of the houses around here are old. Who knows what creatures lived under there munching on your mother's bread. Are you a baker too? I must say that the resemblance between you and your mother is a gift for all who loved her. You look like her, except we rarely saw her hair down like yours."

I moaned, "I have not had tetanus for a very long time. I actually cannot remember if tetanus was part of my barrage of needles before my business trip to Dubai. That trip was more than ten years ago, so my answer is I do not know. Thank you for your kind words about my mother. I miss her every day and miss her more since I have moved here for the short term, living within her house, walking the floors she walked and baking bread in her kitchen. Everything remains as it should, everything is still hers."

Estavia reached into a leather pouch she had laid on the floor. "Short term? I don't understand. I assumed you were here to continue the legacy of your family's winery. Last time I checked there is nothing short-term about growing grapes, and bottling wine."

She raised the syringe, rubbed the alcohol on my arm, and gave me the injection " I would like to see you at the clinic when you can drive, but if your schedule gets to crammed with meetings I can always make time to see you."

"Just so you know, I do not accept health payment from the wineries, I accept wine. You have one of the best Cabernets in this community. I think your mother had plans to enter it in a competition for our AVA, but I am not sure if she ever completed that dream."

Stephen was the first to speak after he uncovered his eyes, hidden from the needle that had pierced my arm. "Short term? What are you saying, Clara? You are here to sell the winery and to return to your home. I do not even know where your home is, or what you do, but you are here now and that winery belongs to your family. You are the fourth generation. You cannot get rid of that winery. Dad, tell her she can't sell the winery."

Ben had nodded off to sleep again, this time with an empty wineglass in his hand that hung over the side of the chair. Yawning, he commented, "Stephen, Clara and I have talked, and she is in a dilemma. She has a very high-status job in Manhattan, lives in a condominium with a door attendant, and never cooks. "

"Hmm, let me see what else I can tell you about her. Oh, yes, she knows nothing about wine. She prefers whiskey, and when she does buy wine, she buys colorful labels and the cheaper bottles. Did I miss anything Clara?"

Stephen noticed me turn away for a moment, clench, and unclench my fists as I felt the pressure of the tetanus shot.

"Clara, this evening is almost like home. I was your doorman tonight, you are not cooking dinner, and we do have a premium whiskey that I would happily pour on some ice for you." He glanced at Ben.

Estavia finished her conversation with me in a quieter tone, picked up her leather pouch, called for Chardonnay to walk her out to her car. "Here are my reminders: ice, no walking for a couple of days, and keep it elevated. I will have one of Ben's crew swing by to pick up some crutches. Just return them when you are through and please do not be shocked if they look like they are handmade and carved from an old oak tree."

She walked over and hugged Ben, looking at his limp arm. "Ben, I have been watching you. I want to talk with you privately and get an idea of how we can get you looked at in Spokane. Not now, but I will be back in two days. I will check on you and Clara. Ben, I will not listen to you say no, or hear you say you are fine. I will see you in two days; both of you."

She left, not saying anything to Stephen, walking in an affirmative waddle that carried her through the kitchen, out the side door, and through the garage door that Ben had left open. Stephen watched her from the security camera. She climbed into her Volkswagen bus, turned on her lights, and slowly backed out until she could drive around the circle.

I pushed up on my elbows, looked at Ben, and back at Stephen. "I certainly will appreciate dinner tonight, and my second wine class, but I cannot spend the night. I do not have a change of clothes or a toothbrush, and I am sure I did not lock the door of my house."

Stephen smiled, "It's all been taken care of, Clara. I sent Thomas the Third with his wife to your house with instructions to gather some clothes, bring your laptop, phone, and lock the house. I apologize if their entering your house would upset you, but Thomas the Third is like my brother. I trust him and his wife as if they were family. You can sleep on the couch, close to the bathroom. It's for two days, Clara, and then we will evict you."

Stephen returned to the kitchen, began to drain the pasta noodles, and toss the salad, clicking the salad tongs against the metal bowl. "Bread, where is the bread?"

I shouted from the couch while resting my foot on the glass-topped coffee table secured on a half oak barrel. "On the floor of the car, Stephen, hopefully not mangled." Between the glass and barrel were assorted corks haphazardly touching, as if to serve as tiny pillars supporting the glass.

I heard the back door close and Stephen returned quickly. I heard him tearing the bread in chunks, laughing, and opening the refrigerator door. "Butter, where is that churned butter from one of our crew?" He peeked through the fireplace, "Clara, would you like a glass of whiskey or some of our Pinot Noir?"

I leaned over to see his smile, noticeable through the fireplace adjoining the living room and kitchen. The flames of the wood danced on his face like a golden beard. "I would love some penny."

With those words, Ben threw back his head, dropped his wine glass in the magazine basket, and shouted with a positive affirmation, "Clara, our new friend Clara, we must enroll you quickly in our wine class."

I heard Stephen talking to someone in Spanish, heard the dishes placed on the dining-room table and the strike of a match. I saw the dining room dim as the chandelier above the table glowed from the candles. Ben limped to an oak cabinet and slid out one of the drawers. "What music would you wish to hear tonight, Clara? Stephen has quite a collection that has taken over my country and rock sounds."

I stood slowly, holding the couch arm that was as high as my waist. "I do like classical music and prefer a violin or cello. However, I prefer your voices during my wine class and no distraction from the music."

Stephen stood at the door of the dining room while their housekeeper moved behind him placing dishes on the table. "I will be serving tomato pesto pasta with thin slices of beef. Our salad is fresh heirloom tomatoes, thin slices of mozzarella made from the cheese shop in town, and basil grown in our herb garden. Only, and I repeat only if you clean your plate, will you be given a slice of lemon cheesecake with one of our late-harvest Rieslings."

Stephen walked slowly to me as he spoke, and waited for me to find a stance that gave me a small sense of independence. I tried to balance myself, but he reached for my hand.

"Clara, you cannot walk. Please let me help you, just for the short term."

He lifted me into his arms, tilted me gently to the side, walking into the dining room that had floor-to-ceiling windows. The deep dark sky flickered with the night's stars, and a moon faded behind one of the clouds. "Tomorrow, you will see our vineyard from here. The windows are one-way. You can admire our grapes, but none of the grapes can see you. I would, however, wish to introduce you to them soon."

Stephen placed me in a high-back, upholstered dark-wood chair covered in an embroidered cotton motif. "You are sitting on the fabric work of one of our crew. She has embroidered all the chair coverings, the table runner, and the valance above the windows. Each holiday we will hang banners down from the ceiling in our home and the winery. Dad and I love color, festivities, and bringing people into our home."

Ben had found his place in the middle of the table that sat more than sixteen people. Stephen sat opposite me at the other end of the table, further away than I had wished. "Clara, I would like you to meet Maria. She has been with our family since I was a little boy, and her sons work with us." Looking at Maria, "Maria, this is Clara. She owns the Long House Winery, and I know you must remember her mother."

Maria spoke fluent English. "Miss Clara, a pleasure to meet you. My family knew your mother and grandmother. My grandfather, who recently died at 110 years, actually knew your great-grandmother in his younger years. He would often sit and tell us stories about her. He told us that he used to pick grapes off her vines but we think he was not telling the truth. My sons Thomas Two and Thomas Three will show you where the first vines were planted, and with more vines, the vineyard grew."

"I will help you tonight and I can sleep in the room by the kitchen if you need my help. We seldom have women in this house, so I would just enjoy talking with you."

Maria placed a salad dish before me and left quickly, returning to the kitchen. She paused and turned around to look at me; winking, she blew me a soft kiss. I smiled and thought, "I have a new friend, a female friend. How I miss my friends back home."

I pushed the tomato around the olive oil and remembered the salad I had with my friends at a tiny bistro in lower Manhattan, celebrating an engagement and a divorce. I remember we ordered two bottles of Barbera wine, one for each friend. I will have to ask Ben where the Barbera grapes are grown in Walla Walla.

I had known my friends for more than ten years, some from high school, and some from college. My move to Manhattan halted appearances at any showers or celebratory parties because I realized my weekends had become as busy as my week. Everyone had planned the dinner for months, teasing each other with their new life changes, coordinating flight schedules, hotels, and agreeing on one Broadway show.

One friend flashed her diamond ring around the table, only for the other friend to blurt out her impending divorce between gasping sobs. The table became hushed listening to her pronounce that her doomed marriage was the result of her husband leaving her for another woman. "Don't women know, don't women understand that there are plenty of men in this world, so why should they pick the married ones? Does this idiot realize that he will not be able to offer her the same comforts once I am out of the picture because I am going to make sure he is penniless? Two children, we have two children and ..." She began to cry again.

"And listen to this, sweet friends, one on the way. I am pregnant. After all, these years of trying to get pregnant, after adopting our sweet, precious twins I am pregnant. She swallowed adding, "I am not sure the baby is my ex's."

I remember how we all just stared at her, and silence swirled around the table. No one knew what to say. The waiter stood patiently waiting for our orders. Two friends only nodded, pushed their chairs back, and left the table. Two more friends left with the excuse they needed to find the bathroom, which left her and me.

I folded my napkin ends forming a tiny triangular shape. Shrugging, I stood, walked to her, and kissed her head. "Take care of yourself, the baby, and your children. Find a place for your anger because you need to love now. Three little hearts need your love."

Choking on a piece of basil, I allowed the memory to drift away and listened to wine pouring into my glass. I looked at Ben and Stephen, pretending to have been listening to their conversation. I stared at my wineglass, checked out my reflection in the window, and in a haughty voice asked, "Who sits at this table if you do not have many guests in this house? This room is amazing; it is right out of a magazine. Do you always have glowing eyes outside your windows staring back at your guests?"

No one either heard me or chose to respond, so I continued, "The music, where is it coming from?" Stephen pointed to six colored tiles on various walls. "Speakers, we had buried within the walls. All the speakers are on for the moment but often we will dim the sound just like lights when we have conversations with our clients."

I nodded, and tears rolled down my face "Ben, you are playing my mom's favorite violinist. Did you know?" Ben nodded quietly, "Yes, but I did not play this to sadden you; I thought we should invite her spirit to dinner. I raise a glass to Clarish and her daughter Clara, our new friend."

Wine Class 101

I reached for my glass and brought it to my lips. Ben tapped his fork on his dish.

"Ready, Miss Clara? Time for your first lesson. Please, just look at the wine and tell us what you see." I saw Stephen looking at me, and feared that I was going to flunk my wine class by saying words, not in the wine dictionary. I held the glass up to the candlelight. "I see a very deep color, the color of a royal robe worn by one of the kings from my fairytale books. By tilting the glass I can see a little light shining through, and I definitely can see the reflection of the candle flames. Is this where I put my nose into the glass and take a whiff?"

Ben smiled, "I never quite knew why people do that and sadly the novices have had to wipe off the tips of their noses from the splotch of wine after diving in for a scent." Stephen sat back and waited for Ben to continue. "Excellent. A perfect description of a red blend, this blend of grapes includes Malbec, Syrah, and Merlot. I am going to continue to talk, and you tell me when I have said something that is not familiar. To introduce you to wine is our pleasure and to your advantage, so please do not be embarrassed."

"I hope you, unlike my son, will learn a good bottle of wine. Stephen's introduction to wine was a truck ride to the river with ten of his high school classmates and a case of our wine. Fortunately, the wine was newly bottled; it was a very young red blend."

I looked longingly at my glass, pretending to be staring at the color but in truth looking at Stephen's eyes. "Red blend like the carafes of wine I drink in the Italian restaurants?" I wanted to tell them about the Barbara wine I had had with my friends wondering if it was a blend, but I did not want to interrupt Ben.

Ben continued, "Blends are just that: several varietals of grapes that we have blended to create a specific flavor, taste, color. Producing blends is the best part, often created by trial and error, followed by repeating the same blend annually. Tourists will often choose a pitcher of beer and pitcher of soda for the children, rather than a local wine, based on cost. However, I do not want to mislead you, because some of our blends can be costly."

I held up the glass, ran my finger along the gold edge, and stem. "These are special wine glasses. There must be a story behind them."

Stephen mimicked my actions by rubbing his two fingers down the stem, watching me the entire time. I found myself blushing but did not look away. "These are gifts, drinking vessels from clients around the world. Occasionally, a customer trained in glassblowing will make us wineglasses, again, as a gift. I know that you are probably not ready to tackle Washington's big city, Seattle, but a world-class stained glass artist, Dale Chihuly, lives there.'

"We have a glass room in the house that I will show you when you are comfortable walking. The room is secure, cameras, special codes, and a lock on each cupboard that holds a display. We treasure these gifts. These wine glasses are, as you have already defined, royal."

"Dad met the Pope at the Vatican more than fifty years ago over lunch. He introduced the Pope to our wine, not the wine offered at Catholic services but wine for the Pope to savor in his private quarters."

"Clara, I must give you a little history of Prohibition. Catholic churches were often exempt from alcohol limitations because of the rituals performed at their service. It often took an authoritative signature from a physician, but the wine was available to the parishioners. During a religious service there is something said about the body and bread; I think the body is the wine." He looked at Ben, laughing. "Perhaps, where we got the term 'full-bodied' for wine." I began to tip my glass back and forth hoping to signal that I wished to move onto another wine. I finished my salad. Maria came to remove our plates and place an empty soup bowl in front of us.

The large bowl was painted orange with tiny replica cacti around the edges. Between each cactus was a cluster of grapes. I looked at the inside of the bowl before Maria poured in the soup and saw dates scrawled next to the initial. Maria smiled, "Made from our community, Miss Clara. Every artist deserves recognition though it might be hidden by a ladle of soup."

The strong scent of onions and beef broth filled my nose. "French onion is one of my favorite soups. I know you did not know it was my mother's favorite, too. I do believe this dinner was cooked before my unexpected arrival." Maria whispered, "Leftovers from Stephen's poker game last night."

Stephen looked at me tilting his head to the side, inquisitive, and wondering what Maria had said to her. I just smiled and soon realized that his head tilting would be one of my favorite memories of him.

Ben took a deep gulp of his soup, the parmesan cheese hanging from his spoon as if it were a rubber band stretching from the large crouton to his spoon. I was not sure if I should eat the soup or wait for class to continue. I followed Ben's lead, watched Stephen release his fingers from the wine stem, and ate my soup silently. The taste, I thought, was unlike any soup I had ever had. "Stephen, how long have you been cooking? The flavors of this soup far exceed anything I have ever eaten."

Stephen scraped the bottom of his bowl, "A very simple recipe. Clara, have you made this before?"

I paused pushing the last of the onion into the fragment the crusty dark piece of bread that stood in the last puddle of broth. "I suppose I could lie, or I could make up a great story, or I could tell you the truth, the same truth that I told your father; I do not cook."

"I order in, eat out, or have all my entertaining done by a caterer. I did not have the luxury of learning how to cook meals with my mother. We did bake, oh, and I do know how to bake my grandmother's recipes."

"Finally, my mother conceded to some outside help in the house when the responsibility of the winery became overwhelming. I speak the truth; a baker I am, a cook I am not." I heard Maria drop a pan, heard some ruckus. I was unclear if their dinner had fallen on the tiles or if Maria was mad, knowing I was not a cook. I picked up my wineglass and looked at Tom, "Step two; I think my wine glass is empty."

Ben commented, "I saw you looking at the sides of the wineglass, the thin spiking lines on the glass; the mark of a solid quality of alcohol, some say it shows the presence of sugar. I am not sure why anyone would think wine lacked sugar in the fermenting process. A wineglass is not a measuring cup. You cannot measure how much sugar is in this glass, but you can look for the legs. Something tells me as you wobble on yours you will not forget that term. Now a big step and we are looking for the right answer. What do you smell?"

"I smell cherries, not cherry pie, not cherry cordial but a cherry that has been dipped into liquor. I am trying to see if I can taste anything else." I looked at them seeing if they would offer any hints. Ben waited; Stephen just looked at me with a thin-lined smile. I continued with finalization. "I taste cherries and I taste nothing else."

"Your reward is you may have a drink of our Pinot Noir, which we considered the best east of the mountains. No gulping, sip so you can enjoy the flavor in each swallow. Most of the grapes we get from Oregon. We do have a few vines, but Pinot is a very difficult grape to grow. Many wines are controlled by the climate, hot sun, to successfully grow the grapes."

I sat back, rested my swollen foot on top of my other foot, closed my eyes, and took a sip. I began to hum, and giggle. "Are you kidding me? I have been drinking whiskey and scotch all my life. Nothing has left this amazing warm flavor in my mouth, slowly sliding down my throat."

Stephen saw me move, readjusting myself in the chair. He took the wine bottle, poured some for his father, and looked under the table to see my foot sliding off my good leg. "Clara, I am so sorry. What was I thinking? We need to get that leg elevated on something besides a chair." He looked around the dining room for something to raise my foot; he called Maria who appeared with a crate topped with a pillow.

When Maria tried placing it under the table, Stephen reached out for the crate, pushed a chair aside, and leaned under the table. I felt his hand gently lift my foot, and put it on the floor. He began to push the crate closer to my leg while I moved my legs to accommodate the pillow. "Ice, Maria, she needs ice. Please bring a bag wrapped in a towel." He kept his hand on my leg, balancing my foot on the pillow, and slowly rubbed his fingers over the swelling. Maria slid the ice bag under the table, and Stephen balanced it on my foot, wrapping it in the towel. He leaned his head out from under the table. "Better, more comfortable, or would you like to finish dinner in the living room?" I wiggled my foot back and forth, pulled my skirt up slightly to keep it off the icepack.

"It is perfect, Stephen. Thank you. I am sorry to have disturbed my wine class and dinner."

Reaching down I touched his perfect chin and tapped my finger against the tiny indent. I repeated, "Perfect." Ben began, "Now, Clara, I have always felt wine belongs to the heart of the one tasted it; to the person who remembered where they drank the glass or bottle. Wine is like driving a car or even perhaps learning how to walk; it is a slow process where every person drinks wine for his or her reason."

"You admitted you bought wine based on the label or the price. Often people will go to a winery and buy the most expensive wine to show off at a family meal. The wine, Pinot Noir, you are drinking is a difficult grape to grow, thus the higher price tag. A pinot grape skin is fragile and often succumbs to weather, especially if it gets too cold."

"Oh, we have had our share of the wine snobs whose noses practically scrape the bottoms of the oak barrels that line our walls. They often take over the conversations at the tasting discussing either their wine collection or where they bought their wine. During a tasting, our focus remains on the customers; we do not care where they have bought their wines or where they have traveled."

"We certainly appreciate the ones who have years of wine knowledge, but try to welcome the newer recruits, usually the ones who like sweet wines. If I remember, you mentioned that you liked the sweeter wines, and we will have one with our dessert. "

"I do remember years ago. I was in Burgundy attending an international wine conference where I was an invited speaker. The location of the French wine region is north of the forty-seventh parallel. In Washington, we are close to a straight line across the continents and oceans from the French wine. I was the only winery from Washington State invited and had the pleasure of spending time with several famous winemakers."

"I am like other winemakers. We are older, wiser, and prefer to leave the management of our wineries to a family member. After my trip, I began to discuss with Stephen the need for him to step forward and take on more responsibility. I promise you it was not an easy sell for my young bachelor who enjoyed travel, and not just for the wines."

He listened while his father continued and began to eat the tomato pesto pasta with chunks of beef. Maria had put the steamed mussels on the side without knowing what I thought of anything that lived in a shell.

Ben spoke quietly, "Pinot Noir was born in France, its birth mother if you will, Burgundy, the gold medal for pinots worldwide. Our Pinot wine has won gold in every competition over the last ten years. We do not grow the grapes, but we can design a perfect wine from grape to glass."

"Essentially, it gained its popularity after the movie about the two young men wandering, bumping, and falling into vineyards throughout California. People are shocked by the price, and constantly question why it is more than other red wine. Clara, it is not like any other red wine. I often like to ask when you think wine came to our state. I know this is a question that just might require another bottle of wine for you to think about the correct answer."

Stephen uncorked a bottle, smelled the cork, and glanced at me. "The next wine is Zinfandel. This is something we started bottling about five years ago. It is a blend of three of our grapes; Zinfandel, Syrah or Shiraz, and Petit Syrah."

"A few wineries have made this their premiere grape, and well deserved because it is a wine we can grow successfully here. Unfortunately, Zinfandel labels can give confusing descriptions like 'ancient vines' or 'old world vines.' Typically, no old vines exist that are dinosaur relics. Perhaps the few vines left in your great-grandmother's vineyard, your vineyards, exist, but they no longer produce grapes. I think the challenge we have is the decision to keep what we have or to begin planting new vines that take more than three years to produce. I think when Stephen and I have a few serious conversations, we will decide if we want to expand our winemaking. However, tell her Stephen, what you would like to do in your spare time."

I smelled the wine that was lighter in color and its flavor was not quite as distinct as the Pinot. I waited for Stephen. I wished he would talk more. I thought his smiles and his laugh would make anyone else wish to laugh. I thought he had remarkable respect for his father by allowing Ben to teach me. I felt the warmth of the wine, and my head felt lighter.

Stephen took a swig of his wine after giving the glass a swirl, "Hard cider is my next goal. The alcohol content of hard cider is similar to beer; about 5 percent.

"The climate has a major impact on the grapes. Grapes like warmth; they like the wind to keep their soil churned and deposited with nutrients. And most importantly, they like water. You will see our irrigation system, something you might consider for your vineyard. Yours is a little antiquated, but you do need a drip system. Grapes are a desert plant and need only minimal water to survive, but they do need some water. I need a fermentation process with apples but I have plenty of orchards to choose from. I mean, I do not need to grow any, plant any; I just need to go down the road and find a farmer that would like to collaborate with me."

"Orchards these sides of the mountains continue to attract farmers from the city, but often there is an overabundance of fruit or they cannot get the prices they want to sustain their farm. I am working on a business plan to discuss with Dad and get down to the hard figures."

I finished the last of my wine, trying to memorize the flavors before I faced the next question. "Stephen, my field of work is analyzing numbers for my clients to give them the raw data they would need to decide what their next step would be in their dreams growing their business."

"I offer pluses because I could play with numbers every moment of my life, however, the minuses are showing a spreadsheet to a client who had hoped to invest in property, or who wished to sell his property to increase his assets. I suppose it is like playing a human game of monopoly."

"I am the caboose and prepare the reports based on the information that our clients disclose. I do not meet with them regularly; I give the report to our marketing team that creates a PowerPoint presentation from my data. Unfortunately, I have agreed to be on call for these meetings. Wherever I am, I am expected to help them answer any questions that the clients may ask."

"The challenge and I promise you it is a challenge, is when the client argues with the final figures. I suppose I am going to sound like one of your wine snobs but I do know my work. I take enormous pride in my spreadsheets that the clients receive and I just do not make mistakes."

"Typically, our clients will give us false, incomplete data. I can only work with what I get and I make that offer to you, Ben. I think I owe both of you a couple of spreadsheets based on this dinner, wine, and the use of your couch." Ben smiled another wide smile, not disguising his honest appreciation of me. Stephen responded, "Well, I suppose we should throw in the carriage service, Dad picking you up and my carrying you around the house. I would love to have your input and it will help us decide our direction. What do you need from us?"

Ben held up his hand, "Last time I checked, or remember, I was discussing where Pinot came from and I did not mention what climate it needs to grow. Now that the interruption is over, Clara, tell us your thoughts." I finished my glass and half of my pasta watching Stephen approach me. He reached under the table, taking the pack of ice off my foot, and touched my toes. Walking to his father, he called to Maria, "More ice please; the towel is soaked." He looked at me in a knowing, sensitive fashion. "Three glasses of water, two and a half glasses of wine and one bowl of soup. May I take you to our baño?"

Ben accepted a refill of his glass and spoke in a very authoritative voice, "Take her but come back. She is still in school and we still have one more bottle of wine to go with our dessert. Check with Maria on the way to the bathroom to see if she has the Riesling chilled."

I lifted my head slowly, listening to Ben scrape his dish and crunch on the last piece of his bread. I put my arms around Stephen's neck and felt his arm under my legs as he bounced me closer to his body. "She seems heavier, Dad. Maybe we have fed her too much." I turned my head slightly, "I do not know when wine came to Washington State, Ben. Have I flunked my class?

Maria came behind Stephen and switched out the pillow and towel. She left the icepack on the table and put the ice bucket with the Riesling next to Ben. She placed clean wine glasses on the table; stemless glassware used at the end of the meals.

Maria looked at the small area around the table's edge where one of their guests was so excited about the wine that he had just drunk that he smashed his wineglass on the edge of the table after throwing the wine bottle across the room. Fortunately, the wine bottle missed the windows and slid across the kitchen floor.

Chardonnay had been sleeping in his large-pillowed bed, which often served as camouflage for him, a match to his light fur, when the wine bottle slid under his nose. Chardonnay sniffed at the bottle, licked the inside with his long tongue, and nestled his head back under his leg with a slight snort. Stephen pushed the bathroom door open, sliding me out of his arms. I kept my arms wrapped around his neck, my face slightly lower than his. "The Zinfandel tastes a little grassy; it is much lighter and does not feel quite as heavy as the Pinot. I do like the flavor, and would ask for more if my head did not feel quite as dizzy as it is now feeling."

Stephen brushed his tongue against my lips. "Yes, I can taste that grassy taste as well on your lips and very distinctly on your tongue."

He whispered. "Please understand; I am not taking advantage of your innocent response to several glasses of wine. I just cannot take my eyes off you. You are lovely. How many men have told you how pleasing you are, Clara?"

"It would probably not be appropriate for one of your clients to touch these lips or to brush this thick hair away from your soft skin. I am so glad I am not a client, but if you help us with our books will that make me a client?"

I felt his kisses on my neck, "I can make exceptions for clients I meet outside my office. I would consider you an exception, exceptional, and exactly what I need now in my life." I kissed his chin, turned my head to the toilet, and watched him back out of the bathroom.

"Stephen, could you just wait for me at the table. I will call you from the bathroom door. Well, you see, I am embarrassed to be in here and you out there when I am going to the bathroom. I mean at the company, we executives have a private bathroom, so I guess I am a bathroom snob, too."

He closed the bathroom door slowly, and I heard him walk away calling Maria to clear the plates. He stood looking out the dining-room windows silently. Where she came from, he wondered and, as if his father had heard his words, he spoke up. "She is her mother, Stephen, and I lost her mother. Do not lose her; I warn you, you cannot manipulate her."

The Petting Zoo

Stephen turned around leaned on the table and looked at his father. "What do you mean manipulate, Dad? Why would I ever wish to change her thoughts or try to make her do something she did not want to do?"

"Stephen, you and I both know that you can be manipulative. How many women have sat at this table, leaned over the table showing their plunging necklines, worn their most expensive perfume, and spent the night in our guesthouse with you?"

"They don't want you, they want your money, they want this winery, they want only to take advantage of all of this hard work to line their purses with wealth, credit cards, fine cars, and take full advantage of you."

"You know what it feels like when they storm out of the house after you have told each one that you are not ready to marry. And only after you have charged three credit cards with the gifts that they expected from you after wearing the title Stephen's girlfriend."

I was standing in the open bathroom door and heard the conversation.

Stephen responded to his father, "Dad this is different; she is different. She does not need me, she does not need this winery, but Dad I need her."

"I will be patient with the hope she will decide that I am equal to her Manhattan clients. I am not sure I could even dress to her expectations. Dad, I do not own a tie. I think the only suit I have is from my high school prom. "

Stephen paused, running his finger along his T-shirt collar and remembered his prom and how he won the bet with his friends after he pulled out a pair of cotton flowered panties from his pocket the next day. They concluded that he had scored on the beach after the prom. He never told the truth; he could not afford to lose his status with his friends, his friends that had lived in the valley with him since his family first purchased the vineyard. Stephen remembered his date slipping off her underwear behind the seagrass, tossing them to him saying she would lie for any man just to be his trophy.

Stephen heard me calling his name and went to retrieve me. "I heard your conversation."

"Please understand I am different. I just do not know what to expect in the days or weeks ahead. We do not even know each other, but I feel there is an unknown purpose for our meeting."

Ben had left the dining-room table having a quiet phone conversation and ignored us when we returned. Stephen placed me gently in my chair, bent over to place my foot on the pillow.

I noticed new wine glasses and lemon cheesecake. "Wait, I thought with a white wine I needed a different shape glass. I feel I've been demoted to a safe cup. I am not dizzy and I would never break one of your glasses"

Ben returned to the table. "Clara, you can drink wine out of anything you wish. We like the stemless glasses and will often bring them out for desserts. It is like marking the end of our dinner. After dessert, I would like you to have a small taste of my port with a thin slice of cheese once we put you back on the couch. Think you can handle more alcohol for testing purposes?"

I quickly began to talk out of nervousness, afraid to look at Stephen whose touch left me warm. "Update time. The Zinfandel tasted a little peppery and fruity. It did not feel as bold as the Pinot but I enjoyed the taste. I guess I should ask what grapes I have in my vineyard; I think I have seen the signs that say Merlot and Chardonnay."

"I do not know anything else; I just read the signs when I went for my walks. I have concerns about some of the vines. The grapes look as if they need more than a cup of water. I thought I saw some bugs crawling around one of the bases of the vines. I saw chickens scurrying around the vineyard enjoying the bug appetizers. Oh, let's see, what did I forget to answer, oh, yes when did wine come to Washington State?" I continued to ramble and did not look directly at Stephen.

Ben sat back, and seemed to be enjoying me, who had enough wine to drink, had probably fallen for his son, and had not spoken of pain in my foot once I had started drinking wine. I sipped the Riesling and placed forkfuls of cheesecake in my mouth. "I am going to guess about wine in your state's history, or should I say my state's history?" Well, it's not my state yet. My state is New Jersey."

Stephen and his father grew quiet as I talked rapidly, acting like the puppet whose ventriloquist had taken over her voice. "Let me think, I know that California had a head start on winemaking, of course, you mentioned France, where the Pinot grape came from. My guess is probably sometime in the last sixty years, and that you, Ben, are responsible for the success of all of the other winemakers."

Slowly, I could feel my head beginning to spin. Ben looked as if he was moving in a circle around the table; Stephen looked as if he was swaying back and forth in his chair. I put my arms on the table, resting my head, looking up briefly when Maria placed a cup of hot coffee in front of me. "Drink, Miss Clara, sips, and try not to close your eyes."

I kept my head down, embarrassed, trying to keep the dinner in my stomach, and not on the tile floor. I twitched both of my feet back and forth, a fleshy attempt to focus on the movement and not think of my overwhelming feelings of nausea.

Stephen walked over, not smiling, and lifted me. "One more trip to the bathroom for you?" I shook my head in sloppy motions, "Perhaps, I should go outside for a few minutes and look at the stars."

He carried me through the heavy copper doors in the front of the house and out to the courtyard to a chair high enough to look over the flowerpots and under the awning. In the distance, I heard the sounds of a guitar, clapping, and noticed that the flags hanging over the gates were jumping in the breeze to the music.

Focus, I thought to myself. Look at one object that is not moving, and focus. I reminded myself not to pass out, not to say something inappropriate, and certainly to keep my hands to myself. I stared out at the courtyard and saw Chardonnay and Pinot chasing a small, furry animal until Stephen yelled inside the house, "Quick, get my air gun!" Maria came running out and Stephen waited for the dogs to come closer.

He shot the air gun at the furry animal, a baby coyote. "Who left the gate open, and how did this coyote get in here? If the baby is here the mother is not far behind." He stomped away from me, across the courtyard and hit the switch on the gates that swung slowly closed. He walked into the garage, and I heard another loud pop.

"Estavia must have left it open, there was another baby in the garage. Somehow, it tangled in the ribbon that

119

had fallen off your wrapped bread, Clara. I was almost tempted to bring it to you as a gift." Stephen yelled into the house again. "Maria, call the crew up here and have them bring torches. We need to check the vineyard and the grounds before morning. I do not want any of our wine-tasting guests frightened away by a coyote, or more importantly, I do not want any coyote nibbling on any of our guests."

I leaned my head back realizing that the animal the dogs were chasing was not furry, only the sleek coyote whose eyes I had seen glaring in the dining-room window earlier in the evening. I started to tell Stephen that I had seen it when he lifted his hand and whispered, "Shhhh."

Stephen edged along the brick wall slowly, moving backward toward the gate. He flipped the switch again watching the gate open. Out of the shadows, a mother coyote appeared carrying one pup in her mouth and the other walking under her belly. Stephen stood still knowing she saw him, but also knowing that he was not a threat to her or her to him with the pup in her mouth.

Just as she ran through the gates, he could hear the voices of the crew in the background. Shouting in Spanish, they showed up at the gate moments after the coyote ran into the darkness.

Stephen shouted for quiet. The torches that I had seen approaching were flameless and there was complete silence.

I heard Stephen talking to them quietly, and watched five silhouettes walk up the pathway.

Stephen called Maria and I understood what he said in Spanish; tequila. I realized they were walking directly to the porch; I attempted to brush my hair with my fingers and straightened my skirt. I noticed the top bottom of my vest was open, a frayed buttonhole that I closed. I thought I should stand but realized that if I even attempted I probably would topple onto the flowerbeds.

Lining up in a semi-circle, Stephen introduced me, "Gentleman, meet Miss Clara, owner of the Long House winery and our guest for the next couple of days. She has a very severe foot injury that will require her to rest. I would like you to help her any way you can and, most importantly, she needs to hear some of the stories that you know of her family heritage."

Stephen pointed around the circle, "This is Thomas One, Thomas Two, Thomas Three, Thomas Four, and Thomas Five. You have met a couple of the Thomases. You do not need to call them by number; they will respond to Thomas."

As Stephen called their names, they nodded. Each dressed in white cotton T-shirts, jeans, and no shoes. Some wore shirtsleeves rolled up hiding their cigarettes, and only the oldest of the crew had a heavy scarf tied around his neck. I thought, if only they wore the same hats throughout the week, I might know each one. Some wore baseball hats, a valley tourist hat, and the oldest was wearing a tattered, straw hat that hung over his ears. Maria arrived with the tequila, set it on the flower wall, and smiled at them.

Looking at me, she whispered, "My family, Miss Clara. They are all wonderful, kind men and they will do anything that you wish to make you comfortable."

"This one," she twisted the ear of the youngest," is my baby. We kept trying for a little senorita, but it just never happened. Although I do think this son has the most delightful eyelashes, kind of like Stephen, don't you think?" The group began to laugh, nudging each other with their elbows, and saying something about Boss Ben. Maria blushed, winked, and began to laugh, "No, no, Boss Ben is not the father of this young one. Oh, my goodness how you talk and treat your mother with such disrespect; I am so ashamed."

Stephen took a quick swig of tequila and stood next to the youngest son. He batted his eyelashes and the youngest Thomas mimicked him. "I don't know, Maria. We could be brothers, except he doesn't have my chin, his hair coloring is way too dark, and I think he was born speaking Spanish while I had to learn mine."

Stephen walked over to me, "So, how are you feeling after a few gunshots, a crowd of Hispanic men staring at you and seeing your first coyote?"

122

"I am much better; I do think the gunfire startled me enough to wake me out of my drowsy state. I hope I was acting appropriately in the dining room. I certainly do not want to give the wrong impression to your father or you."

"Clara, you have given me an impression of a woman one who is so remarkable that I just remain in awe of you. What do you need now to be comfortable?"

"A cup of coffee would be perfect, and perhaps a blanket. I am a little chilled. I did not expect to be wearing this thin outfit outside." Stephen walked to the wall behind me, pushed a button, and an outside fireplace began to warm the back of my chair.

Slowly, he turned me around facing the fire, brought a small, cushioned hassock to rest my foot. He asked one of the Thomases to bring me some coffee and a blanket. Stephen placed the softest blanket on my lap and tucked it under my shoulders. I smiled as I pulled the blanket tighter. "Looks like I have a frayed piece of clothing that I should take to the dry cleaner to fix."

Maria overheard the conversation and spoke up, "Miss Clara, I am your dry-cleaner person. I am not sure I know what a dry cleaner is, but I would be the person to sew your clothes, repair your clothes, and at your request make you a new skirt. You only need to ask. Before you go to sleep tonight, show me what you wish to have fixed and it will be done by morning."

Ben appeared at the front door, leaning easily on its frame, and looked at his crew. "What is this celebration, a party? I know that I need to get up early in the morning to take care of my grapevines, but if there is going to be some singing and music, well, let it begin."

As if on cue, a guitar began to strum along to a small hand drum, and two of the Thomases began to sing. The song was slow and melancholic, which made my eyes fill with tears. Maria came over and sat next to me, adjusted my blanket, and spoke softly. "Did you know that your mother loved this song? My family would sing it to her outside her bedroom before she became ill."

"Mr. Ben would sometimes ask them to sing below the patio that overlooks the vineyard when he would invite your mother over for dinner. It is really not a song for dancing, but Mr. Ben would dance with your mother under the lanterns, and my family could always hear her laughing."

"Your mother would ask my family to play a polka, but Mr. Ben would always say we needed an accordion. I am not sure it is something that my culture plays. I think if your mother were still with us, Mr. Ben would try to find one."

I smiled, putting my hand on her hand. "You are so kind to talk about my mother. I am sorry that I did not get to know you after I arrived to take care of her. I never meant to be rude or unkind, but I just was overwhelmed by so many people coming to our house, all the food left, the flowers, and even the tiny kitty someone left in a box on the porch."

"How is that kitty, Miss Clara? I think my family saw it wandering in the vineyards chasing the chickens. We decided it would be a perfect gift for her, hoping the purring would relax her and help her sleep."

I had only seen the pure white kitten once or twice and it had disappeared chasing a chicken through the vines. I had hoped Maria would not pursue the question, as I was not sure how to tell her that the kitten was gone.

I pulled the blanket around my neck and felt a slight shiver. I handed the coffee cup back to Maria. "I would like to be your friend. I know I will need your help in turning my home into a more colorful home with banners and curtains."

"I just ask that you please be patient with me for now. All this is so different from my home in New Jersey and my job. I know I will need different clothes to replace my suits and the fancy shoes I brought with me."

Maria's eyes twinkled. "Well, I will trade you a new skirt for one pair of fancy shoes. I tire of wearing these sandals and tennis shoes. I would love one day to just put on some makeup, untie my hair, and prance into our bedroom one night to tease my husband."

Smiling, I could feel my eyes drifting shut, and Maria motioned to Stephen. He nodded to the crew who left and he walked slowly over to me, bundled and cozy. I sensed him near me and felt his fingers through my hair. He leaned over and whispered, "It is bedtime for our guest. I will see you in the morning."

He carried me through the front door; the house was silent except for the soft cello music from the speakers. The fireplace was burning with an intense heat that made the room warmer. He motioned to Maria and without speaking she understood, and bent over, spreading the logs and leaving a glowing bed of embers that nestled together to form an ashen floor.

He put me down on the couch where Maria had made a temporary bed. My head fell to the side on the pillow and turned away from Stephen. I felt him trying to tug the blanket from under me; I was holding a piece of rock.

Maria nodded and whispered. "Thomas One gave her a gift of the rock. He told her he would spend time with her tomorrow telling her about the creation of the valley. He wished to share with her his stories about her great-grandmother.

"Leave it in her hand. If she holds the stone, maybe she will dream about grapes, wine, and her winery."

Stephen softly kissed my cheek. I forced myself to keep my eyes closed waiting for his kiss and felt his fingers moving through my hair. My throbbing foot reminded me of why I was on this couch, not in my own home. After he left, I faced the fireplace, watching the embers flicker and fade.

The History Rock

Maria woke me, standing next to the couch. "Miss Clara, good morning. Would you like your breakfast now, or would you like to take a bath?" Maria stood in the sunlight that streamed through the windows, holding a steaming cup of coffee. I eased myself into a sitting position, feeling my foot tingle as I tried to move it onto the floor.

"Is it possible to have a bath before breakfast? I'm afraid I sweat through my clothes in my sleep; the heat from the dying fire made this room feel like a sauna. But I don't have anything to wear; I don't know what I should do."

"I will find you some clothes. Do you need Stephen to carry you to the bathroom?"

I stood, twisting slightly to look out the window and saw the crew weaving through the grapevines. I looked for Stephen but he was not part of the grape gathering. Maria reached out for my hand and I grabbed it, edging slowly between the couch and the table to the open floor. Standing still, I stepped down on my foot and slid it across the floor.

Reaching the end of the living room, I looked out the dining-room window. The night had hidden the expansive patio stretching from the dining-room window outward about twenty-five feet in a perfect square. Unlike the front of the house, the patio was open, with green vines climbing throughout its wood rafters. Wrought-iron tables were spaced evenly throughout the square, their tiled tops glistening from the night's moisture and the morning's sun rays. Maria stood next to me and gave me a visual tour of the winery.

"Mr. Ben owns more than one hundred acres of land hidden from the highway. He often says the wind and sun are what make his grapes grow so perfectly. It does get very windy but it does not get too cold. His special grapes are the ones that he always says need special sweaters, so they do not freeze. We have never had a season recently that threatened the grapes. I know that our winery is not as close to the Columbia River as yours."

"We have an impressive irrigation system that you will never see; it is hidden in the vine roots. My husband, Thomas One, is responsible for the irrigation of all of these acres. Not once, and I know I am probably bragging a little, but not once has there been a lack of water for the thirsty vine roots."

"I know you have an afternoon history class later but some vines in Mr. Ben's and Stephens's vineyard are over one hundred years old. Can you believe Miss Clara, that something that started as a seed can still be alive, and not just alive but producing grapes? Do you know much about winemaking?"

"Maria, I know nothing. I think Ben wants me to consider hiring Stephen to keep my winery running. He fears that I just might sell it."

Maria turned me around facing her. "Miss Clara, you cannot sell that winery. You cannot give your heritage to a stranger. Your soil, your vines, the rocks, the gravel were handled by your great-grandmother, by your grandmother and your mother. For you to let someone else come in and change what has existed since mid-1800 is criminal. Miss Clara, you are giving a piece of your family to a stranger who will never be part of your family, your history. I ask, please, Miss Clara do not give up your winery."

"Ben and Stephen are the most respected winemakers in the valley. This winery, the Bennington Winery, is world renown. If they help you, and if you allow them to help you, your vineyard will survive another hundred years. Please, Miss Clara, think of your mother and your grandmother when you are trying to decide what to do. This land is yours, it is ours, and no one else should have the privilege of joining this community, or our vineyards, for a mere investment."

Maria turned away quickly and began to walk away to hide her tears. I blurted out, "Stop Maria, I did not tell you this to upset you. I just do not know what to do. I do not need the money; I do not need the investment."

"I do need to consider the life I have, the city where I work, my friends, and all the years it took me to reach my current position. It does not matter what education I have but it does matter that I have never taken a course in soil or gravel. Last night was the first time I learned to taste a glass of wine correctly."

"Maria, I am not prepared to learn all over again. I just am too proud to consider being a novice. I have come a long way from my freshman year in college to my existing corporate position."

Maria took my hand and led me toward the bathroom. "I want to understand what you are saying. This land is our families' land; I was born here, my husband was born here, we are not immigrants from Mexico. The work we do and our employers have made us feel like wealthy people."

"Yes, we do send money back to our extended family. Sometimes we visit but we have not been back for more than fifteen years, our responsibility is to our work and this vineyard."

I shuffled behind her watching the floor tiles change in color like a kaleidoscope. Maria took me back to the bathroom where Stephen had left me the previous night. I only remembered the toilet, the freestanding sink shaped like a wine goblet, and the tiny, narrow, ornamental cupboard filled with toilet paper, tissues, and shaving supplies.

"Maria, there is no bathtub or shower."

Maria opened two shuttered doors that faced the toilet and exposed the sunken tub under the stained-glass skylight windows. The entire room filled with the scent of lavender, and candles, tucked into tiny caverns along the brick wall opposite the door, flickered softly. I could hear the music that was floating above the steaming water and stood speechless.

She nodded. "Yes, an island oasis in this house. I think Ben had built it originally for his wife but she could not use it. I am sure you realize that the boys will never use it, but it is so elegant. You are the first female to step into these lavender waters."

I had never seen anything so exquisite, even in some more expensive hotels where I had stayed during my travels. Maria waited. "I will close my eyes. Please remove your clothes. Let me help you step into the tub and let me know when the bubbles hide you."

I eagerly dropped my clothes, struggling for a moment to move my swollen foot from my skirt. My naked self reached for Maria; she guided me to the bath step, grasping my arm as I slid onto the tub. I felt the warmth; my foot tingled with the newfound feeling of heat and not chilling ice. I sat first on the submerged marble seat and slowly eased myself into the water where bubbles began to climb up my body, clutching my tummy, breasts, arms, and shoulders while I stretched my legs.

In a reassuring voice, "I have covered Maria; I am blanketed in lavender. I feel as if I am in the middle of a field, or resting my head on a pillow filled with lavender. Can I stay here all day?"

She leaned over and turned the brass knob to a slow drip. "Yes, Miss Clara, you can stay as long as you wish. But I am afraid if your skin becomes puckered like a raisin." Picking up my clothes, she placed a pair of khaki pants, an open-necked cotton shirt, a thin T-shirt, and a pair of panties on the hook. "Wear what you wish. They are my clothes, but I am sure we wear the same size. Looking at the mound of bubbles around your chest, maybe you are a little bigger than what Maria has to offer."

I rested my back on the wall that surrounded the tub. I rested my head on the built-in pillow. I imagined the luxury of owning a winery, a successful winery. Although there were no windows, there was a skylight and I could hear voices outside of the bathroom walls saying it was time for a siesta, and the barking dogs seemed to run alongside the outside wall.

I looked around the room for a clock and saw a tiny, copper-framed clock face. No numbers, no second hand only the hands that glowed and, to my surprise, pointed to early afternoon numbers.

A part of me wanted to jump out of the tub and do something productive, but the other part of me remained. "Self," I said aloud. "If I am going to learn about winemaking I suppose I need to learn about the pampering of the wine owner."

I closed my eyes and saw Mother lying quietly in our winery bathtub, staring at me, not speaking, but looking directly in my eyes. After giving her a sponge bath, I brushed her hair and placed some rose scents near her neck. My mother was a wine owner but she never had the luxury of stepping into a sunken tub, never had the luxury of having time to spoil herself.

Perhaps this is a reality I thought, the reality of working and never finding the time. Shrugging, I thought it would not be any different from my work in Manhattan: all work, and no play."

Maria knocked softly on the door, "Miss Clara, Stephen requested you have a taste of the new late-harvest Riesling, just a sip or two. He is out in the laboratory tasting. He wants to know your opinion. He was very specific when he told me, just a few sips. I included a churro, fresh from the oven."

I watched Maria place the tray with the small port-size glass and churro. Smelling the cinnamon, I nibbled the churro, feeling its warmth and flavors fill my mouth. "I think I will be ready to get out in a few minutes. Can you throw me a towel? You do not need to leave. Please stay." Maria sat on the empty chair and watched me sip the wine. Raising my eyebrows I commented, "Sweet, almost sweeter than the dessert. Does he add extra sugar to this wine?"

She laughed and smiled at me, now holding the towel. "It has to do with the time it is harvested. We like these grapes to get a little colder to hang onto their sugar. I am afraid you will not find a big bag of sugar sitting in the laboratory."

I gave up trying to hold the towel and began dressing. I leaned against Maria, pulled the baggy pants easily over my foot, and dropped the white shirt over my head. "Perfect fit, Maria. I might just ask for you to start my wardrobe with this exact outfit." I felt the lump in my pocket and pulled out the rock.

Maria smiled, "From my Thomas, he left it with you last night for your first class on how our valley originated. Are you ready for a quick class? He is so anxious to talk to you."

"I will give you an answer to his first question. What you are holding is a piece of basalt or a small fragment. Every time my family digs into the soil, turning it and refreshing the nutrients for the vines, they find pieces of rock. He will tell you all about this amazing valley. Come with me. I am going to have you sit in the private, inside patio next to our outside guest patio."

Maria led me to a small gazebo off the dining room. The door to the gazebo slid open easily as Maria helped me step down one-step to the room that was floor-to-ceiling windows with private screens. "You will be able to see everything going on but no one will be able to see you."

"Mr. Ben values his privacy and the guests that come to the house. In this room, a small speaker projects conversations from the guests on the patio tasting the wines. He will sit here for hours listening, taking notes, and sharing what he has heard with Stephen. They not only want to please everyone with their wines, but father and son want to know what their guests learn about their wines"

"They see this as an opportunity to train the wine pourers in how to anticipate all the questions that the guests may or may not ask. You will see when you go into our winery later this afternoon a variety of wine lovers. Some people come as a social event; we do our share of bridal showers."

"Occasionally, we will have a class for the local college. Mr. Ben turns into a pseudo professor by asking the students questions. He does not have any tolerance for the students who do not take tasting seriously. We take pride in what we do every day. Sometimes it is hard for a tourist to understand how serious this business is. They can go and buy a bottle of wine from a shelf in the store without knowledge of how it started as grape seed.

Did you know that winemaking started with grape seeds stuffed in packages of apple seeds when the first settlers came? Slowly, this world, our world has evolved."

I watched a young couple sit close to the gazebo, away from the limousine that had just dropped off a carful of elderly tourists. One gripped a cane, one a walker and the limo driver returned with a wheelchair for the last woman. Ben greeted them and gratefully accepted hugs from each. "Welcome to Bennington Winery, my college alumni. I am happy you have joined us to celebrate your fifty-year reunion. Now, which of you was the head of cheerleaders?"

The smallest woman holding the cane raised her cane, unable to lift her head, for her severe back curvature prevented her from looking up at Ben. "That would be me, the one who was tossed, caught, swung out to the fans, and did all of the tumbles in the air. Look where I have ended up in life. Weakened, brittle bones, but those were good times, weren't they girls?"

The woman in the wheelchair began to laugh, "Good times for you maybe, Sherry, because you certainly had your own team sports after those games. Some of us tried to get into those parties and we did not have a chance. I do remember seeing you in class with those bruises on your neck; now what did we call them." She paused, "tucker bites, tickle bites?"

Sherry smacked her cane against her wheelchair. "Sucker bites, my dear. If I remember correctly, your flabby chin hung on your chest. I am not sure if any people could have found your neck." The seniors broke out in laughter and followed in a staggered formation behind Ben, as he brought them to the ramp and up to the patio.

Ben noticed the young couple sitting at a table a few feet from Clara, whose hands had left their wine glasses and were groping each other. The young woman would let her head fall back and sigh.

I watched from inside and Maria began to giggle, "This happens so often when couples have a glass of wine here only after visiting the tasting rooms in town. The warmth, the minimal clothing all adds up to a sensual moment. Watch what Ben will do next, he is customer service extraordinaire."

Ben spent a few more minutes with the senior alumni, politely attempting to remember stories and memories. He tried to stay interested when they shared their lives over the last fifty years. One woman asked about his wife. "Did you ever marry the blonde girl who was our class treasurer? She was certainly a whiz with numbers. I remember during our class officer meetings, discussing plans for an event when she handed out papers filled with our existing budget with our deficits. She had our full attention.

We just assumed that one day she would own a business or run for a political office."

Ben sighed, a question he had not heard for years. "Yes, we married and we had a son. You will see him when you start tasting; he looks like his mother with his blond hair, green eyes, and the tiny dent in his chin."

Before he finished, he heard another question aimed at him. "Well, where is she? Can we see her? She was one of our favorites throughout all of college. She always smiled, seemed as if she never judged anyone. If I remember correctly, she would talk to anyone she saw. I think that is how I met her. I was leaning against the giant maple by the biology building with my face in a book, and she just walked up to me."

"I remember, Ben, she was wearing a dress, and she always wore dresses even in the cooler months. She wrapped herself in that deep wool shawl that she would tuck in around her shoulders. It was a multipurpose shawl; sometimes she would sit on it, sometimes she would lie under it, and on those few days of sprinkles she would put in over her head."

"I did see her wrap it around a stray dog that had wandered into one of the classrooms, soaked and shivering. When the professor demanded the dog's removal from the classroom, she picked it up, held it in her lap, and ignored the professor's request by answering a question he had just posed to the class."

Ben found it hard to believe these aging women could remember a story about his wife. A small incident like a wandering dog led to his wife's memories like tiny petals on the paths that she walked. The woman who wore the dress and shawl was the same woman, his future wife, who came to his bed one night and covered him with her shawl.

"Thank you for the beautiful story. My wife and I started this winery but she died more than thirty years ago. Every day when I see Stephen, I see her. He was named in remembrance of his mother Stephena and my name as is his middle name."

They were not ready to let him go until he heard one last question, "Ben, she was young, what happened?" Ben looked up when Stephen motioned to him, looking at the couple embracing at the table. Ben acknowledged him, motioning he would be right there. "Excuse me please, I need to help Stephen. I will ask one of our pourers to bring the wine to your table so you will not have to walk. I would like to offer you a complimentary cheese and fruit tray. Any other foods you wish, just ask your server to bring you the menu. We pride ourselves in keeping our offerings minimally priced."

He left the table, moving quickly to the couple at the back. The man's baseball hat slid slightly down his head exposing bright red hair. He was moving his hands under her halter-top, and a wardrobe malfunction was eminent. 'Well, hello young lovers. I am Ben, the owner of this winery, and I would like your help checking out our latest project." Pointing to the row of teepees, he explained briefly, "We are considering calling them, Suites and Sip."

"We are trying the idea of providing private rooms for guests who would like a place to hide from the heat. We would only rent the rooms for a set number of hours because we are not set up for full-line hotel service. We are thinking of providing a shower, a nice soft bed, a table and chairs, and, for the true ambiance, the entire room will glow with candles. Well, not real candles but the battery-operated ones that will certainly give the room a nice glow. Now, I am thinking about either CD players or a small radio, so why don't you tell me what you think?"

They sprang from their chairs, grabbed their wine glasses, a bottle of wine, and followed Ben down a path between the grapevines. He pointed to the Merlot, Chardonnay, and Syrah grapes forming a hedge along the path, "Look at my beautiful little purple circle of sweetness, just waiting to be picked. Sometimes I think they just push out their skin more when they hear me walking. It is as if they are competing and saying, "Pick me, and pick me."

Ben stopped at the end of the path and pointed. Three single tepees were scattered through the border of the vineyard. "Now, don't let those tepees make you worry about what I just promised, they are the outer covering.

When you walk through the flap you will see the front door of the cabin."

"Only the first cabin is complete, and I will be anxious to get your thoughts on how I can add to the last two." The man began to reach for his wallet, and Ben raised his hand, "No, this one is on me. I will consider you my cabin consultants."

Ben watched them walk under the flap of the first tepee. They stopped, pointing at the painted drawing of a large-red mammal winking down at them, and holding a tangerine-colored fish in one paw. The man gently nudged her into the cabin by pushing on her close-fitting jeans.

I looked at Maria, "Really, he rents those cabins by the hour?"

Maria started to laugh. "No, those are playhouses for the crew's children. The first is complete with a shower typically used for the children. I suppose it functions as a mini water park because the shower sprays come out from all parts of the walls, and there are fountains of water. They love it, we love it, and it is just another kind gesture of Mr. Ben and Mr. Stephen."

I began to nibble on my toast when Thomas One knocked on the gazebo door. "How are the ladies of the winery doing today? How does it feel, my Maria, to have another woman to talk to in this house?"

Maria stood and motioned for him to sit. "Thomas, tell Clara about the rock you gave her. She has held it and I think it might have even gotten a bubble bath."

"I would love to tell you about our valley, Clara. Millions of years ago, the temperatures cooled into giant layers of ice. No, this was not the kind of ice you would imagine in the famous ice-skating rink in Rockefeller Center." He smiled when I nodded my head in approval of his knowledge. "Curious, have you ever skated on that rink?"

I nodded again, "Yes, I have, but the last time I had been drinking too much tequila and, well, I fell more than once. To make matters worse, I slid into the security guard chasing down the high school students. As a united effort, the students decided to form a Radio City Rockettes line which took over the entire middle section of the rink."

This time Thomas One shook his head, "Tell me more about a Rockettes line." I stood, balancing on the table, and began to kick one foot higher than the tabletop, place it back down on the floor and kick the other foot up. "Picture me in a line of thirty very tall women, with very long legs who do everything in measured, synchronized movement.

Simultaneously, we kick our legs, holding onto each other's waists, smiling with perfect, wide grins, and never making a mistake. Now picture a gathering of high school students who can barely stand up to skate, forming this line which essentially acted like a giant sweeper knocking everyone over like the rotation of the windmills."

Thomas One smiled, "Someday you will need to line up the crew and teach them. It would be fun to dance for our Feliz Navidad celebration. We need new ideas for our skit." "The skit that makes Mr. Ben and Mr. Stephen laugh the most wins the first place prize, a gallon jug of tequila. The children win yearly by dressing up like grapevines decorated in homemade ornaments; they win an ice cream sundae party. Now, I know our crew does not wish to take away from the children's prize but I do think a dance line could put them in the first place."

"Back to my class, Miss Clara. The giant layers of ice began to move, slowly they moved. Eventually, they formed a giant ice dam that formed a steep, deep wall. The dam failed to stop the moving wall of water that had pushed against it to move across the land, churning, digging, lifting the soil and rocks."

"Soils that had once stood alone, untouched by any disturbance except the windstorms, were now lifted, pushed higher and became the frame of the canyons that dug deeper pushing boulders aside and forming mounds which flattened into plateaus. This churning, tossing, and digging of the landscape continued over thousands of years until it became the landscape that rests around us. Add the palette of colors when the sky darkens, the sun's morning rays turning it golden, and finally the setting sun turning the boulders into red stoplights."

"I forgot to mention that, before any cooling of the atmosphere happened, volcanic eruptions occurred, eruptions that pushed mountains and forced layers of ash to cover the valley. The ash was responsible for the cooling and eventual formation of prehistoric ice-skating rinks. The great Columbia River that flows to the Pacific Ocean and its tributaries, the Snake River and Yakima River, are the result of geological forces from years ago."

"We, the farmers, like the result; the soil filled with rich nutrients has given us a sustainable home for the grapevines."

I found myself smiling when he expanded his vocabulary with words that he had read or biology he had learned from Ben. "Miss Clara, the flood continued for years, certainly none recently, but when the Missoula flood came through, more lakes and ponds were formed and filled. Our soil was granted a gift of moisture for planted grapevine roots."

"The soil is rich in basalt, sand, nutrients. You will learn from Mr. Stephen how we feed the soil; sometimes one of the biggest costs is the food that these vines demand. Most importantly, over-fertilizing and over-watering can result in more grape leaves than grapes."

"Grape roots are strong and fearless and they will travel deep into the soil, from five to thirty feet, assuring that their vine will survive the elements of wind, heat, and cooler temperatures. The depths of the roots result in their need for minimal water. Our vineyard that overlooks the valley plus the treasure that nature offers equals a lifelong marriage resulting in the quality grapes and the wine that you have tasted. Vintners have the exceptional skill to vary alcohol levels during fermentation, an additional factor in the quality of wines made.

"Now, if you want to impress Ben and Stephen when they start to quiz you, remember that Zinfandel has the highest alcohol content, 14%, while beer is only 5%. It only takes a glass or two to feel that wonderful, warm feeling and perhaps get a light flush on your cheeks. Zin, a nickname by fans, is one of my favorite wines."

"Some of our Zin vines are from pre-Prohibition in the early 1920s. Understandably, before you were born, but clearly around your grandmother's time. This was a sad time for the wine, the alcohol, and beer industries. The ban on alcohol did not last long in Washington State because it was repealed in the early 1930s." Although Thomas One had repeated Zinfandel's alcohol content, the information I had heard from my earlier wine class from Stephen and Ben, I did not mind hearing it again.

I glanced away for a moment and stared at two visitors who had arrived. One was an elderly woman wearing a lavender suit and hat while she held her daughter's arm. Her daughter looked to be around my age with straight, blonde hair, wearing a sundress that barely covered her thighs. Her floral sandals slid along the pathway, while she balanced the woman.

I watched as she walked up to Stephen, and kissed him solidly on his lips. Stephen responded by backing up and looking at her, giving her another hug and kissing the elder woman on the cheek.

Thomas One watched my face blush and quickly gave a quick explanation, "Do not worry Miss Clara; she is the daughter of one of the other winemakers who has had a crush on Stephen since she was a little girl. She may appear older than you think but she is a small one. She will be graduating from high school next year. My sons have told me that she wants to take Stephen to her prom. Sadly, when he says no, he will break that little romantic heart she has carried for him for so many years".

Maria appeared, "Clara, are you comfortable taking a few steps with my help? Perhaps you would like to walk through the vineyard to the laboratory or sit inside the winery to watch the activity from a front-row seat?"

My Nez Perce Great-Grandmother, MaMinny

Over the last half hour of Thomas One's chatting, four buses, two limousines, and four private cars had arrived. In the distance, I saw one Clydesdale horse pulling a decorated cart that was shaped like a giant half wine barrel.

Riding inside the decorated cart was a bride dressed in white with a small veil flying in her face. Next to the bride was the groom wearing a white suit with a burgundy vest. I assumed, with their dark skin, and jet-black hair, that they were family members of the workers throughout the valley. "They look so young, are they relatives of yours?"

Maria spoke up, "No, Miss Clara they are not Hispanic. They are Native Americans. They are from your blood with thick, dark hair that speaks to their ancestors. Often Stephen offers the grounds for photography. The bluff overlooks the Columbia River. It is one of the most breathtaking spots in the valley."

"Below the bluff, might have been the location the original Nez Perce built their homes and fished along the river. The Nez Perce believed the spirit of the wolf appeared on the bluff and along the river. The spirit reminds us who lived here first, and it will protect the vines. When a cold spell came and destroyed vineyards years ago, everyone said that we upset the wolf spirit and in his anger, he blew cold air throughout the vineyards."

147

I blushed for judging the bridal couple based on their appearance. Internally, I scolded myself, promising to be cautious and sensitive to the cultures living in the valley. Thomas One added, "We try to keep peace with the animals. I know you saw Stephen shooting an air rifle at the coyote family yesterday. We have tried to not kill any of the habitats but sometimes it happens."

"Years ago, I remember it happened on my fiftieth birthday. We had other dogs, the same breed as Pinot and Chardonnay, attacked by a pack of wolves. All three dogs were killed and torn to shreds in the vineyard. My sons and I waited for the wolves to return. They did not have a chance, because we had surrounded the vineyard in the dark and had set up a prop of a large-stuffed animal resembling a Dane. As soon as they crept to the Dane, we began to shoot until all four wolves were dead. One attempted to run away, crawling under the vines, but I was right there to shoot it between the eyes. We have kept the wolf claws, a trophy for us, a reward for us, and most importantly a reminder that the wolf spirit is still awake in the valley."

I remembered last evening when Stephen whispered a warning, the hush of the crew, and seeing the mother coyote cross quickly over the courtyard with one pup in her mouth and the other stumbling beneath her legs.

"Thomas One, tell me more about the Nez Perce, about my great-grandmother's heritage. Who told you the stories?"

"My grandfather has relayed many stories to us. I tried to remember much of what he has told us, and I kept a journal. Over time, his mind began to dwindle, and, sadly, his repetition of the same stories became the brunt of family jokes. My sons certainly knew better than to mock an elder family member. However, often grandfather would tell the story five, six, seven times at one dinner. He would get angry if no one laughed at his jokes and would often leave the table only after scolding the boys who would break out in tears or, as they got older, burst out in laughter."

"Grandfather just sits in his rocking chair now and stares for hours. He talks to himself, and we often find him with tears running down his face. We think he might be struggling with a memory that he cannot understand or speak about."

"Where is he now?"

"He lives with our family. Mr. Ben and Mr. Stephen paid for a small addition to our home. We try to keep him involved, but getting him to walk now is very difficult. Often our sons lift his chair, carrying it into the dining room, out to the porch, and on cooler mornings they will load the chair into one of the tractors so he can travel the fields with them. When he is on the tractor, he nods and hums. He never speaks, but points at the landscape and claps his hands. His favorite drink is Pinot Noir. After the wine tasting room closes, we carry him in his chair into the wine tasting room, sit him at one of the wine-barrel tables, while he drinks wine."

"We know grandfather will be taken someday by the spirit of the wolf, and the spirit will give him his legs so he can run, tell his stories to all who will listen, and certainly drink the wine of the heavens."

Thomas One took my hands. "Family and tradition are very important. I know that your life has changed living in a big city where family perhaps has evolved into your work friends or your neighbors. I understand your mother was your only living family member. I know and understand that when someone dies, or when you move far away, distance makes it easier to forget your past."

"Miss Clara, your roots are seeds planted long ago by generations and like the grapevines you see, your roots are buried deep within your heart. Those who walked before you gave you the tiny seeds that grew into your existing talents."

I blushed again and looked away. "I will share your grandmother stories that my grandfather shared before his mind became a little foggy perhaps from age or the tequila he drank like a boy. I think over time the story changed, he may have added extra frosting on the tale, but it will give you an idea. Would you like to stay here and talk or are you anxious to get up and walk this morning?" He watched me stand, stretch, moving my feet from side to side.

"I think I am perfect here. Your conversation, our conversation, can it be heard by the guests outside?" Thomas One shook his head, "No, this room is soundproof. Mr. Stephen and Mr. Ben occasionally will use it for entertaining, but it is very curious to me how their home has opened more doors since your arrival. Spaces we have never used have transformed into welcoming walls for you."

"We had a gift shop attached to this room many years ago. Mr. Ben built it for his wife and she could access it easily from their home when she began to have health problems. She did not want to be far from the house or bathroom. Mr. Ben had one of the staff stay in this room, watching for shoplifters and assuring her safety. What an easy job for the crew to just sit in here all day."

"After she could no longer work in the gift shop and had to remain in her bed, that small building was closed. Only about a year ago, Mr. Ben tore down that building and added a very small gift shop within the tasting room. He has included the wood from her gift shop in those shelves that hold wine bottles and wine gifts to keep her memory alive."

Maria had appeared with a pitcher of cold lemonade, small sandwiches, a green salsa, and fresh-baked tortilla chips. "Every teacher and student needs to find time for their lunch, no cafeteria or lunch boxes required." She kissed the top of her husband's head, softly touched my hair, and left.

"My wife is the best, Miss Clara; she means everything to me and my family. Her love and our love are more than any acreage of grapevines." Thomas One took several sandwiches, chewed them quickly, gulped a half glass of lemonade, and began.

"We have been told that your great-grandmother was from the Nez Perce tribe that originated in the valley and lived along the rivers around the early 1800s. Her tribe raised her initially. Her biggest influence, however, was a family who adopted her. She was a descendent of Chief Joseph, whose name you will find in every history book."

"Your winery has been named Long House, and there is a reason. The houses where the families lived were communal; more than 30 families lived together in a longhouse, or tepees or underground housing. We heard the community included hothouses or sweat lodges, basic structures for religious ceremonies after the missionaries arrived, and there was a hut for girls with adolescent bleeding." He looked away finishing his sentence, "It was a Native-American ritual and tradition to honor the passage of girls from youth to adulthood."

I smiled, guessing that he would not use the word, menstruation.

"The villages were typically located along the rivers or streams, close to the water and forests, but they remained mobile to maintain their dietary needs. Their crops were harvested in the fall, but they would also hunt and fish."

"Salmon was the primary fish caught, and fishermen still fish along the Columbia River and Snake River. Sometimes I grow weary when my grandchildren want me to take them fishing. It is a very long process waiting for them to catch a fish when I could be taking a long siesta."

"Besides fish, the hunters would hunt for goats, bear, deer, and birds to keep the families fed. They picked wild berries and grew onions, carrots, bitterroot, and camas bulbs. Women, like your great-grandmother, learned as young girls how to pick berries and to dig for roots. Often at a young age, they also began to weave, grooming toward a marriage. Tools were basic sticks for digging, hooks, lines, spears, and harpoons for fishing."

"In the 1700s her tribe became involved with horses, specifically the Appaloosas. They quickly gained the reputation of owning the largest horse population. Well, I suppose it was not exactly an industry, but owned the largest herds of horses within the plateau and the valley. The tribe expanded their wealth with the horse. One of the biggest influences of horses was their ability to travel great distances to hunt for bison."

Thomas One laughed, "I know you will not forget the coyote momma. She is the spirit of the Nez Perce. When a child approaches adolescence, they are given a spirit to protect them. I wonder what spirit you have, Miss Clara. Is it a wolf, a coyote, or a horse? You will figure it out in time. Your great-grandmother's spirits cannot be the same spirit you carry. My wish for you is to discover what your spirit is. Once you do, you must call on it, you must ask for its advice and most importantly, you must respect it. I think that today people speak of guardian angels watching over them. Your spirit will become your guardian angel."

"In the early 1800s, the fur trappers began to live with the Nez Perce. There was never any anger or fighting at the time between the French Canadians and the Nez Perce. "I know you are patiently waiting to know how your great-grandmother fits into your history. She was, in a sense, a hero. This is the story my great-grandfather would tell. I do not know if it is true, but he told it many times. One of the fur trappers got his leg caught in a trap that had been set along one of the streams for a family of beavers. When he began to attempt to twist his leg out of the trap, the trap teeth cut into his calf deeper until they were touching his bone. He began to bleed, causing the sand around the stream to darken with a thick puddle of blood. He had lost enough blood that he fainted, or perhaps the heat got to him, and his body went limp; his face lay on the edge of the stream."

"He was unaware of the animals that sniffed him through the night, of the wolves that came near the trap but backed away when they realized that the leg they hungered could not be grabbed quickly. Your great-grandmother, MaMinny, had wandered down to the riverbank, hoping to take a quick bath before returning to the nightly communal meeting."

"She heard his moans, saw the fur trapper, and immediately ran to his side. My grandfather said your great-grandmother thought that a bear was caught in the trap because the trapper's face had a long bushy beard, his hair was curly and stuck out under his fur-lined hat, and saliva gave his face a very animalistic look. He said he heard that your great-grandmother noticed his thin lips were covered by hair, and she could barely see his pointy nose."

"She immediately took off her shawl, covered him, and put her flute to her mouth and forced three sharp sounds. A hollowed willow branch was pierced with small holes along its surface served to alert tribe members that help was needed by one of the tribal women."

"Your great-grandmother knew the flute sounds were heard as distant tribal members began to beat their drums, as they ran toward the water. When they arrived at the river, they saw your great-grandmother lying on top of the fur trapper in an attempt to keep him warm. She sat up quickly putting her hands up and quickly told them that the injured man was dying from blood loss and the cold of the night. Her brothers moved slowly wedging a solid chunk of tree trunk under the trap's teeth. The traps inched open enough for them to slide the fur trapper's foot out before the trap sprang shut."

"Within moments, other tribal members arrived carrying a sling made of two long poles and a leather sheet looped underneath and stitched tightly. Your great-grandmother said that the fur trapper just stared, tried to mumble, but would only fall back asleep. She had wrapped his leg in a strip of fabric from her skirt that was stained with fresh blood from moving him to the sling."

"Once he was carried back to the village, he was brought into the longhouse to a small bedroom she shared with her family. The shaman arrived, unwrapped the wound, sprinkled herbs, and applied clean dressings. Your great-grandmother dipped a piece of cloth into a small pottery bowl filled with bitterroot tea, and put small drops in his mouth."

"When his whole body shook from the fever, her brothers brought buckets of water from the river where she would soak cold cloths and place them on his body. She often said that he would look at her, wrinkle his furry eyebrows and search for something to say."

"His tongue had become so thick from dehydration that fumbling words came out of his mouth. She said he would shake his head back and forth when she would speak to him in her native words, flutter his eyes, and stare at her before closing his eyes tightly."

"When the light of the first full moon came weeks later, he finally woke, moved his hands, and tried to sit up. She never left his side. She ignored the words spoken by her father reminding her that if he were not part of their tribe, he could not be part of her life."

"When he finally sat up and began to eat a very weak carrot stew, he only stared at her face. She said that he kept nodding his head, touching her face, and saying words that she did not understand. When he tried to walk, he would stumble. Her brothers would help him walk, just like my wife and Mr. Stephen are helping you walk."

"When her family realized their guest was planning on staying longer and had shown affection to your great-grandmother, they wanted him to leave immediately."

"Your great-grandmother talked with her spirit for advice, asking what she should do to not lose her family without losing the man who she had begun to love. She knew her tribe had decided whom she would marry. Initially, she had willingly decided to follow tradition by marrying her chosen cousin, until she realized her feelings belonged to the fur trapper."

"One of the times she was bathing him with the cool water, he held her hand and moved it lower." Thomas One pointed to his crotch and wiggled uncomfortably back and forth in the chair. "Please understand what I am trying to say Miss Clara; my grandfather said that she told all the tribal women that the white men were large in their loins."

"When the fur trapper was sleeping, your great-grandmother would trade a peek of his manhood for pieces of fabric from the other women. Soon many women became disgruntled with their husbands and began to question them on their physical bodies. None of the tribal husbands knew the origin of their questions.

I found myself laughing so loud that Maria hurried back in the room looking at me followed by a glance at Thomas One. "What is so funny about a history class? What is Thomas telling you making you laugh at a great-grandmother you should respect."

Thomas One stood, adjusting his cotton pants and whispered in her ear. Maria began to laugh as loud. "Miss Clara, do not listen to his story. I believe there is no truth to this story. It is false. Now really, Miss Clara, if you were part of that tribe, would you trade something to see a man's private parts?"

I thought to myself, "Well, maybe." I looked at Maria, looked at Thomas One, and shook my head yes. "What I have been hearing since I got here is respecting my heritage. If my great-grandmother got to look at some stunning man, well I certainly should be able to do the same." Maria and I looked at Thomas One whose face flushed with embarrassment. He started twisting his hips as if he had an imaginary hula-hoop until Ben appeared in the doorway.

"Thomas One, I have been looking for you and I did not realize you were having a dance class. Do you know how much longer you will be? I do need some help with the crusher. It has been making a grinding noise. The grapes are still pressing but I just have this sense that something is going to stop if we don't check it out before it gets worse." Thomas One had put his hand over his cheeks and Maria scooted out. I tried to stare at Ben with a very solemn face until I burst out laughing. "I am so sorry. I just heard the funniest story about my great-grandmother. I just can't quit thinking about the peep show that occurred around her future husband."

Ben looked at me, his eyebrow raised; his lips aligned avoiding a smirk, "Joke, who said it was a joke, Clara? Native-American women were known to check out "the goods" before they married someone. Now I do know it was quite unusual to share that experience with other women. I do think that you should respect their traditional behaviors."

He continued staring at me, shook his head, and left the gazebo. Only after he was safely out the door and standing outside the gazebo, I heard him say. "I think I got her," he said to Chardonnay. "I think she believed me." I sat back in my chair, embarrassed that I had laughed out of disrespect but knew that Stephen would tell me if the story was true.

Thomas One stepped toward me, hiding a smirk, "I guess I need to finish quickly. A fairy-tale ending, your great-grandmother did marry the fur trapper, however, the tribe banished her. She found herself living among the French Canadians and worked as an interpreter during the growth of the fur trade industry. Sadly, however, the French Canadians' harmony ended after an outbreak of measles and the deaths of a large number of Native-American children. The deaths were blamed on the fur traders, and tension began forming."

"Your great-grandmother was able to have three children, one your grandmother. However, after the birth of the last child in the late nineteenth century, she succumbed to measles and died. I will show you where the simple wood cross is; it is the spot she is buried. "

"Your great-grandmother was part of history. Chief Joseph negotiated land for the tribe before the gold rush took away their land in the mid-nineteenth century. He took the remaining tribe miles away to avoid the restrictive plan the military offered."

"Unfortunately, a war broke out. The military won. Chief Joseph conceded and agreed to the land offered for his people.

"Known as a strong leader, he shrank to a puppet as military actions directed where his tribe would live. One of the largest reservations for the Nez Perce tribe is located in northern Idaho. Perhaps Stephen can take you there someday. I cannot emphasize how important roots are; your family is your roots." Thomas One heard his name called from outside the gazebo. "I need to go. Ask Maria to bring you to the laboratory, one of Stephen's responsibilities. Remember any of your high school chemistry?"

Quick to respond to him, knowing I had no memory of chemistry, I asked, "A chemistry lab, why may I ask, is there a laboratory here? I thought this whole bottling-of-wine process was picking grapes, crushing them, putting their juice in a barrel, and drinking it. I had no idea that there were so many other steps in the process. Thomas One, I know nothing about any of this. Although I appreciate all the time you are spending with me, the truth is I cannot possibly learn what has taken you years to learn. I feel pretty helpless right now."

Thomas One softened his voice, concluding his time with me. "We feel helpless in our life, Miss Clara. What you need to remember is that there have been offers from Mr. Ben and Mr. Stephen to help you and believe me, they can. But, you know what the hard part will be? You and you alone must understand that your winery needs a home in your heart, not on the land, but in your heart."

I nodded, weary of the lectures and the constant reminders of what I should, and should not do. I gave Maria a weak smile as she picked up her ringing phone and handed it to me.

"Hey, hey, how's my man? I asked. "Well, I miss you too." Listening, I kept nodding my head as Maria left the gazebo only to stand outside and listen.

"No, I have no idea when I will be coming back. Besides a bum foot, I have the challenge of adopting this family heirloom called Long House Winery. I know where I belong but the reality is I have never had to choose. Yes, I miss our special times too, but things are changing for some reason as I try to prioritize my life."

Laughing, I replied, "No, I do not have heat exhaustion, no I am not on drugs, and well, at least for today I am not drunk. However, I guess I just need to understand what this winery meant to my family. Yes, I know I had plans of coming down here and selling it or putting it on the market. The truth is that if I sell, a big city wine company will outbid these smaller wineries and it can change everything."

Switching the phone to my other ear, "I do not know why it matters, Samuel," Maria leaned further into the doorway after hearing his name.

"Look, when was the last time you sat and had a real conversation about your past. In all honesty, in two days I have had this feeling that there is more to my life, perhaps another purpose. Come on, don't laugh like that, I am sharing my heart with you."

Unknown to me at the time, Maria had been listening to the entire conversation. "Samuel, what I am trying to say, and what you are not hearing is, that my life is only about twelve-hour workdays, the constant push to move up the ladder, the big paycheck, and luxury."

"Oh, yes, I do love to travel and I will never forget the spa in Venice, the amazing chateau in Burgundy," I paused. "Burgundy, funny, I never really thought about that trip until now. I do remember spending time looking at all the different wine labels to tell my mother about when I got home. She was re-designing hers to mark her journey. I do not think she ever completed it. Perhaps she left that for me to do."

"Samuel, please do not laugh at me and tell me I am going through one of my phases. And please do not ask yet again, what do I want to be when I grow up?"

I listened to Samuel talk, nervously twisting one strand of hair through my fingers and tugging at it. I stood and looked out of the gazebo watching the couple that had disappeared into the tepee reappear. Curious, I thought, the young woman was leaving the teepee, walking quickly and approached Ben.

I watched Ben listen for a moment, and stood between the couple when the man caught up to her. The woman pressed her back against Ben's back while the man faced him. Ben stood in the middle of an emotional sandwich.

Slowly, the woman walked toward the gazebo and sat down on a chair within several feet from where I stood. I noticed the slight bruising on her upper arm and the pink tiny circle under her eye and realized Samuel was still on the phone. I spoke quickly to him, "Just a minute, Samuel." Calling for Maria, "Maria, please come here."

Susan Shate

Maria appeared holding a broom when I motioned toward the woman who was sitting in the chair, alone, while Ben talked with her companion. The man put on his sunglasses, pulled his baseball hat down, and shoved Ben, who stumbled backward, falling into one of the hedges. Within moments, Thomas Two and Three grabbed the man. Stephen slowly lifted his father from the hedge; two additional crewmembers arrived and stood back waiting for direction.

As if a well-orchestrated plan, the crew moved him away from the patio into the garage. The patio had suddenly become crowded with guests holding wine glasses and pushing against each other to get a better look at the man. They did not need to see very much because his voice rang out with obscene words, directed at Ben and his woman companion who was now trembling.

Maria brought the woman inside to sit next to me. She said nothing, just sat in a chair and stared out at the man as he disappeared into the garage. The police arrived, talked briefly to Ben, and moved toward the garage. Thomas Five arrived with a decanter of wine to divert curious guests on the patio and filled the guests' empty wine glasses. Music began to blare over the speakers; Stephen brought Ben into the kitchen and called for Maria. I sat quietly with the woman, not sure what I should do, and realized that Samuel was still on the phone. Hearing his voice I responded,

"Sorry, I can't talk now. Yes, I will let you know when I will be home; yes I will stay in contact with the office."

My final words, unfortunately, were not heard by Maria, "Samuel, I will always love you. However, the reality is that you are gay. I seek a straight man. Please remember, sweet one, I will always love you and you will always be my friend for life. No, Samuel, there is no one in my life at the moment who makes me laugh as you do, who can resolve a botched up accounting spreadsheet faster than you, and who has been to every Broadway musical. However, there is someone special, someone who plays my mother's favorite violin music, is teaching me about wine, and loves to talk about the history of the wine valley." Pausing I looked quickly out the window and whispered in the phone, "His name is Ben. I cannot talk now, later, please "

I put the phone down and remained silent, waiting for the woman to talk. Thomas One came in and whispered to her. She shook her head, "No, I am not going to file a police report. I do not want to talk to anyone. No one will understand, so what is the point?"

A police officer came behind Thomas One. "We are going to take him in and I will be happy to escort you. Are you aware of this man's record? Have you known him for very long?" The police officer had found her emotional switch, and she began to sob uncontrollably. She looked at me and I remained silent based on the look from the officer. "Have you looked at my record, too? Do you know who I am and what I do?"

The officer stood patiently, "Perhaps we should have this conversation in private." Maria and I started to leave the room and the woman held up her hand.

"Please do not leave; this becomes one of those situations where it is just me against all of these men who will judge me. Please stay unless you are uncomfortable." Maria left. I stayed and introduced myself. I waited; she looked at me and began to talk. "My birth name is Susan Shate. My street name is Shaterize, acquired by a reputation known to shatter the mind and bodies of any of my clients who hire me."

"He, well," she glanced at me, looked down, and mumbled, "He is my pimp and we were here to celebrate my birthday. I suppose there should always be a special occasion for birthdays. I never had one when I grew up; I never had the chance to invite my friends over for cake and presents." Her face changed from sadness to a hard look, perhaps the mask that she wore more frequently with strangers who hired her. She waited for someone else to speak.

The police officer looked at me showing my stoic face, the one I would often wear for clients who acted like demanding children in my meetings. I thought, my clients, are like Susan's clients. They pretend, negotiate, and challenge until someone leaves satisfied or dissatisfied.

The officer entered the information and read his computer. "Susan, you do not have any warrants or previous arrests. I do not think you must give me details because anything you say I will need to enter. But I am guessing that you are a highly paid escort hired by this madman."

Susan did not respond, knowing that even a nod would only add information to the computer. "So Susan, he is not your pimp, correct? He must be a client," the police officer continued. "From the looks of him and the helicopter that left you two off ten miles down the road, and private limo, he is very wealthy. Are you aware of this?"

Again, Susan did not respond, the police officer had given her a fair warning and she was going to heed his words. If she spoke, not only was she jeopardizing her job, but her employer. She had not told her employer that she was heading out with a client for the day, her birthday, a client who promised to celebrate her birthday in exchange for sex.

"Well, his record is nonexistent, except for his physical altercation with Ben today. Somehow, he has always managed to pay people off to save his name, to save his company. He is a big name in the wine world and I promise you this valley will not see the end of him. I really cannot do much but take him in, if you will not press charges. I have already heard that his attorneys are on their way."

He looked at me, "We valley folks are not quite used to this kind of chaos. Most of our problems come from our guests and not our locals. We have awful car accidents that take away the young, sometimes too young. That is what always confuses me," he shook his head and looked away repeating, "Too young and distracted by alcohol, weed, or looking at their damn cell phones."

Susan looked at me, speaking directly to me for the first time, "You probably don't understand. I can tell by looking at you that you are not from here. You are probably one of that big-city, educated people who never had to worry where your next meal came from or where you would sleep. I just finished high school, got my GED because my employer wanted me to sound smarter for our clients. I mean, she is hiring tutors for us so we can learn more cultural things; she said it will be a good marketing tool for her clients."

She walked to me and stood to tip her head to the side. I saw the red circle under her eye had now popped like a clear blister, its edges pooling like tiny strings moving into her cheek. "Well, Clara, you probably do not know what it is like to be in my position, to be forced to learn something I have no interest in."

"I mean, you probably had your educational path waiting for you to decide what class you would take when you would graduate when you would go on for higher degrees. Why I bet you even had a job waiting for you the day you graduated."

I reached up and ran my fingers down Susan's hair. "I know we have never met, and I do not know if we will ever see each other after today. But, Susan, we are similar in our different worlds."

"I sell my mind for money, I say things that make others feel good about themselves, and I have gained stature in my profession because our clients ask for me. They only want me and no one else to help them. You see we are similar."

I hugged Susan gently, afraid to touch her arm, afraid to press my face against hers. The police officer waited, and Susan finally agreed to walk to him.

"Please, do not think less of me, Clara. You might meet my client someday, who uses his power and money to get his way. Well, if you ever meet him do me a favor and hit him in the balls with a wine bottle."

I watched Susan leave through the gazebo door, and cross the patio. The police officer met her out front after she looked one last time at the vineyard, the valley, and watched as her client stood with his back to her as he climbed into his limousine.

My New Love

I heard the noise coming from the living room. I limped over and saw Stephen leaning into his father's ear. Stephen was shouting to his father, "Dad, keep your eyes open and listen to me. Dad, do not fall asleep, Dad we are calling the ambulance, Maria is on the phone. Dad, listen to me, please listen."

Stephen knelt by the couch shouting at his father. Maria held the phone dialing 911, speaking rapidly and in Spanish. She kept shaking her head and saying no. I slid my feet over, took the phone, repeated the address, and gave brief information about Ben's situation. "How long?" I asked and looked at Stephen. "I understand you are planning on flying over. I will find out where to land."

Stephen nervously responded, "Tell them to land in the west acre, we have it marked, and to please hurry."

I knelt next to Stephen, "Ben, come on, open those eyes and talk to me. Wake up, Ben, and talk to me."

Ben opened an eye and smiled at me. "Sugar and yeast; remember those two things and you just might graduate with honors." He closed his eyes again and Stephen began to talk to him louder. "Dad, open your eyes."

Ben opened the other eye, "Hey, this is a private conversation; I am talking with your mother. She asked me if you are cleaning your room if you are doing your homework, and if you are going to give her a grandchild. She is waiting."

"No, Dad you are not talking to Mom you were talking to Clara, remember? She was asking you chemistry questions. Mom is not here, Mom is not here."

The medics ran into the house just as Ben took one deep breath, smiled, and his skin began to change into a pale hue of bluish-gray. I pulled Stephen away as the medics put him onto the tiled floor and began pushing on his chest, ordering each other quickly to insert intravenous lines, and placing cardiac leads on his chest. Stephen slumped into my arms, put his head on my shoulder, and whispered. "Please, Clara, I cannot live without him."

I held Stephen as Ben was wheeled on a gurney out the front door to the waiting ambulance. The drivers said quickly, "You two need to come with us."

I climbed in after Stephen as he slid along the seat of the ambulance, close to his father's head, and spoke to him, lifting his oxygen mask strap to whisper in his ear. "Dad, it's me, Stephen. You have had a nasty fall, right into those shrubs."

"I am grateful that I left them all bushy, it kept you from hitting the cement walkway. I think you might be sleepy right now but I want you to listen to my voice please?"

Stephen tugged on my hand pulling me closer to him. He motioned to his father, "Talk, Clara, let him hear your voice. Tell him how much you do not understand about winemaking. Tell him what you remember, please talk to him."

My mouth close to Ben, and began to talk. "Well, Ben, favorite love of my mother Clarish, you need to take a short rest before you begin to feel better. I know you want to jump up and continue my wine class, or better yet get me to tell you how much I adore your Pinot. Now we just want you to rest. However, you must focus on us. Can you hear my voice? Can you move one little finger, or move your head?"

We waited, watching his head move with the jiggling of the gurney as the ambulance dashed along the highway, swerving occasionally around the curves, jolting around cars that pulled along the side of the road. We looked at his hands, resting on top of the white sheet. When his hand slid off the gurney, we smiled.

The ambulance pulled within feet of the heliport. I moved quickly out of the ambulance, followed by Stephen who walked at the side of his father's head, talking. "OK, Dad, just an occasional bump as you are loaded onto a helicopter. Do you remember when you were insistent on us building this helicopter pad?"

"I thought it was the most ridiculous thing that I had ever heard. You said, "Son, I think it is a great marketing tool and we can certainly use it to fly clients around the valley." You also had a classic line, Dad. "Son, I think we could include a Helicopter Valley Ride as one of the auction items for the fall barrel festival."

"I do remember your favorite reason, Dad." You said, "Son, I think you could impress your date by picking her up in a helicopter. Remember, Dad, do you remember?"

The medics shoved the gurney into the helicopter. Stephen jumped in pulling me after him. The medic, Ralph, spoke to Ben, "Just a short ride Ben and we will get you hooked up to machines that will get your lungs breathing. Here we go." Placing earmuffs over Ben's ears, Stephen's, and mine, we lifted slowly into the air.

Stephen knew Ralph: they both went to high school together, always seemed to date the same girls. Ralph had a deeply tanned skin, wide white smile, and black hair that had hung down his back. Both tall, both athletic and both sought after by the valley girls.

Everyone had grown up together, starting the primary grades at various times, every father knew the girl's father, and every mother attended the same school parent activities with other mothers. Most dates were mere "friendships," there never was any romantic involvement because everyone who lived east of the mountains wanted to leave. Ralph's parents were divorced; no one had ever met his father. Rumors were that he moved to Seattle chasing an old flame.

Colleges west of the mountains were more appealing; out of state colleges in Idaho, Arizona, Nevada, were not that far from home. A gradual the stark reality occurred that families could not afford to either pay out of state tuition or afford the universities in Western Washington.

Stephen worked with his father into his late twenties, promising to learn everything he could from his father first, followed by a college education. Ralph spent a stint in the Marines, returned as the hometown hero, and pursued his medical career.

Originally, he had hoped military credit would assist him in applying for medical school but a minor amputation of his right thumb limited his mobility in his right hand and his dream of becoming a surgeon. Only scarred, puckered wrinkled tissue remained where the thumb had been and no one ever knew the story behind the amputation.

No one asked, ignoring how his thin plastic surgical glove fingers drooped when he gripped any object. Stephen had only heard rumors of bar fights, post-traumatic stress, and an accident after chopping a fallen tree.

He looked at Stephen now with eyes filled with concern. When Stephen searched his face for a positive look, gesture, or nod, he only shrugged and whispered, "I don't know."

Ben began to thrash back and forth, pulling on his oxygen mask and pointing at me, "Clarish, what are you doing here? Get back to your winery..."

Ralph talked to him and looked up at me. "Are you Clarish's daughter?" I nodded, wiping my face quickly.

"I know I am much younger than your mother but she was admired by so many."

"This community loved her, well, we still love her. She not only ran that winery but she was so involved in everything within the community. I remember the year that we had the unexpected frost, everyone will tell you about the destroyed vines. We had an impossible time on the roads, ice, rocks, and some fissures that had formed once the ice melted."

He listened to Ben's heart, gave him an injection into his IV. "Something for his blood pressure, it just keeps dropping now and then." He stopped talking when he heard the triage center at the hospital ask for an update. He talked quickly, throwing out numbers, medications, mental status, oxygen level, and color.

He looked back at me, "There was no way we could travel on the roads, so your mother turned your living room into a mini first aid station with the migrant clinic staff caring for strains, sprains, and broken bones from falls."

"We answered all of our calls treating the minor injuries for members of the community. The freeze did not last but a week, yet while we were taking care of clients she was taking care of us by cooking all of our meals, washing our clothes, providing us with a place to sleep, and offering us her remarkable wines."

He started to talk again but Ben began to cough and hold his head. "My head feels tight; it feels like it is going to burst." He let out a low moan and became quiet.

Ralph pushed more medication into the intravenous tubing while giving the triage team an update. The helicopter left behind the green dotted soil, speckles of livestock, and ribbons of highways as it approached Spokane.

Freeways crossed through the city, joining the rural land to the buses, taxis, and cars that drove passing blue exit signs, ducking under overpasses, and heading to jobs, homes, schools, or colleges. The helicopter pad landing was on the top of the hospital and I watched as staff stood at a safe distance from the whirling helicopter. After it landed, they slowly approached as the blades stilled.

Stephen sat back and for the first time took my hand, while gloved hands grasped Ben's gurney, placed it on a waiting bed that rolled him quickly away from the helicopter. Entering sliding doors, the team vanished down the hallway of Eastern Washington Heart Center. One doctor approached Stephen and asked a few questions about Ben while directing us to the intensive care unit waiting room.

I had no words, my fear had silenced me. The hospital staff now had Ben, with all of his symptoms, and it was up to them to move this man in a direction of healing.

The intensive care waiting room was stark, empty, and lifeless like the patients hidden behind the automatic doors that took families into their rooms. Hospital brochures were stacked evenly in plastic containers; the water cooler stood half-filled, with a wastepaper basket overflowing with discarded cups.

A marble counter held carafes of coffee, hot water, and tea lined up under the only window. More brochures stood at attention at the end of the counter offering available information on all the hospital services, social workers, business staff, and hospital advocates to guide families through the system. I wondered how a system filled with stress could direct families. People came for admission, staying or leaving to go home, or transferred when there was no one to care for them at home.

After Stephen and I took seats facing the automatic door, I looked around the waiting room. Every time I wanted to say something to soothe him there would be a public announcement paging a physician, an x-ray technician, a family member who needed to return to the surgery waiting room, and once I heard an urgent code that told me that there was an emergency.

Several times, I heard the tiny bells of a lullaby and I wanted to ask someone what it meant. I wished it were a happy sound and not the sound of a song implying death.

Saving Ben

Every time the automatic doors opened, we would strain our eyes looking for anything that would give us a glimpse of Ben, or his doctor or someone who might be approaching us with information on his progress.

Stephen said, "I forgot what Dad was wearing. I honestly cannot remember what he had on; I was pre-occupied this morning with the chemistry lab and forgot he had been outside. I mean, typically we rotate to break things up and some of the guests can be a little weary of our smiles."

"I swear if one more person asks me what my favorite wine is I might just have to make up a strange story about some ancient wine found in an Aztec temple in a pottery jar that had been carved in symbolic wine symbols. Do you think they would believe me, Clara? Better yet, do you believe me that wine began before Christ?"

I felt his arms tense, twitch, and tremor when one of the staff came out holding a frosty white zippered satchel. She was a younger nurse, spiked blond hair, a floral scrub top decorated in large purple lilies, and lavender pants. "Good morning. Are you Stephen?"

Stephen stood; I followed quickly at his side. She touched his arm as we stared at the nurse waiting for her purpose. "These are your dad's clothes; we have changed him into something more comfortable. I am Anita, his nurse, and part of the team working with him right now. I know you wish to see him but if you can just be patient for a little longer; we must get his entire vital signs stable before we take him to surgery."

I was the first to speak, "Why is he going to surgery, he did not break anything, he just fell back into the bushes? I watched him fall. I know he did not hit anything."

Anita pointed to a little room that I had not noticed. "Please, let us step inside here for a moment so I can give you an update."

Walking into the room hidden by the floor-to-ceiling aquarium, I was amazed at the transformation from the waiting room. Three small couches were staggered throughout the room, allowing a grouping of one couch, one light, one chair, with tossed blankets hanging over every piece of furniture. Soft music was playing; I smiled for the first time in hours when I heard the soft piano notes. She guided us to the couch and sat across from us. The room was empty except an overturned Kleenex box on one table, discarded candy wrappers on the floor, and several torn crumpled pieces of paper from a yellow legal pad.

Anita spoke directly to me after looking briefly at my wrapped foot, "May I ask who you are to Benjamin Thomas?" I gave a brief explanation of my short forty-eight-hour visit to the winery and stated I was a new family friend.

I emphasized that I saw the entire incident from the gazebo and attempted to explain that the couple had just left the tepee.

Stephen looked at me as I began to explain that the tepees were for couples who preferred time alone to drink wine. I found my voice rising. "Ben was so kind to them and so quick to acknowledge that they perhaps needed some time alone, away from the other guests tasting wine on the patio."

"I mean, if you had seen this couple's behavior I am not sure if another winery would have done the same. I am sure they would have been asked to leave. When Ben guided them to the tepee, they were laughing and stopped to shake his hand before they disappeared inside."

"I know that when they reappeared, and Ben saw her face bruised, well, clearly something had changed. I think the police will give you a complete update on their report about the couple."

He nudged me before he spoke to Anita, "I do not want to give the impression that we rent our cottages for afternoon sexual encounters. Our work crew and family typically use the cottages. We built them for the children for a place to play and also a future marketing venture as our winery expands, but clearly, my Dad must have sensed that it was the quickest solution to the couple's inappropriate public behavior. I do want the name of the man who pushed my father." Anita turned her head to Stephen, seemingly not interested in the tepee's purpose. "I just need to ask and understand your father's behavior these past few weeks. What we are observing now is that the incident that happened today was the final blow for some earlier changes that might have occurred."

He sighed nodding, "Well, yes, there have been some changes, but Dad has said it was all related to fatigue or that he had stumbled. He has been dragging his left leg a little and has had some weakness in his left hand. However, he had no trouble picking up Clara from her winery the other day and driving her over here. We had planned to take him to the doctor later this week. Is it his blood pressure? Exactly what are you finding?"

Anita softened her voice. "Stephen and Clara, all this is very preliminary, so you must understand I am just telling you thoughts based on the MRI, or the brain image that was done. He may have burst an existing aneurysm or he has a brain hemorrhage."

"No one knows at this point if either of these findings occurred based on the scuffle he had with your guest. Our focus now is to fix what is going on with Ben."

"The plan now is to stop the bleeding or to do something to relieve the pressure he is feeling in his head. Has he ever talked about his head hurting?"

I added, after remembering his behavior in flight, "Yes, in fact, he commented on his head feeling like a bursting balloon right before the helicopter landed."

"Please do not think the worse, not now. We will have to see how he does after surgery and let our medical team relieve that pressure. Would you like to see him before he goes to surgery?"

Stephen had become silent, words filling his head, questions he wanted to ask but he felt numb, he could not speak a word. All he saw was his father, his partner at the winery, his mother's husband, his childhood playmate, his protector, his mentor, and the person he wanted to make proud.

He could not imagine him lying in that intensive care unit unable to talk about their latest release of wine, or talking to one of the wine shop owners on the East Coast convincing him why they had the best Pinot Noir in the valley.

Aware of his distraction, I whispered in his ear, "Stephen, Anita wants to know if you would like to see your Dad before he goes to surgery."

Stephen looked at me, then at Anita. "I don't know. I have the same fears as when I was a little boy. Dad stood behind me with a shotgun telling me not to move when he saw the wolf creeping behind one of the grapevines. I thought I could just jump off the porch for one second, grab a branch, and run back. I still remember how frightened I was, not of the wolf but Dad's voice. He never raised his voice to me and still does not raise his voice."

"I am sure even with this vile man pushing him today, he was talking very quietly, trying to reason with him, trying not to make a scene with so many guests around. I need this guy's name." Talking firmly to me he added, "Clara, please, don't let me forget."

Continuing he said, "Yes, I am as afraid now as felt then. I am afraid that the wolf is death creeping around my Dad, who does not have his gun, and I cannot protect him. " Stephen looked down and became silent. I spoke, "When Ben is ready to go to surgery, please tell us. Perhaps by that time, Stephen will have decided. Thank you, Anita." I whispered to Stephen, "A wolf spirit will protect him, Stephen; the wolf is not death."

Anita touched Stephen's hand and left. I took one of the blankets and wrapped it around Stephen's shoulders. I felt a chill in the room, perhaps from the conversation or the cloud of anticipatory silence. "Stephen, I will be right back. Let me get you some coffee."

I returned with the paper cup filled with steaming coffee, Stephen stood in the middle of the room putting on his father's shirt that he had pulled from the white plastic bag. "It's his favorite shirt; he told me Mom had given it to him. If you look closely, all the shades of purple are the actual grape colors of our wines that run together."

"He told me he used to wear this every day. After Mom died, he quit wearing it. Then when your mom, Clarish, died, he wore it in the evening at dinner only. His official lounging jacket he would wear every night by the fire, humming to the music. It seems it was his mourning costume, which makes me wonder why he was wearing it today."

"Did he have a premonition that something was going to happen? Why did he put it on today, Clara? Why not next month or next year? Tell me why he wore it today." I reached up to him, pulling his face closer.

"Stephen, you carried me around all day yesterday without even thinking of yourself or how I could be a burden to you or your family. And now, although I cannot carry you physically, please let me carry your emotions, let me guide you when you are too confused to know what to do and let me lift your heart."

Stephen looked down at me, rested his forehead on mine, and let me touch his tears. "My original plan, Clara, did not work. I was to be the conquering warrior that took care of you while you healed."

Suddenly, he started chuckling when he remembered me explaining the tepee to the nurse. "You thought that we grabbed our naughty guests, plunked them in the tepee to

186

have some serious sex, and sent them on their way after buying three cases of our wine?"

I giggled. "Stephen in my heart there was a part of me that hoped I would end up in one of the teepees with a certain wine expert after I graduated from my winery classes."

Stephen lifted my chin gently, our eyes were now looking at each other, puffy from tears, cheeks slightly reddening, and dried streaks lined our faces. Stephen kissed me, rubbing his tongue across my teeth. I responded by licking the tip of his tongue. We kept our eyes focused and took turns kissing each other's face as if to dissolve the sadness that lay invisible to everyone else's eyes.

"Clara, I do not know why you have come into my life. Something tells me that there has been a plan that you and I will never understand. I think your mother talked to my mother. I hope they are both talking to Dad now and telling him to stay put because they are not ready for him to join them."

"What do you think, Clara, was our meeting each other scheduled during our busy lives or has it come along for another reason?"

I kissed him one last time. "I am a focused person, Stephen. My life is numbers that evolve into precise, exact information. These last days have been unforgiving moments of jumbled, unpredictable, lovely friendships and the stirring of many new emotions."

"I guess it started with the mother coyote, burning the bread in my mother's oven, plus all these people coming forward to tell me stories about my mother. I feel her with me as if she is waiting for me to do something, but what I fear is that I might not be doing exactly what she wants me to do."

"I suppose you might call this serendipity, or that the stars have aligned, or that I just have very weak ankles that collapsed after wearing high heels every day at work." We both laughed but turned quickly when Anita called our names.

"Stephen and Clara, we will be taking your Dad to surgery in five minutes. Would you like to come in and talk to him?"

I turned back to Stephen. "Yes, we would like to see Ben, right Stephen?"

We left the small, quiet room, crossed the waiting room that had filled with two other families and one police officer. Anita hit the red button on the wall, a structural invitation into the intensive care unit. Another smaller waiting room was inside the door with hardback folding chairs, newspapers with past headlines, and a two-burner hot plate with empty carafes, a water fountain, and several boxes of tissue. Stephen whispered, "I am not sure what it would take to make this room more comfortable for families." He looked up at the blaring fluorescent lights, tapped the tiled floor, and ran his hand across the pale-yellow walls.

I felt overwhelmed by the sounds surrounding fragile lives. An orchestra of faint, tiny monitor beeps merged with swishing sounds of machines breathing oxygen into hungry lungs. Sliding glass doors opened and closed, curtains slid on ceiling tracks exposing an individual lying quietly, or someone sitting chatting to the nurse, the rolling of equipment across the floors, the hushed voices of staff talking with family, the ringing phone, and physicians were shouting orders.

I thought this is its world, a world where negotiation happens with no guarantee who wins a contract to live. I watched the parents stand outside one of the rooms holding a baseball hat and a giant stuffed teddy bear staring at the ground, leaning with their ears against the glass door waiting to hear a word that would assure them their child would be better. Anita moved quickly past the room, blocking us from the parents and walked toward the end room. There were no curtains pulled around Ben's bed; four masked staff wearing scrub greens and paper slippers surrounded him. "Please, meet the team waiting for you and who will be taking care of Ben in surgery," Anita explained.

We stood by the door, the staff nodded and parted as if it were a choreographed move performed several times each day. Anita whispered, "It's OK, go up and talk to him. I am sure he would enjoy hearing familiar voices."

She nodded to the staff that stepped away from the bed but did not leave the room. I felt he was in critical condition and no one wanted to be far away at this point. Stephen took my hand and we walked to the top of the bed. Ben lay still, his color had faded to a pale gray hue as if someone dipped the tip of a black paintbrush in a small coin of white paint and swirled it.

His lips were glossy. Anita offered, "His lips seemed a little dry, I gave him some clear lipstick." Anita began to point at all the tubes in his neck, arms, and the clear yellow tube that hung on the side of the bed draining his urine. "He looks like we have dressed him in medical technology. The one medicine you can't see is trying to keep his blood pressure balanced to offset the potential pressure in his brain."

Stephen looked at his father's hands, tied with soft white restraints. "Stephen, we are not tying down your father to cause him harm. He keeps moving his arms; a good thing to see movement but we are afraid he will try to pull one of the lines, something we do not want to happen. He is lightly sedated, again to calm his body to keep his blood pressure down." He leaned over Ben and began to talk, "Well, look at you. How many times have you told me that I could not take an afternoon nap until we finished our work?"

190

"I would like to remind you that it is now two o'clock and here you are snoring. I suppose this means I have to get that crushing machine fixed and get those grapes-started. I guess it is OK this time, but really, Dad if you want to take a vacation, you know as well as I know, that harvest is not the time to relax."

Ben opened his eyes stared at Stephen and winked. In whispering words, he asked, "Can I marry Clarish?" The surgical team could not believe he was speaking. Stephen's eyes filled with tears, "No, I do not permit you to marry Clarish. I need you to come to my wedding first."

I put my face next to Stephens. "Hey, Professor Ben, I need to finish this class. I mean, I do not even know what you put in first to the wine; is it the yeast or the sulfite? If I am going to keep this winery, I certainly need your help and if you think you could just sleep this afternoon away, well, that just will not do. And you promised to take me on a ride to look over the valley. Don't you break your promise."

This time Ben winked and spoke very slowly in a sleepy drawl, "Stephen, you find time to love the daughter of my Clarish."

Again, the staff looked at Ben and the two of us, nodding their approval of his responses. Anita whispered, "One quick kiss, and we need to leave."

After wiping tears from his face, Stephen kissed his Dad's forehead, and I followed with a kiss on his nose. "We will be waiting for you. Hurry back."

Stephen looked up at the staff and thanked them. We left quickly with Anita and stood outside the door while Ben's bed disappeared down the hallway. The staff shuffled quickly, making a sharp left turn at the end of the hall to the surgery suite. "Now we wait?" Stephen said to Anita.

"Yes, and we are talking a minimum of six hours. I would like to suggest that you consider going out of the hospital for a walk, or lunch, or just a different change of scenery. You can do nothing now and I am afraid sometimes sitting in our waiting room can just make your day longer."

She handed him a small beeper, "I will call you at intervals to give you an update. Please, do not think when I am calling that something is wrong. If my calling frequently would upset you, I will not."

Stephen looked at me seeking a decision, "Please, call when you can and I agree with you. I think we need to leave the hospital. But I just realized we don't have a car."

Anita reached into her pocket. "So here is the deal, you don't have any idea how you got my car keys. They fell into your pocket accidentally. My car is one block away. Turn right when you leave the parking lot and look for the small grassy park with the beautiful fountain that looks like an angel wing."

"My car is parked right in front of it, my favorite spot in this city. No, I do not park there because it is a sure guarantee no one would dare to steal a car in front of an angel. I just find it very peaceful and I will often sit on the bench before I head home or start my day at the hospital."

"I am here until midnight; please, just get away for a few hours. I promise you that one of the best teams we have in this hospital is taking care of your Dad. Go."

We felt her gentle shove on our shoulders. We walked back through the automatic doors, down the hallway, down the elevator, and out of the hospital. The air smelled like a sheet mixed with the freshness of spring rain. A mist seemed to hover in the air and burnt-orange and brown leaves scattered as we formed a path to Anita's car. Stephen looked back, staring at the row of windows, wondering where his father's surgery room was, which window was intensive care, and what bright green drape would shield the sunlight as Ben packed his suitcase to return home.

I nudged Stephen and pointed my finger at the couple walking in front of us. The parents had stood outside their child's room earlier. A priest and one of the nurses held them around their waists, supporting sagging bodies. I noticed that the mother's arm swung limply holding the teddy bear and the father was wearing a child's baseball hat sideways on his head.

I began to cry, "Stephen, the little boy must have died." He kissed my forehead and looked back at the hospital again. "We don't know what happened, we just have to think about Dad now and perhaps talk to the angel when we get Anita's car. I am not trying to be selfish but I have no room in my heart now for anything but Dad."

We watched the family climb into a pickup truck, battered, dented, and scraped. Stephen spoke quickly, "It's one of the valley's families, and everyone will be impacted by whatever has happened to the family."

The car pulled away, the minister standing stoically, the nurse waving, and once the car was out of sight the nurse turned around and began to sob into the minister's black shirt. We stepped between two parked cars to give them privacy and waited for them to walk past.

Anita's car sat in front of the angel wing made of white marble, folded slightly in against the form of a figure in a kneeling position. Red spray paint that covered the dedication plaque resembled a giant clown smile making it impossible to know who had been acknowledged in the statue. We touched the wing at the same time. Stephen whispered, "Go take care of Dad."

Her small Volkswagen station wagon's interior resembled her lifestyle; the backseat covered in gym bags, several empty water bottles, and tennis shoes on the floor. Two medical textbooks were on the passenger seat of the car, cardiac physiology, and a study manual for advanced life support certification. CD's were on the floor, a local fast-food restaurant sandwich wrapper filled an empty coffee cup, and a punch card for the local coffee shop was sticking out of the empty ashtray.

I carefully moved my feet around the floor mat and waited for Stephen to start the car. A blast of hot air filled the car immediately, Stephen laughed. "Well, our Anita must not be a Washingtonian to need this much heat in the summer months."

"By her looks, I think she lived on the islands. Do not let that blond hair fool you, I think she probably lived in Hawaii' and decided to try the Pacific Northwest. Sometimes people think or assume that this eastern part of the state is warmer. Not true. I hope you stick around, Clara, to catch all the seasons we have to offer."

We noticed all the "No Parking" signs lining the street, parking hours requiring a parking permit, and finally the parking patrol marking tires with the skill of a chalk wizard.

Leaving the tree-lined streets, we followed the road toward the riverbanks. "They do not need to walk far to enjoy Columbia. All we have to do is walk to its edge." Stephen recognized a street sign and began to drive slowly along the line of shops and stores. Pointing to them he said,

"So, Clara, these are the tasting rooms from many wineries. Often people would rather walk from room to room than coming out to the wineries."

"I do not dislike them, because certainly, they have the chance to try out the different wines, but it is just not the same. I mean, how many of these places can offer our patio, our air-conditioned wine tasting room, and just the view? Who would miss the chance to stroll through our vineyards and look at the amazing view? A historical fact is that downtown Walla Walla was a temporary stockade after Fort Walla Walla closed in mid-1850."

"Unfortunately, most of these places might mention the wineries but sometimes they just want to sell the wine. The small shops and tasting rooms that sell our wines, and perhaps soon your wines, are great promoters because we take good care of them."

"Our vendors are invited to come out to the winery for different dinners or new releases. They mean more to us than just people who sell our wine. Perhaps one of the biggest pluses besides the wine sales is the interest we get in people joining our wine club."

I asked, "Wine club, Stephen? Does that mean they get T-shirts and punch cards, like buy ten and get one free?"

"Not quite, my novice vintner. They get discounts and are the first to know if we have an event. Unfortunately, with so many tourists just coming for visits we cannot get a strong, consistent membership base."

"We do ship, so if people like our wines we will make sure they get what they want. Dad writes a newsletter with updates about the winery and he also teaches, he always teaches." Stumbling over his words Stephen found himself unable to continue.

"How about recipes Stephen, does he include recipes?"

He remained silent looking for a parking spot and gulping back his tears.

"Well, I know that my mother had a recipe book given to me after she died. She filled it with recipes including pairings. Now I will be the first to admit, I had no idea what a pairing meant or was not sure I would even care to match wine with a meal."

I offered a suggestion, "I bet it would please Ben to know that this book exists and perhaps he can include it in his newsletter when he feels better." I paused, "Or I can help too. I mean, you have already hired me to work your financial spreadsheet as you increase your wine marketing, why not a little marketing idea?"

Stephen moved the car into a small space, got out of the car, and opened the car for me. An empty water bottle fell to the ground as I got out of the car. Stephen picked it up, tapped it on my on the head, "Why, Miss Clara, I think you just might find yourself a valley job after all and you can leave that city job."

How Different a Day Becomes

We walked over to the street vendor and the beeper chirped. Stephen dialed the number immediately and listened to Anita's voice. He lifted the phone slightly away from his ear for me to hear. "Your Dad has been given anesthesia and a tube has been placed down his windpipe to help him breathe. They are going to begin to drill a small hole in his skull to help release the pressure. Talk to you soon." She hung up quickly.

I walked slightly behind him, looping my fingers in his. We watched the park fill with wandering people guiding children and dogs, throwing Frisbees, running to, running away, walking slowly, or walking toward the river.

Occasionally a visitor bumped into a park bench, tossed wrappers in garbage cans, picked up the flier that had stuck to the bottom of their shoe, searched through their backpack, stared at their paperback book, and poked a text message into their phone. Some took off their jackets, put on a baseball hat, and pointed at a bird to their stroller occupant. Some sat on the river railing staring at the water, leaned against a tree finishing the last of a cup of coffee, cursed words at the bicyclist that swerved past the runner, sat on the grass, lay on the grass pointing at clouds, or strummed a guitar.

I thought life continues. No one's day has been halted, jolted, punctured, or floating in a bath of anticipation like Stephen's and mine. Odd, how life has a way of insulating people from what could happen, what might have happened, and what one wishes never happen. Human beings can become introverted, selfishly worried only about the sounds of the river, or the time of day, or the expired parking meter. No one needs to embrace the fears that we attempt to silence in our minds. Their appearance of normalcy is validated by the sameness of walking, looking, staring, and searching for a place to fit into the grassy park population.

Stephen stood in front of the hot dog vendor who rattled off the available toppings like a vinyl record whose needle had stuck in the same groove. I was distracted thinking about Ben. Stephen ordered two hotdogs with cream cheese and red onion toppings, two drinks of water, and a saucer-sized chocolate chip cookie.

I watched the woman with a giant sunhat reach for its brim when it began to lift from the breeze gently ruffling the edges of newspapers, diverting the Frisbee from its course, and rustling the pages of the paperback book resting on the face of the sleeping college student.

I shuddered at the coolness that seemed to dive into the hotdogs spinning on their rolling cylinders. The blue sky faded into streaks of gray, with clouds stretching like rubber bands. The sun had disappeared, hiding behind the last cotton-ball cloud puffing ivory strands into a billowing sail popping like the failed elasticity of chewing gum.

I felt Stephen's arm around my waist and we began to walk quickly back to the car. No sooner had our car doors closed than a pelleting shower of hail ricocheted off the front window, bouncing onto the hood of the car, and aiming itself like miniature cannonballs at people walking, running, and bicycling past.

So their life has now been jolted, I thought. Just when the park patrons had settled into an anticipated afternoon of sunshine, unexpected stormy bleakness stopped them. "I am sorry all of your day was ruined," I shouted, "but I am glad you are sharing our day."

The beeper alerted us and he called Anita. Looking at me he only nodded and finally said, "Yes, I hear you. We are not far, we are on our way."

Without thinking, he began to back out. We both felt the thump on the back fender and realized that the mother with the stroller had started to walk behind the car. Stephen jumped out of the car apologizing profusely. He listened to her make her point of him being an idiot and needing a driving lesson on backing up.

She asked what if she had not been paying attention, could he possibly live the rest of his life knowing he had killed her child, and ended with the pledge of hoping he would someday have the same fear she had.

He opened the door to the driver's side to find me finishing my hot dog, "I will be driving us to the hospital."

Stephen climbed into the passenger side and put his head on the dashboard. "It is not good Clara; they want us to come back now. Dad lost blood once they attempted to repair the aneurysm, and they are not sure if they will be able to give him enough blood for the loss. His blood pressure is low now. Anita said come back emphasizing come back now."

His head bounced on the dashboard as he cried, hitting his fists alongside his head and repeating, "I just cannot let him go, Clara. I cannot even think of what it would be like if he was not walking in the vineyards, sitting next to me in the laboratory, or telling his jokes to our guests. I cannot believe this. How can one day, one afternoon change a life that quickly?"

The car inched along the streets filled with cars leaving the hospital grounds, students leaving classes juggling books, cell phones, and gulping sips from soft drink cups. The space that Anita had originally parked her car had turned into a mini parking lot for three bicycles and one scooter all chained together, facing the curb. Stephen became more anxious as his beeper went off again. Calling Anita, he heard her whisper, "Please hurry." He looked at me, jumped from the idling car, and began to run toward the hospital. I sighed and looked up, "Ben, hang on he is coming, just wait another minute. Please, Ben, just another minute."

I circled the block, found a load /unload sign that permitted parking after hours. I slid easily into the space, grabbed Stephen's jacket, my jacket, and began to run past the couples holding hands, the parents snuggling their sleeping infant, and the homeless man playing the harmonica, tapping his foot against his crumpled hat filled with coins.

The elevator took an eternity to arrive. I pushed myself in front of the waiting crowd of visitors and spoke firmly, "My apologies. My friend is not doing well and I need to get to his side; I need to get to his son's side. Please excuse my rudeness."

The crowd parted, parted as if they understood or as if they did not need an explanation because the look on my face was all they needed to see.

When I arrived at the intensive care unit, Stephen was standing alone in the hallway. He was staring at me but not seeing me, he was leaning against the wall tapping his foot. His physical appearance resembled a pillar of strength. I approached him slowly, keeping within his sight and hoping he would notice me. He turned quickly and returned to the room. I stood by the door and saw Ben lying on the bed motionless, no tubes were visible on his face, arms, or hands. His color began to match the gray skies. Stephen stared at me, unblinking.

I walked to the bed, put my hand on Ben's hand that felt warm, warm like the first time I had met him and sat with him on the porch with a cup of coffee in his hands. Stephen only looked at Ben, he did not touch him, he did not speak, and he just stared.

I spoke softly, "Ben, I believe you are still in this room and you are watching us. I know that Stephen cannot tell you how much he loves you but you must believe he told me you were his life, you were his world, and that he will never be the same without you."

"I can tell you that I will take care of him for you, I will stay with him in the weeks ahead, and every time I get an answer wrong on my wine course I will think of you? I wonder whether you have found Mom yet. I have no doubt she is waiting for you and she will take care of you, she will help you understand the feelings that she had when she went to Heaven."

Stephen stood behind me putting his arms around my waist. "Please, keep talking to him."

I took one of Stephen's hands and slowly placed it on Ben's hand. "We are touching you now, Ben; we are giving you the warmth of our love. Your son is trying to understand what has happened and how you can be lying in this hospital bed."

"I am trying to figure out why you have chosen to leave us when you should be walking through my vineyard with me. Yes, Ben, did you hear me. Did you hear what I said? My vineyard, Ben, I will stay and take care of my family history. My generation will assume the responsibility that others have given me. Will you help me, Ben?"

I laid my head on his chest and cried, "Ben, thank you for being part of my life. Thank you for bringing me to Stephen. Without you, without meeting you, without you loving my mother I never would be where I am right now." I rubbed my hand across his patient gown that felt newly pressed for our final visit.

Anita walked behind us. "What can I do for you at this moment?" Stephen let go of me and spun around facing her, "Tell me what happened, Anita. I need to understand why my father was alive at this time yesterday and he now is dead. Tell me, Anita, that if today's scuffle had not happened, would my father still be alive. Tell me, Anita, that he was murdered today in his winery."

She stepped back from Stephen. "I am not an expert on the why behind today. I can tell you, Stephen, that the scuffle did not cause his brain to have an aneurysm nor did it cause the aneurysm to burst. What happened today could have happened anytime."

"The aneurysm was leaking and his left-sided weakness might have been a warning. Even if you had taken him to the hospital a week ago, it is doubtful if what happened today could have been stopped."

I put my hands on his arms. "No blame, Stephen, to you or to the unfortunate incident that happened today. He was essentially a fractured egg waiting for one moment that caused his aneurysm to burst. I wish the circumstances had been different. Why could it not have happened while he was walking through his vineyard with a glass of wine or sitting across the table from you at dinner?"

The room became more silent. A quiet stillness filled the corners of the ceiling, the floor, for any murmur of the sound of a heartbeat, or a sigh, or the tremor of lips. Stephen watched his father, not taking his eyes off his chest that remained frozen in the clutch of death's grip. He glanced at me occasionally; meeting his eyes,

I kept my hand on Ben. Stephen kept saying repeatedly, "I don't know what to do; I don't know what to do." He laid his head on Ben's head and kept whispering to him, "I love you, Dad. I love you more than I ever thought possible. I do not think I could go through a day without you. Dad, tell me what to do. Help me, Dad. Please don't leave me now, not now with all our plans just waiting to happen." I hugged Stephen bent over the white sheets covering Ben.

Anita waited by the room door, blocking anyone from interfering or entering the room when the only people who needed to be there were standing at Ben's side.

"Who is Clarish?" she finally asked. "He kept saying her name when he first came in." I turned my head away from Stephen's shirt. "My mother is Clarish, and she died."

I watched Stephen lift his head and stand beside me, two bookends pressing grief between them. "My Dad loved my mother, but she died when I was very young. He had no one else until he met Clarish. I know he wanted to marry her, but she became ill and died."

Pulling me close, he continued. "Along came Clara, resembling her mother, walking into my Dad's life and mine. I have only known her for two days and in that short time, everyone at our house has fallen in love with her. Dad is directly responsible. It is all his fault that she became his wine student, that he was going to be her mentor in managing her winery; and my role, well, my role is still, as we say in the industry, aging."

I felt the warmth of his arm, his lips rubbing across the top of my head, and again he became silent. Smiling, Anita spoke. "Stephen you were a gift for Ben's life, and Clara, a pleasant surprise who came to him two days ago. You gave him the gift of a memory, your mother. Perhaps seeing you reminded him of Clarish and he decided to reunite with her?"

Stephen stood back and bowed to me, "Anita, please meet Clara, the fourth-generation woman to own the Long House Winery. Before her, her mother Clarish, her grandmother Margaret and her great-grandmother MaMinny. I just know my Dad is going to look up every one of those women first chance he gets."

Stephen kissed his father on both cheeks for one last time and walked out of the room. Afraid to kiss the same spot I kissed his forehead and one ear. "You listen to me, Ben. I am going to be talking to you before long, and I need you to guide me. When you see Mom would you tell her I said hello and I miss her so much?

Following Stephen's walk, I left the room after hugging Anita, placed her car keys in her hand, closed the door, and searched the long hallway for Stephen. He was waiting outside the intensive care unit doors. I saw him talking to someone in the shadows. When he moved I could see the five Thomases and Maria. Within seconds, Stephen's body disappeared in embracing tentacles of arms that held, touched, and grasped him. Maria's voice whispered a prayer in Spanish and unison, every Thomas said, "Amen" repeatedly.

Maria saw me and walked to me with her arms in a wide yawn. I laid my head on Maria's shoulder, felt Maria's fingers stroking my hair and my ears filled with sympathetic Hispanic words. Maria rocked me, rubbed my back, and began to say a prayer again. I did not understand her words; I only knew that when she paused I mechanically said, "Amen."

Anita stood in the background, holding a small bag that had Ben's jewelry and wallet. Stephen turned, took the bag, and felt a solid lump at the bottom of the bag. Stephen pulled out the leather-bound book that fit his palm.

Stephen walked to me, took my hands in his, and placed the book in my opened hands. Folding my fingers over the book, he spoke softly. "Clara, this book is for you. Dad had tucked it in his pocket earlier in the day to give to you. Everything in this book is everything about you, your family, and wine. I know that Dad had put this book together when he knew your mother, and now it is yours."

Somehow, we found the strength to walk down the hallway past the other small intensive care rooms feeling the quiet nods from family members who watched them through the windows. The elevator was empty. We faced the doors knowing that the same elevator that brought us to Ben would never open its doors again to his room.

We stood in the lobby, unable to move to the automatic doors where people pushed through carrying flowers, talked on cell phones, looked at pieces of paper with room information, guided a child, or carried balloons that trailed behind them bouncing in the last whiff of outside air. Visitors balanced a cup tray filled with three tall drinks with plastic lids, shook out umbrellas, and stomped their feet on the welcome mat. Each visitor avoided the wheelchair that sluggishly moved, propelled by its owner's gloved hands, the volunteer's eyes searched for someone to help, and the stray pigeon flapped overhead, circling the fluorescent lights, landing on top of the bright-green hospital logo sign.

After the stampede of feet had passed, we moved through, welcoming the rush of wind-filled raindrops to replace our tear-stained faces. Neither of us spoke until a cab pulled up offering services. Stephen shook his head, "No, thanks, we have family coming to pick us up."

Within moments Thomas One appeared, driving an old Cadillac wearing the worn signs of the valley with smudged paint, dented fenders, and hubcaps covered with wet soil with tiny cracks running across the edges of the windshield. Thomas One jumped from the car opening the back door. I slid in, followed by Stephen who sat close to me; he rubbed his hand on Maria's shoulder who looked at us from the front seat.

Death, the Uninvited Guest

The ride back to the valley took two hours, the rain had washed farm dirt onto the highway, and the road had a slick surface forcing several cars to slide off the road. I heard Maria's murmuring reminders to Thomas One to slow down, watch that car, turn your lights on, use your flicker, do not pass the truck it will splash us, you are too close to the horse trailer, and watch out the car next to us is moving over.

I clenched Stephen's hand. Maria passed stemless wineglasses over her seat to Stephen followed by a half carafe of a deep burgundy wine matching the changing evening sky. "Only the best, Stephen, it is his 1990 vintage, which he gave me as a gift. I suppose it is my turn to give his gift to all of us, his Pinot Noir."

Stephen poured the wine freely into my glass, then his own, and leaning to the front seat, he poured a small amount in their glasses for Thomas and Maria who held their glasses high. "To my father" Stephen clinked the glasses. "To our boss," Maria and Thomas One said in unison. I ended with a final clink, "To my new friend and my wine tutor."

We sipped the wine slowly, commenting on its richness, its perfect fruit flavors, and its full body. "This wine is my Dad's mark. Only he knew how to get the perfect blend of grapes and sugar to create this amazing taste."

Stephen looked up, let his head drop, and began to sob loudly. I put my hand over his empty glass, linking a finger into his hand holding it tightly.

Thomas One drove the Cadillac slowly into the winery. He flashed his lights twice and waited. Within moments, winery team members lined the driveway, each holding a candle flickering against the darkness. We rolled down our windows, reaching our arms out, and felt our hands brushed by calloused fingers. Over twenty team members stood with tears, downcast eyes, and trembling lips illuminated by the candle.

When we left the car, we waited as each member came to hug Stephen, and invited us to blow out their candles. With only the scent of the smoldering candlewick, and the strings of smoke trailing up, Stephen repeatedly said, "Thank you," until his voice became hoarse.

Thomas One stepped in and told everyone in Spanish that he would let all know the funeral plans in the next few days, but expected to see them in the vineyard at their scheduled time.

Stephen said something quietly to Thomas who repeated the words. "Mr. Stephen would ask that all of you remember his father, Mr. Ben, in everything you do in the days ahead. When he is not as sad as he is now, he would like to do something for you to honor your love for his father."

Stephen took my arm and walked to the front door that was unrecognizable with the bouquets that lined the front of the door. "How did they know, Clara? How did the entire valley know so quickly?"

Stephen's chest began to tremble as he tried to hold back tears. Thomas One guided him to the garage door, walking into the kitchen that smelled of beans, chili peppers, warm, baked tortillas, and chicken rotating slowly above the fire.

I moved quickly into the living room to straighten the room after Thomas left, only to find it spotless. Nothing resembled the medical chaos that had resulted in Ben being administered first aid in his chair. The carpet just vacuumed, hid the ridges left by the tires of the rolling gurney. I saw Maria nod, smiling, tears staining wrinkled cheeks; she turned and left the living room.

Ben's chair stood stark, his throne still had the imprints in the leather seat from his last moments in his home. Stephen came up behind me and kissed the back of my neck, "Don't leave me tonight, please. I need to know you are close even if it is behind a different door."

I let my hand follow his hair, soft and matted from rain, sweat. "I will not leave you Stephen, but remember your Dad invited me as a guest originally. I am here for him and you. I promised your Dad I would take care of you, Stephen, but I do have a request."

213

I paused. "Keep your heart exposed, let me know what you are feeling; do not hide from me. If you want time to yourself, tell me. If you are angry, tell me. If you want to scream, scream. I will not let you run from what is and hide in your work."

Stephen gave me one last hug, took the plate of tacos Maria handed him, and went to his room. I balanced myself on the stool by the counter, and stared at the plate, realizing my weariness had overtaken my desire to eat. I glanced at the living room, placed my hand on the back of my neck feeling Stephen's lips and went to my room.

I closed the door behind me and sat on the edge of the bed, feeling the lump from the little book in my pocket. I lay across the bed holding it in my hands, Ben's book, his knowledge, memories, and a piece of his life.

Stephen knocked sharply on my door the next morning. He stood, reaching out to me and asked through tears, "Clara, I need you to help me with my Dad's memorial."

"The phone has been ringing all day from vintners in the valley seeking details, wanting to help me plan, offering to send help running the winery. I cannot even begin to know where to start or answer their questions. Clara, I don't know what to do."

I sat up in bed, realizing I was still wearing my clothes from the hospital, and holding the little book. I reached out to him.

Stephen shuffled his feet across the tiles and stood next to me with his red, puffy eyes. When he sat on the edge of the bed, I pulled him toward me. Stephen felt me press my chest against his chest, aligning my heart with his. He held me in total silence until I spoke softly in his ear, "Let us honor your dad with a celebration that he will hear in the heavens. We will respect his friendships throughout the valley and embrace everyone when they come to the celebration. You will unselfishly reach out to the winery team and understand that for the short term they may not be as productive as they were two days ago." Pushing him gently away from me, I sat up, rubbing his shirt with the tips of my finger.

I felt Stephen's lips. "Clara, you are a gift that came to me days ago and I am still unclear about the timing, about Dad bringing you home, and about your foot injury. Your foot, Clara, I forgot your foot and you have been walking on it."

He slid his hand over my abdomen, across my hip, down my leg to my bandaged foot stained with dark blood. I straightened my knee and turned my foot in circles. "Stephen is better, much better. I will follow up in a week or so but I am having no pain."

215

He ran his hand back up my leg, under my skirt, and stopped. My breathing increased, struggling emotionally, not knowing what I wanted, or did not want. I wondered about what his touch would feel like. I waited for him to look at me, stared at the closed bedroom door, and remained motionless until he slid his hand slowly back down to my knee.

Stephen stood, pulled me gently to my feet, and kissed my cheeks. "Maria has started breakfast. I will have her keep it warm until you join me. Come and read my list, which has grown to three pages on my legal pad. I have pulled out Post-its, a highlighter, and printed all the wineries in the valley. Thank you again, Clara."

I eyed the giant soaking tub briefly but headed to the shower. Stepping out of the shower, I saw my clothes replaced with an all-black outfit consisting of a loose peasant blouse and a calf-length skirt.

I braided my wet hair and let it fall on the black blouse. The bandage had fallen off in the shower. It allowed me to inspect the skin on my foot, which had turned a pale yellow. My toes had lost their puffy appearance, and twisting my foot side to side offered only a twinge of discomfort. I noticed two raw openings between my toes exposing tissue. I found Ben's book tucked on my pillow, placed it in the spacious skirt pocket, and walked out to the kitchen.

Stephen was on the phone standing by the windows waving at the winery crew pushing stainless steel wine barrels into the warehouse. Several postal trucks were by the tasting room unloading boxes. A florist truck stopped at the top of the vineyard and followed Thomas One's direction pointing to the patio. I stood next to him while three wreaths decorated with grape leaves and clumps of grapes hung off patio chairs facing the windows. Stephen moved the phone away from his face, moving his face closer to the window, his breath fogged up the glass. I moved my finger slowly across the glass and wrote Ben.

We did not hear Maria call us to breakfast until she spoke over the violin string music that filled the room. "Mr. Stephen and Miss Clara, your breakfast is waiting. Come, sit, eat, and put your thoughts together for the day ahead. I am going to help in the gift shop today. Sandwiches for your lunch are in the refrigerator, I expect you back here by five for dinner." Acting like two scolded schoolchildren, we moved to the counter, smiling at Maria and offering a weak smile while we ate breakfast in silence. Stephen pushed the legal pad filled with asterisk-marked tasks toward me. I numbered them in order of priority.

Stephen reached for the ringing phone and I put my hand on his. "Do not answer. Put in a new voice message acknowledging your dad's death, and ask callers to check tomorrow for updates on his memorial plans. Stephen, they will understand your need for privacy today."

Maria watched Stephen listen to me, wrapping his fingers in mine, and nodding. I looked at Maria, "Please let the phone ring only in the gift shop." Looking at Stephen who had finished the house message, I said, "And your cell phone, Stephen. Nothing absolutely nothing needs your response today. I will be happy to check the messages throughout the day and select any that might require Thomas One's attention. The only voice you have is for yourself; no one else." I took his cellphone, tucked it into my pocket.

Stephen said, "Want to take a walk through the grapevines? Dad and I tried to make it a morning ritual, although we have not been very consistent this past year. Let's walk and talk, please." He looked down at my bare feet, smiled, and disappeared into his room. He brought out a pair of boots, "Not mine. I think your mother left them here once and I kept them to return to her. Somehow, I always forgot when I visited her, and now I know why. I had to save them for you whenever you decided to come into our, I mean, my life."

I lifted my skirt, princess style, and slid my feet into Mom's black boots decorated with tiny paint splashes of sugar pea vines.

When we left the dining room and opened the door to the patio, the brightness of the morning sun bounced off the wrought-iron tabletops putting a light glow around the wreaths hanging over the chairs. Stephen began to walk over to the circular signs of sympathy until I pulled his hand.

"Walk in the vineyard. Show me your favorite grape, show me what a healthy grape leaf looks like, and let's get a bottle of wine from the warehouse."

Stephen held my hand close to his leg, and I moved my feet slowly through the graveled path. I read the signs at the end of each row: Zinfandel, Shiraz, and Muscat, and asked, "All red?"

He smiled, "No. One is white and is very sweet. No quiz now, but I will give you a hint it starts with M."
I wished I could make a quick note in the little leather book, but left his comment to memory. The winery crew nodded as we walked by, not approaching Stephen with any questions, and became silent in their conversations between each other.

Stephen began to say, "It's OK. You can talk to me." I pulled his hand and said quietly, "No, Stephen, no you do not need to talk now, no explanation is needed. Let Thomas One handle their questions."

After walking through the vineyard, Stephen stopped at the stone path that led to the winery to the left and the driveway to the right. He began to walk down the driveway, pausing to look back at the house, then the vines, and continued slowly down the driveway. At the end of the driveway, he paused and gazed at the ribbon of concrete highway carved through the mountains and touched their winery sign carved by one of the Native American tribal members. Standing nearby, I watched Stephen's lips move as he looked back at his home and the winery.

Almost as if he were in prayer, I heard him say, "Dad," several times and stood quietly. I remembered Mother reminding me to stand still and quit fidgeting when she would meet neighbors at the feed store. I thought Mother would be laughing right now if she knew how silent I was, honoring Stephen's feelings.

Stephen looked over at me after hearing my mumble. "Sorry, Stephen, just sharing a thought with my mother. I guess I should have asked her to look for your Dad while she was watching us these last couple of days."

He began pointing across the Columbia River. "See that bluff? Well, Dad and I used to climb it, and we would sit and talk about how this valley came to be. He was quite a historian, which you will soon learn once you open up his little leather book. He once told me years ago that he wanted his ashes thrown off that cliff. He would say, 'Now make sure when you toss them out if they will float down the river. Make sure none of them land on all of these rocks. I prefer transforming into an ashen raft on this river than grey icing clustered on dingy-looking stone walls.' We will go there, Clara, after Dad's memorial, if you will come with me."

Stephen laughed spontaneously, tickling me until I gave him an answer. "Yes, Stephen, I will go with you to the bluff; but, only if you don't have to swim across the river!"

We stood on the grass while the postal truck turned sharply on the curve and drove up the driveway kicking up the tiny rocks. Stephen pulled me into the winery, picked a bottle of Pinot Noir, saying his father told him to pick the best wine to help plan the best memorial.

We spent the afternoon going over all the details. The task list that appeared like putty in the morning had come together with the memorial planned within the week. I patiently wrote, rewrote, edited, and rewrote again the words that Stephen wanted to be included in the obituary. When I called the editor of the valley newspaper with Ben's obituary, the editor responded in a high, squeaky voice, "No charge for Ben. Ben and I went to high school together. He never knew how much I loved him and I guess I never had a chance to tell him. He is very special. His death will cause a ripple in the wine community. I am almost hesitant in publishing this because one of those big corporate wine companies will read it and be here offering to buy the winery."

I looked at Stephen and spoke into the phone, "I do not doubt that Stephen will be more than happy to tell anyone who approaches with an offer that the winery is not for sale. Thank you for your generous gift to Ben. I will let Stephen know."

I paused, listened, and answered, "No, I am just a friend. I am the owner of the Long House Winery which belonged to my mother, grandmother, and great-grandmother." Nodding to the phone, I ended the conversation, "Thank you again, and yes I would love to meet you someday. I am sure my mother enjoyed your friendship." I hung up quickly and watched Stephen smiling.

Stephen asked, "I suppose our established editor told you she loved my dad and still loves him?"

I nodded, sipping on my wine.

"Well, the truth is that she went to school ten years before Dad and has him confused with one of the other winery owners who died ten years ago. Partly because of her age and partly because of her poor sight, Dad never had the heart to tell her she had the wrong Romeo. Watching her follow around him at wine functions was quite amusing."

"She did know your mother, however. She tried to get close to your mother and it is unclear to me why. I think she wanted to get some dirt on your family's history but your mom was protective of your grandmothers. I think the only person your mom talked to about her past with was Dad. He took notes from her conversations and added notes from the crew. I caution you about her attempting to have you disclose family history. I think you will find when you read the valley newspaper that she does not qualify as an expert historical writer by writing a four-page bi-monthly publication."

I looked at the empty wine bottle and watched Stephen check the shelves under the kitchen-serving counter. "Lesson time for Ben's student, M stands for Muscat to drink with the coconut cream turnovers Maria left us?"

Shaking my head as he stood with a platter of dessert, "Stephen, we have not even had the sandwiches that she left us. How can we jump to a dessert?"

Not responding to my inquisitive look and question he asked, "What, your household never had a backward meal?" I waited, tipping my head to the side, slightly lifting an eyebrow to my bangs.

"A backward meal is when you start with dessert. After Mom died and I became a challenge for Dad at mealtime, he found a new idea. We did not have a Maria at that time, just the two of us, so the desserts were the chocolate cupcakes with white filling, or jelly doughnuts or cream-filled eclairs. See a pattern here? Yes, I like cream-filled desserts. Maria figured it out quickly once she joined us. Now here is the deal, rules of a backward meal. You must finish your dessert or you will not get your dinner and there are no second helpings of desserts."

I looked at the clear wine, swirled it, and took a sip. "I taste a subtle sweetness. I can see myself drinking this

223

easily, quickly, and not realizing that I had finished a bottle. It isn't chilled."

Stephen smiled, "Yes, it would be much better chilled or sitting in a bucket of ice. But after one bottle of wine gone, I thought we would not care, Ben's student gets an A." I bit into the turnover with spurts of cream coating my lips and the corners of my mouth.

I giggled through dinner, spitting out the kernels of corn when Stephen talked about his early days picking grapes. The first time he crushed grapes with his bare feet, and when he made his first bottle of wine he said he told Dad, "I wanted to mix all of the grapes, put them in a blender, add a cup of sugar, and serve it over crushed ice. Dad did not say a thing, did not give me any direction or rules and watched me bring twenty bunches of grapes. I washed them under the faucet, soaked them in a large bucket mixed with the sugar, and threw them in the blender with their skins and stems."

"I kept adding water since the grapes clung to the blender blades. I had to keep dumping the grapes out when stems would prevent the blades from moving. Finally, I thought the best thing to do would be to put the semi-smashed grapes in a sieve, run water over it, and hope the stems would not go through, Clara; I could not get the grapes to soften, liquefy, or even appear like a jam. I did not want to tell Dad that I had failed, so I made up a pitcher of grape

Kool-Aid, and poured that in the blender with the macerated grapes."

I coughed out my tortilla chip when Stephen said, "It worked. The wine turned into a purple, red, green color. I got several empty wine bottles and poured the wine into each one finally pushing a cork in with a rubber mallet."

"I needed a label and it had to be my label. I was not sure what to call the wine, or what the wine should represent so I just drew three labels of the Columbia River surrounded by the plateaus."

"I think I might have even included a tepee with smoke coming out of the top because I had several Native American friends. I think I might have thrown in a horse. I am sure none of the labels would be appropriate these days."

"Finally, the big night came. Dinner with Dad and it was a backward dinner. I took two of his beveled wineglasses that I think he and Mother got for a wedding present. I went to the local market and bought an assortment of desserts that included two brownies, one sucker, two cordial cherries, and two chocolate fruit pies."

"I heard Dad talk about how some wines do well with chocolate. At that time I did not know that none of ours could be paired with chocolate fruit pies."

"Dad read the label, smelled the wine when he took the cork off and watched me as I poured the wine into the glasses. I had seen him taste wine in restaurants, a small pour before he would accept the bottle. I gave him a pour which included a layer of grape skins, twisted stems, and one very wine-soaked bumblebee."

"Clara, he put the glass to his mouth and with his teeth closed sipped the wine. He finished the small pour leaving the residual vineyard scraps at the bottom of the glass. "Stephen," he said, "How did you make this wine?"

Eagerly, I gave him the whole process, discussed my problems with the grapes mushy appearance, and how I thought the Kool-Aid was the secret additive. I had noticed that Dad had consumed one brownie, one chocolate pie, and one cherry cordial in one shoveled gesture into his mouth. Finally, he asked if I had tasted the wine. Proudly, I put the beveled glass to my lips after pouring the wine close to the rim. I do remember keeping my eyes closed fearing the sight of bugs and I drank the wine quickly. I tried to swallow the stems sitting on my tongue and pushed the grape skins clinging to my palate with my tongue. I never said anything, I smiled, nodded and promptly excused myself to go to the bathroom, where I threw up the wine, a half cup of stems and left the grape skins to float like deflated parachutes."

I finished my wine, "So where is this treasured first bottle? Will I be able to taste your adolescent adventure?" Stephen looked up at Maria and shook his head when he saw her reaching above one of the kitchen cupboards. Maria stopped, pushed the wine bottle back in place, turned around gave me a wink, and pointed back to the bottle.

Speak His Name

Several days of planning followed the dinner. Stephen told stories and I offered him gentle guidance for his father's memorial. The memorial morning had come and I stood in front of the mirror in my bedroom wearing a plum-colored peasant dress that slipped slightly from my shoulders. Maria had left me a bottle of sparkling purple nail polish that I painted on my fingers and toes.

Stephen knocked softly, opened the door and we looked at each other. He was wearing a plum-colored shirt with a burgundy tie and suspenders. They were reflective of the vineyard grapes, and the wine racked within the warehouse cellar.

He stood in front of me, "I wondered what you would look like dressed today."

He took my face and gently lifted my chin. Resting his lips on mine, he moved them gently as if etching memories into a template of emotions that had filled his heart for the past days. He kissed my eyelids, ears, neck, and finally my hands. "May I hold these hands tightly today?"

I raised his hands to my face running them down my cheeks and returned the kisses on his fingers.

Together, we walked to the living room an urn with Ben's ashes sat on his chair. A family friend, a prominent glass artist in Seattle, had made a blown-glass cluster of grapes the size of a basketball. The sunrays had penetrated the purple, bumpy surface, illuminating the glimmering emerald leaves twisted around brown vines resting on the glass.

The grapes were light and dark shades of lavender and green as the sun rays shone themselves through the glass. Stephen walked over to the urn, "Hi, Dad. Today is your day, your party, your celebration, and we have invited all your friends. If you can see us, if you can hear us, sit back and enjoy."

I watched him lift the urn, place his lips on one of the protruding glass grapes, and hug the urn to his chest. I waited as he walked slowly past me and out the front door. Thomas One sat in the horse-drawn carriage with a handcrafted oak barrel that would clasp the urn gently on its top with two fabric-covered screws holding it in place.

Stephen's wreath hung on the barrel, a purple fusion of the mountain's wildflowers shaped like a wine bottle. At the bottom of the wreath was Ben's name in brilliant, shimmering, silver. The carriage was filled with empty wine bottles and blank labels.

Stephen climbed up on the carriage next to Thomas One. Reaching down for me, he gripped my arm tightly and waited as I stepped on the carriage runner. I balanced myself leaning against the carriage seat as Stephen pulled me gently to him tucking his hand around my waist.

Thomas One shook the reins and the Clydesdale horses pulled the carriage slowly past the vineyards, shaking their manes. At the bottom of the driveway, Thomas One paused while Stephen turned, nodded to the urn, and looked at the plateau across the Columbia that was waiting patiently for Ben's ashes.

The local police had blocked the highway with motorcycles for the short ride to the memorial field overlooking the Columbia River. Six police officers saluted the carriage, their hats held in their hands, each nodding to Stephen.

Stephen told me he knew all of them, high school classmates, cousins of vintners, and the oldest his father's poker friend, Sarge, whom Stephen called Mr. Sarge. The only rule his father had on poker nights was there would be no firearms in the house, no boots to mess Maria's cleanly mopped tiles, and no swearing if Stephen was in the room.

Stephen shared his memories of poker nights. He sat at the end of the table and collected any winning coins for himself. He played a Go Fish card game with his dad, progressed to Old Maid, War, and finally poker. He remembered his dad explaining the new release of Syrah. He laughed often when Sarge would talk about a small town crime like chasing a tourist who had stolen pewter wine glasses from the museum. He tried not to look at his Dad

230

when the card players complained about their wives; he knew his Dad wished he had a wife.

When Sarge traveled in his Winnebago with his family, the dog, one cat, and a canary through Montana, he told his father that he always looked for a postcard with a poker theme. Ben had postcards that included anglers hooking a poker card, or three bears sitting around a campfire playing poker, or the entire postcard was a royal flush spelling "Greetings"

I closed my eyes and listened to the purring of the motorcycle, the hooves of the horses on the cement, the slap of the reins against Thomas One's lap, feeling the carriage turn off the highway as it finished the short journey down the gravel road to the billowing tents by the river's edge. Stephen nudged me whispering, "Look." Wine valley workers lined the driveway with hats in their hands, nodding to Stephen as the horses pulled the carriage slowly down the slope. Each worker formed a single file behind the carriage, the first touching the carriage and the following workers with one arm on the shoulder of the worker in front of him. The horses plodded slowly as the recent rainstorm had left hoof-size holes filled with muddied water.

Thomas One spoke. "Miss Clara, I am going to ask that Stephen help you down before I move the carriage down the slope. I am not sure how the horses are going to respond to the slippery soil, and I think it would be best for you to sit over on that rock until we can come back to get you. We will walk you down the grassy slope; it will be safer." Stephen slipped over the back of the carriage, reached up for me, and carried me to the boulder. "I will be right back. Don't move." The muddy slope sucked the soles of Stephens's shoes; he quickly leaped onto the carriage next to Thomas One

I looked up at the plateau, nature's painted backdrop for Ben's memorial. The sun's brushstroke of pinks, magenta, gold, and orange hung from a row of white clouds forming a thin path of white fluffy stones.

Staring at the transformation of the plateaus, I remembered a hike when I came to visit Mother. Slipping on my hiking boots, I grabbed a knapsack, hung binoculars around my neck, and hiked to the plateau. From the plateau, I saw the valley, the other vineyards, and my community. I did not know at that time that the peaceful valley would find a deceitful corporate bigwig buying eggs at the country store, purchasing crocheted oven mittens at the church bazaar, and holding a fishing pole with the migrant workers along the river.

Along the way, I stepped over bright red Indian paintbrush that lined the path; and saw scattered sagebrush. The morning was quiet, with a hint of rain in the air but after months of no rain, it was doubtful if there would be rainfall.

I rarely saw raindrops, or a black cloud covering the valley. However, it smelled like water; it smelled like the freshness of my shower, or when I washed the dishes in the soapy basin or hung the sheets on the line and they flapped nervously in the wind.

I slowly walked through the boulders and saw the windmills standing alone and stark in the fields. Lined up in a straight formation, their propellers moved in slow motion, stopped to a gentle back-and-forth sway, and quickly began to beat in a quick circle when the wind rushed across the valley. I watched an eagle move quickly away and thought of the recent newspaper article about two dead eagles found lying between the phlox.

I tried not to look or think of the beak smashed into the right eye, the talons strangled in a hold around one of its wings and its head pushed into its spine. I hoped someone had buried the eagles as ceremonial respect, I knew my great-grandmother would not have forgotten the animal spirits.

Someone surely would want to save the amazing bird that represented one of the spirits, a spirit guiding a life's journey I was not sure I believed in spirits or the spirit stories my mother told me. I knew I should understand my heritage, roots, and my great-grandmother, a Native American who planted the first seeds for the vineyard.

I had sat on one of the plateau shelves, munching on a chunk of bread smeared in a cherry jam and remembered how Mother would tell me the story of the valley, a giant lake filled with water unable to drain like a bathtub. My mother said her grandmother had a different story, and would only tell her this story in the daytime to avoid nightmares.

My great-grandmother spoke of a monster with giant hairy feet that came down from the heavens. He was looking for animals to eat and became madder and madder when he could not find anyone or anything moving. He thought he would get the attention of everyone on Earth and he began to stomp his feet, he began to jump; he threw his body down onto the soil forcing it to shudder and shake.

Finally, he spotted a tiny raccoon that tried to run between his legs. The monster caught him between his toes, tossed him up to his mouth, and with his giant black tongue flipped the raccoon back into his throat. His neck was so long that the raccoon punched his fists from the inside, tiny bulges rippling down the throat until the raccoon disappeared into his stomach.

Mother said when I was older and I would learn about the geology of the Earth from my teachers and it would be different from great-grandmother's story. I would agree, tuck my head onto Mother's shoulder, and wait for the story. Mother brought out the geography book from the library and began to point at pictures. She would pause, waiting for questions, and sometimes I would tip the book from side to side to look for a monster. In 20,000 BC, a glacier-covered land, the ice walls eventually failed, and the land flooded. The flood grew until it formed the Columbia Valley. I always nodded and asked, "Our land and our home, right?"

I worried when Mother began to talk about the boulders, the boulders that would turn over grinding the earth and piling it up into mounds. I remembered fearing that the existing boulders would begin to grind and move again or that a new flood would push against the boulders to force a new shape. Mother assured me that the Columbia River had been born a long time ago, and the boulders we saw were not going to move again. I learned that the soil in her vineyard had become rich from the constant turning of the rock. The more the boulders worked, the soil would churn and begin to form layers of dirt, layers that would supply the land with the richness the grapes would require.

I asked mother if great-grandmother MaMinny had a canoe. Mother shook her head no and reminded me that hunters used the canoes. She did think great-grandmother might have ridden on a riverboat after she married the French trapper. I always thought the name trapper was funny and wanted to see a picture of a trapper. I knew there were traps around their house for the occasional rat or for the coyotes that attacked their chicken. I imagined if the trapper had big teeth that would snap shut, or if he had big arms that would cut someone's body. Mother explained to me how the Native Americans worked for the trappers and traded the animal fur.

I wanted to know if great-grandmother lived in a house or one of the pointed teepees, I saw on the television shows. Mother would sigh, put down the local geography book with the enlarged dimensional pictures, and replaced it with great-grandmother MaMinny's book with a raccoon-skin cover.

Inside, the pages were empty, or scattered hand-drawn maps were illustrating the vineyard, the plateau, and the Columbia River. Mother never knew what the symbols on the cover meant, but she did point to the C in the middle and tell me it was the first letter of our names. I noticed an envelope tucked in one of the pages, but Mother left it and returned to the history picture book. She pointed to the flat dirt that covered the underground homes. My grandmother was a Nez Perce, one of the many tribes that had settled in Washington State close to the Columbia River.

I wanted to know if they could breathe in their houses underground, or if they had to push a straw push through the dirt to get air. Mother told me each home had a chimney where not only fires were built but provided ventilation. Each home as shared by three or four families. I remembered one day digging with a stick along the bank of the river to try to find a piece of the chimney or a toy from the buried houses but was always unsuccessful.

As a child, I watched the kaleidoscopic natural changes of the valley, looked across the river, and saw the land, once barren, now acres of vineyards. I watched huge trucks dig into the boulders, carry them to flatbed trucks, and change the appearance of the landscape. I remembered sagebrush swaying in the wind like the movement of Polynesian dancers.

When the sun came over the plateau brushing a palette of oranges, yellows, deep maroons, and fading pinks. The sunrise was never in a hurry to greet the day. It would ease slowly over the rock formations, stretching its colors like an elastic band and snapping quickly back to allow the sun to emerge as if it were a whale hidden, waiting to surface.

I watched barges move down the Columbia River and tried to imagine what it was like years ago for a canoe to share the river with a steamboat or riverboat. Although salmon still swam freely in the water, pollution had cut back the quantity. What was once a source of food for the Native Americans washed against the shores, lying against the rocks, mutilated by the coyotes that wandered down to the water.

I remember the small group of children poking at a skeleton of a dead raccoon, pushing it back and forth, and trying to flip it up in the air. Smiling, I thought of my great-grandmother's story about a monster marching through the valley and destroying wildlife. Perhaps great-grandmother never knew humans would be responsible for diminishing wildlife, not monsters.

I blinked, opened my eyes wide, and realized I was not sitting on a plateau, but I was at Ben's memorial waiting for Stephen to return. I looked down at the horses, tossing their heads and neighing loudly at the memorial guests who stood along the road.

As a child, I laughed at the wild horses chasing their leader up and down the slopes, charging along the riverbank splashing each other, flaring their nostrils against the wind. I had seen pure a white colt chewing on a dried twig, and staring at me. I spoke to the colt in a childish whisper, attempting to imitate the sound of a horse, "I won't hurt you, little one. You need to find your mother. Everyone needs someone for protection." When the colt stared back at me, I asked it, "Do I know you? Are you one of the spirits that my great-grandmother talked about? Are you going to protect my mother's vineyard, our grapes?"

The colt neighed, tossed his head to the side, scraped the earth with his hoof, and ran after the mare with the chestnut hair. I felt I had met my spirit and knew, at that moment, I would meet this colt again.

My heart felt heavy from the memory of youth, of my mother, of my spirit. Touching my heart I whispered, "Ben is heading your way, Mother. He wants to love you in Heaven." I heard the blare of the bugles followed by the wail of a bagpipe. I watched Stephen walk up the grassy slope and take my hand, as we walked toward the carriage. The horses stomped their feet and shook their heads, swaying the carriage slightly. The urn remained secure on the wooden wine cask.

Two workers held the reins of the horses, while the rest of the men surrounded the carriage. Each grasped a piece of ribbon in one hand, and in the other hand, they held a glass bowl of corks.

Together, we walked between the tunnel of human forms reaching us through voices, extended arms, and hands acknowledging Stephen's grief. I smiled at the strangers, hoping they eventually would find a place in their hearts for me. Hundreds of people waited patiently in the afternoon setting sun as Stephen walked to the podium. I waited beside him, feeling Maria's hand in mine.

Stephen took a sip from the wineglass waiting. "I knew what this wine would be, and I knew it would be Dad's favorite Pinot. I suppose, when I look at all of you, I would have to say besides his winery and his awards you were gold ribbons of life. You were his first-place prize, his mentors, his support, his lifelong story, and his competition. It always

239

amazed me how your wines would stand side by side in judging, and not once did any of you attempt to dismiss each other's amazing craft. Oh sure, some of you tried to be better, tried to find the secret behind each other's success, but always in good humor. I knew that I grew up as Dad and Mom's only son, but you became my brothers and how grateful I am that you became part of our family."

Stephen paused, looked at me, and smiled briefly. His eyes gazed at the wine, as if he was searching for his father's image, he would take a sip, look again, and finally finished the remaining wine. He lifted his glass to the guests, "I honor you as I will always honor my father. Today is a difficult day; this past week has been unforgiving, but I am through with anger at the spirit that took my father."

"This evening the sun will set, as it did last week and the week before. Tomorrow, when the sunrise reaches over the plateau and for the sunrises to come, I ask only that you speak my father's name. He is giving you another day, warming your vines, and encouraging all of us to prosper. I am thinking he might ask you to check in on me, or better yet, watch for the next judging; he just might be one of the judges!"

The guests laughed, applauded, and began to chant Ben, Ben, and Ben. I moved closer to him and refilled his wineglass. He pulled me close, "I would like you to meet our latest member of the community, Clara, daughter of Clarish, now the owner of the Long House Winery. Please, take a moment to introduce yourself to her; she will need all of our help in the months to come."

The guests waved at me, lifted their hats shouting, "Hello, Clara." I returned their waves while Stephen finished his second glass and spoke, "I invite all of you to the carriage where the blown-glass grape urn holds our Ben."

"Per his request, his ashes will be tossed over the Columbia River from the plateau that he and I often traveled to in my youth. Each of our team will hand you a cork and pen to sign the bottom of the cork."

"I admit that these corks are the improved, latest invention made from a sealed foam material with a membrane that will not break. I ask that you write your name on a cork."

"I plan on hiring an artist to create a hanging with your autographed corks that will be displayed in our tasting room. At the bottom of the art, there will be a list of each of your names. I have thought of creating a memorial in town for Dad, although I do not have any definite plans. I will make sure each one of your names is included in that memorial."

"Starting next month, we will release our newest red blend with a sketch of Dad on the label. Part of the proceeds will go to the intensive care unit at Eastern Washington Cardiac Center to renovate the family waiting room."

While Stephen was speaking, guests turned around to look at the urn on the carriage, others stared at me, and finally, once again they began to applaud. "Thank you for coming, please enjoy the food, wine, and beer."

Stephen stepped back, listened again to the chant of his father's name that ended once the mariachi band began to play and move through the crowd. We walked hand in hand with Maria and Thomas One holding our glasses of Pinot Noir.

Together, we walked to the cliff overlooking the Columbia River. Stephen shook his head, "I cannot believe I just stood in front of the entire wine valley talking about my father. I feel him here, I feel his presence, I cannot figure out why, but I just know he is not too far."

We watched the guests mingle, walk up to the carriage, sit at the round tables covered in purple linens with vases of wildflowers, and pick appetizers from the trays held by the catering staff. "What a party, and how Dad would have enjoyed every minute of this. I am trying to imagine where he would be now."

"I think he would be sitting over at that table with his wine buddies who own the oldest wineries in the valley. On the other hand, maybe he would be sitting on the ground with the descendants of the Nez Perce listening to their stories. Where do we begin?"

Thomas One moved Stephen slowly through the crowd and Maria stood next to me as we began to walk, listen, stop, accept hugs, and drink the wine from our glasses constantly refilled. Stephen walked to his father's wine friends, accepting their thoughts humbly while acknowledging each vintner. "Where are Mario and Herbert?"

The men shook their heads until one spoke up, "Herbert headed into Seattle to have a chat with one of the corporations who convinced him that he was getting too old to run his winery alone. You know, there has been a man around here quite a bit lately talking to us."

"I have to admit, Stephen, not all of us have a talented, educated son like you. So many of our family have left the valley and our crews run our wineries. It gets to be too much, as we get older. Did Ben ever say he was getting old?"

Stephen asked, "Who is the person? I have not seen any stranger around our vineyard. Why are you even talking to him? Don't you think that any property sales should be offered first to someone within our community? Better yet, sell your property to that eager city winemaker who is anxious to expand beyond his garage. We all have our favorites who buy our grapes or a cooperative that invests in our grapes for their wine club. There must be other options."

All of the voices spoke in unison, slamming the table with their hands, "You are right, Stephen. We need to stick together, and we are a community. This person has to deal with all of us."

I had planned to tell Stephen about Crenshaw Mildsgate later on in the week and was surprised when I saw Crenshaw walking toward him. Mildsgate carried a bouquet of dozens of lavender and purple roses, "Why, I would be that person, Stephen. I am sorry we are meeting for the first time under these circumstances. Your Pinot Noir deserved more than a gold medal in last year's competition. If I may, I would like to stop by and talk with you later about expanding the marketing of your wines."

Stephen stared at the man, his face flushed in confusion, adding another layer of red to his skin tinged by the sun, multiple glasses of wine, and the barbecue sauce that lined his lips. I whispered to him, "It is the man who has been coming to my winery. I have not, and will not talk to him. He should not be here, Stephen; he is here only to recruit other vintners."

As he began to hand the flowers to Stephen, Thomas One, Two, and Three stood in front of him. Thomas One reminded him that the event was only for guests took the bouquet, and both the sons took an elbow, moving him toward the parking lot.

Mr. Mildsgate shuffled his feet in the grass avoiding the muddy shoe strings from Thomas Two's sneakers that fell near his polished shoes. His driver waited with the limousine door open, handed him a cell phone, and closed the door after he slid across the seat, never looking up. Stephen shrugged, not hearing my comment, assuming an uninvited guest had been removed, which occurred occasionally at private events.

Tourists who had spent the afternoon in a winery tasting room would attempt to walk into the home of a vintner, thinking if they had just bought a few cases of wine they should automatically be invited. Ben had several experiences when guests would walk from the patio, through the door of the gazebo and begin to talk with him while he sat in his chair reading the evening paper.

He was gracious, answering their questions while directing them back through the gazebo door. He always would end his conversations by phoning Thomas One, assuring that the guests he had just met in his living room were able to find their way back to the wine tasting room. Stephen returned his attention to the table. One vintner spoke up. "Hey, Stephen, I asked you if your dad ever thought he was getting old. We do not remember him ever saying he felt older. He never admitted any problems with his health, though we saw how his walk became more difficult."

Everyone at the table began to talk about the past. One vintner said, "Remember the old days when we would jump up on our tractors to head down to the vineyards, or better yet when we had the old-fashioned grape stomping? I

think a couple of the newer wineries are advertising fall
stomping to lure in the tourists, but after the first time, we
did it I will never do it again. Can you all imagine what was
in the press after the grapes went through?"

Stephen began to laugh at adjectives describing the
residuals left in the grape skins, "broken toenails, the skin off
a wart, chipped nail polish from an expensive pedicure, lint
from black socks, and dried skin from ankles, oh yeah, and
the worst--peeling skin from the bottom of the feet."
Stephen waited. "Here we go, Clara; watch and listen. This
information just might be on one of your future quizzes.
These guys do this at every gathering; even my dad would
throw out a word or two. Some may appear to be bragging,
but I promise you they are seasoned vintners."

Stephen took our glasses for another refill. "The best
Merlot in the valley, tell me what you think, Miss Clara."
She did not realize that Maria, Thomas One, and sons had
introduced her on the microphone as the daughter of Clarish
before the carriage arrived. After inviting the guests to
welcome her, the comments flew into the tent.

"We will welcome her," one vintner shouted."
Another asked, "Is she as beautiful? Just like her mother and
is she single?" Thomas One did not respond to the questions,
"You will see her and you can make your own decisions.
Ben visited her at her the Long House winery and, like us,

246

and became fond of her, and began to teach her a few things about wine in the short time she knew him."

Another shouted, "Is she a wine drinker?" Thomas One asked them to not only be sensitive to Stephen but to the new person who has come to the valley.

I sipped my wine after placing my nose on the rim. He looked at me, tapped his glass against mine, "And?" "I taste plum, just like the jam Mom made. I think a little flower smell, but I could be confused with all the flowers on the tables."

Stephen winked at me, rubbed his finger on my hand, and returned his attention to the vintners' table. "Who has had a guest say their wine tastes like a rotten egg, throw in a quarter?" The clinking of the coins tossed onto the center of the table happened quickly. "Who had a guest say that the wine tastes like a morning newspaper that had landed in a puddle?" Again, the coins were tossed. "How about a musty, wet basement?" This question brought a groan from two of the vintners, but the rest held their quarters. "Two of my favorites are the wet dog smell or the smell of burnt rubber." One of the vintners spoke in a quiet tone, "What I wouldn't give for a rubber so worn out it smelled burnt."

The pile of quarters had begun to topple, especially after the vintner who had a momentary fantasy about rubbers dropped a handful of quarters on the top.

Several men looked up at Stephen after giggling like boys in a high school locker room. "Well, if we are talking about rubber, I mean burnt rubber. How about the wet sweater?" Again, everyone snorted and burst out laughing, spitting their wine across the table. Stephen laughed and I nudged him nervously.

"There you are, Miss Clara, you are one of us now if you can laugh at a bunch of aging, or should I say aged men, or should I say aged wine, or should I say Old World, or should I say the estate owners? What should I call us?"

Empty glasses filled with more wine. Soon, appetizer plates placed in the middle of the table offset the fluid-versus-food intake. A platter of salami, crackers, and wedges of Camembert, Cheddar, and Swiss stabbed with sharp knives greeted the vintners who began to cut the cheese in chunks while putting salami on the crackers.

"So, who is going to cut the cheese next?" Again snorting laughs, tears rolling down their faces and one vintner hiccupped, "Oh yeah, we forgot to mention the guest who said their wine tasted like farts."

"I still remember that day, with my wine tasting room overflowing with guests who drove from the college football playoffs and were drinking away their home team's loss. I was pouring, and four volunteers were walking around the tasting room to keep the pours continuous. The entire room became still after the guest shouted, "My wine tastes like someone farted in the glass."

"Everyone looked at me; the volunteers froze where they were standing. All I wanted to ask the obnoxious, barrel-chested men wearing the opposing team's sweatshirt was when he last tasted a fart."

"Being the elegant vintner that I am, and a descendant of Sam Hill, I put forth my polished Quaker kindness, walked to the man, smiled, took his glass, and offered him a tasting from my 2005 Viognier."

Someone asked, "What? You brought out the gold medal bottle, the coveted national winner?" The vintner smiled, "I said I brought out the bottle, I did not say what kind of wine was inside."

Again, the table began to laugh, shaking their heads. "Tell her, Stephen, who Sam Hill was and why the only person at this table claims he is one of the descendants."

Stephen looked at me, my face a pink glow, and my lips a thin outline of wine purple. "Sam Hill came here for a short time in the early twentieth century, around 1910, after falling in love with the Columbia River."

"There is more history about this man than we could fit into one afternoon, but he was a brilliant businessman and attorney. He tried to move his wife, daughter, and son to Seattle, but after six months, his wife returned to their Minnesota home. Sam's wife was the daughter of the founder of the Great Northern Railroad, which had an amazing impact on the valley and our wine."

"Sam had a house in Seattle and built his mansion, called Maryhill locally, with the plan to lure Quaker farmers to join in his mammoth dream; a community of farmers with the same religious beliefs. Even when Sam built paved roads around Maryhill to prove to the Washington government the value of an accessible surface for travel, he could not gain support from any of his community."

"Not far from Maryhill, he built a structure honoring World War I veterans which resembles the pillar structure of Stonehenge in England that is three thousand years old."

"Oh yes, Sam liked cement, big block structures. Now, nothing he built compares to Napoléon's Tomb in Paris. Maryhill is now a solid cement museum, as is his home in Seattle, and he built the Peace Arch at the border of Washington and Canada. Sam is history here, but you," he nodded to the one vintner, "are not a descendent anymore then I am. "

I asked, "So Maryhill is not a winery?"

"Yes and no. The Maryhill mansion is a collection of artwork initially donated by the Queen of Romania. There is a winery west of the museum, a four-generation vineyard. Miss Clara, you are not the only winery in this valley that has longevity."

"You will learn over time that our vineyards, our grapes are a treasure for vintners. You and I use only the grapes from our vines, but it is common for winemakers to seek grapes from a particular vineyard to avoid growing all of their grapes. We do both, we grow our grapes and we buy our grapes from vineyards in Oregon."

"Clara, you will soon learn that buying extraordinary grapes is not all it takes to make a premiere wine. When a winery establishes an award-winning wine, there is more to the equation than grapes."

"Quality grapes are certainly part of the equation, but how the grape becomes a winning wine becomes the responsibility of the viticulturist. A hard lesson for many, and I am standing firm that our grapes will continue to produce our wines."

He turned away from me, while the table of vintners became louder. "No, you are wrong. The first grapes came from France as tiny vines. I know I am right." The other vintner stood up, staring down at the vintner who had smashed his hat on the table in an act of righteousness. "You are wrong; tell him, Stephen. Your dad had that massive history book of wine on his coffee table for years. Tell him, Stephen."

Stephen shook his head, "I hope Dad can see all of you, drunk from wine, arguing like you would at poker games. I love all of you."

Stephen's speech was a little slurred; he lost his balance. "Well, you are wrong. The first grapes were not vines but grape seeds and they arrived in 1825 around Fort Vancouver. They were very English, my friends."

I looked puzzled, "Fort Vancouver? I had no idea that this place has so much history. I mean, I knew that my great-grandmother married the fur trader, but I honestly know nothing compared to the conversation that I have heard. Why do so many of you know, or better yet, care about the history?"

Stephen looked at me and shook his head, laughing. "There is true history, Clara, and there are tall tales told only by vintners who have been drinking all afternoon. I will give you a historical tour when we head to the plateaus and I will show you our library at the winery where you can learn to become a tall-tale teller, too."

Again, laughter. "Hey Stephen say tall-tale teller three times," shouted the vintners leaning over the table." I found myself giggling again, watching Stephen as he struggled to say the rhyme a second time.

With help from the vintners, beginning a choral shout of fragmented rhymes after pushing out their chairs, forming a line, and kicking up their feet. Stephen toasted them until his face flushed and tears streamed down his face. The chorus line stopped abruptly and became silent.

"You know, Dad would have loved to be here, he loved all of you so much, and you are so special to me. I cannot thank you enough for being here. I love all of you, thank you." He turned away wiping his eyes on his sleeve.

"Stephen, it's OK." I squeezed his arm. "No one expects you to laugh all afternoon. They are your friends. They understand. Do not be embarrassed."

The vintners disappeared in search of catered tables filled with cheeses, salami, crackers, salmon, prime rib, baskets of French baguettes, and towers of chocolate brownies. A local mobile espresso vendor had arrived, and a jazz trio was setting up on one of the small hills under a canopy of tiny lights readied for the evening. Maria and Thomas One walked us to a small round secluded table with four chairs. "This is our table," Thomas One announced. "Maria will bring you your food and I am going to get you a latte. We want you to have some time without having to talk to anyone and, most importantly, get some food in that stomach."

Stephen began to look around and Thomas One pointed. "Behind the trees, we set up the port-o-potties. Do us all a favor, Stephen; do not go in the bushes." I laughed, respecting the relationship that Stephen had with Thomas and Maria. After this afternoon, and watching Stephen disappear behind the trees, I realized there were vintners, friends, and the entire community to take care of him.

He emerged from behind the trees with his arm around a tall female with blond hair that reached her waist. Maria had left the table so I could not ask her who she was or why she happened to be near to Stephen. I watched her put her arms around Stephen's neck and kiss his lips repeatedly. Swaying away from him, she turned around and blew him a kiss.

Maria had returned to the table and I began to eat keeping my head down. Maria had seen Stephen and the woman. "Miss Clara, she is an old story and I will tell you about it another time. Do not worry Miss Clara; she is part of the community. For every older vintner, there is an adult child or two. So many adults you see here grew up with Stephen, and so many of the senoritas were in love with him throughout the years. He must be kind to them today." Stephen wove his way back to the table. The guests linked arms with him, hugged him, and tugged at his shirt to offer their thoughts.

"Clara, I can see why people sometimes call a memorial a celebration. I am not celebrating Dad's death, but just to hear everything said about him lifts my mood and makes me for the moment, happy. Some people have said in the past do not wait until someone dies to say you love them."

"The closeness of this community has been our second family for so many years and has shown their love to him, to me, to my mother and Clarish. I wonder how long the warmth I feel will last."

Thomas One had brought a plate of food for Stephen that had distracted him for the moment. Smiling at another guest who put a bottle of Rose, chilled in a bucket of ice, on the table, Stephen thanked them while they poured the wine into clean glasses for us.

Stephen tapped my glass. "Clara, why the silence? If I have done anything to upset you, please tell me."

I took my wineglass and brushed his wineglass, "I am sorry, Stephen, and no, you have not intentionally kept me alone. Yes, I will tell you what is wrong; it is the stunning, attractive women consoling you."

"I had no idea there were so many other women in your life. Silly me, I would have thought you could have told me all about your love life in the week I have known you. I just feel awkward, perhaps out of place. I would appreciate it if I could ask Thomas One to take me back to your house." Stephen saw the guests dancing on the wood floor rented for the event. Lit torches surrounded the grounds and his crew was standing with lanterns at the path near the port-o - potties. Stephen did not respond; he just finished his plate of food quickly, refilled his wineglass, and took my hand. "Not without a dance. Let's call it our first dance, and do not even think it will be our last dance."

When I began to shake my head no, Stephen began to pull my chair away from the table. Looking at my face, he gently wiped the smudges of mascara that had slid from my eyelids and kissed my forehead. "Clara, please, one dance." Walking on the outside of the circle of tables, we merged in the middle of the couples that were just finishing a jitterbug. The band nodded at him and began to play a slow waltz, one I did not recognize, but the snare drums' swishing sounds confirmed slow movement.

Stephen held my waist tightly against his, pressing his fingers in my lower back, and clutching my hand in his against his chest. I pressed my forehead against his chin letting my body mesh with his releasing any doubts about his past. Stephen pointed to the band once again and they began to play the familiar exit song, "Good Night, Ladies." I looked up to him, smiled, and said, "Listen, Stephen, listen to what the crowd is singing."

Without realizing, all the guests had surrounded the dance floor, holding hands and singing in whispering voices, "Good Night, Ben." Muffled sobs, blowing noses, and the final toast of the night interrupted the music as wineglasses lifted to the stars.

Stephen turned slowly in a circle holding my hand. He bowed and I curtsied to the guests. Thomas One waited at the edge of the dance floor, the guests parted and we moved quickly to the waiting car. Stephen asked Thomas, "The urn?" Opening the door for us Thomas said, "Safely belted in the back seat Stephen, time to go home; let's take Mr. Ben back one last time."

We slid into the back seat; no last glance at the celebration, only at the beam from the headlights moving up the hill to take Ben back to his winery. I was surprised to see a motorcycle officer waiting for us at the top of the hill. Turning on his blue flashing light, he escorted the car back to the winery. I kept my hands in my lap; Stephen put his arms around the urn. He laid his head on the thick glass vine that toppled from the top, and said nothing.

Driving up the driveway, I pointed to the mother coyote sitting with her pups at the edge of the lawn, "She came to say good-bye to your dad."

Pinot and Chardonnay came out to greet them, Stephen held the urn close to his chest, ordering them to sit after Pinot licked the urn, and Chardonnay looked up at his owner sensing something was different. Stephen rubbed their noses with his free hand, "I know you know something is different. You miss his car, you miss him giving you your treats, and why didn't you chase the coyote away? He will miss you, too."

Thomas One held the dogs while Stephen walked slowly, whispering his father's name. When he walked through the kitchen he thanked Maria for cooking Dad's favorite dinner, he nodded at the two bottles of wine, uncorked, breathing in the air after months isolation. Stephen looked at the fireplace, painting shadows of the couch, the coffee table, and his father's chair against the darkened window shades.

He placed the urn on his father's chair with Thomas One at his side, securing the urn with several bungee cords. Pinot and Chardonnay followed Stephen to the chair, waiting patiently.

When Stephen stepped away, the dogs moved closer to the chair and lay where Ben would rest his feet. I wrapped my arms around his waist. "You have made him comfortable, Stephen. He is home once again. It is time for you to rest. I think I will just leave the two of you alone and take a warm bath before bed."

Stephen turned around looking down at me. His eyebrows in a simple line, his eyes puffy, and his face reddened from the sun and wine. "No dinner, no wine?"

"Not tonight, Stephen. Tomorrow will be a long day." He held me, looking into my eyes seeking the true reason for my leaving him alone.

I watched Stephen tug the tie around the urn; I kissed his cheek, and went to my room. The celebration was over and I had to decide about the days to come, where consoling would be replaced with communication, where kissing would be halted until I understood Stephen's history with the women in the valley, and further pursuing wine education would weigh heavily on my decision to stay or sell the winery.

Sitting on the bed, I felt Ben's leather-bound book deep inside the pocket of my skirt. Sliding the book out, I rested it on my lap, running the palm of my hand along the binding. Speaking low, I asked, "Ben, why did you give me this book, why did you come to my house, why did you introduce me to your son? You are gone now and I am left with too many unanswered questions. How I wish I had your knowing self here to guide me."

Ben's Empty Chair

I awoke the next morning, fully clothed, with a light blanket tucked under my chin. Maria knocked. "Miss Clara, I did not wish to disturb you last night. I have started your shower, and your clothes are hanging on the hook for today."

Handing me a cup of steaming coffee, she did not wait for an answer; she turned around, closing the door with a soft click. I thought I heard the soft strings of a violin when the door opened, silenced when the door closed. I peeled my clothes off and left them in a pile on my bed. I had a fretful sleep, tossing, sweating, and dreaming about mother meeting Ben.

I tried to picture Mother, sitting patiently on a small bench in a vineyard-covered with frosted white grapes, waiting for Ben to come on a sparse wisp of a cloud. Mother had white ribbons in her hair. She was sitting away from a crowd of people who gathered around a large wine barrel staring and pointing at something inside. I dreamt someone said, "Look, it's the leather book, the book of wisdom and wine."

I walked across the cool bathroom tiles, and between the small tiled walls that had filled with steam from the raining shower. Holding my head back, I felt the water run down my face, past the last kiss Stephen had left, down my lips that had lost their pouting appearance, jumping from my chin to run between my breasts, forming a steady stream of heat. I faced the wall, feeling the rush of heat between my shoulder blades and lower back, ending with a slight bounce off my buttocks to a waterfall of soapsuds and mineral-scented shampoo.

I began to trace the tiles writing random letters, random symbols, escaped feelings that had yet to solidify in my heart. I rubbed the moist letters with my fist, an emotional eraser seeking the correct answer for the formula of my undecided struggle. The tiles became the invisible chalkboard of my internal turmoil, needing a correct answer to the puzzle that I faced: the family winery, and Stephen.

I wrapped myself tightly in the tablecloth-size towel, its cotton fabric absorbing the moisture on my skin while wrapping me in its cocoon of warmth. Smiling, I saw the pale-lavender jumper hanging on the ceramic wine bottle hook. Maria had searched for mourning clothes with a tinge of lightness in the flowered long sleeve blouse.

I found the apron pocket in front of the jumper where I deposited the leather book, pulled my hair in a clasped braid, and walked out to the living room.

Stephen sat on the couch, reading the local newspaper. A section of the paper protruded from under the urn, and Chardonnay was sitting next to the chair licking the paper.

Maria motioned to the chair at the counter where a glass of fresh-squeezed orange juice and a cheese omelet waited for me.

She watched me, sensing I was upset and recognized that she could not interfere. She reached her hand across the counter and met my eyes after I looked up. Wiping away my tears, I held her hand and mouthed a silent thank you.

"Maria, wake Clara. We have a long day before us." Stephen called from the living room followed by, "Chardonnay, put that paper down now."

We watched Chardonnay dash out the front door after Thomas One entered, and began to laugh. I slid off my stool and waited for Stephen to look up from his newspaper.

"Maria," he began to shout again.

"Stephen, I am right here."

He patted the couch, "Please, sit for just a moment with Dad. Today is his last time in his living room, his home. I thought we would take our time driving to the plateau. He needs to see the valley for the last time."

"You look lovely. I never thought very much about the shades of purple until I saw you in the grape-colored canvas you have worn these past days. Can you believe it was not long ago you lay on this couch, healing? Even with a limping leg, I thought you were striking." He leaned over to kiss my cheek, but I put my hand over his lips, accepting his kiss on my finger.

Not now, I told myself, not today. I stood by Ben's urn, running my fingers across the green coil of the glass grapevine lid. Patting my jumper pocket, I said, "Ben, I promise to take good notes."

Maria and Thomas One watched Stephen slowly untie the urn, walk around the living room, and stand in front of the fireplace. He walked into the gazebo and stood in the doorway overlooking the patio, the empty wrought iron tables, the vineyards, the wine tasting room, the warehouse, and the tepee houses. Thomas One had told the crew to work inside the warehouse until he gave them orders to return to the vineyard. He wanted Stephen to have privacy in these final moments.

Stephen smiled when he noticed a bottle of Pinot Noir and a single glass sitting on the farthest table on the patio, near the flower boxes, and next to the steps that led to the vineyard. "Your wine, Dad, our wine, and your last taste await us."

Stephen slowly poured the wine into the glass, clinked the glass against the side of the urn, "Soon, without you, I will be taking care of your wine, your winery, and your vineyards. Please watch over me, I do not know if I can do it without you."

The wine cork, which had been resting on its side, slowly rolled across the table, landing first on the chair seat before teetering at the top of the steps and bouncing down to the gravel path. Stephen toasted the urn, "Dad, if that was your sign or a way of saying yes, and then I know I will be just fine."

Stephen looked around for me but I stood in the kitchen respecting the last time a son would have with his father in the house where Ben learned to be a single father. Maria rubbed my shoulders while saying a prayer quietly. I put my hand on top of Maria's hand, the woman who had adopted me over the past two weeks offering me strength in my weakest moments.

Stephen hoisted the urn in his arms and walked to the front of the house. I waited for him next to the convertible, fixing my eyes on his reddened eyes. Stephen hesitated when Thomas One offered to take the urn from him.

I reached out with my arms, "Let me hold the urn. Ben would be very angry if his last ride in his cherished car had the top-up. I will secure him inside the seat belt and I am sure nothing will happen."

Thomas One and Stephen helped me into the car, treating me like a child incapable of strapping itself in. Stephen put the urn on my lap, pushing it gently against my chest while securing the seat belt. He smiled and whispered in my ear, "Dad you are closer to her now than I have had the opportunity. "

I giggled, pulling my arms around the urn. "Your dad earned this front seat position; you have a way to go."

Stephen edged slowly out of the driveway, unaware of the crew that had lined up on the edge of the winery behind them. Easing the car onto Highway 12, he glanced at me. "Are you ready for a little local history?"

I felt the weight of the urn on the leather book in my front pocket, "I do not know if I can take notes. Please tell me everything about the history. I may need a refresher course later."

Stephen began slowing the car every time a truck passed, pulled over several times on available shoulders when a farm truck or tractor drove behind him. "We are on Highway 12, which starts in Aberdeen, Washington. I am guessing you have not been to Aberdeen, but we will visit the city one of these days. What are your thoughts about pirates, pirate movies, and pirate ships?"

Shrugging, "I have never really seen a pirate ship close up. I suppose you are going to tell me that Washington State is known for pirate ships?"

"Well, yes, one of our ships, the Lady Washington, moors in Aberdeen and has left its mark on the pirate movies that invaded us years ago. I have been on the ship. It's a historical, crafted beauty, immaculate and protected by a staff of volunteers. Unbelievably, you can train on one of the pirate ships, and climb one of the masts. I did when I was younger, Dad was beginning to market our wines in some of their stores, and I spent an afternoon on the Lady."

"Clara, you have not lived until you placed a foot onto the rigging, and slowly edged your way up. A movable rope, a ladder, I navigated slowly, while harnessed with another mate next to me."

"My goal was the crow's nest, but a couple of wakes from passing passenger boats caused the ship to tilt slightly, enough for me to lose my grip and dangle momentarily with one hand. What a rush, Clara! We will go back and, no, you do not have to climb a mast. But I would like you to be my winch for the day."

"Do you still sell your wine in stores?"

"Yes, we could make it a business trip to introduce our wines and yours. Our red wines have been successful and several shops want me to teach classes. In the past, it might have been possible, but I am not sure now. Dad would rotate dinners throughout the summer and invite groups of wine-shop owners to our winery. This was a worthwhile marketing tool that benefited our wines throughout the city markets."

"Discounting cases of wine, no shipping fees, and partnerships were born. He truly was the spirit of wine, and those are hard shoes to fill. I preferred to be in the background answering individual questions, but I did enjoy teaching."

"Where did guests stay, in the tepees?"
Stephen laughed, "No, the teepees are rarely used for guests. I think our winery needs to catch up with other wineries with

lodging, concerts, limousine services, helicopter rides, and four-star gift shops. We have kept our store simple since the cost of our wines is substantial and we want the dollars put into our bottles, not into a vase made out of pressed corks. I do not know if you realize all the requirements of running a winery, owning a vineyard, researching varietals, and producing wine that will win you the Gold Medal."

"I don't know all the details that Dad handled. We divided winery responsibilities according to our skills. We were quite a team, right, Dad?"

"Look at the Columbia River Basin, formed millions of years ago by glaciers. The one community that you will learn more about, your heritage is the influence of the Native Americans. The rivers had a tossed a variety of names throughout the years, each tribe with its interpretation of the waters and how it influenced their lives."

"You will still see some fishing along the Columbia, you will see boats, and the parks have all attempted to incorporate water activities depending on their location. We certainly do not have as many rivers as wineries, but rivers do converge and join the Columbia River in multiple locations. Behind us are the Tri-Cities, Kennewick, Pasco, and Richland, whose location marks the merging of the Yakima, Snake, and Columbia River."

"You are certainly are here at a scenic time of year, but I promise you we have distinctive seasons. As a winery owner, you will see seasons as your wine calendar, but it gets cold here plenty of snow and plenty of worry for our grapes. More than ten years ago the frost was so bad that 75 percent of our grapes were lost. The frost happened again in 2010 and impacted the Cabernet Sauvignon grapes, resulting in a 12 percent decrease in wine production."

"What happened to my mother's vineyard?"

"Your mother's vineyard had plenty of white grapes, but your reds were destroyed. When your mother became ill, I think she was unaware of the destruction and focused more on her condition. Her crew did the best they could, but production decreased. Typically, it takes a solid year to rejuvenate the affected vines."

"I don't understand. If it gets cold here, why does it not happen more often?"

"The temperature needs to drop below 32 degrees Fahrenheit. The biggest threat is when we start to see the flowers pop and the first buds starting to show on the vines. Once the buds and a few small leaves appear, typically flower clusters will follow, marking the new crop. Frost can reduce or wipe out the vines. You will see next spring."

"Look, Clara how the hills roll with green pastures, interrupted by brown desert, and is dotted with trees. The soil within this valley is the major contributor to our success in winemaking. You will soon learn the impact of the soil on the various grapes."

"Yes, weather, wind, temperature, water are part of the equation but the terroir, the soils are key. Terroir is a French term referencing the combined elements of soil, climate, and a variety of subtle growing conditions. Look over there at the windmills. I do not think you will ever see so many concentrated in one location. This wind farm is one of the largest providing electricity to the valley."

Walla Walla History

Stephen pointed to the burgundy highway sign and turned right toward the Whitman Mission. "I know you are anxious to learn about your heritage, and I know that Native Americans are part of our country, but often their past is minimized depending on how they preserved their heritage. Native Americans firmly planted themselves here."

"This is one of the first missions run by Dr. Marcus Whitman and his wife Narcissa Whitman, around 1830. They were determined to learn the language of the American Indians, the Cayuse, who settled in the area, by creating a book pairing their words with English words."

Stephen sat in the car, pointing, and "The museum is a National Park Service center, free to the public. The signs along the cement path will point to structures: a home, a gristmill, and a blacksmith shop. This mission is actually on the original Oregon Trail."

"The story ends sadly when an outbreak of measles killed many Native Americans and children. The Native Americans blamed the Whitmans, accusing them of poisoning the children. The Whitmans along with approximately ten others were killed by an angry group of Native Americans which ended the Protestant mission. The tall white structure is the Whitman memorial acknowledging their death. On the bottom of the hill heading to the

270

memorial is the great grave where the slaughtered were buried."

He edged the car closer to the path where I had a clearer view of the memorial. I wondered, "Stephen, an entire family gone when all they were trying to do was help. My great-grandmother was not a Cayuse; she was a Nez Perce. Her challenges of living in this region with the appearance of the white man must have been difficult."

I wanted to walk the pathway up the hill and touch the memorial. I wanted to apologize and say that my great-grandmother would never hurt them and promised to find a way to remember them.

Stephen watched me clutch the urn, as I tried to imagine what it was like to have been the Whitmans who gave of themselves only to be murdered by those they had helped. He decided we would not go to French Town this trip but would travel into downtown Walla Walla before heading back to the Columbia River.

I stared at the long rows of shops, the art sculptures, the tourist strolling past wine shops, bars, and restaurants. No mannequins posed in the windows wearing the latest couture fall dress, no jewelry store aligning small, open-mouthed boxes with diamond rings, bracelets, or earrings. "It is a little Western, a small home town, a neighborhood where I am guessing everyone knows everyone," I asked about the hotel, noticing a black limousine parked in front.

"That is the Marcus Whitman, built in early 1900, a name you are now very familiar with since our last stop. A name stamped throughout many locations in the Northwest. Something has caught your attention?"

I motioned at the limousine, "That's his car, Mr. Crenshaw Mildsgate, the uninvited guest at Ben's memorial. He wants to buy my winery, perhaps your winery, or maybe the entire valley. How many wineries did you say exist here?"

Stephen pulled under a large, shaded elm, next to a mailbox, a bike rack, and the sign pointing to Whitman College. "How do you know him? Have you met him? Has he offered to buy your winery? How many vintners know about him? I mean, does he travel only in a limo? Can't he be a little less obvious and rent a car?"

"I honestly know very little, except he has been to my house and I have not come to the door. I have heard he wants to take over the wineries and produce the wines in giant production factories that will essentially increase quantities and lower the costs. I am surprised you had not seen him before the memorial."

"He will certainly not be the last or the first who has tried to convince us that our wineries are outdated, that we could make more money if we formed a cooperative interest. We heard yesterday from my dad's friends that the wine generation is aging, with fewer children willing to assume the role. Sound familiar, Miss Clara?"

We looked at a female passer-by, dressed in a tennis outfit, whose Chihuahua had had its collar caught in the spoke of the secured bike. Smiling, she looked at us, bending to untangle the dog that began to squeal and run its claws against the wire spoke. Exposing a tanned cleavage and a black lace bra, she looked past me and shouted to Stephen. "Hello, Stephen. I have not seen you since college. Are you returning for more classes?"

"Last time I saw you we were stomping grapes together at the school graduation party. You know I never did find my thong panties that somehow slipped off into the growing vat of grape juice."

He sensed my tension as I clicked my nails against the urn. "I am sorry I forgot your name but sadly my father just died so I will be assuming all responsibilities. I hope you have had the chance to do something with our education." He did not wait for an answer, eased the car forward after she successfully disentangled the dog. Stephen watched her walk in the opposite direction.

"Stop, Stephen, stop the car." I watched Crenshaw Mildsgate walk out of the Marcus Whitman. Another man walked alongside him talking on his cellphone, slipping a piece of paper from his suit coat pocket, and quickly taking notes. I gasped. "What is he doing here?" What is he doing with Mildsgate?"

Stephen heard my fingernails tapping the urn again; grateful for the momentary reprieve of explaining who the dog walker was, but curious about my reaction. I pulled down the visor and looked down. "Just tell me when they are in the car, please."

I heard the limousine car door close, its tires turning sharply on Main Street. Stephen whispered, "The mysterious man has left." I moved my head up slowly, "One bad man and the mysterious man, perhaps someone from my past? Discussing past relationships is not part of our infantile "get- to- know- you" phase. Not today, but someday I will tell you about him, about Christopher."

He cringed, recognizing our barrier of unknown past relationships; the women from his past relationships. Like the elephant sitting in the wine vat, he had a social history within the valley. My relationships, however, were states and cities away.

Stephen moved slowly, looking back assuring the limousine had left, and began his tour, pointing. "The farmers' market over there opens mid-May and closes in October. I might lure you back for another dance in a few weeks. The pavilion, where the market is held, is one of the newer installations. If we did not have Dad, I would buy you the biggest Walla Walla onion I could find, or a bouquet.

Our official state vegetable arrived here courtesy of the Italians."

"We will need to walk these streets to familiarize you with the businesses. My favorite statue is right there." He waited for the bus to move and pointed at the firefighter. "We value our community support teams that keep us safe from fires and crime."

"Look at the buildings, Clara. Why that one with the arched windows was built in the 1880s and is known as the red light building housing brothels. Remember now, we are talking late 1800s and early 1900s on so many of these buildings. There is the courthouse, the oldest pharmacy in the state, and the oldest independent bank in Washington. I know you fear the absorption of our wineries, but clearly, we try to maintain the heritage of this community. Age is not only good in wine but it is good for a city."

"Street art is everywhere. I keep thinking perhaps we need to acknowledge Dad somehow. Now everything is too raw to consider turning him into a monument, but I think it is something I need to consider."

I began to tap my fingers against the urn again, which caused Stephen to turn quickly to look at my face. Staring at me, as I showed no anger, no pout, no furrowed brows, and asked me, "You are clinking your nails for some reason, please tell me."

Ignoring his question, I focused on the idea of a sculpture for Ben. "Why not something similar to this urn? Create a sculpture framed in the words written on the corks yesterday. The sculpture will be a permanent acknowledgment of your dad and the valley vintners."

Stephen looked at me, adding. "I have another thought. We could make a giant piggy bank sculpture for donations to the Walla Walla Community College Enology and Viticulture Program at my alma mater. A scholarship fund for future viticulturists, yes, I know Dad would want to support education. Clara, what would I do without you?"

He smacked his hand on the steering wheel causing the horn to beep at the innocent older woman pushing her wheeled shopping cart into the crosswalk. She stepped back quickly and Stephen stood up in the convertible apologizing. Waving, she said, "Is that you, Stephen? Does that voice sound like Ben's son and my violin student from more than twenty years ago? Look how handsome you are and you are married. I knew you would be a fine catch."

Stephen pulled the car over and walked to the woman, hunched over, and turning her head to the side to see him. Reaching up to his face, "My eyes are not as good as when you and I worked on learning music, but from what I can see you look like your father. A blonde man, yes, blonde like your mother but tall like your father."

She moved her hands down his arm, "Oh, and lifting those wine barrels has given you a few impressionable muscles. How is Ben? He owes me a bottle of his Pinot. We won a bet when you started the classes that you would stay for a minimum of two classes. Well, Stephen, you were with me for more than four years."

He knelt noticing her neck was shaking from holding it to the side. "Miss Taylor, my dad died a week ago and we just had his memorial. I am sorry you did not know but I will bring you a bottle of Pinot. I think if he was here, he could invite you to the winery for that Pinot. That said, I would like to invite you to dinner."

She smiled at him, "Yes, you are still the kind Stephen I knew. I would love to come to the winery but I do not drive. I am so sorry to hear about Ben. He was and will always be a pillar in this community."

"Do me a favor and try not to wrap your feelings too quickly. You two were very close. You cannot possibly move on, memory-free for a long time. Please, no need to be the strong, determined violin player; it is time to be the grieving son."

As Stephen continued kneeling, she bent slowly kissing his head, "How I remember the curls; the curly topped angel I would call you. Who is the cook in your family, you or your wife?"

277

I pushed the urn between the fabrics of my skirt closer to the floor, commenting as I leaned out the window, "A pleasure to meet you, Miss Taylor. Do come for dinner and we will fill the house with violin music. Stephen will come and pick you up."

Miss Taylor turned her head, "You take care of my favorite student." She noticed the transit bus stopping across the street and began to walk, "Can't-miss my carriage. I am in the phone book Stephen; I will look forward to your call." Stephen took her grocery cart in one hand and took her hand to walk her across the street.

He whistled a deep, whistle waving to the bus driver who looked out his mirror, "Hey, Stephen. Hello, Miss Taylor. Please, take your time. I am in no hurry." Stephen lifted the cart into the bus and helped her step up the two rubber matted steps. "I will call soon and, Miss Taylor, my friend is not my wife. Her name is Clara, daughter of Clarish. She may be assuming ownership of the family winery. She will not be cooking, I will, as she does not cook. She says she is a baker but she brought burnt bread when Dad invited her to dinner at our winery. It was the first time I met her."

Jaunting across the street and climbing into the car, he apologized, "Now, Clara, you just met another of my women. She had an allegretto impact on my life, not only a teacher but as someone who introduced me to classical music. She is why you hear violin music. I have not seen her for ten years if not longer."

Driving again, he pointed at the Macy's department store that consumed the block. "Time to continue our history class. Next time you shop there, check out the historical plaque. After the abandonment of Fort Walla Walla, this part of this city became a temporary stockade. Can you imagine being punished in a stockade a block or so from a brothel?"

Approaching Whitman College, Stephen pointed to the library. "Next time you wish to dive into your Native American history this is where you can do your research." He drove past Whitman College. "The Whitmans will not be forgotten, as you will see on a stroll through the campus. Historic houses, dating from the later 1800s, line these streets."

"I always dreamed about living in this neighborhood until the night I parked my car not far from one of the student houses nicknamed "The Outhouse," where environmental students lived. Well, I had Dad's car and I came back to it after dining at a local restaurant to find it filled with bags of dried leaves. I guess one of the students decided to rake leaves at midnight and through his blurry beer eyes thought the car was an open city recycling can."

I pictured Stephen trying to shovel leaves so his date could sit. "Do tell me, Stephen, how you solved the dilemma?"

"I didn't. The students saw me returning with my date and began to whistle, inviting her to share a beer. When they realized it was my car, they descended like hungry maggots and cleaned out the car. I do remember the line of young men holding the passenger door open for her, and bowing to her once the door was closed."

Stephen drove behind the Carnegie Art Center where a marker stood. "That marker is part of your history. It commemorates the treaty signing in the mid-1800s with members of five tribes including the Nez Perce. The Nez Perce though hesitant essentially signed away their freedom away by agreeing to live on reservations."

He stopped under giant maple trees that lined the street. The open convertible top attracted the beam of warm sun. "The original site in the mid-1800s of Fort Walla Walla is now the Veteran's Hospital."

"Fifteen original buildings stand throughout the ground. Dad and I walked through here many times throughout the years. I probably have overloaded you with too much information, but I have to guess the history here has no comparison to your cement city in New Jersey."

I tilted my head back, "Stephen, I love how the trees form a ceiling above the sidewalks. Such giant leaves here and I am sure I missed the blossoming trees in the spring. Well, there is always next year, right?" I imagined Native

Americans moving up the street on horses, and my white spirit horse swishing its tail at the end of the pack.

He leaned over and kissed my cheek for the first time since the ride had started, "Yes, there is always next year, Clara, and the year after, and ten years after. Your words are the exact words I have been waiting to hear."

I took his hand, "Be patient with me, Stephen, and you too, Ben. I had a whole different life in New Jersey. My feet are aching to be squeezed into a pair of red pumps, I am dying for a pastrami sandwich, and I will miss my theater evenings. I never expected this journey. I have made many friends and at my age, it is hard to create a new circle of friends. This is your community, your world. I am not sure I can separate myself from nearly a third of my big city life to start over and be part of your life."

"Nothing here is the same as what I had. No one I have met is similar to any of my friends or business acquaintance. Where do I take my dry cleaning? Who will deliver my favorite Kung Pao noodles? Where will I jog for miles? Where is the airport to take me to my favorite Caribbean island?"

"I know I must sound like an entitled bitch, what you must understand is I worked so hard in college. I fought, clawed, and climbed my way over male barriers to get the position I now hold, and finally, when I have earned success, I am facing a life-changing experience."

"Do you understand what I mean? Have you ever thought of what your life would be like outside this valley? Have you ever wanted a different lifestyle?"

The Reality of Two Different Worlds

I noticed that Stephen was listening, driving, and saying nothing. When he touched the urn at the last four-way stop before entering the highway, I asked him what he was thinking. At first, he only looked at me and nodded, finally he spoke is voice escalating from a whisper, "Clara, in thirty minutes I will leave my father to float, disperse, sink, and land in the bottom of the Columbia River. In another thirty minutes, my strength, the life that guided me, the voice that assured me, the hands that toasted and the arms that embraced me will be gone. In thirty minutes, the heart that held all of my secrets, the mind that taught me, and the lungs that breathed grapes will disappear."

I became irritated, wondering why he was yelling at me as if my ability to sense or understand him had evaporated. All of a sudden, he slowed the car, pointed to the plateau across the fields: and said, "You know Clara, that sky that has become an afternoon shade of purple and pink could care less that Dad has died. Tomorrow that same sky will glow with sunrise; life does go on doesn't it?" He hit his turn signal with his fist, waited for the next dirt road to appear, and abruptly turned the car onto the road.

Pressing on the brakes several times, he stopped the car, got out, and walked over the fence where a black colt was turning its head side to side, unafraid of the approaching person.

Surprised by the abrupt turn, I asked, "Where are you going?" I waited, but he did not turn around. I watched him gently touch the black ears of the colt, while the mare stood behind her colt without fear. Her coat was black with small freckled white circles under her neck, on her legs, and the tips of her ears.

I put Ben's urn on the driver seat, covering it with a blanket from the back seat. Stepping out of the car, I realized I had been sitting for an hour and my legs were cramping while my healing foot looked swollen. I teased him, "Let me know if you are watering the fence."

Limping over, I looked back at the car, assured the urn was safe. The mare neighed, shook her head, and nudged the colt softly, prompting a small prance and one last glance at Stephen before it walked back to the center of the field. I waited and did a quick mental rewind of the last twenty minutes, nervously sputtering, "Stephen, oh my, what have I done? Have I added something to your sadness? Will you please accept my apology for being a selfish self-centered city girl?"

Stephen turned around and walked within a foot of where I was standing. He looked down at me, ran his fingers through my hair, tracing my collarbone in a small circular motion. "I accept your apology. I cannot for this moment or in the weeks ahead find the emotional energy to substantiate an argument of why you should stay here in the valley. I no longer have the energy to woo you, to beg you to stay, to even think that someday we could be together forever."

"Now, all I can think about is that I must dispose of my father's ashes and give him to the spirits that surround this valley. I want my mother, your mother, your grandmother, and great-grandmother to be waiting for him, to greet him, to care for him. I do not want him to be alone. I am now the selfish one, I am the grieving one, and I am the lost one without my father. If you need me to help you with your decision, I cannot and will not. Now I am empty. If you choose to leave I will add you to my heart's deepest vessel that holds my frail emotions."

"I cannot defend my past, my friendships, my valley romances, my elderly teachers. We have only known each other for two weeks, two weeks where our lives have been changed by death, a raw, sensitive attraction, scattered fragmented life memories, and an invisible wall of two separate occupations, dreams, goals, and lives. I know we have a common ground, I know that we have a foundation that unknowingly has formed from grief, but please do not ask me to try to pitch winery real estate choices."

I reached up touching his cheek when he wrapped his fingers around mine.

"I will never be able to thank you for all you have done for me, for Dad, for your acceptance of our crew, for your presence at Dad's memorial. However, except for our last dance and your introduction as Clarish's daughter, you have no ties to this valley."

"Just as a baby colt, you have the freedom to return to that field you call New Jersey, surrounded with all that is familiar to you. I cannot promise you your life here will be easy. I cannot assure you that even with my help your family winery will flourish, and I cannot say with any certainty that the attraction we feel for each other now will last."

"I can offer you for this moment only, a grateful, grieving man who will spend the weeks ahead committing to the winery that Dad and I built together. You are welcome to be part of my wine day. I will happily teach you, but only if you are ready to commit to your family winery will I come to your vineyard."

I looked into his eyes, seeking their softness, eager to feel his lips against mine, waiting for him to pull me into his arms, but it did not happen. He kissed my forehead, reached out for my hand, and walked slowly to the car. He opened my door and walked over to his door. He lifted Ben's urn gently, holding it tightly while facing the plateau, "That's where we are headed, Dad. We will let you go before sundown. I will put you back into the trusting arms of Clarish."

He crossed in front of the car, handed the urn to my waiting arms. I put the seat belt around the urn and clicked it in place. The road was narrow, and he drove further down to turn around. Passing the field of cows and sheep, he came across a sign that read "Fresh Eggs." He edged the car into the narrow driveway, cautious of the tricycle that rested on its side near the battered van.

Backing out slowly, he returned the car to the dirt drive and came to the soft shoulder leading to the highway. "One more turn and we will be on our way to the plateau. No history class along this stretch of the road, but I dare you to guess how many colors that sun will give us this afternoon." I was embarrassed, realizing what a selfish fool I was thinking I was the reason for his silence. He looked at me when the black limousine emerged from one of the open, metal gates leading to a winery not seen from the road but hidden beyond the fields, beyond the creek, and looking down at them from a small hill. I wanted to ask Stephen whose winery we had passed but I did want to draw attention to the limousine.

"Clara, we just passed one of the oldest wineries in the valley. Not a generational ownership; however, it has had frequent buyers throughout the years, viticulturists who hoped to make it a viable vineyard. Often city folks realized quickly making wine was not only growing grapes."

"Winemaking in your garage, basement, or apartment is very different from caring for a vineyard. Sadly, that winery has been nicknamed The Hobby Vineyard, based on the multiple, unsuccessful owners. I think every winery with the proper knowledge, investment, and nurturing of perfect conditions can thrive, but it takes time and patience."

I tapped my fingers on the urn, trying to erase the last hour when I left a crack in our fragile relationship. Stephen realized that he had almost passed our turn-off, and swerved the car quickly to the right past two carved structures resembling frowning owls.

I stared at each wooden pole guarding the path to the cliffs, each owl looking at each other, each set of claws gripping the carved branch of a fractured branch. "The owls are several protectors of this land. Typically, tourists will not go down this road often, thinking it is Native-American land and off-limits to curious travelers."

"Native Americans once owned the land but now it is the secret path for all of us locals seeking a peaceful refuge. Prepare yourself for a breathtaking moment."
Stephen slowed the car to a crawl, swaying back and forth to avoid the dirt bowls that dotted the road like a pinball machine. Shrubs, trees, and dark ashen bulky rocks lined the road, forming a solid fence-like wall, a barrier discouraging off-path exploration, temporary toilets, or an open field for garbage disposal.

He pointed up. My eyes followed his muscular arm, tanned, with sparse light blond hair. An eagle balanced with ease on a v-shaped bare branch coveting a nest the size of my clawfoot bathtub. "I can't see any movement in the nest, but he is guarding something. Or maybe he has the nest for sale and he is looking for any potential buyers."

"The nest reminds me of when I was younger and came this way with Dad with a couple of my friends exploring the forest for our science class. Right in the middle, I mean right in the middle of the road, was half an eagle's nest, severed down the middle by what Dad had said was a commercial chain saw."

"I stared at this mammoth architectural home with awe, curiosity, and respect. At first, we were afraid that there were unhatched eggs pushed under the twigs and moss. Dad told us, on that hot August day, that mothers only hatch two eggs in the late winter months. Dad eyed the line of trees for other metal blade destruction, noticing two trees leaning against each other where the other half of the nest wedged itself between two tree trunks."

"I remember taking several small fractured twigs, torn from the nest by shuddering vibrations of the saw. I still have them somewhere in one of my boyhood treasure jars. Do you have any shoeboxes filled with treasures, Clara?" I thought of the jar filled with mother's ribbons, mother's cookbooks, and the photographs in my living room. I had forgotten Stephen had not spent time in my home, Mother's home, my undecided future home.

"I do not have a special treasure box, a diary, an old yearbook, or even any of my toys. When I moved to the city, I had the choice between moving into a nine-hundred-square-foot apartment with minimal boxes and furniture or staying in the suburbs with unlimited furniture, boxes filled with accumulated memories, and pet bowls filled with daily food. My New Jersey condominium is compact, clutter-free, and pet free."

Stephen ran his fingers softly on my hand gripping Ben's urn. "I am sure Dad has never sat in a woman's lap for a long time. Something tells me he is smiling at me now, reminding me of where he is and I am not."

I shivered and looked up at the sky. "It got cold. Are we pushing the time right now, or will we have time to say good-bye to Ben?"

"It's the trees, Clara. They are covering us preventing any warmth, and when we reach that pale-blue cloudless spot in front of us you will see the difference."
Stephen moved the car the last six hundred feet on a paved road with a border of goldenrods staggering throughout Douglas knotweeds, patches of dried grass, swaying randomly with the whispering breezes squeezing out from the dense woods.

The trees parted, yawning, twisting their branches to the blue sky hanging like paste-free wallpaper over the landscape of irregular shapes, steps, and jagged lumps of bedrock forming the plateaus towering over the Columbia River. I felt the warm sun on the back of my neck. Stephen turned off the car, stood, grasping the window frame, and rested his head on his elbows.

"Clara, Dad, and I spent many days here. I grew up learning the history of the land, appreciating the soil, or, as you have learned, terroir is a gift to our valley. Can you imagine, over fifteen million years ago the earth carved, sliced, cut, tumbled, and performed airborne somersaults with gypsy volcanic rock rearranging the landscape to create the Columbia River?"

Stepping out, Stephen stretched, rubbed the back of his body against the hood of the car, finally standing next to me sighing, "I am not sure who I should hold first, Dad or you."

I lifted the urn to Stephen, opened the car door and stood, bending from the waist, moving my neck in circles, and marching my legs. "Not sure why I am so tight. We have not been driving too long. I think I embraced Ben with every muscle in my arms, legs, hands," I paused, "And my heart." I tugged at my boots, pulling them higher.

Turning around talking to the urn, I noticed the tattoo on the back of his neck. The collar of his shirt covered the top part of the deep-blue symbol or letter. He seemed to know I was staring; he reached back and pulled the collar up to his hairline hiding the tattoo.

Walking slowly, we approached the steel railing, the metallic accessory crowning the top of the plateau. Geological signs described the height of the plateau and the dangers of slipping on the unpredictable soil and rocks and the depth of the Columbia River.

One of the boulders held twelve painted crosses illustrating visitors who died after ignoring the hazard of attempting to traverse down the plateaus. Stephen placed the urn down, standing on the bottom ledge of the railing. He swung one leg. Bending, he focused down the hillside and put his hand to his ear. "Listen, Clara. Do you hear the waterfall?"

I shook my head no, folded my fingers on Stephen's waistband, one foot bracing the urn against the railing, and bent my head listening. "I hear nothing, Stephen, not a bird, not a car; the stillness has suddenly covered us."

"I feel as if this location and your memories with Ben are respectfully silent waiting for the arrival of his ashes. I feel the stillness and the hushed anticipation that Ben has returned to the river. A muted celebration from Nature welcoming him to the riverbank, to its gravel, to the river silt floor. I feel as if I, too, should not speak. Stephen, can you feel the calm?"

Stephen slid off the railing. He picked up Ben's urn and began to walk to the right, toward pale-orange and grey boulders forming a fortress of crackled, rotund formations. Stephen stood in front of the fortress, took a sharp turn left, and disappeared behind it, "Clara, follow my footsteps, I will wait for you before we begin our descent to the waterfalls."

A Son's Goodbye

I began to shiver from the anticipation of leaving the metallic, protective railing. I felt a tingle of excitement, like the time I hid under the high school bleachers waiting for my girlfriends to bring a pack of cigarettes and a lighter from one of their father's jackets. I was not afraid of breaching house rules, or its consequences, only the reality that my status would change once I did something earning me the friendship in the inner circle of popular girls. Even now, I felt that I wanted Stephen to know that I was not afraid, that I was climbing down these rocks to show him that I was not a wimp.

I crept over to the boulders, sliding my hand into one of the crevices; waiting to hear Stephen's guiding voice. I felt stillness, vacant air without direction, and finally, Stephen's words, inviting, reassuring, and coaxing me. I moved to the left, slid my hands over the jagged rocks, wishing a small white button would open to an elevator. I felt the edge, straight, rigid, a structural corner without a roof that opened to a narrow path covered in pine needles, wide enough for me to walk to Stephen who waited, leaning against a tree trunk, holding Ben's urn. He turned and began walking to a smaller clearing surrounded by towering trees and a horseshoe-shaped circle of tree stumps.

Reaching him, we looked down at the plateau steps nudging the mountainside. A small stream of water threaded across each flat, smooth rock, spilling from one step to the next. "Keep your boots on, Clara, walk behind me, stay in the middle of each step. We will be to the bottom in just a few minutes. Do me a favor and look at my back, do not look down and do not look behind."

I glanced down at the stream reflecting the sun's rays as it jumped from on each step to the next, like a child jumping from one puddle to the other. The forest stood congested with branches embracing each other to assure they would not fall or lean on a younger sapling trying to bury its roots deeply into the sandy sediment. Stephen walked slowly, holding the urn with both arms against his chest. I followed, hearing my boots squeaking against the rock's surface. I kept my feet close to avoid sliding and stared at Stephen's back.

I counted each step with a meditative focus; I stopped at sixty when Stephen reached around to take my hand, stepping onto the gravel shore of the Columbia River. "I feel as if we are in a cathedral looking up at all the silhouetted rock formations. The river's color is a bronze reflective glass. You climbed down those steps with Ben as a little boy?"

Stephen nodded and walked to the river's edge, taking gulps of air as if he had an ice-filled soda in his hand

He stretched the urn with his arms. His voice at first muted said, "Remember, Dad, when we would come here and spend a whole day looking for pieces of Native American pottery, fish skeletons, and bent fish-hooks? Dad, I know the stories you told me were not all true but I do remember you pointing down the river and telling me that there were islands in the river and someone constructed a cable with a box that carried people across the river to the falls. I found myself wishing I could swim across this river or ride on a steamboat, or sit along the bank fishing with Clara's ancestors."

I remained quiet, knowing Stephen needed to remember his past and hoped that his voice had found its way to his father's spirit.

"Maybe I never told you, Dad, but I loved your stories. I loved having the time with you when I was small, and even now as an adult. When I went to school, all I heard was students wanting to leave the valley and move to the city."

"No one wanted to stay here in this desert: hot summers, cold snowy winters, the same neighbors, the same stores, the same roads to tricycle, bicycle, practice driving, ride horses, drive tractors, pull carts, ride on buses, taxis, or depending on the latest punishment, walking. You never gave me restrictions, Dad. I guess I gave you no reason, but I always knew somebody, somewhere, and somehow was watching me making sure I did not get in trouble. Thank you, for talking about Mom. If it were not for her and you, I would not be here."

"You always apologized to me and said that you wished I had a mother to take care of me, someone to offer me more understanding, who would hug me more, who would help me with my school projects, who would help me pick out my clothes and who baked sweet desserts for me every day."

"We did just fine, Dad. We cooked together; we somehow made school projects that gave me a decent grade. I always had plenty of desserts from my community mothers who adopted me. I will never forget Clarish, your second love, and I loved her, too. She had the best hugs, always would sit on the floor next to my bed and hum, or play with my hair, or tell me stories about her mother."

Stephen sat down. After he motioned, I joined him. "I know you probably do not know that Clarish tied my hair at the back of my neck with one of her leather ties. She did not want me to cut my hair; she wanted me to be both her son and daughter. It lasted only until one special daughter by the name of Clara came into her life."

"I loved her, Dad, sometimes I think as much as you did. I think I loved Clarish because she loved us. I do think through our lives together we became not two but three. I will miss just us, Dad; I will miss you in the morning, by the fireplace, in the vineyards, in our tasting room, at the dining-room table, sitting on our patio drinking wine. I will miss us planning the future of our winery."

"I hope you won't mind if I still talk to you, ask your advice on anything Dad. Dad, will you hear? Are you hearing me now, or have you already started pairing wine at Heaven's Happy Hour with some of your favorite cheeses? Somehow, I just need to feel you near. Please do not leave me, not yet, please."

Stephen laid his head on the urn that sat between his crossed legs. He cried loudly, he wailed, his body shook, his arms trembled, tears slid down the urn forming a damp circle in the sand. "Dad, Dad, what am I going to do?"

I stroked his head, rubbed my hands along his shoulders, his neck, and his back. "Talk to him, Stephen; I know he is listening. Talk to him."

He put his head on my shoulder, pulling the urn closer. "Dad, you brought her to me, and now you will not be here for us, Dad. She needs you and I need you, Dad, why did you leave me?"

As if a whisper he kissed me gently touching my cheeks, nose, chin, and lips. Holding my head tightly, he pushed his lips against mine, no movement, only the pressure as if sealing our lips. For a brief moment, I felt his anger and knew my presence represented life, while the urn validated the reality of the moment.

Moving his face away from mine, he said, "Clara, I need you. Give me the chance to show you how much I need you. If you must set a timeline, if you must think about me, the valley, your winery, I will give you the space you need. I do not know why you came into our lives when you did, but I ask you to please stay."

I slowly raised myself from the ground, kissed his head, and moved my lips down to his neck. I licked the moisture on his hairline and saw the tattoo, two letters S and C formed as two separate grape leaves on a vine. I thought it was an old tattoo.

He brushed off his pants, slipped off his shoes and began to walk to the river's edge. "I am ready, Dad; I am ready to give you back to the river." Slowly unscrewing the lid of the urn, Stephen began to tilt the opening over, when two small plastic bags fell out.

The bags were wrapped together by a small note. Stephen read, "Keep a little of me for you and who you now love until you find a purpose to memorialize me in your lives." Stephen held his head down looking at the two bags. "Something he must have arranged with the crematorium; a final request from him to me, and you."

I picked up the bags and began to cry. "He was the most unselfish man I have ever met. I do not know what I would do with his ashes, but I will treasure them." Kissing the bags, I nodded tucked them inside my pocket next to the leather-bound book.

I took off my boots and stood next to Stephen. He shook the urn once and a puff of ashes floated briefly, landing on the river haphazardly, spreading out in a fan-like shape. Pausing patiently, we waited for more of Ben's ashes, to follow until a half-moon circle began to move slowly away from us. We put our hands in the water, touching the ashes, guiding them away, holding our hands under the water. A warm breeze floated over the ashes, stirring the water gently causing it to ripple moving the ashes further away.

"He's gone, Clara. He is gone."

I lifted our hands and placed them on Stephen's chest, "No Stephen, he is right here in your heart. He will never be gone."

Stephen lay back in the water, floating toward the ashes that had formed a blurry, hourglass shape. His head centered in the middle of the hourglass, his hands touched the grey water as it pulled away from him, splintering off in a spoke of downriver movement leaving Stephen's hands wet with clear, cool water. I watched, felt the wind stir my skirt, my hair, felt the chill of reality. Ben was gone. He sat in the river and began to wave. "May the spirits of the valley surround you. Goodbye, Dad, goodbye my only father, goodbye my best friend." Slowly he stood, his shirt clinging to him, his pants wrinkled, wet and dripping into the water like mournful tears. He backed up slowly, measuring his steps until he reached the bank. I wrapped my arms around him, whispering, "He loved you, Stephen; he loved you."

A sudden cracking of the shrubs along the riverbank, a whimpering neigh, and a white Appaloosa stood looking at me. Sipping the water, touching the river with his hoof, he drank knowingly, respecting our moment. As quickly as he appeared, he disappeared pushing his body through the shrubs. I looked at Stephen who did not act as if he saw or heard the horse. He stood next to me shivering and looking up the rocky steps of the bluff. I knew I saw the horse, my horse spirit.

"It's time we return to the car. I do not want to leave but I have no choice. Clara, what will I do tomorrow, in the next hour, at our next wine event?" He grabbed my elbow when we heard a stuttering motor, and Thomas One coming around the curve with a dilapidated fishing boat. He was throwing flowers into the water, moving the boat in a large circle; then he drifted to the shore.

"Mr. Stephen, Miss Clara, I knew you would be here. I remember, Mr. Stephen, coming here several times when you were little. Your dad would call and tell me you were too tired to climb back up the boulder stairs. Come, I have warm blankets and a half-empty bottle of wine. I think you should pour it into the water for Mr. Ben." He stepped out of the boat offering his hand to us.

Smiling at Stephen he asked, "Were you attempting to swim across the river again? Oh, how you would beg your father to let you swim across, and how disappointed you were when you came home with your failed attempt to convince him." Looking at me, he said, "Miss Clara, today the water is calm, but it can move quickly, especially if there are any larger boats, barges or, in warmer weather, the occasional sightseeing boats."

As Thomas pushed the boat away from the shore, Stephen wrapped himself tightly in one blanket, me in another, throwing a large fur cover over our laps. He pointed down the river, "Thomas, please follow the ashes; you can barely see them but there is still a small trail glistening in the last of the sun's rays." Thomas turned the boat slowly around. Stephen balanced the empty urn under the fur between his knees, his hand resting on my lap.

The fishing boat engine murmured behind the thinning ashes, pointing like grey arrows at the boulders, the shores, a fading compass at the river's mouth. Pointing, Thomas commented, "Over there, is the Wallula Gap, Miss Clara."

"The winds flow through the valley balancing the climate, assuring that the wind will protect the vines from diseases. Moisture control in the valley helps increase the carbohydrates or sugar in the fruit. The Gap is an important ally for your vineyards."

Thomas continued, "In the early 1900s, there was a railroad track running in the fields along the river with loose gravel among the bluffs, crumbling, I am grateful that you and Stephen got down to the riverbank safely. I think you have shown what a city girl can do."

Stephen ran his fingers in the water along the boat, tapping it, swishing it, scooping it in his palm, allowing the water to run through his fingers, touching the moisture in his hand again, in his mind touching his father. Thomas increased the speed of the boat. The skies had darkened. The sound of wolves wailing and coyotes barking bounced off the boulders. Maria was waiting for us near their truck with more blankets, a carafe of hot coffee, and down jackets. Stephen's car was behind the truck with Thomas Three sitting behind the wheel, smiling and waving. Thomas One looked quickly at Stephen, "No, he did not drive your car; I did. I followed him, driving the pick-up truck. I am grateful there was no traffic, based on the fact he had trouble staying on the highway and he drove on the shoulder."

Maria approached me, helping me put my arms through the dark down jacket smelling of a new, dry-cleaned odor. She wrapped a blanket around my shoulders, while Thomas One handed Stephen the jacket and the poured cup of coffee. I hugged her, a spontaneous gesture for the woman who was a stranger two weeks ago and now a protector and friend.

I gulped the coffee quickly, unaware of the slight burning sensation on my tongue. Stephen watched me drinking, but I avoided his eyes. I gazed at the river thinking again about Ben, and the morning we sat together on my porch.

Stephen walked over and put his arm around me, accepting another steaming pour of coffee. "Shall we have dinner together to celebrate Dad's spiritual life?"

I pushed against his arm, "If you don't mind, I think I had better go back to my house. I have been gone for a while. I honestly have to say, I think I miss my work. I will need to check my e-mail, find out what is going on in the office, and plan for a trip back."

Stephen, Maria, and Thomas One all stared at each other. Maria spoke first, "Miss Clara, why would you need to go back to your office? Why would you leave your winery?" I flushed, partly from anger at being questioned and partly because the heat from the down jacket, blanket, and coffee sent a spray of pink from my neck to my ears. "I need to go back to the office and may need your help watching things while I am gone. We can talk tomorrow, Stephen. I will come over in the afternoon."

Stephen gulped loudly and smiled, "Let me help you into the truck. Please do not make any decisions without me,

Clara. Yes, we will talk tomorrow. Rest. Thank you for today, for yesterday, for last week. I said it once and I say it again; I could not have done it without you."

Thomas One and Thomas Three had pulled the boat onto the trailer. Thomas One offered direction, "Thomas Three, you ride with me. Maria drive Miss Clara to her house and see if she needs anything before you leave. I will see you back at our house." I waited for Maria to hoist herself on the truck seat swinging her leg easily into the truck, and after I climbed into the passenger seat Stephen pushed the door shut. "Take care of her. Tomorrow is too long to wait to see her again."

Thomas One's truck eased away from the embankment, displacing gravel as the fat wheels tugged the trailer up the slight incline. Maria looked in the rear-view mirror and said Stephen was waving at us. I could hear him honk his horn, and quickly move his car in front of our truck and enter the highway.

I found myself looking at Stephen's convertible blending into the dark road, its beaming headlights spotlighting the motorcyclists heading in the opposite direction. I realized it was close to dinner and I had no food in the house. Maria must have read my thoughts because she said, "Miss Clara, we have been to your house to fix the stair step, finish the laundry that you had started, and clean up the kitchen. I did open the windows while I was there just to

305

release the lingering smoke from your baked bread. I have cooked a few suppers for you and they are in the refrigerator."

I squeezed her hand, "How lucky I have been to meet you, all of you. You have taken such good care of me; I don't know how I will ever be able to thank you." I began to cry with abrupt sobs that sucked in the air before bubbling out in residual coffee scents.

I arrived in this valley to decide if I could become a winery owner. Today, I still do not know. I just need to go back to my comfortable condominium without swaying banisters and think about my options."

"Maria, you and Thomas One, have not only generous hearts but your acceptance of me has been overwhelming. I know it is hard to understand because you have met me after my accident and we all faced heart-breaking turmoil within days. Who would not have reached out, who would not have cried when Ben died? Who would not have stood next to Stephen? In truth, such behavior is not me; I am distant around strangers. My job is objective facts, and do not become personal with anyone or anything."

"I have friends, acquaintances, that I spend evenings with, dining and drinking, comparing our desk challenges. In my world I am surrounded by professional peers, colleagues, whose lives revolve around boutique-stores, three-inch high heels, leather briefcases, social media, calendars too full for volunteer work, they are singular islands away from families or relatives, craving only the fast lane with no desire in rewinding their lives."

Maria turned up the road to my house, dark skies dangled low hanging stars daring to be touched, wolf eyes brightened by the headlights disappeared, and grapevine silhouettes perched in dance line positions. We approached my house, the outline lit by a single porch light.

I slipped out of the truck, inhaled the cool evening, the flowers bowing to me from the steel arch, the scent of the caked dirt from the truck tires. The winery doors rattled slightly in the subtle breeze, enough to remind me that it held full barrels, empty barrels, and winemaking equipment. Maria stood next to me. "You have a home, Clara, which has withstood your mother and grandmother. Thomas One said that structurally this house will last another hundred years, and he will help you with any repairs; you will not need to carry a hammer. You may need to carry shears for your vineyard, but I know Stephen will help you as you begin to learn about your heritage."

"I will tell you a secret. I still know very little about wine or winemaking. When a bottle of wine sits on my counter, the cork lying next to it, and I smell the first pour knowing that I will always love the simple reality that grapes were transformed through the patient love and caring of my husband, Stephen's team, and Ben's guiding touch. Their commitment to the vineyard is the key to their success. My one question for you: Can you commit your life to these vines?"

I stood in front of Maria. "A question I cannot answer. I again offer you a sincere, grateful thank you. I will come tomorrow afternoon, but I doubt if I will attempt to bake anything again until I get that oven figured out. Good night, Maria." I hugged her and walked slowly through the gate and up the path to my front door.

Great-grandmother MaMinny's Letter

I looked at the two chairs sitting side by side on the porch; one was the last to have held Ben weeks earlier. Scattered fireflies lit the grapevines like random strings of fading Christmas lights. I watched a bat blend into the night sky, its wings swooshing and stretching in circles over my house. The large L on the stained-glass front door glowed from the house lamps. The living room filled with the warmth of a furnace, which someone had figured out how to work since I left. A triangular wood stack waited patiently with a jar of long matches sitting next to the hearth. I lit the fire, where staggered branches rested like wooden hats on the crumpled newspaper. The fire crackled, spit, smoldered with curling smoke, bursting with a shot of golden flame reaching to escape up the chimney.

I looked at the photographs of Mother, Grandmother, and Great-grandmother sitting on the mantle. "Help me decide, please help me decide."

Reaching into the pocket of my skirt, I pulled out the small sack holding Ben's ashes and placed it next to my mother's picture frame. "Have you found him yet, Mother? I know he is looking for you. I think, at first he may seem lost. He had no plans to enter the spiritual world, but I know you will take care of him. You'd best find some wine because he has not had any for a couple of weeks. I promise I will toast the two of you each time pour a glass."

Kissing their photographs, I eyed the couch, the small table with two wine glasses and a bottle of Merlot. A stack of books and photo albums pressed into one of the cushions with a hand-scratched note lying on top. "Look at the pictures, take notes in your journal, learn about your family." I thought of the steaming bath I had anticipated, looked at the polished new banister, the steps solid without broken gaps, and sat on the couch. "For just a moment, family, I will look at some pictures and I am off to a well-deserved pampering of this aching body."

A carved coyote wine stopper topped in the bottle of wine. Looking back at Mother's frame on the mantel, I said. "Yes, I know I should let it breathe for a few minutes, but I am so thirsty. I will let the next glass breath." I watched the deep-red wine fill the wine goblet, placed my nose over the rim of the glass, and inhaled the smell of berries.

Toasting Mother, Grandmother, and Great-grandmother, I opened the first album, the cover rough as if made from thin layers of wood. It opened stiffly, perhaps resistant to another pair of hands prodding into the past. The first parchment page was stained, smeared, and streaked with ink, displaying a deep, brown muddy color. I sniffed the page, inhaling the earthy scent combined with a faint smell

310

of potato. The corner of the page curled from curious fingertips and parts of the pages stuck together.

I could not read the hyphenated dates. I quickly followed the smudged letters forming a wave of handwritten words on the page, MaMinny. "Great-grandmother MaMinny, this is about you. I will finally get a chance to meet you."

Pouring another glass of wine, I turned the first page to find black-and-white photographs stuck to each page with dried candle wax; photographs of a fort, cabins, livestock, and tall firs around the perimeter. The second photograph was blurred, showing a woman standing next to a man, neither showing any emotion, just staring at the camera. I searched in the kitchen drawers for a magnifying glass from my childhood. I used it to count how many legs each dead spider had when I found them dangling from a web that had flattened itself against a porch post.

I reached to the back of the drawer and found my magnifying glass covered in crusted cookie dough, a chunk of dried bubble gum, and flecks of burnt toast crumbs. Running the glass under hot water, I watched the dough slide over the metal-framed edge, followed by the bubble gum. I opened the refrigerator and saw a platter filled with thin slices of salami, carved tiny squares of Brie, a mound of grapes, apple slices, and circles of a pitted peach. "Thank you, Maria," I whispered.

I returned to the album with the magnifying glass and rested it above the couple. The woman's hair hung in two braids; one down each shoulder, her dress fell to mid-calf. A small necklace hung around her neck reflecting white against her skin. The man wore a white shirt. Suspenders held up his dark pants, boot tops ended right below his knee and he clutched a dark hat in his hands.

The third picture was the woman holding an infant, wearing a white, high-collared blouse, a long black skirt, and her hair coiled on top of her head in a tight roll. She was smiling, tipping the baby to the camera. A small, box-shaped house was in the background, f surrounded by a fence with a white horse tied to the gate. I leaned into the magnifying glass, "It's you, you must be the horse who keeps appearing in the vineyard. Is it you?" My breath fogged the magnifying glass as I lifted the album closer to my face, and a folded letter fell out.

The letter was thick, several pages, and creased evenly along the edge forming three folds to the center. Feeling brittle at first, it unfolded easily, allowing a dried flower petal, several seeds, and a root attached to the end of a toughened stem to slide out.

The letter was dated March 1901.

"The words of this letter are spoken by MaMinny Von Shantman and written by her lifelong friend Rebecca Sally

Smith on a cool evening inside my log cabin. I have known Rebecca and her family since I was an adolescent. I ran from the Indian battle hiding in the woods, alone without a family. I was a descendent of Chief Joseph who fought to keep the Nez Perce tribes on their land, but I have no proof. Living within the protection of the forest with tall, towering green-leaved trees had been easy for the earth provided me with food. I picked gooseberries, blackberries, elderberries, wild strawberries, and pine nuts. I was not far from the river and although I could not fish, I was able to pick at the carcasses of fish that had washed ashore especially when the steamboats began to travel back and forth. I forget how long I had lived in the forest but my life changed when I met Rebecca who had been chasing a chipmunk, crawled under an elderberry shrub, and found me sleeping. She poked at me with a small stick, giggled when I opened my eyes, ran her fingers through my dark hair, and asked if I wanted to be her friend.

I did not speak English but she took my hand and walked me to her family's' cabin. I easily understood the loud voices, the pointed fingers at me, and the broom that held up brushing imaginary dirt in the air. I walked backward, knowing the path to my hideaway and knew that my darker skin would never be accepted in their home.

I never saw Rebecca again until the day I ran to her cabin with a blood-soaked shirt and pointed to the river. Her father grabbed a rifle and followed me with a growling dog, and two older brothers who laughed the whole way to the riverbank. I pointed to the white man, lying on his side, with a bleeding wound. The two older brothers grabbed me, shook me, and yelled in unknown words. The white man spoke and said four words, "Not her, white officer."

Rebecca's father recognized him," Jeremy, my favorite fur trader, what has happened to you?" Jeremy's eyes fluttered and he did not speak, his body turned an ashen blue, and the bigger brother pushed past me, quickly threw him over his shoulder, and began to run through the woods.

I followed, stood at the edge of the forest at the end of the path from the cabin. I watched people rush in and out, I saw the brothers carrying armfuls of wood, and run down to the river to fill buckets with water. Rebecca would stare at me from a window, pressing her face between the thin fabric curtain and the glass. I had no idea what was happening until Rebecca came out, took my hand, and walked me into the house. The room was silent, radiating heat from the open fireplace, and smelled of vegetables cooking on the stove. I waited, feeling the stares of her family, two men dressed completely in black, and one Native American who spoke to me explaining Jeremy would have died had I not found him.

He invited me to sit by his bed while he slept and assured me no one in the house would harm me. He explained to me that he knew Jeremy for he sold him animal pelts for flour, metal, and fabric. I noticed the father was wearing a grey fur hat. The mother came over and covered Jeremy with pieces of fur.

I accepted the metal bowl filled with steamed carrots, potatoes bits of greasy meat that I learned later was bison. I slept on the warm floor grateful for the blanket that Rebecca had placed over me and woke several times throughout the night to offer Jeremy water and bits of bread soaked in the vegetable broth. I left him only to drain my bladder and expel my bowels in the woods. Rebecca offered me a plain blue dress to wear when she saw my animal skin dress, soiled from pulling Jeremy from the river's edge. The dress was thin; it gave my body no warmth.

Rebecca brushed my hair one day; the dark ends reached my waist. Compared to her short, curly blonde hair, her mother's blonde-haired braided hair, and the father's shoulder-length blonde hair and pale-white skin; I was someone different. Jeremy became stronger and spoke a few words, translated by Rebecca's father.

I kept waiting for the family to get their broom and sweep me out the door, but one evening they put a metal bowl on the table and invited me to sit on the bench next to Jeremy. When everyone held hands and bowed their heads, I waited to begin eating.

I learned that Rebecca's family was one of fifty cabins in an area called Frenchtown, known for fur traders

*and trappers. Jeremy's role as a fur trapper ended after the
tribal wars. His trade with the European countries started to
change silk became the desire of rich women.*

*I cannot remember how I got my first name, but I got
my last name when Jeremy and I married at St. Rose's
Church. A law passed to forbid white people and Native
Americans to marry but Rebecca's family said they told
everyone we were married before the law passed. I do
remember I never returned to the forest, Jeremy, and
Rebecca's family built a cabin for us not far from the river,
near the path that led to their home, and close enough to the
sounds of the lapping water, the nighttime coyote howls, and
the occasional chatter of canoe riders going down the river.
They cut down the tall Douglas firs, making a mud and stick
chimney, and surrounded the house with a small picket
fence. I had braided a heavy piece of twine that hung outside
the front door to ease our entrance. I had never lived in a
house above the ground before. My family had built and an
underground home, which we shared with four other
families, but I remember very little about it once left seeking
from the tribal wars.*

*Rebecca's mother taught me how to cook and bake. I
made bread daily using the skins of grapes as the ingredient
to help the bread rise. Oh, how I loved the smell of grapes
when we would buy them from the market. I learned how to
skin rabbits, pluck chickens, and milk the goats. Jeremy*

bought cattle, pigs, chickens, and began to plant wheat, and the local blacksmith made the wheels for our buggy. The white horse that you see in the photograph was a gift to us from Rebecca's family, I never named her, but I found her love reminded me of Jeremy's love for me.

We planted apple, walnut trees, and several dark twisted vines with roots that seemed to burrow into the moist soil once planted. The vines were gifts received on a trade from a German settler; they were vitis vinifera and grew Cabernet Sauvignon grapes. I did not know the vines were grapes, but soon realized I could make a juice from them and wine. Your father and I made wine for social gatherings and we donated wine for Sunday morning services at the Catholic Church not far from our community. Members with more than twenty acres sold their wine to the saloons; many had plans to ship their wine on the new railroad but the rails never came close to us. I learned to be tough my dear Margaret, I learned to assume that one good day would roll into another, I treasured every moment I had with your father. Within the community, I learned to love and embrace the new life that I had been given.

We loved our house not far from the river, and oh the fish that your father caught for our dinners. He would dry the salmon and all winter, we would have fish when the river became too cold for fishing. In the 1860s, the rivers froze completely, except our river the Columbia, which froze to a depth of fifteen feet. The salmon and the vines we had planted were ruined.

I was so sad to see my first grapevines frozen and brittle but I managed to salvage some roots. The river once filled with salmon grew lifeless after more dams were built, a sad discovery for us and for the salmon who could not return to their spawning grounds.

My daughter, Margaret, our first-born came into the world in one of the first established towns, Walla Walla. I had tried to have you at home but you were stubborn, I often wondered if you became a stubborn adult too. Sister of Providence hospital in 1889 was your birthplace not far from the library, bank, and the state penitentiary.

We had electricity then; thus I was able to see your smooth face and wide yawning mouth while holding you in my arms. What a special baby you were, you became best friends with Rebecca's firstborn, Stephen. Your father and I opened a mercantile store a year before you were born where we sold basic food staples, grain, fabric, and I made small baskets. We were busy once the gold rush settlers came through, and we were able to maintain as more immigrants moved to our state.

I was very grateful for these immigrants, Margaret. Their hair was dark like mine, few spoke English, and their clothes were simple. Your father and I soon had new friends who would come to the cabin with their meals, including homemade alcohol, much stronger than my wine.

I tried to bring you a baby sister or brother but I got very ill and could not have another baby. I know you would have been the best sister and I am sorry. I hope as your life went on you found a special friend, like my Rebecca.

You will see there are other pictures in this album of all of me and my friend Rebecca and your home. My white horse died, when we buried her I asked her to watch over you, so please look for her in your dreams.

I write this letter, older and very tired. Your father died three years ago, his healthy body became weary, and his heart longer beat strong. The doctor said it was as if he had leftover changes from the diphtheria epidemic. We had nothing to stop the awful epidemic. I know when you have children; dear Margaret there will be medicines to protect against illnesses like measles, cholera, and typhoid fever that affected my ancestors. For the safety of your children give them medicine that will prevent them from dying like so many did, in my time.

I have lived a good life. I learned to be independent, I learned about my ancestry, I overcame hatred, I embraced others, not my color, and I married your father who brought me you. I give you my life and lessons dear daughter. Carry yourself with pride, do not judge others, find a place in your

life for wine, plant my grapevines near your home, look for
my beautiful horse to guide you, and offer you peace.

  Wearing the claws of our spiritual protector, the
wolf, I wish you love."
Your mother always, MaMinny

I folded the envelope slowly, gently rubbing my nail across
the crease. "So you are my family, Great-grandmother,
MaMinny. You are the one who began the cycle of women
that I now follow. You found love, survived against odds in a
white man's world and became an entrepreneur, a mother, a
wife. You were the mother of my grandmother, Margaret.
Your letter is different from the story that Thomas One's
great-grandfather shared. Perhaps Thomas One's grandfather
remembered it differently or did not know about Rebecca. I
do feel stories need to be told, and now I know the
importance of heritage, family history, and belonging. Now,
with your words, this letter, I know this is a true story."

  "I sit here wondering how I could ever fulfill the
same dreams you had for my grandmother that you instilled
through passionate blood passing through the placenta. How
did you fill her soul with the drive never surrender to a
challenge, to seek only the chance to risk, and to erase failure
from her mind like a chalkboard?"

  "What was the power that enabled you to succeed
despite your different clothing, inability to speak the

language, and lack of skills to fit into your surrounding culture. How did you feel the first time someone laughed at you, imitated you, or ignored you? What is it that made you wish only to blend, to look at others with eyes seeking only to understand them, not to threaten them? Was a cabin a luxury for you, did you miss what was familiar to you, the woods, the berries, the water? What made you leave what you knew to transition to an unknown world and face an unpredictable outcome?"

"Were you in a situation where the warm earth's seasonal coolness led you to seek warmth or were you convinced that living a changed life was your only chance of surviving? How did you ever fall in love with a man when you could not speak his words, nor he yours? What was so appealing to you? Was it his appearance, his weakness that needed your strength, his appreciation of you for saving his life, his desire to challenge the community that found difference something to shun?"

"Did you ever feel equal? Grandmother, you were cooking, cleaning, and harvesting food, working in the store, sewing, caring for him, and others. How could you feel equal striving daily to maintain a capable image while suppressing surrounding and unknown fears? Rebecca was part of your life probably the one person who understood you and helped you grow."

I eyed the bottle of Merlot and realized three hours had passed, and a final glass of wine waiting to be poured. The fire glowed, its firefly embers, releasing wisps which rose and disappeared.

Pouring the last of the wine, I walked to my front door, stepped onto the porch, and smelled lingering fire smoke. Looking across my dark vineyard, I saw the faint glow of a fire at the edge of the bluff. I could see no one's shadow, no horse, just a cone of bright flame.

I began to step off the porch when two pairs of deep yellow eyes peered through the gate. Nudging the gate open with their muzzles, they began to walk slowly to me. By their size, I realized they were wolves, their paws anticipating their movement on the stone path, their heads down until they stood within a few feet of the bottom step. I moved back slowly, willing my feet not to trip, reaching behind me to find the latch of the screen door. Opening it softly, I stepped inside.

The wolves never moved, watching me intently. They turned and disappeared into the darkness. I reached for my phone to call Stephen but changed my mind. Walking to the photographs on the fireplace mantel, I touched MaMinny's photograph. "Thank you for keeping me safe."

It is time for a bath. "Good night, family," I murmured as I climbed the stairs. The banister did not move when I grabbed its polished surface, ascending slowly to my bedroom. Entering the bathroom, I smiled when I saw unlit candles balanced on different pieces of tree trunks about my bathtub, a new CD player sitting on a shelf that had been empty before I left with two new violin CDs resting on top. One of the dining-room chairs held my robe and slippers, and a tiny dish of rose petals perched on the side of the tub next to lavender bath salts.

I dropped my clothes to the floor, pulled Ben's leather-bound book from my skirt pocket, and placed it on the tiled floor. Sliding in one CD, I turned on the faucets filling the tub with water and lit the candles. Untying my hair, I stepped into the tepid water, sank in until my chin rested on the water, and closed my eyes. I did not have a bathtub in New Jersey. I thought of how I would brag to my friends how I could shower, dress, apply makeup, and style my hair in a half hour. Relaxation, candles, stringed music was not part of my financial life.

Reaching down to the floor and lifting Ben's leather book gently, I noticed for the first time that the book was divided by a piece of cardboard in the middle. The first section was my wine-making primer with a simple, systematic, directional guide. Each page had a set of parentheses at the bottom indicating a visual demonstration to be followed by practice sessions. The pages after the cardboard held small invitation-sized envelopes, one glued on each page with discolored cracked edges.

Closing my eyes, I drifted into a light sleep imagining downtown Walla Walla in the late 1800s with the city transitioning from horse-drawn carriages and great-grandmother unaware that Washington State had officially become part of the union. I pictured great-grandmother walking past scattered vineyards with her French- Canadian husband.

Love bound her to him, love ignorant of how their relationship was viewed outside their cluster of log cabins, a love that did not need anything except embracing their private moments of laughing, pointing, learning languages, and finally, learning diligently how to write.

MaMinny left her family, surviving with a hesitant acceptance of people whose skin was white. I pushed the warm water around my shoulders, turned on the faucet dripping hot water between my feet pressed against the bathtub.

"And here I am," I said to the candle closest to the tub, forcing its flame to shimmer in a slight hula movement. "Although I no longer have a family; I have a condo building filled with established friends. I must choose between leaving the security of my New Jersey home to live in a vineyard, a tasting room, a home begging for upkeep, and a handful of new friends."

"The only connection I have here is my mother who brought people into my life even after she died. I had never met any of these people when I made my monthly visits, as they often left food on the porch or placed clean linen in the cupboards when I was in New Jersey. What do I owe this community? Am I an extension of her? No, I am not," I shouted, forcing two of the candles to blow out, and sizzle from my flying spit.

"I am not my mother; I am not my grandmother or great-grandmother. I am the granddaughter and daughter who lives in the city."

I slammed the water with my fists shouting again, "Who is going to listen to me? Who is going to understand that I do not want to leave my familiar surroundings for something I do not know. I am not you, great-grandmother. I do not need ways to survive, I do not need to change who I am to be accepted by others, and I do not want to sacrifice my past to find my future."

I listened to the banging on the front door; reaching for my phone without hesitation, I dialed Stephen, "Someone is at my front door. It is midnight, what should I do?"

"Clara please let me in. I promise not to stay long."

Visit from a Native-America Spirit

I reached for my robe, blew out the last candle that had survived my bathroom rant, and walked down the steps. Stephen stood on the porch with Thomas One.

"Clara, there have been multiple wolf sightings, and several goats were found dead along the highway. I know you do not believe in guns and it is too late to teach you tonight. Thomas One will stay with you through tomorrow."

"You can come to our winery, or I will come here to teach you to shoot a gun. Wolves are not too common and I am not sure why we are seeing them this time of year. We were all worried about you. Please understand I am not trying to see you for any other reason." Stephen smiled brushing away the wet hair from my face.

I pulled my robe tighter, realizing bathtub bubbles glistened on my neck and ran down my chest. "I have seen them, Stephen. They were in my front yard over an hour ago." I point to the path, saying, "Right there, right behind you; they stood and looked at me." Stephen stared at the spot as if a laser beam directed their gaze. "They left after I backed into the house. They just left, leaping over the fence and disappearing into the vineyard. Please do not harm them; please, they are part of my spiritual heritage. I think they are here for me; I think my great-grandmother sent them to protect me."

Stephen eyed the empty bottle of wine, the charred wood, the stack of albums on the couch. "Clara, wolves kill; they do not hover over you with wings. They will kill, perhaps not you, but if they are hungry enough you could be their dinner. I do not think they are here to protect you, I think they may have killed your chickens that waited patiently for you to return."

I cried out, "No, not my chickens; not the mothers with babies! I am sure they have found shelter under the house or pushed their way through the winery door. Please, Stephen, do not tell me that those beautiful babies are gone."

"They were so cute, how they followed their mother in and out of the vines. I held each one. The mother trusted me with her little family." I found myself looking at him with wide eyes, shimmering in a thin blanket of tears.

"How could a family be destroyed by one hungry thing, something bigger than them, something that could have easily chased a rat, mole, or even one of those squirrels that continues to chase its tail on my roof? Stephen, those wolves belong to me. I will not shoot them."

I think Stephen knew these past few weeks I was not one to easily change my mind, or explain how or why the valley was not my home or even that an entire community was on standby waiting to support my winery. He had learned to listen and offer me his presence for this moment. I was trembling as he touched my arm. "Thomas One, grab the couch for tonight and we will talk in the morning. I will take care of the crew and you take care of her. Clara, stop by in the morning. "

I knew looking at his eyes and realizing how afraid I was, that I did not argue, and prepared the couch for Thomas One and return upstairs. I heard Stephen talking in low tones to Thomas, the door close softly, and heard Thomas latch the door.

I tossed all night, trying to imagine the baby chicks disappearing into the jaws of a wolf, the mother circling them to protect them and finally clamped in the same jaw. Who would want to destroy an innocent family whose only daily ritual was to find food, shelter, and take care of each other? I sat upright in bed, covered in sweat. I woke to the sound of music, the smell of coffee, and a breeze traveling lazily up the stairs from the front-door screen. "Maria, are you down there?" I shouted from the top of the stairs.

"No, Miss Clara, just Thomas One preparing a light breakfast before we head out. Take your time, I think I burned the first batch of scrambled eggs, so I will start over." I dressed by the bedroom window, pulling the drapes into the long bent nail that served as a hook, scanning the horizon for any wolves, any horses, any chickens. Seeing nothing, I descended the stairs to Thomas One's awaiting smile.

"I am not a cook, but I cannot let you starve before we walk around your vineyard. I thought I might point out a

328

few things to pique your curiosity. I heard coyotes last night, but after sitting on your porch until early morning, I did not see any more wolves. Perhaps they were just stopping by our valley for a short visit and they have continued to another location. I hope so."

I looked at my plate of runny scrambled eggs, dots of hot sauce, and big uneven chunks of bread balancing on the edge. Thanking Thomas One, I attempted to eat the undercooked yolks, dabbed my bread in the center, while gathering tiny strands of egg whites.

Thomas One talked nervously. Smiling I nibbled on the edge of the bread until he announced where the eggs were from. "Miss Clara, I looked in your empty refrigerator with only a few jars of pears, apple butter, and pickles from Maria. I began to wander around your yard and heard sounds behind your winery door, muffled clicks, and all of a sudden one little chick hopped out followed by two more and they began to run in tiny circles. I pried the door open and a very scolding mother hen ran after her babies."

"My chickens have not been eaten? The babies are all well, all four of them?"

"I only saw three Miss Clara, but one may have left the winery sooner. I did find a beautiful nest of eggs from the mother, your morning gift from her. I will show you where her nest is so you may gather them yourself."

"We do not have any chickens at Mr. Stephen's winery. The dogs were eager to chase them and visitors with children raced through the vines to catch one. I love them; my culture loves them, I hope you will take care of yours."

"I can, if you wish, build a little pen for them to prevent you from fearing the wolves attacking them. You just need to let me know, I have several sons who, according to their mother, are not busy enough, so a project would be perfect to keep them out of trouble. "

I swiped the last piece of bread in the remaining puddle of eggs and chewed quickly. I took several quick swallows of coffee, and thought of my favorite breakfast place in New Jersey, in a corner brick building across from the train station. It was an impossible location to find a table during the week, but on weekends it was my trophy after a morning walk. I would sit at the long stainless-steel counter, close to the cash register so I could talk with Mazie, the owner, and have free access to the glass coffeepot for limitless refills.

Mazie was a widow, had no children, and her last living brother lived in Florida. Multiple attempts to get him to travel to New Jersey for a holiday visit were always fruitless, so Mazie would open her restaurant and offer free breakfast each Thanksgiving and Christmas morning. All the locals came, all her regulars came, and I volunteered to pour coffee, and hand out steaming plates of pancakes.

330

Mazie knew when I had returned from a visit with Mother. She placed a plastic flower in a cracked saltshaker, had silverware, and a coffee mug waiting with a tiny sign on my seat that said, "Reserved."

She would listen, nod, and rub my hand when my eyes filled with tears or my face flushed, ignoring the customers standing at the cash register waiting to pay. "Just a minute, Bill; come on, Joe, since when have you ever been in a hurry; Charlotte, you do not have an appointment to go to; Harold, just leave your money on the counter if you are sure your dog leashed out there needs to go to the bathroom."

I would laugh, listening to her manipulate her impatient fan club, which always relented when she scolded them, turned to each other discussing the weekly crossword puzzle, the impending winter storm, and diminishing attendance at the Friday night tavern dart tournament.

Mazie collected their monies, focusing her eyes on me while offering an occasional wink to the customers. I knew she never kept any tips stuffed into a cookie jar resembling a black cat. She put all the tips in her safe, hidden behind her annual calendar from the car repair shop around the corner. The tips paid for the holiday meals, sent flowers to a regular who had become ill, sent a monthly check to her brother in Florida and bought bags of cat food for the stray cats who hugged the back door of the restaurant with yowls of hunger. The milkman occasionally would leave an extra plastic jug of milk with a rubber-banded tag, "feed the meowers."

Mazie knew everything about my family and the winery, but I had not been back to tell her about Stephen or my struggle with the reality of leaving New Jersey, my job, and my friends to assume responsibility for the winery.

I needed to return to New Jersey soon, to get away, to have distance between the valley, Stephen, the winery, the memories, and reestablish what was familiar to me. I missed sitting at my beautiful mahogany desk, looking down seventy floors to the streets below, walking to the bars where the staff knew my name, and having my friends divulge their latest conquests with men, or spending a weekend sleeping in, walking, shopping, and having dinner along the river.

I thought of the drive-through Walla Walla with Stephen, the quaint street, the sculptures on each corner, the historical markers, and the tree-lined streets, the bus that seemingly rolled unhurriedly past the stores. There were no taxicabs, bicyclists, clusters of people waiting at intersections to cross, police officers directing traffic, neon advertisements, newspaper stands, food carts, homeless holding paper cups looking up and down when the sound of footsteps shuffled by. I wondered what Maize would say when told her I was thinking about moving to the west, running a winery, leaving New Jersey.

I did not know when I would reach a decision, I just knew I could not continue to limp on one foot and wear stiletto on the other. I realized I was deep in thought when Thomas reached for my empty plate. I put my hand on him, "No, I can do my dishes. You have spoiled me too much already. I do not know what I will do when I go back to New Jersey to face my dishes."

He put his other hand over mine, "Miss Clara, what it will take for you to know that this is your home? We, my family, and Mr. Stephen and all the wineries want to be your new family. You need to give us a chance to show you that this valley is as exciting as your New Jersey home. Why won't you give us a chance?"

"Certainly, Mr. Ben's death was not the right time for you to meet anyone, although I do know he was so very fond of you because you look like your mother. How he loved your mother, not in a romantic way, to us who saw them together, but in a respectful way. He was not far from her at a social function, he was the first to refill her empty wine glass, and he was quick to answer a question during one of her wine tastings. He never laughed when she made a mistake and oh, she made plenty of them."

"She felt responsible and protective of you as you grew up. She had the best laugh and she was always humming, no particular song, just humming in a very happy, satisfying way."

"She told stories of how her great-grandmother's best friend had a son called Stephen. I am sure you have heard that story. If not, I know that many will repeat it."

"On the other hand, if you visit our homes in the evening, someone will be telling the young ones about MaMinny. Everyone knows the location of her grave that will never be without flowers or trinkets and occasionally candy."

I began to put on my boots and he tugged me away "Let's go barefoot; I want you to feel the richness of your soil. I will carry your boots just in case it is too muddy. Come, Miss Clara."

I moved my legs in a marching motion and followed behind. Standing on the porch, I caught my breath as I looked at the beauty of the vines to the left, the winery facing me, the arbor vines entwined with other vines as if they were racing to the top. The path to the gate was solid soil. We followed a strip of grass that led us to the vineyard.

A car pulled up just as we stepped from between a row of Merlots. A man with a baseball hat sitting crooked on his head, a pipe clenched between his teeth jiggling as he spoke. "Hello, Miss. I am hoping there will be some tasting today of the Long House Cabernet. This winery was the first on our list today, wasn't it, Suzy?"

I looked in the window expecting to see a female Suzy next to him, only to see a Golden Retriever with a purple scarf around its neck. I recognized him as the man who drove to my winery weeks ago, hitting the winery with his car and the man who appeared at Ben's memorial. I knew with the baseball hat firmly planted on his head, Thomas One had not recognized him.

"I am sorry to disappoint you, but there will be no tastings. The winery is not open. I am not sure when it will reopen but I would be happy to check if there are any bottles of wine available, if you would be interested in purchasing a bottle."

"A bottle, oh, no, I want a case; actually, I want three cases. I want whatever you will sell me. This winery has the best Cabernet Sauvignon in the valley, and if something is happening to this winery then I had better get what I can. How much is a case?"

Thomas One stepped in, "Bottles are $45.00 a piece so you are talking $270.00 per case. How many did you say you wanted?"

The man unbuckled his seat belt, reached into his back pocket. Opening his wallet he pulled out a stack of bills, all hundreds." If you have four I will take four, and I will give you payment in cash. Do you know what is going to happen to this winery? Do not tell me it is going to be sold. I would buy this beauty. Now, I know nothing about wine, but this Cabernet needs to stay in this valley. My grandfather knew the grandmother who owned this winery; it would be a shame if anything happened to it."

Thomas One nudged me as we walked to the winery. "Put on your boots. His storyline is getting muddier. Plus, when we open the door, there will be a field of chicken and poop. You have plenty of cases to fill his request but I am going to make him think he is getting the last bottle produced. It makes for grand storytelling when he is sharing it with his friends."

Thomas walked to the back of the winery, unlatched the sliding door, and stacked three cases on a dolly. I had not been in the winery storage room since my past wine tasting event. All the cases were stacked behind the counter.

"Thomas, I had no idea I could sell cases. Had I known, I could have sold so much more wine during the wine tasting when Mother was still alive. What do I do with this cash?"

Thomas One gave a simple answer. "Open a bank account."

The man took off his baseball cap, exposing his matted red hair clinging like a spider web to his moist head. "My name's Jess. I'm from New Jersey. I am here for a long weekend. This is my favorite get-away; this one got expensive quickly with the wine I have been buying. You don't ship, do you?"

Thomas One's eyes widened when he recognized him and attempted to move the conversation along quicker, "When we are in full operation we do. If you are flying out of Spokane, you will find several shipping locations. It is going to cost you additional money, but I think it will be worth every sip."

Jess looked at me, "You look familiar. Have I seen you around? I mean, in New Jersey or Manhattan. Your hair, it is your hair, that jet-black color. You look like someone who rides my office-building elevator; her hair is your color. I think she gets off on the 70th floor. Mine is 75th."

Thomas waited for me to speak up; I was quiet. I had recognized him, the perfect-suited man with burnt red hair, each in place. He spoke to everyone in the elevator, often had a bouquet, and impatiently tapped his foot on the elevator floor.

I looked down at his leather shoes, slid my eyes back up to his face, and knew he was trying to place me in our mutual office building. Suddenly, the dog hanging out the window, panting, slapping its tail on the car's interior was equally familiar.

I had seen the dog with him on the elevator. The dog was his service dog, standing patiently next to him, his fur pressed against a perfectly tailored trouser, his nose sniffing the briefcase that hung level to his eyes. The dog would nudge the owner's hand occasionally who stared at the blinking elevator numbers, listened to the automated voice announcing floors, and wishing the passengers a good morning. I never petted Suzy. I always found the corner closest to where the elevator doors would slide open, quietly, yawning its metallic lips while people entered or left its carpeted floor. The elevator's ceiling lined with soft lights and a floor-to-ceiling mirror gave everyone a chance to brush away the bagel crumbs resting their lip, wipe away the subtle, faded shadow of the final latte sip, and beam a final toothy grin assuring no sliver of adorned a tooth after the protein shake. A television with subtitles sat embedded in the corner gave everyone a digested version of the world news from the lobby to their floor.

"No, it couldn't be you. Why last time I checked, I did not see anyone wearing overalls and braids, although I must say, the resemblance is striking. I am thinking you must be the smart one who has made this valley your home; no towering buildings for you, just the rows of leafy vines that produce this wine."

He counted out the bills into Thomas's hand, unlatched the trunk, and peered around again to look at me. "Hey, if you ever come to the finance district, look me up. I own the building."

He shook our hands and opened the door for Suzy to leap out and run free, finding plenty of soft dirt to relieve herself. Her service-dog backpack caught in one of the lower vines. She tugged once, running back with a green vine flying behind her like a canine kite.

Jess apologized and handed it to me. I responded in a monotone voice, "Keep it and find a vase to put it in your office. Who knows? You may grow some roots and start your vineyard in Manhattan."

He put Suzy back in the car just as the mother and her chickens zigzagged by, heading back to the barn. Suzy pressed her nose against the front window with pleading eyes, and barking at Crenshaw.

Finding the Baby Chick

Thomas One turned to me, "You know him?"

I nodded, "I know of him but never worked with him. He owns most of Manhattan, so he easily could have bought every case of wine we have. I am not sure why he came here; I am equally not sure why he only bought a limited supply. Something just does not feel right about his visit."

"I know he knows who I am, if not from the elevator ride then from my photograph in the lobby as part of the advertisement for my company. He may have noticed me on the elevator, but I think he had a plan when he drove up that driveway. I am not sure what yet, but I have a sinking feeling at the moment."

"I am surprised you did not recognize him as the man who showed up at Ben's memorial, and he was the man who hit the doors of my winery years ago, destroying some of my oak barrels."

I walked toward the driveway and watched the car ease between the vineyards. I could not tell if he was taking photographs or if he was on a cellphone, but he was not in a hurry to leave. Thomas picked up his phone. Speaking in Spanish, he directed someone to do as he asked and kept saying in English, "Now, Now."

"Who are you talking to?" I asked.

"I called one of my sons to follow him. He certainly will not be suspicious if a beat-up truck follows him with a few noisy Hispanic boys. Just curious, I want to know if he is truly heading to the airport exit or returning to Walla Walla."

"He did have luggage in his trunk, but I am not sure if he is coming or going. I had the same feeling, Clara, that I had seen him before, but I was not sure. The dog and baseball hat certainly were not part of what he wore to Mr. Ben's memorial. What is he going to do with your wine?"

I shrugged, "Perhaps he is going to send it back to the wine conglomerate in Seattle, who he clearly must have a partnership with to be out here."

I stood by the winery listening to the mother hen scold her chicks. "Whew, she sure is bossy. I am so glad they are all here except for one. Maybe it is lost and we will find it as we walk through the vineyard."

I followed Thomas who reached down to the soil, feeling the moisture. "It was in the early 1900s that irrigation systems were introduced to the vineyards, assuring that the roots have adequate water."

"Someday, I will show you the winery that is planting vines in rocks; hard to believe, I know. The rocks certainly can keep the roots solid, hold in the water and heat. The rocks offer the vines a challenge, as their roots need to work to burrow deeply. Your soil is perfect, needs a little tender loving care weekly, but I will take care of it for you.

341

Water and vines are the perfect marriage. The leaves are valuable for photosynthesis, the weather is responsible for the tannins in your grape skins influencing the amount of sugar, helping to retain acidity, and determining the size of your grapes. Your grapes are healthy; these temporary orphans have done well, probably because of the work from your mother and ancestors."

"A vineyard cannot survive isolation, but for the short term, it can maintain itself. Look, Clara, at the Columbia River, the warmth, the evening cool, but no cold winds; all these add up to a vineyard's success. "

Thomas noticed a swarm of birds diving into one of the rows of chardonnay. "There's a problem, and it is something we will take care of immediately. We can put nets over the vines to prevent the birds from feasting. We try not to use pesticides. It may sound a little corny but we honor Nature, who assures that our vines and the earth survive to contribute to our grape crops."

Thomas One stopped when his phone rang, "Thanks, son. I will tell Miss Clara."

He gave me an update, "He is going to take a late flight to the East Coast. I hope he has time to ship the bottles unless he had already set up a drop off location. We could find out who shipped our wine and their final destination. Stephen and I work with all of the local shipping offices; not sure it's worth the effort at this point."

As I walked through the vines, plucking a few grapes, I thought of Ben when he tasted my grapes with glowing comments. I wished I could remember which vine and grape cluster he touched, so I could touch it and connect with him. I realized my heart was still heavy thinking about him. I wondered where he and Mother were at this very moment.

Thomas One pointed down a path that followed close to my fence. He continued to talk about the impact of the weather on grapes, and stopped and pulled several vines apart. Behind the vines was a tiny cross made of animal horns and tied with thick, braided twine. Tucked under the twine were several claws, brittle, and slightly disintegrated.

"We think this is your great-grandmother MaMinny's grave. We have no actual proof it is her grave, but my grandfather told me that his father brought him here once to show him her grave."

"It has been here for more than 150 years since her death, and we keep it hidden to prevent anyone from taking her away from us. She needs to stay here even if this is not Native-American grounds. She is respected, kept warm, and we silently acknowledged yearly. We think the claws are wolf claws, just like the necklace you are wearing around your neck."

Thomas found a vine that formed a thick mass at the bottom, a nest of dried grape leaves, sand, bits of gravel, and his hand touched something soft. In the middle of the nest was a tiny chick, startled, glassy eyes gazing, beak opened in a final chirp, one twig-like leg sticking up, the other folded against his wing.

"Clara, I see this as a gift to her. I think this was the chick with a limp; it always fell behind from the rest. Perhaps it died and a wolf carried it to MaMinny's grave. Its body is whole, unharmed."

I stooped next to him asking, "Should I touch it, should we say a prayer, or must we take it back to its mother? What should we do; it is so cold in the evenings." I began to cry and realized my tears went beyond the little chick, beyond the hidden cross, my heart spun as I felt the loss of Mother, my mentor, Ben, my valley family, the winery, Stephen, my grandmother, my great-grandmother.

"Thomas, why must things die? This little chick did not even get to say good-bye to his family. He probably died alone, and he did not even know that his death was coming. He was quite happy limping behind his family, nibbling at the feed they missed, burrowing himself into his mother's feather breast. He didn't have a chance."

I remembered my childhood when I found a dead duckling along the river. Mother wrapped it in the embroidered towel that had held fresh slices of bread smeared with apple butter, handed the duck back to me, and talked about the duck's life.

I knew it was a fairytale-like others Mother would whisper at bedtime. I wanted the fairy tale to have a happy ending. I remember asking Mother if the little duck would wake up if Mother asked the family wolf spirit, or if the duck drank some of Grandmother's medicine. Every time Mother shook her head no, I tried to convince her that the duckling was under an evil spell and it would wake shortly.

Angry with my mother, I ran upstairs and put the duck under her pillow. Mother waited, knowing I would eventually come to my conclusion after I researched my science books to understand why or how young ducks die. Fables, stories, Native-American history, they are all remembered and interpreted differently, as the story of MaMinny's love, Jeremy.

Thomas waited patiently, watching me touch the little chick cautiously, speaking softly to it. He spoke, "You are special, not like all the other senoritas that Mr. Stephen has brought for dinner. I know why Mr. Ben liked you so much; you are like your mother, soft heart, but a hard, protective shell." He reached down to help me up, "Do you wish to walk further?"

Nodding, I wiped my nose on my sleeve and kept my hand in his as he stood. He became a momentary protector from my swirling feelings, the continuing uncertainty, and the constant reminders that I was part of a winery generation, and my vineyard held the spiritual self of my great-grandmother, MaMinny.

The path of the vineyard ended and I walked to the location of the nightly bonfire. Looking back at the house porch, I remembered where I stood and watched the distant flames and smoke.

"Nothing is here Thomas; no ashes, only dry pieces of wood, perhaps blown around by the wine, nothing resembling the fire I see nightly. Why would someone clean up the spot and leave each evening?"

Thomas dropped to his knees and dug into the soil. He brought a handful of soil to his nose. "Miss Clara, I do not smell anything resembling burnt wood or ashes. Are you sure you saw a bonfire and not perhaps the headlights of occasional cars traveling down the highway?"

I nodded, affirming my story, and started saying, "Also there is a hor…." I paused, realizing my visual sighting of a horse belonged to me; I certainly was not going to add an Appaloosa horse to the mysterious equation. "I do not understand. I know I have seen it. Perhaps next time I should just walk down here and confront the person on my property."

"Miss Clara, next time you see the bonfire, please call one of us, and we will walk with you. Do not walk through these vineyards at night alone until the wolf-pack issue is resolved."

"I ask you to listen to me on this one and not ignore what I am saying. I know enough about this valley and land to know when there is danger. This wolf pack is a danger. Are you listening?" He gently turned me directly facing him.

My head remained downcast, "Why won't any of you let me just be independent? You know before I met all of you I was a capable, successful woman. I put on a pair of boots, tramped around the vineyard, burned one loaf of bread, sprained my foot for the first time, and suddenly, I am someone who needs all of you."

I looked up at him, "You must understand, you must understand! I am not a city idiot. What does it take anyone to listen to me?"

Standing within a foot from him, "I am not one to be told what to do, I have made my mistakes and somehow have survived, I rarely ask for any help, so I do not understand how I have been corralled into a helpless, dependent behavior. I will always appreciate all of your help when I was injured. I am healed now, physically, and what I do going forward is my decision, not yours or anyone else's decision. Why will no one understand me? I am speaking English."

I realized when I used the words speaking English I had offended him. His face turned bright red; he stepped back from me and began to speak quickly in Spanish while he walked quickly up the path to his truck. "Thomas, I am sorry. I did not mean it the way it sounds. I would do nothing to offend you. I am so sorry."

I tried to hop behind him, with hollow versions of sorry, only to see him pull away after I touched his arm. I did not notice Stephen leaning on the tasting room door. "Not sure what you said, Clara, but I have not heard Thomas One swear that much since Maria told him she was expecting Thomas Five."

The Long House Winery

He added, "Not my business to ask, so I will not, but I would find some way to let him know you are sorry. He is not the best person to have on your bad side."

I stared at Stephen, his white T-shirt moist from a morning in his vineyards, a bottle of wine tucked under his elbow, and two wineglass stems in his right hand. "Stephen, I do not think I can continue to pretend to like being here, to make any of you think I plan on staying here, and I am weary of being nice. I need to end this little charade, talk to whomever I need to talk to about selling the winery and going home. I mean, I do not even feel guilty that I just saw my great-grandmother's grave. I don't care if she is buried in the vines, I don't care if her cross has been hidden, Stephen I do not care."

Stephen waited and watched my face turn from a sun-kissed tan to pink, to red. He watched my eyebrows furrow and, in a now-familiar pose, hang my head. When I began to cry, he stood as I leaned my head on his arm. Slowly, I moved my arms to his neck, wrapped them tightly on the back of his head, and held him tightly.

He placed his free arm on my head, "Cry, just cry, Clara. You have been too strong for your mother, for my dad and me. I remember meeting you at our house with your injured foot. You demonstrated to us that you were strong even when your eyes showed your pain. You did not know me, but you unselfishly became my protector. I know your decision weighs heavily on you and you are the only one who can decide. I am here to help you run the winery, to help you sell the winery, or to throw you the best farewell party this valley has ever known."

My mind flashed through my return to the valley. Meeting Ben as Mother's love, burning bread in the same oven Mother had used without incident, the broken step on the staircase, Maria's motherly care, Ben's death, and his life celebration.

I still savored the introduction to the wine community standing next to Stephen, disposing of Ben's ashes, reading great-grandmother's letter, the appearance of the wolves, Thomas One introducing me gently to the vineyard, finding the dead chick on MaMinny's grave, and the missing bonfire. I felt weak, slid down, and when I woke, Stephen sat on the floor next to the couch dabbing my forehead with one of Mother's kitchen towels.

"You are just fine, Clara. I think either the sun or Thomas One's cooking was too much for you. I made you a sandwich with fresh tomatoes and basil. For you a tall glass of ice water to assure hydration in this heat. I have learned my lesson the hard way when I get dehydrated from the wine." When I heard Stephen's voice, my dream of sitting in the corporate conference room with my latest PowerPoint on a client's cost projections began to fade. Sitting up slowly, I took a bite of the crusty bread, tomato juice running down my chin, as I nibbled on the leaf of basil. Stephen leaned over, pausing first before he licked the juice from my chin and kissed me.

"You are exhausted and I blame myself for your added stress. I have been selfish in wanting to keep you near, wanting to show off the valley, the town, introducing you to people who would be your future friends. I take the blame for not giving you space after Dad died. I should have been gracious and thanked you for your support while I drove you back to the airport."

"This is not the time for me to think about what I need, this is your time to decide what you want to do. I have so much to say about your decision, but I will not. I think it would be beneficial if you did go back to New Jersey, go back to what you know, surround yourself with your friends and co-worker, and give your other life a second look. I will take care of the winery; harvest season is coming with plenty of work."

Handing me a small glass of wine he said, "Should we toast your return with just a little wine and a glass of ice water?"

I looked at him and spoke up. "Return to New Jersey, make my decision, and return to my winery? Yes, let us toast a return to the valley. I do think before I go you need to tell me what I have here, besides the tasting room. What in heaven's name is all that equipment out there; what is in the kegs? Will my leaving add a burden to you? The only thing I could contribute at this point is looking at Mom's books to get a feel for where her winery is financially. Hard to know if there was a profit or whether there ever can be."

Stephen refilled my glass with water, "I happened to bring dinner with me, compliments of Maria, so when you feel ready we will go into the winery and I will tell you what you need to know."

"The bottled wine I believe is from harvest right after your mother died. I can check with Thomas One, but I think we have been in a maintenance mode until your arrival. Your vines have been pruned, and your grapes have been used by my winery with yes, my label that is according to a written agreement between your mother and my father."

"Originally, we had thought of putting your label on the bottles, but if we had done that, there would have been no one to promote the wine. Typically, a label offers a known generic location like Columbia Valley."

"We have included Long House vineyards on our label. My dad wanted to preserve your mother's memory in the label. When clients ask about your vineyards we are not specific about your location. Perhaps you may have noticed your vineyard does not have a sign. You are the only vineyard in the valley that has a lone mailbox with a carved post resembling a wolf. I think Thomas One had said once he found some visitors wandering around apparently looking for a petting zoo."

Stephen handed me the bottle and I reviewed the back of the bottle reading aloud "Cabernet Sauvignon a medium, full-bodied wine complemented by dark tannins and aromas of currants and vanilla. Grapes nurtured in the valley sun, wind, and soil at Long House vineyards." A tiny sketch of a wolf dipping its tongue into a wineglass finalized the wine description. I kissed the label, drank the rest of my water, and refilled Stephen's glass with wine.

"Clara, some of those Merlot grapes are just aching to be crushed; I think they are talking to us now."

"No stomping?" I smiled for the first time in hours. "Ahh, yes the French term "pigeage," or grape stomping in an open container. Clara, if you wish to return to New Jersey with purple feet, I am sure I can arrange a stomping for you. Just let me know what your heart desires."

"I wish I knew what my heart desired, Stephen; I just think what be easier for you, for me, for the future of the winery. Thank you for understanding my need to return to corporate America. I promise you I will not prolong my decision; I will let you know when I plan to return. I will not expect you to be responsible for selling the winery. I will be here for any finalization. Would you like to know what I find in Mom's accounting books when I reviewed them?"

"I knew that the winery was dying just like my mother because she did not have the energy to organize a maintenance crew. I know she cared; her emotional self just could not face the reality of what was happening to her winery. And every check she ever sent me was dated in her ledger."

I sighed, anticipating his thoughts and discomfort, "I know what you are thinking. I did not need Mother's money. For some reason, she had this need to send me monthly checks. I put all of the checks in the bank and used that money to pay for her funeral expenses. Mother always wanted to take care of me when I could take care of myself easily enough."

Acting like he did not hear or chose not to hear what I said, Stephen pointed out the window at two unpruned vines and the underground sprinkler system where two segments had burst resulting in no watering of the roots. A tiny pale green bud attempted to push out from the dried bark; however, a tangled web of dried grape clusters and fractured stems blocked it from emerging.

When he returned to the couch, I continued. "You know you are part of this decision. You are the part that makes everything much more difficult."

He held me. "I promise you that once you decide I will not do anything to further complicate your life."

Walking out the front door, we crossed to the winery. Stephen pulled the doors open, exposing the spotless tasting room. Empty wine boxes were stacked adjacent to the bar, wine glasses secured inside low plastic boxes, spitting bowls turned over, pottery bowls for crackers at the end of the counter. We looked behind the bar; a wire held a clipped row of laminated wine lists which ran along the back of the bar. The cash box, receipts, and single wine bags were on the lowest shelf.

I opened a small notebook, which described each wine including the appropriate descriptive sales pitch for each varietal. A monthly schedule of tasting room hours with the names of volunteers was listed. "Mom, had others working for her?"

Stephen pointed to each name and gave a brief description of who they were. "Most volunteers have since moved on to other wineries. I do not think you would have any problem luring them back but you may have to adjust your times to synchronize with other wineries. I think you saw how we run our tastings. We start with whites; move on to reds and occasionally, we will throw in a surprise, like a port, or a late-harvest depending on the time of year."

"Everyone charges a tasting fee. Part of the reason is to encourage serious wine drinkers, and part is to recoup the cost of the wine we have opened. Typically, the tasting fee is waived when a bottle of wine is purchased. Most importantly, we try to discourage the social drinking party. Our goal is to avoid drunken tastings, but multiple tastings in an afternoon by any guest, plus the wine they buy may also become a serious concern for all of us in the valley."

"Your winery only pours wine. Our winery also sells charcuteries or cheese platters with our wine, and we do encourage clients to bring their picnic lunches to our patio. In truth, it is so much cheaper. I do have a problem with the peanut butter sandwiches followed by sips of our Pinot Noir."

"I cannot give a reasonable response to the client who has just had a bag of barbecue chips and complains that our wine tastes funny. So tasting is just that, giving each client the chance to taste and decide what he or she likes or does not like."

"For me, the most difficult part of managing a tasting room is the client who truly has expertise in wine but will often intimidate the other clients. When I host a tasting, I always have several volunteers on hand. I typically introduce myself to the scholarly taster and offer a personal tour or the taste of uniquely aged wine. I find no disagreement with an expert, but I always fear that their behavior may discourage others from learning or from asking questions. I am amused, however, when anyone loudly announces that our wine tastes dreadful, the worse they have ever had. Yes, those are the awkward times when they are encouraged to use the spit bucket and have a fresh wineglass to move on through the other wines."

"I love tastings, Clara. I love to meet people, and I love to hear what they think of our wines. I am always slightly embarrassed when they ask me to autograph a bottle yet I am happy to do so specifically to the recipients, the newlyweds, the special anniversary, the retirement, the new parents, or even for the memorials."

Stephen paused, walked away from the tasting bar holding back tears remembering his father's memorial. I followed, looking at my reflection in the bar-length wall mirror with the stained-glass letters spelling "Long House". I realized I needed a haircut, my eyebrows looked like a joined bridge, the natural tan has made me look more like a tea stain, and my lips were chapped.

Toward the back of the tasting room, Stephen slid another set of doors aside on their track. One of the doors jammed in the track. Stephen pulled it back and forth until it slid easily open. A nest of twigs fell from the track on my foot. "Whose house did we just destroy?" Winking at me he said, "Probably Cabernet Canaries, known to migrate in the fall with an attraction to empty wineries." I felt the coolness from the processing room "Is it always this cool?"

"Yes, the room is temperature-controlled 60 to 65 degrees. In the winter, we heat it slightly y to keep the wines stable at the same constant temperature. If this room becomes too warm it will affect the wine by speeding up the aging process. Are you cold?" He put his arm around my shoulders.

"We also try to keep the room slightly humid, although there is no exact science to the perfect humidity. I try to keep ours around 70 percent because you need to make sure the corks do not become too dry."

"You notice that all your finished bottles are on their side, so the cork touching the wine is kept wet; however, there is the part of the cork exposed to the air. If it becomes too dry, the cork may shrink, and allow air into the wine." From where we were standing, rows of bottled wines stacked high in deep brown bins with dark, sealed tops. "You will notice, Clara, that unlike the tasting room which has a sliding door entrance and windows on both walls, this room has no direct light. We want our grapes to enjoy the sun when they are on the vines, but when they are fermenting or in storage, there is no additional illumination."

Stephen checked the humidity of the room, which registered low at fifty-five percent. "We need to look at all of your bottles, something my team will do after you leave. I am afraid that this room has lost significant moisture. That may have affected the wine's aging process."

He began to walk through the rows of barrels, "Looks like we have some Chardonnay and some Sauvignon Blanc which needs to be bottled now. In a few months, your Syrah and Cabernet grapes will be ready for bottling. We will need to plan our schedule for racking the wines soon. I only see the dates after fermentation when the wine was placed in the barrels. I thought I heard Thomas mumble after your lover's quarrel that you had sold four cases of wine. Let me know what he was talking about when you get a chance."

"I do not wish to give you a class on the chemical additives for your red wines, but we may not be able to save them if there have not been sufficient doses of sulfites and/or bacteria to feed the malolactic acid. Nor do I wish to be the bearer of bad news, but there is a possibility some of your red varietals may not have survived the lack of attention which they required."

Surprised, I asked, "I do not understand how I have lost my wine. I assumed once the wine was in the barrels it just took care of itself. Perhaps another deciding point for me; why should I want to keep a winery that is clearly in the negative. How long will it take to start a new batch once the grapes are picked, I mean, when will I have wine to sell?"

"Clara, it will be nearly two years for reds. Your white wines are ready now. We can get those bottled, and I have no doubt you will get a healthy profit from sales. I will not know until we test your reds if they are ruined. Please be patient and I will let you know."

He found the frayed green sweater hanging on a hook next to the sliding doors and placed it over on my shoulders.

"Is this Mother's sweater?"

"I think the story I heard years ago was it belonged to your grandmother. I guess Clarish wore it everywhere outside of the house. She never brought it near the house for fear that something had left buried eggs in one of the sleeves."

I pulled one of the sleeves closer to my eyes. "I do see tons of little spots, but it looks like spurts of dried red wine to me."

Putting the sweater back on the hook, "I will have Maria take it to a dry cleaner."

"Let's take a look at your inventory before the equipment. I would like to see what is in your barrels first."

I looked at three rows of barrels; each row held twelve barrels stacked three high. As I looked higher there was a small platform with additional barrels, and white, square containers tucked into each other in two long columns resembling colonial pillars.

Stephen pointed, "Everything above you is empty; the barrels probably cannot be salvaged by now, I have no idea how long they have been up there. They need a gassing with sulfur dioxide. "

"Rather than buy new barrels, we will let you use some of ours, decreasing the cost significantly. I know we have quite a few that we can send this way after harvesting."

He read the writing scrawled on each barrel," Cabernet Sauvignon, Merlot, Chardonnay, and Sauvignon Blanc." He pulled a cap from the Cabernet Sauvignon, capping it quickly as he looked under the barrel. Pointing to the cap he said, "It's called a bung, rhymes with tongue.

Returning to the tasting bar, he commented," I am looking for the glass tube to withdraw some wine from the barrel". I moved my hands on and over the barrel, trying to imagine Mother's touch. "Hello, Mother," I whispered.

I recognized the handwriting on the light-blue tape across the barrels. I smiled when I saw a cartoon face smiling, or winking, or with closed eyes depicting fatigue. Stephen returned, drying the tube and holding two glasses.

"This glass tube is called a thief, one we like to say is not a robber of belongings, but the official messenger from the depths of the wine casks reporting what your wine has been up to since placed inside. What I do not see on these barrels is any date of racking. That again is of concern."

"Racking is not putting bottles in a rack; it is removing the wine from the barrels, cleaning the barrels, and adding a little sulfur and bacteria to keep the fermentation process continuing. By now, that process should be complete and the carbon dioxide should be eliminated."

Pointing to the bung, he said, "It's your wine, Clara. Remove the bung and place the thief inside the hole. I think we should start with a taste of your Cabernet Sauvignon."

I felt the thief touch the liquid, and the tube filled with a faded purple wine. We looked at the wine as I poured it into the glasses, "It looks odd, Stephen. It looks diluted with water. When I look at it, I am seeing a thin, transparent liquid."

I followed Stephen's motions as he sniffed the wine. "What do you smell?"

"It has a strong sulfur smell."

"Good job. My father must be guiding you from afar. The wine is ruined, the sulfur is too strong, and I am thinking there was no consistent schedule for adding yeast, so this wine never really fermented. My thoughts are there was no follow-up or appropriate racking of this wine. I am afraid that this barrel is a discard. We will save the barrel for harvest unless you will be here for harvest,"

I stopped him from negotiating my stay during harvest, "Stephen, please. I need to leave. Please do not make this harder than it is."

"Ok, how about a day of bottling before you go. You can ship some of your wine back to celebrate your return with your friends?"

I became more annoyed. "Why are you asking me to do this today?"

He walked away from me toward the equipment covered with tarps, standing like three separate islands. "Not today, Clara. I can get my crew to help you within two days, so please consider one final bottling before you book your flight."

He pulled the first tarp from the stainless-steel machine that stood above his head. "This is your de-stemmer, Clara. The opening is a giant mouth for the grapes to be dumped, the machine is turned on with this simple switch, the grapes fall below into the bin, and the stems are spat out into this container." Resembling a marionette, Stephen pointed to the different parts of the machine, lifting an arm, pointing, or turning his head to the different components of the machine.

He looked into the container that held stems. "Well, it appears that this container is empty of grape stems and the home to something else."

I looked inside and saw a pile of shredded paper and bits of cloth forming a nest. "I am assuming not where my mother hen lays her eggs?"

"I am guessing it is the mother rat's nest. This is something we will need to get rid of and set some traps. I am sure that is something you will not choose to be involved in. We will keep the circle of life protected by putting the dead rats out on the drive for coyotes." I certainly did not believe he had a desire to include my wolves in the circle.

"This piece of equipment will be in use shortly after we clean out the stem barrel. I want you to picture us picking the grapes, loading them into large crates called "lugs", using your forklift, driving it through the back doors, lifting it, and tipping the container into bins for fermentation. Based on what your vines yield, we are going to have a successful harvest, and next time you come you will taste a different wine."

"Now, your white grapes do not go through a de-stemmer."

Pulling off another tarp, Stephen looked like the magician uncovering an illusion, "Your presser, Madame Vintner. Your white grapes go directly into this. They are pressed with this simple, computerized pad for a couple of hours, the juice is collected below and off to the fermentation bins. Look inside, Clara. It resembles a space capsule but the sides are like an accordion that squeezes together, crushing your Chardonnay and Sauvignon Blanc."

I put my head inside. "No creatures and a clean smell. Do the white grapes go into the plastic fermenting bins?"

"No, pumped right to the barrel. You have ready wines, which we will bottle with or without you. I will sell them at our winery and give you the profit. If you wish, we will include your whites in the tasting. Again, we will be careful how we describe where the grapes originate. We must keep your winery a secret for now."

I stood in front of the wine racks that held bottled white and red wines. "All my Cabernet in the bottles will be destroyed?"

"No, your bottles should be just fine. I did notice there were some random bottles behind the counter standing upright. I am guessing that, without offering their corks a little moisture by resting them on their side, those may be a loss. But I will check them for you."

"Where do you suppose Mom's books are? Do you think she kept a record of sales? She did not do a very good job documenting her winemaking process. I forgive her; she had so much to handle her illness. How long did it take all of you to realize that she was dying?"

"I think my father said it best at her service. He knew when she refused to marry him and told him that her disease had taken over her body."

Making a Decision

I began to rummage through boxes while Stephen put the tarps back on the equipment and commented, "Seeing grapes become wine will be a gift you have given me even if you are away."

I pulled books from one of the boxes. "Look at this, Stephen. It looks like Mom's high schoolbooks, but they are all history. Maybe that explains why she did not do very well with her bookkeeping, I see no math books."
I opened the first book and saw Clarish written on the top corner. "What are these torn notebook pages for?"

Stephen walked over as I balanced the books in my left arm. "Look, this composition book is titled <u>Grandmother Margaret 1890-1955</u>, dated June 1, 1977; mother's high school senior project."

"To think I was born more than ten years after she graduated." I flipped through the book as we glanced at handwritten words page after page, with occasional newspaper clippings taped in the book.

"Looks like you have a little reading for your flight back. You have found a treasure. What else have you discovered hiding in that box?"

I ducked my head back into the box. "There are a couple of knitting needles and what appears to be the leftover ball of green yarn. Green yarn, the color of the sweater I was wearing, my mother's creation. Oh, Stephen, I cannot get rid of that sweater; it was part of my grandmother. I was too young to remember what she wore, but I do know that she was always shivering. Looking back, I often wondered if she was cold or if she had a constant fever causing her body to chill."

I looked around and saw the green sweater on the hook. "I will take care of this sweater. I have a dry cleaner right by my condominium that will clean it and give it proper storage. There is no need to bother Maria."

"Maybe I will ask one of my friends to teach me how to make a scarf with green yarn or just keep the knitting needles in a safe place. I think I need a place to put all these memories, old and new."

My eyes clouded up with moisture as Stephen stood to hold the stack of books, kicking over the remaining boxes. One of the boxes spilled out with a handful of corks. He tossed a few of them in the air, "They are all used, Clara, probably from tastings, so you probably can just toss them."

Juggling my mother's composition book, the knitting needles, and the sweater, I picked up the corks and placed them in my pocket. "I need to take some with me."
He walked over, hoisting the books onto the tasting bar, brushing off his shirt, and turned around to face me. "This building, all of the vineyards, your family's home cannot be put into a makeshift treasure box. Everything you have had

with your family will be a lasting memory each time your feet touch these grounds."

"Every time you close your eyes, I will be with you. Please find a place for me, Clara."

I felt like a mannequin as I stared at him, unmoving, poised with one foot aimed at the entry of the winery as I thought about my job, my New Jersey life, all I had for so many years.

Thomas One walked into the winery. "Mr. Stephen, I looked all over for you. I need your help at our winery. We are ready to bottle the wine. I think we may need a few more volunteers. Some of my crew decided to party in town last night and I do not think I want them operating the machines today."

"I have already had words with them. They are embarrassed, but in truth, I could not quite understand what they were saying." He turned to me smirking, "I am pretty sure they must be speaking drunken English."

I started to apologize, but Stephen interrupted. "Look, I need these six casks taken to our winery; you will find twelve cases of empty bottles along the wall. We need to get the white bottled quickly. I will make a few phone calls and I think we can round up several volunteers if Maria will make her famous quesadillas and salsa."

Thomas One looked surprised, "If you give my team a little time, they should be ready to bottle Miss Clara's wine

368

in a few days. No, Thomas; now. Clara is returning to New Jersey soon and I want her to take some of this wine with her." Stephen's voice was firm, a voice that Thomas One rarely heard.

Stephen turned and walked out. "Thomas, take the books from Clara and put them on her porch. I will see you back home."

I watched Stephen walk away, heard his car start, and saw the thin veil of dirt that followed the tires past the winery door. Thomas One said nothing; he shrugged, took the books, and walked past me. He put the books on the rocking chair closest to the door, nodded at me standing in the winery door, and left.

I realized the two men who had entered my life disappeared down the driveway, past the grapes. I picked up the books from the porch chair, Ben's chair where his soft-spoken words had offered me some direction for the winery's future. The house felt cool, too. Perhaps the afternoon wind had brushed through the open door, or the comfort it had afforded me these past weeks was slowly withdrawing, preparing for my exit. I put the books on the couch, walked to the fireplace, and stood in front of Mother's photograph.

I spoke to her in words that began respectfully but slowly escalated, "Mother, why have you left me to struggle with your dream, your winery? I grew from the strength you gave me as a child, adolescent, and woman. I remember feeling your touch, your words that guided without demanding, you're approving nod. We spent hours tracing the family trees and hearing your reflective thoughts of how I reminded you of yourself as a child. I remember, Mother, I remember your subtle ways of disciplining me."

Grasping the framed picture in my hands, I walked toward the kitchen. "I will never forget the day I came home from school and you knew I had not gone to school because a phone call about my absence preceded my entry through the front door. Like any other day, a warm slice of bread, and a glass of milk waited on the dining-room table. You sat with me and listened to me describe my classes, the latest school gossip, and asked about my homework for the evening."

"Somehow I came up with a project that required me to look at the sugar content of all of the milk products in the refrigerator. Oh, how excited you became, Mother. You pushed your chair back and began to pull out everything that might have had some level of sugar."

Setting the frame on the kitchen table, I continued my conversation with my mother's portrait. " I watched you line up jellies, juices, bottles of wines that were down to their last drops, peanut butter, carrots, apples, Asian condiments, ketchup, leftover slices of bread wrapped in waxed paper. I was shocked when you opened the freezer and pulled out two containers of ice cream and three grape Popsicles."

"Mother, you told me I needed to taste them all and write a simple graph on what tasted more sugary. I remember looking at the ice cream, lifting the lid to see the brittle frozen edges of chocolate."

I took a soup spoon from the utensil drawer in the kitchen, returned to the table, and tapped it on the picture frame. Smiling, I continued, "You gave me a spoon and told me to eat as much as I wished and hand drew a chart listing each item on the table. I was to place a dot on the number that showed if the sugar taste was high, medium, or low."

"All I remember, Mother, is for every item I ate, you pushed another in front of me until the ice cream containers were empty and the popsicles were gone. I ate a sandwich slathered with peanut butter, grape jelly, slices of apples, and squirted with blobs of ketchup. Finally, when I eyed the wine bottles, you poured the Chardonnay in a glass, followed by the Sauvignon Blanc."

"You laughed with me when I laughed; you danced with me when I started to hop around the room like a gluttonous king completing a banquet. I remember Mother, how you stood outside the bathroom door listening to my project heaving repeatedly into the toilet bowl. You never said anything when I said I needed to go to bed, but you did cover me with a blanket, hum softly to me, and comb your fingers through my hair. Most importantly, Mother, you never asked about the project, you never asked me how I felt, for you knew that lying to you. I had hoped someday we would talk about that afternoon when I was older; I often wondered how the conversation would start or how it would end. I guess, Mother, you never needed me to say I was sorry, you never needed to anticipate that I would lie to you again, and I never did." Hugging the picture frame, I pressed it against my chest and whispered my secret feelings to her.

"Until now, I could tell you that I do not want this winery. I could tell you that I love my New Jersey job and home. I could tell you that by selling this winery, I am closing my life and the memories that this valley held for me."

"I will not lie to you, Mother. Can you hear me? I cannot lie and tell you I wish to close the doors of this house, the winery, and close everything that meant something to you, my grandmother, to great-grandmother in one sale. I do not need the money, Mother, but I am stubborn, very proud like you and I wish to choose my direction."

"What did I learn from my sugar high when I was young? Perhaps having something handed to you, something which you do not need to work for or even something that leaves you satisfied for the moment will eventually backfire."

"I am talking about my New Jersey job, Mother, clearly not handed to me. I worked so hard that I turned into an absentee daughter until I realized how sick you were. I love that job, Mother. I love being in control and knowing exactly what to do each day, knowing exactly what to anticipate, and most importantly how to fix anything that goes wrong."

I whispered into the picture, "Mother, I cannot possibly be in control, plan a day, figure out the next weeks, or even fix a problem here at our Long House Winery. I know nothing, except today I learned about the equipment, that harvesting season is coming, and that some of the wine is ruined because there are no records of when you tested the wine or added chemicals. Some bottles are ruined due to dehydrated corks. How do you expect me to keep your winery?"

"Are you asking me to start a new career? Are you asking me to keep the winery and have someone else run it? Are you asking me to quit being stubborn and to quit being selfish and to think about the big picture? Mother, everyone loves you in this valley, but I am not you and I cannot try to be the person who you were to so many."

I tossed my hair back, "Yes, we look alike. I am one neither worries about nor cares about anything or anybody unless it is on a spreadsheet, a PowerPoint, or a database that will benefit me. Please understand I am not rude to people, but I am all about me."

"What you should know is that my self-indulgence has disappeared since my involvement with Ben and

Stephen. Do you think this is the problem, Mother? Do you think I do not want to become empathetic for the long term?" "Are you listening to me? How will I know what to do? What if I am wrong, what if I make a mistake, what if my decision will negatively impact everything you worked so hard for?"

I held the photograph tighter, feeling warmth envelop me, similar to the afterglow of a glass of wine. I balanced the frame, at eye level. Mother stared back with a satisfied smile, the smile that always told me everything would be just fine if I believed in what my inner heart was saying.

My mind became still, the room silent except for my whispers. "I understand Mother; I understand what I am to do. You heard me, you helped me, or perhaps I helped myself by talking to you. I know now what direction to take next."

I put the picture frame back on the mantel, wrapped myself in a blanket from the couch, and walked to Mother's office. Her desk was filled with stacks of different colored folders, a phone with a blinking message light, the windows framing each spider web dangling from the lights, and an outdated wall calendar. Brushing away the thin layers of dust from the folders that clung to my fingers like grimy thimbles, I found a small, pale-blue book labeled "Monthly Sales". The book lacked any numbers; each page began with a month, no year, and no week. "Mother, where are your records; how much wine did you sell? Did you have a bank account?"

I sat on the wicker chair, lacking the rolling wheels and leather cushions from my Manhattan office. It creaked; small pieces of broken wicker poked at my bare arms, and it swayed when I leaned forward to open the desk drawers. Piles of papers, stuck in the drawer runner, filled two of the lower drawers. I read an invoice for wine purchases, several maintenance slips, and a handful of future purchases for wine bottles.

The top drawer pulled out an inch and jammed. I forced it open with a pair of scissors, leaning back in the chair when a large spider scurried across the desk, hopped over her scissors, and disappeared down the back of the desk. Stuffed inside a burgundy, fist-sized cloth bag were two key rings, one attached to a small cardboard circle with the handwritten letters "SAFE." The other keyring had only a cardboard circle with a capitalized "S. C."

I looked around the room for a safe. The stark absence of furniture made my visual scoping quick and simple. I lifted a few posters mapping the Washington State's American Viticulture Areas, marking all the wine regions with their specific grapes.

Mother had circled the valley including the Long House and all of the vineyards that surrounded their winery. Tiny pins corresponded to a tiny chart on the side of the map that named each vineyard. Pushing on the pin for the Long House Winery, the adhesive tape holding the poster wrinkled and the poster fell on the floor with the pins scattering across the wooden floor. Looking at my bare feet surrounded by haphazard pins, I tiptoed back to the living room. I slipped on my boots, laughing, "What would they say in New Jersey if they saw me wearing these boots with my blue suit?"

Standing in the doorway, I scanned each wall one more time. My eyes rested on the empty wine cask, cut in two, holding dried flowers resembling a funeral arrangement. I marched across the floor and stood in front of the cask.

I pulled out the dried flower spray, looked under, and caught the barrel as it began to slowly tip. Catching the rim of the barrel, I rested it on the floor and saw the small-keyed door hidden in the wall behind it. Fishing the key from the cloth bag, I inserted it into the slot and opened the door. A wooden box stood facing the opened door, exposing rows of more than thirty cylindrical boxes held in place by a thick leather strap.

I pulled out one box, levering the nail under the hinge and the top popped from the force of the stacked bills inside, slightly faded with the dark print of "one hundred dollars" distinguishable.

I counted the first stack, a total of ten thousand dollars.

I realized, without opening all the boxes, I was looking at Mother's bank. Looking up at the ceiling, I started another conversation with Mother. "Mother, what am I supposed to do with this money? I am leaving in two days and I have to leave this winery. Now I have to do something with this." "I don't understand why you never opened a bank account. Why didn't you ask me to help you set up a bookkeeping system? Was I meant to find this or did you worry about someone else had finding it? What would have happened to your life's work?"

The Key Chain

I was startled when I heard Stephen's voice. He shrugged and spoke carefully, "I knew, Clara, my dad knew, but no one else knows. I think we counted it a long time ago with her. It is close to a million dollars, guarded only by a wooden wine barrel filled with dried flowers. All I know is that she asked us to count the money, not to hide it for her."

I twirled around, eyes wide, shaking the stack of bills at him. "Were you going to tell me, Stephen, or were you just going to watch over the winery until I returned? Better yet, were you going to sell the winery and let the new owner find this little treasure? Tell me, Stephen, were you planning on taking me on a treasure hunt?"

Stephen put his finger to his lips and turned to talk to someone at the front door. "Yes, all the white grape kegs go to our winery and we will get the reds at a later day. Please ask Thomas One for direction; I am in a meeting."

I saw one of the crew's outline fade as he disappeared and walked down the steps. "Clara, I did not know where your mother hid the key. I have not been to her office. This is not my home, and I would not come here snooping around. Now that you have found the key, we should plan on where you will deposit or transfer the money"

"Our local bank manager was a close friend of your mother's and I have no doubt will follow your request. I think the challenge is the amount of cash, a credible story about its history, and your decision."

I walked over to him with a handful of bills, "Credible story? Do I look like someone who robbed a bank and stashed money in a house that does not belong to me? Do I look like someone who would steal money from my mother when I did not even have a key to the house until my last visit? What do you mean by credible, Stephen?"

Speaking softly, "Clara, I know you, my dad knew you. The vintners have met you, but you remain a stranger to most. You have not considered establishing any roots here. Look, Clara, you have been here a few weeks with everyone expecting you to own your inherited winery. Word has already hit the grapevines that you are leaving, so there goes your credibility."

"No one here understands why you would consider leaving this winery that has so much history with so many in the valley. This is a small community. We are not the cement sidewalks of New Jersey; we are dirt roads, grapes, equipment, and sharing lives over glasses of wine. I have protected you since you arrived, your mother's resemblance has served you well, but in truth, no one knows you."

I pushed files from the top of the desk, batted a horsefly away from my face, and sat on the edge of the desk.

"Stephen, you are the one person I trusted. You knew all along of this secret stash and I just am led to wonder when you were going to tell me, or if you were going to tell me."

Stephen moved closer, "What else was in the bag with the key, Clara?"

I reached into my pocket, "Just another keyring with initials written on a cardboard circle. " S. C."

Stephen put his hand out. "May I?" His fingers grasped the keyring; he turned his back to me, got down on one knee, and put the key ring on the edge of his neck. I looked at the tattoo on the back of his neck matching the letters inked within a circle.

"I do not get it. Why is there a match between the money and your neck? Come on, Stephen, this is getting very strange. "S" equals Stephen and "C" equals my mother, grandmother, and great-grandmother? Or the first letter of your dad's dog, Chardonnay, right, Stephen?"

Stephen sat on the floor and looked up at me, "No. It stands for "C" as in Clara. We never knew much of each other when we were younger. I worked on the farm, you stayed here, and only when your grandmother became ill did I hear about a girl who lived in this house.

"We never met; Dad came over or sent one of the crew over with meals for you and your mother. I was not interested in girls; well, that ended quickly when I went to college. After your grandmother died, you eventually grew up, left for school and our parents met."

"They knew everything about each of us. I suppose we were the easy conversation topics where our accomplishments were compared, our youthful menaces were shared, and parental bragging rights were a nightly, emotional report card."

"One of my weekends after finals, Dad told me about your mother and her daughter. They had both thoughts we should meet, but I was too busy with my female vintners to be at school. I made it clear to Dad that I had no interest in someone who had a finance degree; I wanted to settle down with someone who planned on working in the wine industry."

"He tried several times for us to meet but I somehow managed to find something else to do. I only knew that your name was Clara and your selling feature per Dad was that you looked like your mother."

He stood. "Turn around," I said brushing off the back of his khakis. "Just checking if any map pins chose to map your bottom. Nope, it looks like you are not an AVA." Putting my arms around his neck, I said, "I am listening, S-is-for-Stephen,"

Stephen rested his lips on my forehead and whispered, "C is for Clara, for you. I did not put this tattoo on my neck. I was in a sound sleep I was incapacitated, held down my four friends who considered themselves part of my graduating celebration. OK, Clara, I was drunk after tasting all the wines we made for our final project. A little drunk and major sick based on the lack of quality of the final products." He searched my face for a response as I waited for the story to end.

"So, a new tattoo parlor opened a block away from campus and we all decided we would have our graduation year engraved on our biceps. Yes, proud graduates of the Viticulture and Enology Program, and we wanted everyone to know, especially the women."

"We planned to meet at the tattoo parlor, which we had reserved for our group. I was late; I had my celebration back at our winery." He looked into my eyes; I supposed I had to look as if I believed him so I listened, backing away, and stacking the files, and waited for the story to end. My eyes pierced the wall, realizing that I had another hurdle before I could return to New Jersey. Mother had told me she had felt the residual impact of the Depression and was afraid to trust banks.

Stephen's eyes followed mine, "So that's how it happened. Clara, are you listening? It was graduation gift predicting whom I would marry with initials. We had not met, Clara, but, whenever they were around my dad, he would talk about your mother, Clarish, and her beautiful daughter, Clara. Sometimes I think my Dad paid them to have that tattoo put on the back on my neck. It was extremely painful and I avoided touching my skin as it burned. I let my hair grow long for a few months until I met your mother. Seeing your mother's beauty and knowing she had a daughter equally beautiful, I became the clean-cut vintner you see standing in front of you."

I dangled the safe key ring in front of him, interrupting his conversation, "Stephen, we need to talk about this now and what is behind that wall. I will not stay by myself until we have taken care of the money. If you would give me a temporary guard for sleepovers, I would appreciate it. Why does one key have initials and the other has the word SAFE?"

Stephen pointed at himself with an eager grin on his face. "My father and Clarish said to me that the key equaled a will, a non-legal will, giving all of the money in the safe to S and C when they marry. No, it does not belong to me, for the simple reason we are not married. I think I could easily fill the shoes of a safeguard for one evening. Can we agree?"

He left the office, wandered into the kitchen, and opened the refrigerator. "Clara, hasn't Maria left you any food lately? She was busy making chicken mole; I will have her bring some for us. We can talk over dinner and decide what we will do tomorrow."

Looking at his watch suddenly, he buried his hands in his thick blond hair. "I will call the bank and set up an appointment first thing in the morning. I think we can easily transport the money in empty wine cases. They should stack

easily and we would only require a couple of them. You and I will travel together; Thomas One will be in the car in front of Thomas Two and behind us in the truck. They know only that we are making a delivery. I will keep your secret."
He added, "Do you have an account you wish to have the money transferred?"

I stepped away from Stephen and walked upstairs. He could hear my muffled voice behind my bedroom door as I dialed the bank and was put on hold. Stephen sighed realizing that I still did not trust him or believe him.

I pushed my fingernails across my wolf-claw necklace, sliding it across my chest, moist from residual sweat. Droplets slithered down my neck, pooling in my collarbone before dripping on my blouse. I waited for the banker to return to the phone, weary of listening to the sluggish romance songs; I opened the armoire and reached for my briefcase.

Smelling the soft scent of leather, I unclasped the lock as I heard, "Clara, I am so sorry to have you on hold; I have a slight emergency that should resolve in moments with the arrival of the police." Emergency? I thought one of the largest banks in Manhattan with six guards at the front door, a metal detector for clients who enter the bank, additional security staff to search all bags and how could there be an emergency.

My fingernail felt between the file folders, the piercing end of an earring post. Balancing the phone, I slowly pulled the attached strand of tiny moon-shaped rubies. Placing the earring to my earlobe, I remembered. "Earring, I thought I had lost you in Mr. could-not-be-more-manly chaise lounge. I wonder whether your match is inside or if he kept it as a souvenir of one remarkable whiskey nightcap."

I yanked out a pile of paper with a torn bistro coffee cup warmer, the wrapper from a wedge of cheese, a punched-out foil strip with two heartburn medications, two condoms awaiting desire, and three handwritten notes reminding me to remember the reminder I would not forget to remember. Shaking the briefcase, I heard the small pill case, my six colors of lipstick tapping each other, and my CD player jostling against the bulging folders. Pinching one pen, I lifted one folder to take notes when the banker returned to the phone.

"Clara, Clara, please tell me you are still on the phone. I cannot apologize enough for keeping you on hold for so long. Thanks for understanding. I am all yours."

I heard the creak of a floorboard at the bottom of the staircase and walked to the window. "I will not take up your time; I just want to let you know that you will be receiving an impressive money transfer tomorrow afternoon. I need you to be at your desk, waiting for it, and I wish an immediate call of confirmation."

He clicked his pen several times, a habit I found unnerving whenever I went to his office. "Clara, I will do whatever you ask, but why don't you just take your building elevator to the lobby, walk out the revolving doors, make a sharp right, and enter the bank. I will meet you in the lobby to assure you can bypass the Queen's Guards."

Laughing, and with an impatient response, "I cannot walk to you. I am in Eastern Washington. Not White House Washington, but desert, wine country Washington State. "I have inherited a substantial sum of money that I will be depositing at the local bank. After the banker counts the money, I will have it transferred to my account starting with numbers 785. I am not sure I know the name of the transferring bank, but I expect my transfer to go smoothly."

He sighed, clearly annoyed my vague information. "Clara, please, I need the bank name and a general idea of the transfer total."

I walked to the top of the stairs, "Stephen, may I have the name of your bank for my banker?"

Stephen had moved outside and heard my voice through the screen door. Sitting on the porch rail, quietly watching the burnished red hummingbird prod its beak in the verbena, moving its white chest back and forth. He stood slowly, the hummingbird flew over his head, and Stephen shouted to me, "Baker Boyer Bank; the team has been with our families for a long time. They know your mom, my dad, and me."

I confirmed the bank's name on the phone and listened to the banker clicking his mouse and ignoring the ringing phone. "Clara, I will need to move around a few appointments, or I can have one of my colleagues help you. What was the exact amount?"

I spelled out the amount, "Around one million dollars." The banker coughed on the liquid he had swallowed and repeated it once. "Clara, I will shut down my bank to wait for your transfer. Give me your phone number, an alternative number, the bank's number and I will be here. Do you have any idea who will be helping you?"

I did not want to ask Stephen, so I answered. "Some local banker who allegedly has worked with my family for years. He will count the bills that will be stacked in wine boxes. Do not ask, do not wonder, I only hope we are not traveling by stagecoach and masked bandits are waiting at the local self-service gas station."

He asked, "Wine boxes and cash? Please do not tell me you are taking this trip alone or, better yet, that you have decided it would be safer to wait for the local bus to pick you up and deposit you at the bank."

After a sucking snort, the distant sound of him slapping his hands on the desk, he grew silent. I had to ignore him or I would have ended the entire transition.

"I am not happy about finding this money in my mother's house and less happy when I think about the possibility of where the money would have ended up if I had not found it. A fellow vintner assured me that he and his father knew about the money with plans of telling me that it was somewhere in my mother's house. Although I want to believe him, I closed my eyes and saw him sitting in the middle of Burgundy, France pointing at the vineyards he wishes to buy."

Packing Wine Boxes

The banker validated my comments, "Oh, the playboy scumbag. I get it. We see it here when the boy-toys appear with their bejeweled, gray feathered ostriches gripping their elbows, whispering into their shriveled ears, dabbing their clown red cheeks, and smothering their lips with rooster pecking kisses. I find myself gawking at their bulging trouser pockets after their manicured, open hands push the crisp roll of weekly allowance bills deep along pocket's edge."

"The ostriches' brittle curled fingers tremble signing their name in broad, irregular letters resembling the kindergarten attempts from eighty years earlier. Turning her head slowly she thanks her fledgling for his kindness, love, attention, and his gentle hands at their bedtime massage. I have trained myself to not to inhale when she stands, and to quickly spray my office after she leaves to rid it of her morning flatulence odor."

"I have a stack of antiseptic wipes for the leather soaked chair seat to clean the puddle of urine she leaves. Her white leather shoes squeak, her face flushed from the embarrassment, and her gentle escort wraps his cashmere sweater around her waist to cover the plate-size stain."

"No, you have it wrong," I added. "He and his father have been unexpected mentors these past few weeks. Sadly, his father died recently and he was my mother's, special love. Even sadder is the fact that I am the fourth-generation owner of this winery."

I watched the sunset lighting the grape leaves resembling tiny Christmas tree lights in the evening dew. Barn swallows formed a military formation buzzing with opened beaks among the fruit flies that touched down in the vineyard like a momentary tornado. I reached for my binoculars, following the rows of vines down to the end of my property. Squinting, I thought I saw the swish of a long white tail disappear over the bluff.

I talked rapidly, anticipating an interruption, "Ben, the deceased father, and Stephen, the son, are the kindest men I have met west of New York. The crew that cared for their winery and their house helped me daily. I mean, when was the last time you came home and your refrigerator was filled with prepared dinners or someone you had just met sewed custom-made clothes for you?"

The banker interrupted me, "Hey, Clara, you don't have to sell me on people you have met. Sounds to me like you need to sell yourself. I would be happy to see you for dinner when you are back. I can be one of the best banker shoulders east of the mountains."

I brushed away the tear settling within the tiny crevice between my nose and cheekbone. Looking in the mirror, I watched a tear roll down my face and thought of my adolescent experimentation with face powder. I had stood facing mother's dresser mirror, closed my eyes, sucked in my lips, and patted the pink ribbon handled powdered filled puff over my face. I waved my hand in front of the airborne dust, added three more thick layers of powder until the last puff landed in my eyes causing my tears to wash away my ghost foundation.

I sighed at his offer. "Thank you, but for now I plan on submerging myself in my work simulating a planned walk into quicksand. I do not wish to think about anything but work, no grapes, no wine bottles, no wine tasting, no wolves, no horses, and no dinners."

"Horses? I did not know you had horses. Now, riding a horse through the farmlands would be a definite selling factor for me. What kind of horses do you own?"

Stephen pushed the bedroom door hard, his silhouette in the doorframe, leaving an echoing thump in the room. He waved his arm and pointed at his watch.

Nodding, I hoped he had not heard my comment on horses. "I look forward to talking to you in the morning. I will call you when we leave for the bank. I understand we have a thirty minutes' drive from the winery to the bank in downtown Walla Walla." Laughing, "Yes, I will let you know if our stagecoach is robbed. Talk to you in the morning."

I wiped away the stray tear, watched Stephen pull out a bottle of wine from behind his back. "Have everything you need for tomorrow? I think we should celebrate before we pack the wine boxes. The porch table has our wine glasses and cheese."

I forced down my first response; why was hidden money a celebration, why does he need a glass of wine every time there is a problem, is a bottle of wine a solution, and what about my lack of trust in him and the future? I tucked my phone in my pocket and followed him down the stairs.

The sunset etched a glowing path through the screen door, offering me a golden carpet to the porch. I stood near the railing as the furnace-like summer heat stopped me. I felt the cool breeze against my ankles where Stephen had put a metal fan connected to a heavy industrial extension cord sliding under the gate. I listened to the fan blades scrape against each other and heard the mumbling whirl starting and stopping in exhaustion.

"My fan, you found my old fan. As a child, I would sit in the fireplace playing in my imaginary world and Mother would place the fan on the floor to keep me cool. She would always say it was the wind carrying my dreams, brushing my heart with happiness, as I read my latest adventure book."

I liked my wind story and I hope it was one Stephen would remember. I sipped my wine, ignoring Stephen, humming quietly when the hummingbird circled its feeder. Looking up, we spoke in unison, "Wonder whether it's Mom or your dad." Laughing, I looked at Stephen. "Do you believe someone can return in a different form?"

"Clara, I do believe our parents are spirits hovering beyond our visual sight but not far from our souls. I know with your Native American heritage that the wolf is generational, and I was honestly afraid that we would need to destroy the pack that appeared on your property. I have not said this to anyone but I do think it may have been your grandmothers making a very brief visit to check on their granddaughter. I am sure if I shared this story with anyone else I'd be accused of drinking too much tequila or sampling too much wine. Do you ever have the same thoughts; I mean, you know that someone never really leaves us?"

I felt the warmth on the back of my neck; I touched the wolf-claw necklace. "Stephen, the logical part of me would analyze any theory that life does not end in an urn or the ground. I would review statistics, I would perform web searches on scientific evidence, and I would seek black-and-white evidence. The emotional side of me that has surfaced with my mother's death craves a sign to tell me she is not far from me. I sensed my mother when I heard the violin music at your home, when I burned the bread, and when I found her high school project. I agree that this is something we don't usually share with anyone."

393

"I ignore logic and savor the brief dusted moment when I feel my mother's presence. I think I have my spirit animal, not a wolf. I have seen my spirit, a white horse, several times as a child, and since I have moved here. When we were saying goodbye to Ben at the Columbia River, I saw my spirit horse briefly before it disappeared. My spirit white horse has appeared and disappeared over the bluff after spending the night at a campfire at the end of the vineyard.

Thomas One walked with me to search for embers, but there were none. I cannot prove my spiritual sightings, yet I feel they are real. I wish to keep my private struggles with the emotion-quivers of false hope that the spirit horse is my mother, or grandmother, or an invisible angel sent to protect me. I think anyone who has felt a loss craves to grasp a single second bringing them back to what was and what can never be again."

"How selfish of us to want our parents back in our lives when Ben's brain hemorrhage destroyed his able body and when my mother's cancer crawled through her body ingesting every living cell. Is it selfish, Stephen, to wish someone to never leave your life? Is it an act of unbearable self-indulgence to savor the value of someone in your life? Tell me, what are your thoughts?"

Stephen picked up his chair, sat precariously in front of me avoiding the descending porch steps inches away. He sat and took my hand, "I am a selfish person, unbearably selfish, wishing my father was here at this moment, wanting your mother to drive with us to the bank, and quieting my heart blistering with sadness knowing I may never see you again. I acknowledge your spirit; I respect your desire to keep its presence secret. However, I do believe you have a spirit that may follow you beyond your vineyard."

"Sometimes, Clara," he leaned forward, his lips touching my wineglass. "Sometimes a spirit clings to us to assure a sense of calm, to comfort our sadness, to validate our feelings. As you have said, the logical self always dresses in protective armor, ignoring any resemblance of grief. We know there is a place for logical thinking, and I feel we both have successfully shed that armor momentarily."

"I continue to believe our childhoods, our parents' romance and deaths, had a purpose in our lives. Neither of us knows what will happen in the future. We each have jobs to do; yours in Manhattan and mine here. The only logical next step is to permit ourselves to return to our jobs, to the work we love."

We looked up at the hummingbird, wearing a coat of emerald feathers, circling us, clicking softly before flying toward the vineyard. Stephen kissed my little finger and touched it to his lips. We had nothing else to say.

I walked through the screen door to my mother's office and waited for Stephen to bring the wine boxes. With calculator in hand, I began to line up the stacks of fifty bills each on Mother's desk. Stephen counted packages and placed them around underfilled, screw-top wine bottles each standing upright in wine boxes.

"Stephen, please do not waste your wine on this bank deposit." He held up one bottle, pale pink to my eyes, "Our cheapest wine, Clara. We like to call it Red Velvet; no sugar, no harvesting, just water with red food coloring. I have a couple of our winery's bottles on the bottom as a thank you gift to the banker."

Working silently we filled the boxes and watched the office windows darken with the evening eyes closing slowly. "We are done. Tomorrow we will start early. I will ask Thomas One to bring some of Maria's warm churros to eat on the way."

The next morning, I came down the stairs, Stephen who had been sleeping on the couch, called out the screen door to Thomas One who was inside the winery. He appeared with a dolly, rolling out the wine boxes to Stephen's car trunk and his truck.

I ran upstairs to collect my briefcase, bank documents, and calculator for the final deposit. Running back down the steps, I tripped, falling down a step only to have Stephen's arms around me.

"Not again, young lady. One sprained foot permitted during your visit. No hurry, we have plenty of time. Cars are gassed up; my crew is ready to go. Would you like the top up or down on my car?"

Staring into his eyes, I felt the constant internal conflict of wanting him but knowing I must leave him. "Please put the top-up. Somehow, I imagine the money flying out of the trunk and covering the highway. Perhaps, the top will ease my concerns about drifting green pieces of paper covering the cow pastures."

Thomas One nodded but remained silent toward me. Stephen started his car, waved to Thomas Two behind him, and followed Thomas Ones's truck that began to move down the drive. He commented, "I do not think I will have any history to share with you but we can count cows, horses, or depending on the slower animals, roadkill."

I looked ahead, fingering my briefcase and wanting the morning to be over quickly. The caravan of three cars moved along the highway until a roar of motorcycles startled them. Fifteen motorcyclists with riders passed all three vehicles once the highway stretched in a straight line, no curves, bends, hills, or turns by bulging boulders.

Stephen slowed the car while looking in the rear-view mirror at Thomas Two honking his horn and waving at the motorcyclists. "Thomas thinks a parade just went by, the way he is waving at all of them. I am sure he has harassed his parents for a motorcycle but they are firm about him not owning one. These highways can be brutal with speed and too many young ones have lost their lives on the curves." He pointed to a cluster of wooden crosses covered with dried flowers, deflated helium balloons, and framed photographs.

"This curve is one of the worst. An average of two deaths happens yearly. Typically, the motorcyclist speeds around the car and collides with oncoming traffic from a car in the passing lane. My dad would not let me own a motorcycle. I tried, I begged, I came home on the back of one when I was in junior high school. I cannot remember Dad ever being that angry. I do remember, clearly, my punishment was to clean all the wine barrels and sanitize the de-stemmer."

I turned my head quickly after the roar of motorcycles passed the motorcade of three cars. Pairs of two wheels jumped behind their car, in front of our car finally easing along Thomas One and disappearing. "I feel like the little kid counting railroad cars, I counted eighteen motorcycles and each had a passenger. Did you see the one, Stephen, with the stuffed, four-foot-high horse? Cute, maybe they needed a date and the horse was the best thing they found."

Stephen was not listening; he was watching the black limousine that had abruptly driven behind his car, braking quickly to avoid hitting his car. The limousine flashed its lights, a signal for Stephen to pull over or to speed up, he ignored the car, turning on the radio to divert my attention.

He watched Thomas Two slow, giving the car additional space but the car continued hanging close to his car as if it were trying to either unlatch the trunk and climb into the back seat or check the small lettering on his license plate in Spanish letters that told any car to back off.

I commented. "Sounds as though you should have an ethnicity award for all you and your father have done for the migrant workers. What employer in the valley would provide a safe environment for his or her workers, plus housing, bonuses, embracing their lives, and celebrating every cultural celebration? You and Ben have created a four-star community for your workers and your families."

I realized he was looking into the rearview mirror and not responding to my question. The black limousine had turned onto the fenced road leading to the winery hidden behind the bumps of dried grass.

Stephen commented, "I know that winery very well; the owner had talked about selling for the past ten years after his diagnosis of Parkinson's disease. The valley vintners decided to offer an employee from each of their vineyards to help him until he decided to sell. Hugo was a reclusive vintner, rarely coming to any meetings, traveling often to small wine boutiques in Seattle to sell his wine, and running his vineyard solo for years."

"The valley filled with rumors about him, about his previous marriage and about the tragic death of his teenage

399

son who drove his three-wheeler off a bluff. No one ever knew if it was an accident or a suicide attempt, but neighbors who taught at the son's school disclosed the boy rarely came to school but when he did, he usually had bruised eyes."

"Estavia, our close-lipped nurse practitioner, confided to me and Dad about the police visits to the house twice. One time Dad drove up the unpaved road to the hermit's vineyard with a plan of offering neighborly assistance, only to have his car surrounded by Doberman Pinschers. One jumped on the hood, one clawed at the driver's door biting at the glass with scrapping motions, and two were fighting each other on the roof."

"My Dad backed the car out slowly, fearing harm to the dogs, getting a flat tire, or a window shattered from the teeth determined to reach his face. Later, he called the hermit to tell him of the incident but heard a screaming voice respond with, "This is private property, man. I don't know you. Did you hear me, private property? I do not care who you are or what winery you own. This is my land and my grapes. Stay away from me. If you come back, you will deal with my rifle. Do you understand, man?"

Stephen smirked, "I hope that the limousine was making a neighborly visit to encourage the hermit to sell his vineyard. I hope the Dobermans are there to greet the black demon vehicle."

Pointing he laughed aloud, "Look, Clara, that limousine is screeching out of that driveway, and two Dobermans are in hot pursuit." The driver passed Stephen's car and sped past Thomas One's truck.

I ignored the limousine and focused my attention at the orchards, dangling their apples like a wicked witch waiting to lure someone into her lair. "Stephen, what is that row of outhouses? They look like the ones we had for your Dad's memorial."

Stephen glanced at me "A little bigger than an outhouse, these are migrant worker's homes. You are looking at seasonal homes provided by the farmers for the orchard workers who come during harvesting; one-room structures with a bed, table, hot plate, small refrigerator, electricity, and some of the windows with screens. I was embarrassed when I saw the offering for so many migrant workers whose minimum wage barely compensates for the work that they provide.

Stephen continued, "Sadly, some of those houses have a wife and one or two young ones. I think of these migrant houses and keep myself in check to assure I am doing enough for my crew. I would have nightmares if I offered my winery workers and families such dismal housing. I think it is shameful and a disgrace. The workers rarely complain."

"Estavia provides her free service at her clinic. If there is an injury requiring hospital care, the vintners have set up a fund where, with our approval, the money can pay for medical expenses. Unfortunately, each case needs evaluation individually as occasionally a migrant worker will fake an injury to pay for a long-standing medical condition that had progressed from his early life or was the result of degenerative changes from aging. I know how that may sound," Stephen paused, watching the limousine turn sharply around the curve, one hundred feet in front of Thomas One's truck.

I realized Stephen's attention had been on the limousine after he slowed his car. "What is that limousine doing here? Do you think Mr. Mildsgate knows what we are doing? Why is he going so fast? Stephen this makes me nervous. Maybe we should wait, or call your friend from the sheriff's office to let him know where we are and where we are heading."

Motorcycles

We saw Thomas One's truck brake in front of Stephen's car slowed and came to a complete stop as he turned the curve. His truck's flashing lights became a static warning. Stephen jumping out of the car shouting to me, "Clara, stand outside the car close to the boulder. Do not leave the car."
He began to run around the curve until I could no longer see him only heard his shouts, "Motorcycles, accident, motorcycles on the ground."

 I left the car, cars. I ran around the curve and began to count quickly. Twelve motorcycles were lying on their sides like swatted black flies, sprawled bodies of drivers and passengers pointed their arms in directions like the face of a clock, helmets rocked back and forth, and three bikes without riders in a ditch with license plates reflecting the sun rays. I found myself unable to move, shocked by the scene before me.

 I watched Stephen move quickly, listening to the moans, hearing one passenger shouting in the ear of her mate telling them to open their eyes and talk to her. The black sleeveless leather vests worn in the warmer months exposed their arms, with tracks of crimson abrasions from the road's surface. Thomas One was on the phone, Stephen knelt next to a large motorcyclist, face down, and his legs spread unevenly, who mumbled. "My wife, where is my wife?"

Stephen's hands felt the man's neck, the arteries in his neck throbbing. "Don't move, and don't turn your neck. Can you breathe?" He heard a faint grunt. He felt the wetness of his neck, smelled the thick, musky odor of his hair, saw his arms decorated with tattoo images defining the man's diary of life. One arm had a snake's tail ending at the back of his wrist while its body wound itself under his elbow, displaying diamond-shaped pink, green and ocean colors. At his biceps, a furry tail and two hind legs of a rat showing the struggle of the reptiles feed. His other arm had no visible tattoos; multi-colored rings covered all of his fingers except his thumb.

"My wife, how is my wife?"

Before Stephen could ask for a description, a woman wearing a pink bandanna, blood trickling down her face as if Halloween blood mascara, was crawling to him. "Hank, it's me, I am fine. Do not move; please do not move. The medics are on their way; please stay still."

I watched her touch the man's face with her skinned fingers, "I am here, babe, I am here. Do not move. Talk to me."

Stephen watched the man's body shake, an emotional rumble quivering onto the hot asphalt highway. Looking up, he saw Thomas One give him a thumbs-up gesture assuring that he had been to each victim.

Once I heard the siren, I ran to Stephen, "Is everyone all right? What can I do? Stephen, please tell me they are injured; please tell me they are not dead. Stephen." Thomas One guided the first three ambulances to a safe distance from the carnage.

"They are going to be fine, Clara. Do me a favor, grab that first medic team, and bring them here."

I ran, pointing, directing them to Stephen as each team arrived. Immediately, they placed a board next to Hank, told him to think like a tree trunk, still and unmoving. Two medics, Thomas One, and Stephen rolled him onto the board; his helmet was eased off his head, and he began a barrage of obscenities.

"Who the hell does that driver think he is to cut in front of our group, slam his brakes on twice, swerve back and forth, and speeds away? What is a black limousine doing on these highways?"

We stared at the swollen-faced man, saliva spitting from his mouth like an oral geyser, his wife's hand on his cheek attempting to quiet him while the medics tugged at the gurney straps, pulling them over his bulging belly. "I want him found, I want to report him. I want him dead for what he has done for our motorcycle club. Please help me, please find him."

One of the sheriffs stood above his head, paper pad in hand taking notes as he talked and listening to the few ambulating motorcyclists describe what had happened. "We had no choice sir, we had to lay our bikes down, or we could have killed each other running into each other's bikes. I was the first to lean over and feel the heat and weight of the bike with my body wedged between the highway and the bike. We train for this; we do not expect to do this maneuver to save our lives. I do not know if there are any witnesses except us, and perhaps that person in the pickup. Maybe there are some skid marks, or maybe just maybe the jerk will tell the truth."

Thomas One walked over. "I saw it and I offer you any assistance I can. This is my employer, Stephen, driving behind me, my son behind him. I stopped my truck when I turned into the curve; I put on my flashing lights to warn them. I thank the Heavenly God for saving these lives. I will have nightmares for the rest of my life seeing each motorcycle drop over as if they were pushed with an imaginary force."

"The limousine acted as if it was playing with the motorcyclists, or daring them to race it. By braking frequently, I think it was trying to frighten them or make them mad. Not one motorcycle accepted the challenge; they remained in the formation and slowed their speed. This man, he pointed at Hank, put up his hand motioning for them to all slow, They obeyed him, and perhaps he is the leader. He is also a hero; I think he may have saved their lives by warning them."

Hank tried to move his head from side to side, attempting to say no, but the cervical collar around his neck prevented him from moving. "I am not a hero, these are my friends. Any of them would have done the same thing. Some of us have been biking together for thirty years. Officer, I promise you, we are all over legal drinking age and too young for a nursing home."

Everyone began to laugh, his wife began to cry, and I went over to her. "He is going to be fine, just fine. The officer might need your help walking around and identifying your friends. Would you be able to do that, and may I walk with you?"

She took off her pink bandanna, wiped her face, and nodded. I saw her shiny, bald head, and my eyes filled with tears. I pulled her closer, listening to the soft-spoken words whirling over the heads of the motorcyclists, tiny buzzes of reassurance, confidence, leaning against each other like frail fences, riding partners limping toward the ambulances. I watched Stephen slowly lift one of the riders in his arms.

Thinking of the bald woman, I hoped it was just a hot summer shaved heard and not the residual effect of chemotherapy. The woman nodded, "If I can survive, he can survive." I looked at the trauma, a road painted like a canvas of flushed faces; wound dressings saturated with bloodied saline, smeared lipstick on faces dotted with tiny acne pimples from road gravel, and felt the grip on her hand. "My name is CeCe; my friends just call me C. I think we have a date with that officer either trembling from fear or sheer excitement from witnessing his first major traffic accident. And your name?"

I remembered Mother's pink headscarves tucked under her cowboy hat, her pink hair ties, her routine attempts to apply makeup on her gray-toned face where chemotherapy kidnapped color. I felt a little light-headed. C squeezed my hand, "Hey are you OK, or am I going to need to lay you down next to my husband?"

I looked at C, a head shorter, her leather vest zipper opened slightly, exposing a chest vacant of breasts that had been guaranteed to grow after adolescence. "I am sorry, C; I just need to catch my breath. I will be fine."

Stephen knelt next to me, his arm secure around my shoulder. He knows what I am feeling, I thought; he has always known. He handed C a bottle of water, handed one to me. Smiling at C he said, "All I have to say is I never knew what beauty was hidden under those bulky helmets. I am Stephen, Clara's friend."

C smiled, tapped her water bottle against mine "A pleasure to meet you and to see your color returning. Stephen must be your first aid. I would like to walk with the sheriff to identify everyone. Are you ready to walk with me?"

Stephen whispered in my ear, "She's not your mom, but I think your mom sent her. Big breath, you can do this. They need you and you need to be part of this moment." I took C's hand as we walked toward the officer who greeted us and began to walk with us. C joked to her sitting friends and watched her husband lifted onto a gurney. I put my hand on her arm, "Stephen is with him, and will not let the ambulance leave until you finish with the officer. From here, he looks pretty good waving his arms around, waving his fists and oh, well, I suppose giving the finger to the sky is equally a good omen he will be fine. I am sure the officer will let you ride in the ambulance. We are almost done."

C bent to hug one of the women passengers who was staring and not speaking. "Shirley is deaf and blind and has no idea what is going on. It is imperative that she have an interpreter at the hospital and equally important that she is handled very gently. She just lost her partner of forty years. We invited her to come with us to give her a chance to think of something besides death, funerals, a future empty life, and the reality that he infected her with HIV. He was not one of us because our men have more respect for their women and their responsibility to them."

C began to push her fingers into Shirley's palm, folding and pivoting them she said, "I know enough sign language to tell her where she will be going in a few minutes. Please take care of her." The medic came behind the officer, "She is mine. I will stay with her at the hospital. My son is deaf, I will not leave her, I promise."

Finishing the interview, the officer carried the clipboard bulging with identification papers as he ran to direct the arriving tow trucks. Medics jumped from their ambulances to assist the motorcyclists still sitting on the ground.

Semi-trucks wagging their metal flatbeds edged slowly across the highway, parking in perpendicular lines around the perimeter of the scene. Silently, they moved to each motorcycle, lying like flattened steel platters, curled, stretching, and tangled in the asphalt web. I walked C to the ambulance, talking with her, prompting her with helpful words to say to her husband, and reminding her of how we would like to meet her again someday.

No sooner had we reached the cavernous opening of the ambulance than C touched his boots sticking out of the white sheet, "You better get better Hank, you had better not get sick on me and die. You hear me, Hank?" I hoisted her up as she put one foot on the bumper of the ambulance, grunting to pull herself up.

Hank did not respond. The medic looked out at her solemnly. "We have had to medicate him momentarily for the transfer. He is fine, I promise you. I have learned more obscenities, more threatening glaring looks, and salvaged my fingers multiple times from his snapping jaws." Reaching out to her, he offered a hand. "Please, be extremely quiet, and do not attempt to wake him. He will be more comfortable sleeping while we transport him to the hospital."

C sat next to the medic and focused her eyes on her husband's chest raising and lowering the sheet in white waves. She blew me a kiss after moving her flatted hand from her chest to me. Whispering she said, "I am saying thank you in sign language." I watched the doors close quietly, afraid to awaken the sleeping giant, and the ambulance edged away.

Stephen stood behind me; we watched the last motorcycle loaded onto the flatbed truck. "The sheriff said they have pulled over the limousine in town. I want to know who, and I want to watch him cuffed and in the back of the cruiser. I am in awe of the bond the cyclists share. Did you see how each rider had someone next to him? I never knew angels wore leather jackets."

I clasped his hand as we moved to his car. The line of vehicles that had sat in the sweltering heat for three hours waited quietly. "A sacrifice for everyone, Clara, based on one idiot who selfishly chose to play a game on a two-lane highway. We will need to do something for the riders, maybe invite them to the winery tomorrow. A simple celebration, a reality celebration acknowledging that life offered them another chance to live. I will see if the bank will copy a quick invitation for us and we can drop it off at the hospital."

We waited a few moments until the sheriff's cruiser lights flashed at us letting us pass. He got out of the cruiser and began to direct the line of traffic. The convertibles, delivery trucks, postal trucks, several bicycles, one purple limousine advertising wine tours, and a tow truck pulling a battered Volkswagen camper slowly began to drive away. Passengers leaned against cars, sat on the hood of their cars drinking beer, chased the children through the gaps of cars, took their leashed dogs to the shoulder, and stretched their necks to attempt to see the cause.

Scurrying over the tumbleweed and up the small mounds of browned dirt, bladders were seeking privacy for quick relief. Homeowners hidden by the tiny hills drove down to the end of their dirt driveways offering cold water and diffused radio updates to the questioning drivers. Another sheriff cruiser drove by slowly, assuring everyone that the accident victims would recover, and thanked them all for their patience.

I looked back, remembering the wife surviving her journey, her sleeping husband, and the motorcyclists limping down the highway, the ambulances, the sheriff cars, and the image before and after the rescue. "Life is so unexpected, Stephen. I have been so absorbed; I forgot why we were driving to the city. Right, I remember; we are depositing money. If Satan had his way he would have deposited the motorcyclists quickly into his vault."

"When I reflect on my life this past year, you think I would have considered choices and grasped the security of a solid family memory. Sadly, I am like a child on a playground waiting my turn for the swing, waxing the slide for a quick ride, and wishing my frolicking afternoon would never end. Why have I not grown? Why am I still packing my lunchbox and not packing my life into a new journey? I am not my mother or grandmothers. I do not have their genetic strength. I think I truly am a self-centered, corporate snob."

Stephen knew my self-talk was my emotions working overtime. "You know, she reminded me of Mom. She had that shiny, baldhead. I wonder whether she had someone to buy her a wig or if she could afford a wig. Maybe a wig would be too hot under that helmet. Do you realize, Stephen, what could have happened if they did not have helmets? I think those railroad track abrasions seeping blood were impressive without any broken bones. How did that happen? I think they must practice what to do in these situations, don't you think, Stephen?"

He nodded, and then answered his cell phone, "Yes, we are on our way, a little delayed due to a motorcycle accident along the highway. No, everyone is alive but I am sure you will hear plenty of sirens echoing through the streets in a matter of minutes. Yes, we will park in the back.

We have three vehicles; one will block the alley while we pull into your parking spots. We will see you soon."

I thought I must remember to remind Stephen how dangerous it is to talk on his cellphone while he is driving on the curvy highways. What I would do if anything happened to him?

I sat quietly until I heard two ambulances with flashing lights pass us and continue down the highway. Stephen saw the highway had opened, a parade of impatient cars nudging each other along following him. He called Thomas One, telling him to go faster to avoid the cars passing them with another potential accident. As he turned on the last curve before the town, he could see in the distance two tow trucks with their headlights flashing, circulating red beams across the pale sky.

Baker Boyer Bank

I saw Stephen pull out something from his pocket, kiss it, and tuck it back inside. When I asked him what it was he just said it was a reminder worklist for Thomas One as he bottled my mother's wine for shipment. Odd, I thought. Why would he kiss a worklist?

Stephen slowed the car at the first stop sign on Main Street. The bumper of the limousine had just turned the corner by the pharmacy when two police cars sped by him and rounded the corner. Stephen could hear them on their loudspeaker, "Everyone out of the car, hands above your heads. I repeat everyone out of the car." I leaned forward in my seat listening to loudspeaker voice that vibrated against the brick building and put my hand on the car door to exit.

Stephen stopped me and laid his arm across my chest, "No, Clara, not yet. I promise you we will learn the details, but we cannot leave this car again." Stephen saw Thomas One pull into the bank's alley and waited for Stephen to pull in.

Behind the bank, garbage cans, recycling containers, stacks of empty boxes, and cats leaped from windowsills, as he entered slowly. He honked the horn several times to warn anyone on a smoke break outside the stores back doors that a car was coming. One young couple stared blankly at Stephen when he drove by. "We caught them, Clara. Tell me how much more romantic an alley is for exploring each other's bodies with the scent of garbage, coffee grounds, cat pee, and the sound of whirling air conditioners?"

I read the graffiti on the cemented walls; a pallet of colors changed by layers of spray, dripping rain droplets, and wide brushes of black. "Class of 1990, 2001, and look at the one right above the discarded water heater, 1987. Where did you leave your mark, Stephen?" Stephen only smiled knowing he did not leave a mark on the brick, only adolescent curiosity in the backseat of Thomas One's truck, and inside one of the teepees.

Both parking spots had small orange cone barriers, removed by the banker who ran down the back steps, waving them into their spot. Thomas Two came behind, blocking the alley with windows rolled down, with music blaring from the truck's oversized speakers. When Stephen stepped out of the car to shake the banker's hand, Thomas One turned off the radio and moved his truck next to the car.

Stephen popped the trunk and Thomas One unloaded wine boxes He effortlessly lifted each box and seemed to recognize the lightweight as he transferred the wine to the dolly. He pushed the dolly over to his truck and stacked the rest of the wine boxes.

As he moved the dolly to the bank door, He pointed to a rotting piece of lumber balancing between two four-foot iron pedestals. "Miss Clara, picture horses being tied up here, before this was a bank before there were cars, owned by individual farmers, resting before they carried passengers in a hackney or carriage. Imagine a beautiful, enclosed carriage with four wheels embedded with spokes, small oil lamps burning, a uniformed driver, and statuesque horses guiding you through the streets at nightfall."

"Perhaps your grandmother rode in a carriage as our Mr. Ben rode in our century's replica during his celebration." I thought of the stagecoach ride at an amusement park in my younger days; the bouncing, swaying, jostling from inside with the uneasy gait of the horses weary of repeated circles around the dirt enclosure. The coach leaned to its side, balancing on the wheels moaning from the passenger's weight.

Walking to the rail, I ran my hands along its surface. "I can picture my grandmother riding in one of the carriages delivering wine to the local church during Prohibition. " I winked at Stephen. "I have been reading my mother's senior project, and my grandmother was a wine delivery maiden to all the churches, which were exempt during Prohibition. So, I guess she was not a bootlegger, but perhaps a red-wine angel."

Stephen introduced me to the banker, who offered me his hand as we walked up the asphalt steps missing chunks of cement, no handrail, and a steel door that scraped the sides of the bank when opened. "I am so pleased to meet you, Clara. I

417

am sure you have heard this before, but the resemblance to your mother is as if I were talking to her now. She was my first love until a certain winery owner captured her away from me and every other businessman in this town. I hope our community has welcomed you. I will be happy to help you settle into your winery."

Stephen guided Thomas One to the banker's office and looked back at me, rolling his eyes after the banker's comments, to assist me in settling in. My eyes met his as I listened to the banker prattle about his infatuation with my mother.

After the dolly rested on the carpet in the banker's office, Thomas One left. Stephen closed the door, waiting for the process to begin. Stephen and I began to place the bundles of bills onto his desk; the banker quickly calculated each, putting them in a safe security box. "Yes, Clara there is one million dollars to be transferred to a bank in New Jersey? Am I correct that you do not want to leave any here for your business needs?"

I sighed, leaned against the credenza which held three softball trophies, two beer steins, several frames with black-and-white photographs of the bank dated 1920, and a stack of astrology books. "At this point, I would like all the money to be transferred. I will decide soon where the money will find a permanent home."

The banker verified my bank information and transferred the money. Within minutes, his phone rang and it was my banker in New York verifying the transfer. The banker handed the phone to me. I responded, "Yes, I will stop by the bank when I return next week. Shall we celebrate with dinner? I am not sure how my schedule will be once I return to the office. I have quite a bit of catching up; we can discuss dinner after I look at my schedule. Thank you, again."

As I began to hand the phone back, his voice continued and I responded quickly, "No, I do not need a ride from the airport, but thank you again." My face flushed as I looked at Stephen. Shrugging, I said, "He is an old friend. I am looking forward to my coming back."

The banker, feeling the awkward visual path between us, spoke quickly. "Stephen, I did want you to consider an offer from our bank. It would be an honor if you would consider a permanent memorial to honor your father outside our bank. The rocky waterfall near the front steps has been empty for years; the community garden club maintains the flowers that surround the arbor. The benches resembling toadstools are a favorite of locals and tourists. Take your time thinking about our offer. I understand if you have chosen another location, just let me know."

"Clara and I will look at it before we leave. She has a great idea for a memorial that would not only acknowledge

Dad but also the college's future vintners. Thank you." Stephen reached in the bottom of the last box and brought out two bottles of wine, "One from our winery, and one from Clara's winery, Long House. Your confidentiality and trust are sincerely appreciated by both of us."

Stephen shook his hand and watched him walk to me after I extended a hand, giving me a strong hug. "I feel as if I have just held your mother for a moment; I hope she felt it in heaven."

Ben's Sculpture

I followed Stephen out the back door, around the corner, and to the front of the bank. In the distance, we saw the last of the police cars leaving the corner where the limousine had been. Stephen guided me to the small, circular garden that stood between the bank and the street corner just as the banker had described. We watched a teenager holding his skateboard and posing on one of the toadstools, pretending to shoot an arrow into the sky, an older gentleman sat in a wheelchair next to him.

Stephen, whispering, told me about this man, a vintner who had retired a year ago and sold his winery to the Seattle conglomerate, with plans to spend more time with his son's family. Stephen said he had heard that within weeks of selling the winery, a CAT scan diagnosed his frequent bouts of headaches and blurred vision as inoperable brain cancer. The man, leaning toward his grandson from his wheelchair, was now legally blind. He spoke softly with plucking exact words. He wore a turban to cover the growth of the tumor that pushed itself up from under the fabric.

"My ears can hear a voice. Is that you, Ben, have you come to put all your wine money into the bank?"

"Hello, kind sir. No, this is Stephen, his son. You may not have heard that my father died a few weeks ago. I apologize for not calling you. I am sure all the valley vintners would have been excited to see you and share their wine during his life celebration. Why I think your wine flowed just like this fountain did years ago. You have a handsome grandson. He resembles you."

"Is he wearing a turban?" A sarcastic comment followed by an attempt to find his grandson's head, traveling up his arm, toward his shoulder, his neck, and resting on his ear. "No turban for him, not with this long, straight hair covering his ears. I am sorry to hear about Ben. Did he suffer for long?"

Stephen walked over, knelt by the wheelchair, and put his hand on his arm. "No, it was sudden. He felt sleepy, went into a coma, and died on the operating table after an attempt to repair a bursting aneurysm. He did not suffer, but he left us hurting and filled with sadness."

"Who's that, Clarish? I would recognize her voice anywhere? Except, I do know that she died. Has she come back to take me with her?"

I stepped up, put my hand over his, and sat on the cement. "I am Clara, her daughter, who has inherited my family's Long House winery. Stephen tells me you were one of the best."

Sliding his hand from under mine, he followed my arm to my neck, moving his head closer to me. I could see his eyes were dark, glossy circles set deeply in his eye socket. His eyes nested within their bony skull frame, sinking back into a brain softened from leaking spinal fluid and pooling around the diseased tissue. His arched eyebrows were fixed in a permanent facial feature of awe or residual laughter. His gleaming dentures smiled, exposing shreds of toast crumbs, a clinging apple peel, and droplets of cream.

Touching my face, he spoke directly to me, as if Stephen and his grandson had evaporated. "You must not make the same mistake I made, Clara. Whatever it takes to keep your winery, whatever sacrifices you must make, do not give up the Long House winery. I am sure you have heard of its history. I suppose you have wandered through the grapevines, and I have no doubt you have tasted the wine. Do not make the same mistake I made. I gave up everything to spend my days with my family. Look at my grandson, perhaps not quite as handsome as Stephen yet, but had I been smarter, I would have saved my winery for him. I would have disciplined him in the vintner's art like Ben taught Stephen."

"No doubt Stephen has told you what he sacrificed as a young man to learn the craft. Equally, I am sure that he does not regret where he is in life, except for losing his father. Stephen could have run their winery when he was a teenager; we knew he was ready."

"Ben offered his knowledge to Stephen from sunrise to sunset and he readily accepted his father's teachings." The old man touched my hair. "Is your hair black like your mother's and grandmother's? It feels thick, thick like your Native-American heritage."

I nodded, "Yes, it is black like my mother's hair, and many people have told me I look like her. What is your hair color?

He pushed his turban back exposing a dry, taut transparent skin stretching over protruding bumps on his bony skull. "Now, or four months ago before I was diagnosed?"

I touched his forehead, remembering tiny chick-down sprouts my mother had felt months after her chemotherapy. Gently, I slid my fingertips across his head, "If I were to look into my magic ball and touch the tiny filament of red hair tendrils, your hair was shades of Rose blended with a splash of Cabernet."

His laugh, which combined a cough, burp, and hiccup in one snorting sound, shook his body, forced his hands to clap uncontrollably on the wheelchair arm, and he beckoned his grandson to hold the chair to prevent it from tipping forward. Swallowing, accepting a swipe of the strand of yellow, thick mucus swinging from the corner of his cracked lip, he scrambled for words, avoiding another outburst.

"Clara, how quickly you have learned our trade. How astute you are to imagine my hair burnt red that I proudly slicked back with globs of gel. Your touch, so gentle,

424

sincere, and caring, must define who you are; don't you agree, Stephen?"

Stephen helped me stand, "She is what you hear, she is what you are visualizing, and she has been a gift that appeared weeks ago. Sadly, she is leaving to return to her home in New Jersey and my winery crew will maintain her winery until she returns."

"Perhaps you can help us decide if this would be a perfect location for a sculpture to honor my father. I would remove the water fountain; fill the perimeter of the circle with flowers and put in wine barrels as seats."

"The sculpture would combine grapes and vines. I would have it framed in the words left on the corks that vintners signed at his celebration and finally, a slot would collect coins in a locked box with proceeds going to Walla Walla Community Colleges, Enology and Viticulture program."

Stephen began to check in his pockets; I pushed through my purse finding a cork and pen. "Could you please sign this cork; I will include your name in the sculpture." The vintner slid the pen in circles, lines that jumped off the cork's surface, and dots resembling residual mold flecks.

"Thank you, Stephen, thank you for including me. Thank you for being your father's son. Thank you for giving me this Clara gift." He leaned forward, pursed his lips that fell against each other limply, "One kiss please."

I kissed his lip. "So this seals our agreement that you will answer all my questions."

"I will not be here to answer your questions when you return after the harvest. Ben, Clarish, and I will be throwing corks down from the heavens. We will be watching you, Clara. "

"Choose your path, choose wisely, and that includes not just running a winery. I do not know what your job is now; I am guessing it has offered you security both financially and personally. Owning the winery will duplicate those feelings; give it time, learn the craft, and you will sense the same security"

My eyes filled with tears. Stephen changed the topic quickly. "So, have you heard the sirens? I just saw the sheriff handcuff the responsible idiot unless another redhead is riding around in a limousine in the valley."

"He challenged a group of motorcyclists on the highway causing a horrible accident. Most of the motorcyclists are at the hospital, alive with abrasions and eager to be witnesses to his idiotic behavior."

"He may have been the buyer for your winery and is spreading his tentacles throughout the valley. Clara said he stopped by her winery. He showed up at Dad's memorial but was quickly escorted out by my crew. I am sorry if he was the buyer for your winery. I promise you it will not happen again; I promise."

The vintner yawned. "Rumor has it we were related because my hair had dark-red streaks. This is a rumor, that needs to squelch or, how do we say it in our industry, squeezed." The vintner had begun to nod off as his grandson slowly began to wheel him away. Nodding to us, he remained silent, wiping away a tear, pointed to the sky one last time with his imaginary bow and arrow, and left with his grandfather.

We watched the grandson slowly tilt the wheelchair down the curb, rolling it between the crosswalk lines, walk past the historic Falkenberg clock, and disappear around the corner. The sheriff passed them, put his hand on the grandson's shoulder, and approached us.

Smiling broadly, the sheriff said, "We got the bad guy. The famous Mr. M who promises to bring the best New York attorneys to defend him. He placed all the blame on the erratic, drug behavior of the leather-clad motorcyclists. I am heading to the hospital to complete the witness reports while he pleads for bail."

"He claims he is heading out tomorrow but emphasized he would be back to finish what he started. Not sure, what he started or why he needs to come back. He says that is his plan. Have you met him?"

Stephen commented on his uninvited visit to Ben's memorial. I told him about his visit to the winery and that he works in my building in New York.

427

The sheriff tipped his sunglasses onto the bridge of his nose. "You work in New York and own a winery, an official bi-coastal woman. Not sure how you can handle both, but I am not as young as you are and I suppose anything is possible once paychecks influence your lifestyle."

"For me, my life is in this community where I have lived since I was born. Perhaps there is not as much money or excitement as in your skyscraper city, but there is not much crime, either."

Stephen changed the conversation. "We were heading to the hospital to invite the motorcyclists to the winery for a true celebration of life. I am not sure when they are heading out but I would like to extend the offer." He handed a flier to the sheriff, "You, your team, and the medics are welcome to come."

The sheriff's radio crackled with a voice. He leaned his ear into his shoulder, listened, waved, and walked away.

"I guess, Clara, we have a memorial site for Dad. Maybe it will be finished by the time you return. Let's head to the hospital to hand out the fliers."

The banker knocked on the window, waved, and watched us return to the parking lot at the back of the bank. Thomas One and his son were tossing flattened beer cans from around the dumpster into an empty barrel. Both looked up when Stephen approached.

He nudged his son to return to his pick up at the end of the alley. "Time to go. Mr. Stephen, the wine is delivered, sirens have stopped, and I think it is a perfect time for tequila and tamales."

We began to talk at the same time to Thomas One. Stephen specific to the memorial and I told him we would be stopping by the hospital emergency room.

Stephen patted Thomas One on the shoulder, "You head on home. We will not be very long, and please check on the labeling process. Everything should be corked and foiled. I had hoped to spend time with Clara placing the labels tomorrow. Ask Maria to have a light supper ready for us when we return. It has been a long day."

I motioned to Thomas One and we walked to the future site of Ben's sculpture. Stephen watched me moving my arms in large circles, pointing to the future bench sites, and the flower planting location. I hoped to reconcile my relationship with him after my innocent, insulting comment about his English. I know Stephen realized I was making an effort with Thomas but I sensed he had grown distant realizing I planned on leaving.

Pioneer Park

Returning to the car, I began to flip through mother's senior composition book, running my fingers down the table of contents labeled "The Town." I slipped one of the ribbon bookmarks into the handwritten page and read it to Stephen.

"This is what my mom wrote about the town when Grandmother was alive. The wooden buildings slowly evolved into brick, Oldsmobiles arrived at the end of the nineteenth century followed by Studebakers whose tires sunk, spun, and parked along the curb, blocking the hitching posts. Her mother traveled through town in a carriage or a bicycle. Rainy seasons caused the dirt to become muddy, hoof-holes, scattered throughout horse droppings. Horse-drawn water sprinkling wagons or straw controlled the dust. It is hard to imagine, but my Grandmother rode an electric streetcar that ran on the main street. Horses, bicycles, buggies, carriages shared the street, probably too early to consider traffic lights or stop signs."

"Mom wrote, although cars were gaining ground, it certainly did not reflect the end- of -the -year sales at most advertised dealerships, less than one thousand initially."
I pointed at the next sentence, shaking my head. "She said streets were made of asphalt and she goes on for pages about the difference between asphalt and concrete. Perhaps she needed to complete a specific number of pages for her paper

because, no offense, Mom," I looked up, "but who cares what roads are made of?"

"I have a question for you, Clara. What is asphalt made of and what do you think your New York taxi's drive on east of the mountains?"

Not knowing, I waited while Stephen continued. "Most roads are made of asphalt, which is a crude-oil process. Anything left becomes asphalt cement for pavement like sidewalks. I bet your mom does not include that in her report."

I tapped my finger on the notebook. "Well, she mentioned wooden walkways and the transition to sidewalks. I am sure it's just a minor oversight that she does not mention how asphalt was created."

"You should see this chart, Stephen; she has crammed more information about the two substances in two comparative columns. Funny, her teacher circled some words with a red pen, pulling the line outside the chart and wrote, "Check spelling." I have no idea how anyone could read any of these tiny, slanted letters without a microscope."

Stephen laughed. "I think we can solve the mystery behind her paper. The paper was probably written for her science teacher who taught English composition, and was responsible for giving the final grade for graduation."

"Stephen, can you imagine no curbs or sidewalks existed? My grandmother had only wooden walkways to walk. I wonder why she came to town. If she had the winery and the farms nearby, did she get her supplies here? Her medications, if she needed them? Perhaps she needed grain for the animals, or maybe she delivered her wine to customers."

"I am curious about this grandmother of mine. Do you think she came alone? Somehow, I am picturing a Western town backdrop with boots, horses, saloons, perpendicular buildings, women filling baskets with food, men waiting outside of the stores, and kids falling on the walkways getting enormous splinters or tearing their cotton pants, a recent hand-me-down from a neighbor."

Stephen interjected, "You will need to learn where Prohibition impacted this town. No saloon sales, but the churches may have benefited from your grandmother's deliveries. Let me show you Washington's oldest Christian churches."

He turned the corner and pointed to the First Congregational Church. "The church was built over one hundred fifty years, and, can you imagine, it was built in the mid-nineteen century? It has survived a fire or two and rebuilding, yet that building speaks to the strength of prayer."

"I wanted to show you one more street before I head to the hospital. This is one of my favorite picture books of historical architectural homes, none bought by vintners, purchased by physicians, lawyers, and company owners."

"Look at the leaded glass in the front windows, the columns, the carvings of the gables, and those large front porches. I have never been inside one of the houses, well, perhaps a few backyards for parties in my younger days, but rumor has it some houses have ballrooms on the third floor."

Stephen shook his head and said, "I find it hard to believe a ballroom towering over the house on the third floor I wonder how many steps to the third floor? Is there an elevator, maybe an escalator? I could imagine dancing with you as we danced at my Dad's celebration. Promise me, Clara, if you come back, you will dance with me in the ballroom of that house."

I felt his hand. Looking down at my mother's sketches, I closed my eyes. I imagined wearing a long, silver, metallic lame' dress and a matching silver cloche hat, walking up the stairs, lifting the skirt with my fingertips to avoid tripping, with my chin held high as I moved toward the sounds of the chamber music. Stephen, dressed in his black tuxedo with tails would grasp my elbow and lead me up the stairs tipping my head slightly; I would look over the wooden banister at the guests admiring the young couple.

"It's a date, Clara. Come back and make it happen." Stephen smiled imagining Clara wearing a long purple skirt and blouse Maria had made her for Ben's celebration, he wearing a matching shirt, boots, and clenching my hand skipping up the stairs to the blaring horns of a Big Band.

Stephen moved his hand pointing to the sign, "Pioneer Park is still a favorite of mine and is historical for our city. It is not a youngster; I would say its an oldster from the early 1900s. Maybe there's something in your mom's report about your grandmother trying to climb the amazing trees or, better yet, listening to music at the bandstand."

He slid the car into an open space by the curb in front of the postal carrier truck, and behind a row of bicycles chained together. "Quick, for one moment, come with me." I stared out the window at a massive lawn. Frisbee-throwing college students, dogs tugging on leashes to growl at the man walking with a parrot on his shoulder, parents encouraging their wobbling toddler to walk, the postal carrier sitting on a park bench chewing on a wrapped submarine sandwich, balancing a soft drink cup between his knees, while reading a folded newspaper. I moved from my seat before Stephen had the chance to come to my side of the car.

"Stephen, don't forget we are heading to the hospital." Stephen pointed up. I sighed. "Breathtaking." The tree branches formed an umbrella over the park. "I feel as if I am walking inside an eco-friendly tent. You should sell real estate when you grow weary of selling wine. Visitors to the city who wander the streets for winetasting need to explore this amazing beauty and historical setting."

I slipped off my shoes, Stephen followed, and we walked between trees, dodging the occasional couple pressed against the striated bark, and faced the bandstand. "Shall we?" Stephen took my hand and we walked up the stairs, running our hands along the railing. "Imagine, Clara, over one hundred years ago this bandstand belonged to the children who grew up listening to its music, sharing the park with soldiers, attending weddings, singing patriotic music."

"The rose garden is over there; there is an aviary along the pond. I came here with Dad." He paused, glancing at the ceiling of the bandstand as if talking to his father. "I remember how Maria would give me a stack of corn tortillas in a brown bag. 'Feed those ducks,' she would say, 'give them some of Maria's homemade cooking.'

"Dad and I would sit on a rock by the pond and I would tear off pieces of tortilla, throwing them to the cluster of ducks who gathered at my feet. I guess they were responsible for me learning how to tie my shoes. Untied laces that tangled in the water became instant bait for the ducks."

"Dad always had a book and a paper cup filled with his favorite wine. I still cannot believe how much time he spent with me, how he always tried to find the simplest places like the river for us to just have our time together."

"Surprisingly, probably something you would not have known, but he was quiet. Oh, he could easily expound on his latest Pinot to winery guests or friends and the words flowed like the wine. Yet, around the wine crew, he was quiet."

"I always felt he just absorbed every moment. He never forgot one thing that we did; hard to imagine."
"He hardly ever carried a camera, never had a life diary-like your mother only his wine journal. I know that our planned time together was firm; he never let anything interrupt our time together"

"I mean, he never said, 'Stephen if you don't finish your math we will not go to see the Space Ship Challenger memorial,' or 'Stephen, if you don't finish washing the glasses from the tasting room we will not go sledding in Pioneer Park."

"He valued me, our time, and life." I moved closer, looking up at him and pressing my forehead against his chest.

"Speak his name Stephen, speak of the times you spent together, your memories of him is his gift to you. Perhaps he left without wrapping it, putting on a bow and tag but his gift has a place within you. I want to hear all the stories, and when I am not here, you must continue to tell stories. He has died but you cannot let one fragment of a moment with him disappear."

Stephen pressed the back of my head against him, running his fingers down the length my hair before he began to tremble and tears dropped onto my head. He touched the back of my neck, its moisture, and subtle heat. "I am sorry, Clara. I find that each day when I try to step away from his death, I am drawn back to him like an undercurrent to him: that day at the house, the hospital, the celebration, and the river that carried him away. I hope you do not think I am weak, but I ask that you understand, knowing that I will grieve again when you leave."

I stepped back, licked the tear droplet from his chin, and spoke softly. "Stephen, my leaving is not meant to be as permanent as death. My leaving is a transition for us, a complicated journey for me, and most importantly, for you to focus on yourself, the winery, and your future. I know my staying would impact your direction and confidence as you establish yourself as the primary owner."

"You are strong, Stephen; I do not see sadness as a weakness. What I see is a man whose heart is visible to eyes which seek to feel its warmth and compassion. In this short time of our relationship, I have seen you costumed in strength, control, sensitivity, knowledge, optimism, pride, guilt, and reflection. How many women could have seen what I have seen?"

I waited for an answer and Stephen put his lips close to mine, breathing his answer into my mouth, "No one, Clara; I promise you no one."

He kissed my lips, cheeks, eyelids, and forehead, he repeated, "No one." He felt my warmth, He looked down at me asking, "Feeling well, my Wine Princess?" I began to respond, "Well my foot is…"

I paused after we were both startled by the sound of a squeaking clarinet at the end of the steps followed by a hoarse voice as a white-haired man moved his mouth in whistling movements. "Sorry to disturb you folks, my buddies will be arriving soon and I was just warming up for our afternoon concert. We have been coming here every third Thursday during the warm weather."

He rubbed his clarinet with his fingers. "Some of us can hardly hear, our lips are shriveled due to decayed teeth but we are all World War II veterans whose responsibility is to entertain until we die. The fighting is behind us, we are all widowers, and we have found each other. I guess life is all about finding someone and moving on."

"You two are welcome to stay on the stage; you can sit behind us. The only rule, no singing or kicking your feet into our bottoms while you keep time to the music."

Stephen walked down the steps, shook the man's hand, and thanked him for the offer. "We have an appointment. However, now that I know your schedule, I will try to make your concert next month. "

I smiled, touched the man's arm whose skin resembled parched, desert dunes, and followed Stephen. I thought of how I had changed in the valley. In the city, I was quick to shake hands, dominate a conversation, control a group of clients with jokes or stories, and quickly acknowledge a comment. With Stephen, I recognized I did not need control; I savored his ability to take over in social situations.

Stephen drove quickly to the hospital. "Clara, look at the time. I hope we did not miss any of them."
Just as our car pulled into the parking lot, a tourist bus was leaving the front of the hospital entrance. The side of the bus was a canvas of advertisements for local businesses; tire stores, bookstores, and three churches welcoming tourists to their Sunday services.

"Stephen, please go in. I will wait here for you. I had several quick trips here with Mom when she needed blood work and one last visit when her port required maintenance. I am not sure if any hospital staff would remember me, but today I rather not talk with them about Mom. If you don't mind, I will just read my mom's senior project."

He adjusted the air-conditioning, found a classical music station, and left the car with the invitation fliers for the motorcycle club. I looked at the composition book, tracing Mother's sketches with my finger and talking to the imaginary image sitting in the driver's seat. "Well, it's just you and me, Mom. I am learning everything about Grandmother. You know, I remember so little about her, but

I do remember how you cared for her. I remember wanting to not be left alone and waiting for you to come out of her room."

"I guess when I think about it now you too were a daughter needing her mother. I need you now, too, I need to know what will be right about leaving the winery and returning to New Jersey or what will be wrong about staying with the winery. How I miss the conversations we had before you became ill."

"You know, you never really told me what to do, but you listened. I wonder whether between the thin layers of clouds you can hear my voice, knowing you left me with your ability to resolve a problem or anticipate a problem. I guess Mom, through your report on Grandmother; I will have a few clues on the winery, or perhaps the struggles both of you faced."

"I wish I did not waiver, Mom. Remember how you were when we were going through the wig catalog and you struggled with wanting one until you finally decided to buy a wig. Remember how you felt when you wore it, your confidence in the beauty that had never left you. I guess I am there now, Mom, minimal confidence on what I should or should not do."

I saw Stephen approaching the car. He squeezed through two parked cars, and I ended my conversation with Mom.

Charges Dropped

Hearing Stephen's knock on the window, I ended my conversation with Mother by blowing a kiss in the air at the driver's seat. I closed the composition book and unlocked the car doors.

Tossing the fliers in the backseat, he announced, "Missed them. The bus we just saw was taking all of them to the airport. No one seems to know who arranged for the bus, but I am guessing it is the guilty Mr. M trying to make amends. I knew a couple of the women receptionists and they shared with me a little background on the riders. I will be the first to admit I thought motorcyclists that travel in packs have a raucous social life. I truly have been misled."

"Shirley May, who I know from high school, told me that their professions ranged from two lawyers, one physician, one professor, a grandmother who babysat her granddaughter, a couple celebrating their thirty-fifth wedding anniversary and a couple who just got engaged after dating for the last ten years."

"Sounds like a few of them will need stitches removed in a few weeks, two have on soft casts on their legs, and there was only one broken arm. The big guy, he is a minister whose congregation is a homeless camp. I guess he has the most bruise. I am surprised about his vocation based on the language that came from his mouth while he was lying face down on the cement."

"I have a couple of addresses, unofficially against hospital rules, so I will follow up and invite them to come to the winery next year. Maybe we can offer to be the winery for an event for them or offer our grounds away from the winery for camping. I would like to do something; those of us in the valley owe them something for what happened on our highway. Will you come back?"

I answered firmly, "Stephen next summer is a long way off; please does not ask me to make any plans. Please. These next few days are going to be difficult for both of us. The last thing I want to do is make promises that I may not be able to keep. Do you understand? Our conversations are the same stuck needle on a record, me standing firm, you asking, and me trying not to refuse or hurt your feelings. Was your dad as stubborn as you?"

"I checked my work e-mails last night. I have over one thousand emails that I need to address now. My clients will not only leave me, but they will leave the firm. I might not have to decide to stay or leave the company; I wish to avoid being fired."

Stephen paused at the crosswalk where pedestrians took bright purple flags from a holder before crossing and placing the purple flags in the opposite holder. "I got an enormous amount of flack once I offered to make these flags.

My purpose was strictly to promote our wineries but the community felt I was promoting the rival football team west of the mountains whose colors are purple and gold. Took a few town hall meetings until the town voted on keeping the flags purple, and not before we ran the gamut of color; white for the Walla Walla onion, red for the apples, oh yes, and brown for wheat. I have a feeling you would have done a much better job convincing them to keep the color based on your solid education, the way you present yourself to others, and your professional demeanor."

"I think the banker was intimidated by you. Who would not be, if they had the responsibility to handle a million-dollar transfer?"

"I forgot you asked about inheriting stubborn genes and the answer is yes. My Dad would not have the name or respect from the valley vintners if he did not stand for what he believed. He had his way, Clara. Well, you saw him in action with his sly smile, twinkling eyes, raised eyebrows to punctuate a point. In a short time, you knew him; you saw his kinder side and his approval of the city maiden."

He took one hand off the steering wheel, pointing. "Geography class continues. There are two ways of leaving the city. One way will take us through the wheat fields, the Palouse, and the other direction is a small climb that will take us toward the Blue Mountains. We are heading away from the mountains tonight."

I ignored Stephen's comment about being the sought-after city maiden and absorbed the evening landscape as we entered the two-lane highway. The skies left streaks of fading pillars of light through the rose hue resting atop the hills. The windmills whirled slowly, catching a gasp of air from their marathon day of slicing the sky with their blades.

The fields were shadowed by the cloak of evening crawling down the hills, across the swaying wheat, and forming a shady path for the cattle lumbering back to the barn. The vegetable stands at the end of the gravel driveways were empty from daily sales of potatoes, onions, apples, eggs, home-baked bread, and goat cheese. Plastic buckets, vessels for bouquets, rested on their side, the fertilized water dripping on the wooden table legs. The "OPEN" sign tilted against the table's edge, hand-painted red letters declaring "CLOSED" under the sketched, two-foot-high owl with closed eyes.

Two colts chased each other through sagebrush, while their mothers faced each other as if saying, "Do you think they will sleep through the night?" I squinted past the horses looking for my white horse, my spiritual protector, but only saw the open gate with a child waving a brightly colored cloth attempting to get their attention. The horses lifted their heads toward the colts, waiting for them to return to their side.

The ponies raced to their mothers as if they had yelled, "you're it," one colliding into its mother's swishing tail, the other lifting its head for a nuzzle. They walked between the mares, a maternal playpen restricting any further play.

The lettering on the highway visitor signs began to glow in the final sun's rays; yellow road signs on the curve began to brighten, slowly preparing for the long night of warning and reminding drivers of the winding, curved, asphalt geography. A raccoon stood analyzing the road, moving its head forward and back finally returning to sit behind a mailbox.

The sky changed from lavender to a deep purple and coal darkness. Stars hiding behind the clouds breathed light into their starfish, twinkling arms, finding their position within the night constellations, or breaking rules and wandering off like rebellious adolescents. I tipped my head back knowing that the skies in New Jersey were never black, only reflective mirrors of the lights from the towering buildings. I remembered the last time I left the office to meet my friends at a tiny bar at the end of the pier and stared up at the skies.

My friends knew Mother died and said they would help me search for Mother's star. They assured me the shuffling breeze from the water was Mother's voice. I remembered my friend's smiles, looks of concern rising from their seats, surrounding and hugging me,

How quickly I recognized the value of friends. I never had to explain why I would stop mid-sentence and stare at a woman who had passed our table, a mirror image of my mother, or why I would interrupt someone when a fragmented memory of my mother burst out like a pin in a balloon. My friends hovered close, allowing me to be without speaking or expecting me to explain a blank, non-responsive stare while stirring an empty gin and tonic. I missed my friends.

I focused on our drive. Each home, barn, and grain tower resembled silhouettes of a board game identifying private property that gradually expanded from a house to newer buildings. In the distance, flashing squares of red lights framed the school bus hopping from one fenced drive to the next. Dim, ghost-like shadows outlined children swinging baseball bats, petting the family dog stretching from his daily watch by the light pole. Hands waved and feet ran up the drive to the tall, adult figure standing a short distance from the end of the drive, the child, parent, and dog's path lit by a light beam from the swinging flashlight in the adult's hand.

Stephen sped by a lone hitchhiker whose cardboard-sign letters were invisible in the nightfall. "What is that kid doing hitchhiking this time of the night? I could barely see him. I am going to give the sheriff a quick call to see if he is another adolescent runaway, a valley visitor returning home, or a college student who gave up after their first week."

"Sometimes I pick them up, or at the least pull over to see what they need. I have given them cash through the years and pointed to the closest bus stop. I just hate to see anyone on the highway. Some nights it looks as if tar was poured into the sky."

Stephen pointed out the window, "Check out the glowing eyes. I saw only the red eyes that faded quickly after the headlights passed, "Wolf or coyote?"

"It's a coyote; they are busy this time of night. No more wolves, I hope. I would find it difficult to kill any knowing now what I know about your family's spiritual beliefs."

I touched the wolf claws bound at the end of my necklace. Stephen's hand was on my fingers, squeezing them, as he said, "I wish I could be your protector, I would not disappear. I would be by your side."

I took his hand and placed it on my lips. I did not kiss them; I only pressed his skin against my mouth. He circled his fingers under my chin, took the steering wheel to turn his car slowly up the drive to his winery. The silence in the car ended when the crew houses along the drive echoed with music from a stereo system. His car tires crunched loudly on the gravel, as a final, high-pitched chorus drifted above the trees.

"I need to know what is going on. It's a little early for dinner, or we are late, but typically, they are not quite this animated in the early evening. I know we will not hear them in the house but I am just curious to know what they are celebrating."

Chardonnay and Pinot barked in unison while Stephen eased the car into the garage. I reminded him, "Stephen, this is where we met, do you remember?"

He reached into the pocket of the door panel to snatch a few dog treats. "Clara, how could I ever forget carrying you to the house and feeling you in my arms? When we have talked about all of our memories that is a memory on my heart's first page. Between inhaling your existence and ignoring Dad's exaggerated eye-winks, this garage evolved into the high-school first dance. I walked to you, held you and ..." he paused "I almost forgot; we needed to feed the dogs their treats."

Stephen reached out his window to Pinot; I followed, giving Chardonnay the tiny bone that resulted in residual thick mucus from the grateful tongue.

Leaving the car, the dogs pushed against us, circling us, and running to the kitchen door waiting for us to follow. "I wonder whether they still miss Dad, if they wonder when he will be coming home, or if I will be a substitute from now on."

Maria greeted us with a hug and invited us to the patio for dinner. "The bottling is done, the seals are on, and all that is left is to apply the Long House Labels. Thomas thought you would want to show Clara, and the two of you can pack a box for shipment. The family just finished and Thomas told them to head back to their homes with the reward of a few bottles of tequila."

"You know, Stephen when you ask for something to be done, it is always done. I do not think anyone expected this done in a day. I might also add that no one knew that Miss Clara was leaving, myself included. I mean, I knew that you might leave, but …" Maria's eyes filled with tears and she ran down the hall to her room.

I looked away from Stephen. I walked into the living room when Chardonnay was lying on the floor by Ben's chair; Pinot was sitting in the chair. I laughed, "Look who is playing Ben now, and you have been replaced as the winery owner."

Stephen walked to the chair coaxing Pinot down only to receive a guttural growl when he demanded the dog to climb off the chair. He waited, repeated his command and Pinot stepped over Chardonnay, walked out of the living room, and out the kitchen door.

I looked at the lighted grapevines; the winery doors open with lanterns hanging from the ceiling. "Stephen, we all miss your dad, and I have been so selfish needing your time that you need to spend time with your crew, Maria, and your dogs. Each one of us needs to mourn in their own way" Stephen stepped behind me wrapping in his arms. "My growl is that I will mourn my Clara, my bark will be how I deal with the pressures of running the winery, and my whine will be missing you."

The phone rang, Maria now composed, announced dinner, then interrupted us and handed the phone to Stephen. He took the phone call out on the patio. "Really? He is gone, out on bail, off to his New York tower. What next?"

Listening, he watched me pour wine in each of our glasses, tip my nose into the wineglass and twirl the stem while watching his face. 'What do you mean the charges have been dropped? Just because he agreed to handle the bike repairs, cover the medical costs, paid flights back, he is redeemed? How can that be? What were you thinking?"

Stephen banged his fist on the table, "I don't care who he knows or how much money he has invested in the wineries he has purchased! We know that accident could have been worse, there could have been deaths, or some riders could have long-term recovery. I don't get it. Do the motorcyclists know this?"

"They dropped the charges?" Emphasizing, "THEY dropped the charges because of his generosity, or bribe might be a better word. I am stunned, disappointed, and shamed that we have bowed to this man."

As Stephen listened, I watched him open and close his fist, swinging it back and forth by his side. "You know he will be back, you know he will be the monster with tentacles gripping our vintners with promises of wealth if he buys their winery."

He nodded his head, shook it side to side. "I cannot talk now. I will promise you he will regret the day he meets me, my attorneys, the city council, our Congressman. I remember our high-school days when you were the one who always broke up the fights, always took the side of the bully's, and never defended the guy whose $100.00 sneakers were taken."

"Things never change, do they? The only thing different now is that I eventually got my sneakers back, and my spine. The motorcyclists are alive. I am grateful, but he will someday pay for what he has done. Do not forget my words." Stephen slipped the phone into his pants pocket, grabbed his wineglass, walked down the patio stairs, and stood in the middle of the grass.

Words Filled With Anger and Sadness

I nodded at Maria, who placed silverware, dishes, and water glasses on the table. Whispering, she said, "Mr. Stephen rarely gets angry, and I have never heard him threaten anyone. I do remember the stolen sneakers in high school."

"Mr. Ben talked with him right there on the grass, they were both sitting on the grass facing each other. I think Mr. Ben told Stephen had to decide what to do, which he did after walking around the grapevines until dusk."

"I do not know how he got those sneakers back, but the next day he had them on and was high-fiving all my family. He was too young for tequila but he was giddy, laughing, rolling in the grass, and chased Thomas Three after he took the sneakers and hid behind the wine barrels until Stephen found him."

"I worry, Miss Clara, about Mr. Stephen. Too many things have filled his heart with bubbles of anger and anxiety. Mr. Ben's death, his life celebration, leaving his ashes in the river, wanting to remember him with a memorial, running this winery, taking care of your winery, the appearance of Mr. Mildsgate, and anticipating you leaving."

"I know a heart cannot burst, like Mr. Ben's big vessel, but I have never seen him like this. When I pray with my rosary each night, I thank my God for your presence in our lives."

Maria sat and took my hands in hers, "I will worry about you too, Miss Clara. Alone in a big city trying to forget this valley life while you return to your very busy life; it will not be easy. Once you are here, once you touch a grape, taste a grape, smell the scent of a wine you produced, you can only miss this small introduction into life among the vines."

I put my hand on Maria's face. "I have so many wishes, Maria. How I wish someone would tell me what the right thing is. I wish that the stair-step had not broken at my mother's house so I would not have fallen. I wish my mother had not died, I wish Ben had not died, I wish I had not found Mother's mon..." Startled by my wine-tongue slip, I waited for Stephen to sit at the table.

"What did you find Clara? Did I miss something?"

Maria stood quickly, mumbling something in Spanish with distinct high pitches. "Dinner is almost ready; I will leave you two alone."

"Sorry, Stephen. I know I could trust Maria if the secret slipped; an emotional evening for us. I do not think she knew what I was going to say. I just have to think of other words that start with M-O-N."

Pushing the wine bottle toward Stephen, I teased him with the first word, "monarch butterfly." Stephen swirled his wineglass, "Monastery and I raise you with a monsoon." He slid my wine glass toward him, filled it while winking.

My neck and chest flushed with the warmth of his flirtation. Scrambling to find the next word, I suddenly found myself regretting the trip back to New Jersey. Clinking the wine bottle I half squealed, "Monopoly game, monster, and I raise you one with a monocle."

Stephen felt Chardonnay's nose under his elbow, "Mongrel, sorry Chardonnay, monkey, and monitor; yes, monitors whose silent sound announced Dad's death."

I waited, watched Stephen finish his wine, and pour another glass. "The New York buildings are monoliths, I always hated when Monday came, and someday I will have a monogamous relationship."

Stephen roared with laughter while I shouted, "I won, I am the winner. "Standing first, he lowered himself next to my chair, "Quite a monologue, Clara. I will be patiently waiting to have our initials monogrammed on this winery's label."

Whining, followed by my best pout, I said, "No fair. I cannot think of another word." I pushed Stephen; he fell back pulling my chair down; I fell onto him, and Maria stood in the doorway mumbling in Spanish, words merging a prayer with a lullaby and ending with an alleluia Bible chorus.

Stephen stated, "We have a couple of choices, Clara. We could roll to our sides and get up or we could stay like this and sip our wine through straws." Maria's sharp tone sliced the darkness, "Your dinner is ready, and if I put your dishes on the ground next to you like Chardonnay and Pinot they will never go back to their dry food bowls. I think the only choice you have is to get up, open the Cabernet Franc, and continue your word game over my Polo As ado and fresh Pico de Gallo. You forgot the obvious word, money. How could you forget money?"

We waited for the patio door to close, giggling. "I know we did not forget money, or will ever forget THE money."

Realizing our hunger, we returned to the table and began to eat. An occasional giggle or reminder about who won the word war ended with tugging a corn tortilla to wrap around the refried black beans.

"Stephen, do you understand that us and the winery future is not over, perhaps delayed? Do you think I could walk away from you and never talk to you again? Do you think I have someone waiting for me in New Jersey? Tell me what you are thinking, please."

"Clara, I know you have seen past loves over the past few weeks. Each required an explanation, and revelation of the past, a promise that they were a forgotten relationship. I need someone in my life now, not in the distant, unforeseen future. Your leaving me will leave a void."

He spoke with apprehension, "I will not give you an ultimatum, nor will I ask for a deadline. I want you to understand that I can wait for a reasonable time but not forever. I am not saying this to threaten you. I just need you to understand when you walk away from me I will be empty. I cannot and will not stay empty for long."

I stood and leaned over the table within inches of his face and, shaking my finger, said, "Now you listen to me, Stephen. I know we have something special, something that can easily grow in time if we allow it to ferment." He smiled, pleased at my use of a wine processing term.

"I have no idea at this point what I will do. I can promise you I want you to be part of my life though there are mountains, plains, rivers, highways, bridges, airports, and national parks between us. I would accept a deadline from you; my work is all deadlines. If you want an answer on a specific date, I will give you an answer about us."

"This is not just our relationship; this is my moving here, owning and running a winery, and leaving my friends at my work in New Jersey. I do not think you realize that I had a full life before you."

He put his hands on my shoulders. "I am being selfish, totally selfish. I want you, and I want you here. I do not want to talk to you by phone or e-mail; I do not wish to fit into your meeting schedule. Maria said you were talking to a Samuel the other day, a business phone call a romantic phone call. I will not ask but I want you to know, I want you."

Maria walked out with two plates of flan, shaking her head and, watching the shouting match, injected her own words. "Stop arguing, you two. Please stop it. You have had many glasses of wine, you have had a very long day, and Thomas One is asking me if you will be heading into the winery or would you like to wait until tomorrow morning. Stephen, I am disappointed in you. I have never heard you yell like this."

"Miss Clara, I just know that you would not yell at people in your office or, how do you call them, clients? Clara, you decide what day you will be leaving, leave contact information with Stephen and me, and that is all we can do for now. Stephen, are you listening?"
We looked at her. Scolding was not part of Maria's soft-spoken approach with anyone, not even her family.

I spoke to her quickly, "I apologize. I did not think we needed a referee, I appreciate your intervening. I adore you, Maria, I adore your family, and I have told you more than once I could never have survived my first few days without you. This is your home, and I have no right to yell nor should the crew have to listen to the two of us argue.

Maria placed the dessert in front of each of them with a French Press filled with the scent of strong coffee. "No, Miss Clara, this is not my house. This house belongs to Mr. Ben and Mr. Stephen. Just as you, I am a guest, a privilege I will never abuse." She turned and burst into tears, the second time in one evening.

We ate our desserts in silence. Chardonnay moved closer to Stephen after hiding under one of the patio chairs during the argument. Pinot appeared, putting his head on my knee. The distance between them resembled two domestic canine bookends protecting us during our time of reflection.

My spoon hovered my plate looking for a safe landing, "I am sorry, Stephen, for my words. Tomorrow we will talk about dates, deadlines, and expectations. If you will excuse me, I need to go to bed." I stood feeling the numbness in my feet from the wine, kicked my sandals from under the table, and accepted the one Pinot gripped in his mouth. I thought I could make it from here to my room; I just need to take one more sip of coffee.

Stephen was next to me and scooped me into his arms. "One more arm transportation to celebrate our day." I felt the moist tongue of one of the dogs licking my toes. I nuzzled into Stephen's neck. "I will miss you."

He placed me on the bed after lifting the fan-folded blanket; my head creased the fluffy starched pillowcase. Stephen kissed my forehead. "I will miss you too, Clara, and

I love you." He tucked the blankets under my shoulders, and the bedroom door closed. He opened the bedroom window and before I closed my eyes, I heard the music and his voice outside.

"I think I love you too," I garbled. My eyelids closed as if tiny magnets lined my tear ducts.

While I Slept

Stephen walked to the winery, listening to the loud mariachi music vibrating against the ceiling speakers that had hung in the corners of the winery since he was an adolescent. He and his father discussed the soft, sleepy sounds of chamber music and the music's impact on the working speed of the winery crew. "Something upbeat, Dad," he remembered saying. "Something they would enjoy, get them dancing, singing, and clapping and I think it will make a difference in how fast they work."

He remembered the months of negotiations between Thomas One and his father. No matter what the arguments were, he and his father denied his request for an afternoon nap for the crew. Thomas One had grown savvy in Washington State labor laws knowing the government had approved limits for lunch, morning, and afternoon breaks. Thomas One argued that his crew fathers needed to spend time with their children and drive their wives to town for shopping or doctor appointments.

Ben agreed to paid time off for requests specific to doctor appointments or transportation if there were no other options. He gave Thomas One the responsibility of evaluating requests and the crew adjusted to the permission-required system.

Thomas One pulled the sealing tape from the dispenser and stopped to look up at Stephen. "I sent the team down to the end of the grapevines to look for wolf paw prints. Rumors started when several sheep were found dead along the highway shoulders with their throats ripped open and their intestines in the mouths of crows. The first rumor we heard was the sheep's death was the result of an automobile accident, but the sheriff feels it is a wolf."

Stephen leaned against one of the wine casks, "Do not even mention the sheriff to me after he released the owner and driver after the limousine assault on the motorcyclists." He proceeded to tell him about his recent conversation and realized that Thomas One had moved closer to him, taking a seat on one of the casks.

Stephen shook his head. "You know, since I have been an adolescent you have rallied as a friend? I do not think I have ever asked you outside of work to help me but you always have been there for me. Like now, you are listening, just listening, all I need for the moment."

"And today, no questions asked, you escorted us to the bank and today you came to the river when I was in the river saying good-bye to Dad. You are unique, Thomas, beyond working with me, being Dad's right-hand man, and protecting Maria. I am honored to know you, and will always consider you a friend."

Thomas One hopped from the cask, "If I was your friend you would have told me what was in the wine boxes. I guess you did not trust me enough or thought I would rob you, or maybe you just did not think I was enough of an equal to you to share in the secret. I knew what was in the boxes. I did not know how much, but I am not an idiot."

"The weight of a few bottles of wine did not equal the weight of twelve, twenty-six-ounce bottles of wine. You trust me to pack the surprise wine labels for Miss Clara, for overseeing the cash flow of our wine sales, for organizing the security for Mr. Ben's celebration, but I can see your trust has boundaries."

Stephen walked away from Thomas toward the bottler, "Understand me; it was not my secret to share. It was Clara's mother's secret. Someday Clara might choose to share, but it is not my place. As a friend, you must understand if you trust me with a secret, a problem, an unexpected need you can trust me. I will not share your confidence with anyone. A promise I will keep as your friend."

Stephen had not noticed the bottle of Sauvignon Blanc, candle, and wine glasses sitting on a cask draped with a colorful blue, green, and yellow shawl. Thomas shrugged. "I thought you would be coming out here with Miss Clara so I thought I would create a romantic setting. I only provided the wine. Maria added the final change. My Maria is such a romantic woman, lucky for me."

Pursing his lips, he began to blow out the candle. "No, let the candle burn, please. Honestly, I will need as many candles as possible in the next few months to soothe my heart. Maybe you can be my date?"

Pouring the wine, Thomas clinked his glass with Stephen's. "To love my friend; new love, old love, remembered love."

Stephen inhaled the wine, "Subtle buttery finish. Any problems bottling?"

"Yes, we really could not save two of the barrels, too acidic. One tasted like vinegar. Perhaps I could have bottled some salad dressing for you. We had enough of her Cabernet to take some cases back. I have hidden the ones with your special labels; I can take them down tomorrow for shipment. Did you think of all those labels yourself?"

Stephen walked into the direction of the hidden bottles, lifting one of the bottles. He looked at the small indentation on the bottom of the bottle. "Look here the punt has our first name initials. I had asked Maria to try to paint the bottom of each bottle. I do not think it was necessary to put them in a heart, with X and O's around them."

"Yes, the labels were my ideas based on moments with Clara. I want her to remember me, remember us, and come back to her winery. I hope the labels match her heart

463

when she reflects on our weeks together. I have no doubt you remember what each represents."

They took turns sipping on their wine, lifting each bottle, and placing it gently back into the individual cardboard holders. Stephen looked at each sketch, "The little chick, the hummingbird, the oven with a spiral of smoke, a jar filled with hair ties, the yellow slipper, a violin, and ... what's this?"

Thomas looked at the label. "It's the tail of a horse, Stephen. She believes her spirit is a white horse who has appeared to her during this visit. If anything the image will transport her back to us."

"She has mentioned something about a spirit, but I got a little confused because she wears the wolf claws around her neck. I know you spent time with her helping her understand that the chick lying on her great-grandmother grave was an offering from a wolf."

"I think now that Dad is somewhere in a spiritual world or a Heaven, or a perpetual cloud winery, I have had to think about this idea of a protector, an angel, a reflective self that appears as a reminder of security. I want to believe Dad is somewhere near, that the ashes I left to float down the river have morphed into him, somewhere. I am still trying to understand it logically."

Thomas placed the Long House bottles of Cabernet Sauvignon, Chardonnay, and Sauvignon Blanc in a box." Do you wish to put any of our wines in the box?"

Stephen swirled his wine in the glass, "Yes, but only one each. I want her wines to dominate her mind and all social conversations when filled with impressions of its quality."

Thomas held up the emptied wine bottle, nodding as he opened the Cabernet Sauvignon. "I do believe in a spiritual world. Not ghosts, not the skeletons of our celebration of Day of the Dead, but there is something beyond. I do not think it is above the clouds, or beneath the earth of the vineyards for the bad spirits, but that spirits exist."

Taking an audible sip of wine, the red residual stain on his lips, he continued, "I feel your father. I cannot define what that means, but I think he is watching us, you, his winery."

"I met Mr. Mildsgate, the bad guy, once when he came to Miss Clara's winery to buy wine. He is slicker than the hair gel my sons use."

"He has the smile of someone whose teeth would bite you, but he has something wrong with him, undefined and not noticeable but he does have one of those dogs that travels with him. Miss Clara said she saw them on the elevator in the building where she works. She seemed to think the entire building knew him."

"Be careful, Stephen, he is powerful and I do not want him to do anything to impact this winery. I do not think we have enough attorneys in the entire valley to match his corporate attorneys."

"I suggest you support the wineries, prepare vintners to destroy his evil, and work together as a united force to prohibit any future winery sales to the corporate conglomerates. I would start by making sure everyone knows who and how the motorcyclists were injured."

"Wasn't there someone at the newspaper that was a hopeful sweetheart of Mr. Ben? Call and ask her to write an article about the accident and invite her to your first meeting where you teach the vintners about the potential corporate consumption of our valley."

"I do not think you need anger now, I think you need to gather what is inside and make it work to the benefit of the valley. This is not just your battle against him; it is everyone's battle."

They heard a sound like a screech of laughter coming from one of the crew's homes, followed by a scream that had them running out of the winery, stopping, and staring at what they saw. Three wolves were sitting on the gravel at the bottom patio step looking at Chardonnay whose head was in a headlock by Clara. Chardonnay growled, whined, and lurched, but Clara did not loosen her grasp.

Stephen spoke softly without moving, "Clara, back into the house, do not turn your back on them. Maria is standing at the door; she will open it very slowly. All you need do is to step backward. Chardonnay may follow you; just say firmly, "Follow if not, do not try to hold her, just get yourself inside."

<u>I woke, found myself on the porch, facing wolves</u>

I heard Maria encouraging me to back into the house. I smiled at the wolves, I heard Stephen talking slowly to me from outside the winery. "Stephen, they are not going to hurt me; my grandmother has sent them. They might try to hurt Chardonnay, but as long as I am holding her, I know they will not approach us. I am not afraid; they are the spirits of my ancestors. Please do not try to shoot them; I think I can handle this." I directed my words to the wolves, lifted my claw necklace displaying the spiritual tie I had with my grandmother. I crouched low, almost in a crawling position, speaking to Chardonnay first and watching the wolves tipping their heads to the side before pointing their snouts at Chardonnay's trembling body.

Thomas One had pressed an alarm button in the winery that alerted the crew. Two pushes meant there was danger; the crew would arrive with rifles in moments.

Stephen ejected forceful words in a louder voice, "Clara, the crew is on their way with guns. If you leave and go into the house the wolves will leave, and they will not be hurt. If you do not, in a matter of moments, bullets will fly across the grass. I can see three of the crew near the front of the grapevines, and to your right, I can see four more. Clara, I beg you, please, back into the house now."

Once again, I heard Maria's voice, "Please, Miss Clara, move to me. I am right here waiting for you. Chardonnay, good dog, I have a treat for you."

With that, Chardonnay twisted herself away from me and ran through the open door. I sensed the wolves' displeasure in the disappearance of their evening meal as each stood, stretching their necks to me, almost touching the first step.

Maria whispered to me, "Miss Clara, by saving yourself you will save them. Do you want your grandmother's spirit wounded, do you want it to die and never visit you again? Miss Clara, listen to me."

I stood and began to step back almost within arm's reach of Maria when I stopped and smiled, pointing over the grapevines. "There it is, my horse, it is telling me what to do. I think it is protecting me from the wolves, I think Mother must-have…"

I only faintly remember the image of the white horse. Maria told me later that I had fainted, my head resting on her shoes, my legs splayed out on the patio. She said the wolves backed up, looked over their shoulders, unaware of the crew's rifles braced on their shoulders, and ran along the winery, down the path disappearing over the bluff.

I felt someone pulling me inside and heard the banging sound of the screen door.

I only remember pieces, waking mumbling to mother, asking grandmother to tell the wolves not to harm Chardonnay, and asking the white horse to wait for me until I return. I remember crying, sobbing, and pushing Stephen away from me. I looked at Maria and kept asking for a warm bath as I felt so very cold.

As I lay in a semi-conscious state, I heard Thomas One asking Maria, "Has she taken any medication recently? She had quite a bit of wine tonight and the combination might have been too much. Maria, did you hear her in her room, was she having a nightmare. What has happened?"

I felt Maria lift my head on something soft, perhaps her lap. "I checked on her ten minutes ago and she was sleeping with this notebook lying on her chest. All the covers were thrown on the floor, she had wrapped herself in a robe, and her eyes were streaked with black mascara as if she had been crying."

Maria's hand was on my head as she continued, "I was sitting in Mr. Ben's chair with Chardonnay and Pinot at my feet and she came running out of the room, looked at me with wide eyes and said I think they have come.

"Grandmother said they would come, I need to talk to them. She ran to the patio door, Chardonnay right on her heels. I heard the door shut and heard her voice saying, you have come, you promised me you would come. Tell me, which one is mother's spirit, grandmother's spirit, and great-grandmother's spirt. I am so glad to meet you."

"I think the wolves moved to her and Chardonnay when you heard the scream. What would we have done if you were not in the winery? She could have died, Chardonnay could have died, and I would have died trying to protect her."

I felt Maria's body shaking, felt her tears on my face, and someone else covering me with a blanket, a hand resting on my neck.

Passage of Vines: Clara

Returning to My Mother's Hospital

I felt my eyes fluttering and I tried to speak but I could not make my mouth move. Stephen whispered to me, "Come back to us, please. You have had a nightmare and you need to waken. I want to hear your voice; I want you to tell me who I am. Tell me whose breath smells like stale dog biscuits."

I had felt like I was in a dream; white horses, wolves, Mother, until I felt Chardonnay's tongue on my eyebrow. I struggled to pet Chardonnay but my hand waivered like a leaf and fell back on my chest. My words were blending, and I was aware that I kept saying, Grandmother hurt, saloon, cold, Grandmother, cold, glass, and saloon. I remember falling into another dream, yet I could still hear their voices.

Maria covered me with another blanket when I began to shiver; I felt a pillow being placed under my foot and Maria's stern voice, "Stephen, look at her toes, they are pink balloons with flaming red with blisters popping open on the top of her foot. What is this, did she fall again? How did she ever get her foot in a shoe? How did this happen?"

Stephen spoke defensively "She ran her foot into the edge of her mother's desk when we were getting ready to leave this morning. She never said a word when we were in downtown Walla Walla looking at sites for Dad's memorial. We have spent the day driving around as I showed her historical sites, we stopped and got out of the car at Pioneer Park and we returned here for dinner. Could something have bitten her?"

I heard Thomas, "It could have been a rattlesnake. We have them, and with our warfare with the wolves, perhaps the rattlesnakes felt they had free rein in our vineyard. I have not seen one here but I am thinking of the dead baby chick I found In Clara's vineyard. She and I walked barefoot through the vineyard on that day.

I heard Estavia's voice. "Somebody speak up, tell me where she has been and what she has been doing while I examine her. Someone call the Medics, I think we need to transport her to town."

I felt something tight around my arm. Estavia announced, "Her blood pressure is dangerously low. Where was she before this happened?"

Stephen's voice sounded distant, "We went to Pioneer Park, took off our shoes and ran through the park, and we stood on the bandstand, and returned to the car."

"Now that I think about it, she never put her shoes back on; she carried them in her hand. I did not notice anything different about her walk; she was running through the park with me." Estavia, can you tell what is going on with her foot, her behavior?"

I heard the beginning of Estavia's interrogation and tried to say, it is not his fault but my tongue would not move. "Stephen, how much wine did you two have?"

"I think two or three bottles over time. The wine is fine, there was nothing wrong with the wine, or if there were, I would be lying next to her. Somehow I always manage to drink more than she does."

I felt her hands on my foot as she continued to talk, "Her foot is hot, hot as a cup of brewing tea. Something has infected the foot, this swelling, heat, and little blue veins mean she has an infection that could be traveling to her body. Stephen, is this the foot that she sprained in her earlier visit?"

"Yes, it is the same foot. I do know that she took the medications that you prescribed and only initially had pain."

"I do not think she has taken any pain pills since the first week. But I must say I do not know except she walked easily and even walked down the bluffs to the river when I disposed of Dad's ashes."

Estavia raised her voice, "You took her to the bluffs and walked down to the river? Maria check out her room and look for any prescription bottles in her purse or the bathroom."

I could not hear if Maria had found any bottles but I did hear Stephen say, "Good boy, we can always depend on you to find something under a bed. It looks like the bottle is empty, Estavia."

"Stephen, it does not mean anything that Chardonnay found an empty pill bottle; it could have been there since her injury. It does not mean she took them tonight, but it is something we need to consider. I know you two have been together for weeks now. How is your relationship, and how is she adjusting to running the Long House Winery?"

"She is planning on returning to New Jersey in the next few days. I have tried to be supportive and understanding that her career is what she strove for before her mother's death. We have had many discussions about her leaving. I have promised to oversee her winery; she has promised she will remain in contact with me."

"Today, I did not give her an ultimatum but I did tell her that I could not wait for an indefinite time for her to commit to the winery and to..."

Estavia finished his sentence, "And to your relationship, Stephen?"

I wanted to say to both of them that I could hear them, I tried to move my hand to my ear but I would not move.

I did hear Estavia say, "Are you going to treat her like you treated me? Introduce her to the community, take her away on weekends, and just leave her. Stephen, what were your plans?"

I opened my eyes wide, slowly moved my hand to Stephen's face. "Someday, you will be sorry that we met, that I came into your life, that our parents knew each other, and that I drank all your good wine."

I began to cry and heard Estavia's scolding questions, "Clara, did you drink more than one glass of wine tonight? Did you take any medication when you went to your room? Was there a reason why you took the medication?"

"Yes, I drank wine, so much wine but it was so good. Yes, I took medication; my foot was burning, and sharp needle sticks were in my ankle."

Estavia pulled the blanket off my entire leg. "Clara, oh, Clara, how long has your leg been this hot, swollen, and splotchy? You look like a road map with the red lines running from your foot to your ankle. How long have you had pain in your foot?"

I bent my leg, trying to look at it by curling my head toward my chest, "I do not know. Sometimes it was hot; sometimes it was cold. I could walk easily, so I just thought I was responding to the weather or the alcohol. I have not done anything to it since the first injury. "

"I am going to have you admitted to the hospital to start a quick, intravenous antibiotics treatment that should only last a few days. Also, we will need to check if you have any possible insect or snakebites. You are very sick for the moment, but I believe that you will recover quickly once you have hospital treatment."

"I can't go to the hospital; I have a plane to catch in two days. I have scheduled meetings and my wine box will be waiting for me. Just give me some pills; I promise to take them. Do not put me in the hospital, please. I tried to push myself with my elbows, struggling to stand and felt the point of a needle piercing my left arm, I found myself back in a dreamy world.

Princess Vintner Awakens

I was confused when I heard Stephen's voice sounding like he was talking into a well; he was so distant.

I tried to move my lips but they felt like they were immobile, stuffed with cotton. My eyes tried to focus on the faces next to Stephen's leaning down and calling my name. I wrinkled my nose, a shapeless drop transformed into a white lab coat, or a hand flashing a light into my eyes, probing my mouth, or resting a cold stone on my chest. I would feel sharp jabs in my arm or a cool cloth on my face.

I was sitting up in bed, crunching a cube of ice, holding my mother's composition book when Stephen came in, I asked. "Where have you been, and what am I doing in the hospital? Everyone tells me I was so sick that I was in a semi-coma state, and you brought me here. I do not remember anything except hearing mumbling voices, being extremely hot, shivering from cold, my foot throbbing, and having dreams about my mother."

"Clara, you do not look like the person who came here two days ago. You look like the Clara that I love, disheveled, inquisitive, and I am so grateful to say healing. You have been a sick vintner, high fever, infection, delirium, and incoherent. I couldn't wait to hear your voice."
Stephen sat on the edge of the bed, ran his hand under my gown sleeve. I tipped my head to the side, "Stephen, I do not

remember even when I last saw you, or what we were doing, or where I should be going after I leave the hospital."

One of the nurses walked in with a bowl of soup, a cup of tea, and substituted the glass of ice cubes for a can of ginger ale. "Clara, the medication is wearing off and you will begin to remember everything. We kept you pretty sedated to reduce your fever, and you have received enough fluid to last you for two weeks. I hope to get you to walk to the bathroom tomorrow morning. But for now, sips, take your time, and I or Stephen can help you."

I challenged her, "I can feed myself, and I will be fine. I cannot stay here. I need to leave. I know there is somewhere I need to be." To show proof of my recovery, I tried to catch the wavering straw between my lips but did not have the lip coordination to clasp it firmly. Stephen put his hand on mine, held the can directly in front of my mouth, and pushed the straw gently between my lips. "You are going to be just fine especially when you can look forward to eating Maria's homemade enchiladas."

I felt the cold liquid drizzle slowly in my throat; my dry lips ached from the minimal weight of the straw. I smiled as a nurse encouraged me to drink; unaware that she had placed her hand in Stephen's pocket. "Stephen and I started our freshmen year together at college. While I was dissecting frogs, he had grape skins under a microscope. Remember,

Stephen the day you brought me some grapes to feed my dead frog?"

She smiled at me; I saw her slip a piece of paper in Stephen's shirt pocket. Stephen leaned in to kiss me, a kiss that felt like an intentional distraction from the nurse.

I moved my lips away from the straw, looked at her, "Were you in love with him?"

"No, I did not love him, but I would have loved to know him. A long time ago Clara, long before I graduated, married, had two kids, and now live as a single mom. Keep sipping, I will be back shortly."

I focused focus on Stephen's face. "Tell me are you the only blonde handsome man in this valley? How many girlfriends did you have? Tell me now, because I know that I will forget what you tell me until I am feeling better." Stephen sat back watching me and I began to relax into a light nap.

I woke frequently to questions from the medical staff, searching their faces before looking to see if Stephen was still sitting near. A short African American woman answered my question, "He went home Clara to sleep. It is one in the morning and he promises to return to have breakfast with you."

I asked, "Did you love Stephen too? Did you go to high school with him? College? Did you work at the winery?"

"No, Clara, I do not know Stephen. I am a traveling nurse who takes temporary assignments throughout the United States. I just left a year assignment in Hawaii and I am working my way back to New York to spend the holidays with my family. The plus of a traveling job is the flexibility of my schedule especially during the holidays."

I added, "I live in New Jersey and work in New York. I will be moving back when I get over the incident that has set me back. Are you married?"

She lowered the head of my bed, changed my pillowcases saturated from sweat, laid a clean patient gown over me maneuvering my arms through the sleeves without tangling the intravenous tubes, "I was married to my Prince Charming until I found him in our bed with my best- friend. Although it has been more than three years ago, I think I still am healing. Why do we need men or relationships? I am very cautious now and my true armor is travel, can't stay in love if you are miles away."

I listened, appreciating the soft, warm blanket and pillows positioned to hold my head like two soft bookends. "I will be leaving Stephen and I have not decided when I will return."

She nodded, knowingly, "You will know when you wish to return, and most importantly, you will recognize why you are not returning. I cannot explain the feeling, the emotional compass directing your heart seeking a balance between your logical self and the warmth of love. Now is not the time to decide, you have enough medication in your body to sabotage every transmitter from your brain to your soul."

"I know Stephen is quite the talk of the nurses; some knew him and some would like to know him. From what I understand, this valley has few men willing to commit to a long-term relationship. How long have you known Stephen?"

My eyelids grew heavy as I searched for words, "Not long; two days, no two minutes, no not two years, I think maybe two or three weeks. I think he loves me, and I think I might love him. Do you believe in spiritual guides?" Once again my eyes began to close as I heard her last words,

"I think you love him Miss Clara but keep your eyes open. I think you will be guided somehow."

My voice began to return I found myself laughing and talking loudly into the phone. "No, I cannot come before the corporate annual meeting. You must cancel it for me, and set up a conference call so I can talk with the number-one boss. I hope you have been giving him updates on my original planned return, and what has happened. Please do not be specific, I do not want to come back and face the typical sorrowful stares, like those I had to deal with when my mother died."

"I don't care if our number one client keeps calling and wanting my phone number. I have told him too many times that I do not want to see him again and how we left it weeks ago. Do not give him my number or tell him when I am coming back. I might need to get some corporate intervention from security. I think this guy is turning into a stalker. He calls me all the time, sends flowers to the office and threatens to have me fired if I refuse to see him again. I do not care how much money he has, how important his business is for the company, I will not see him again."

My nurse whispered to me in a soft voice reminding me not to get upset and to end the phone call.

I sighed heavily as I finished the conversation, "Thanks. I appreciate what you are doing. Yes, I have a bottle of wine for you. I may add not just any bottle of wine but a bottle from my family winery. One last thing, check on the company in our building owned by a guy named Mildsgate, you know, the red-haired man whose portrait is in the corporate conference room. I want to know everything about him before I return."

"Thanks again. Schedule the conference call, and I will let you know my timeline for returning."

I turned my head slowly looking at Stephen as if taut strings in my neck were preventing me from quicker movement. "I missed you; I had so many dreams about you and us. I think this medication is playing with my mind. I woke in the middle of the night and thought you were riding a horse out of the room and when I called for you, you ignored me."

Stephen bent over, kissed my face. I looked at him with eyes open wider, clearer than yesterday. Smiling he asked, "Was it a white horse?"

Bragging on my progress, "I walked this morning; felt good to finally put some weight on my foot. I am hearing I can leave tomorrow, but I need to follow up before I return to New Jersey. May I stay with you until I leave?"

Stephen clapped his hands, "Absolutely. I will put you to work putting on the final labels, and then a walk through the vineyard to see how the grapes are coming along. We will be harvesting after you leave and it would be a great winery experience for you to see how hard those grapes work to show off their color, skin, and sweetness for your wines. I will need to check with your physician to see what you can do but I have a feeling Maria is waiting to spoil you."

I heard a rap on the door, followed by a petite woman carrying a food tray, and a smile that covered her face from dimpled cheek to the other. "Miss Clara, you can finally eat a sandwich, but I did add a few touches to make this meal more appealing; a fruit cup, a chocolate shake, and a pudding. Take it slowly. Try to get more food into you. Now that all of those tubes are out of your arms you can move more freely."

Putting the tray near me, she pulled a creased newspaper from her blue scrub pants. I do remember us talking about our great-grandmothers.

"As promised, here is a newspaper from my grandmother's hatbox. She saved everything from her mother. Look at the advertisements; a condensed history book."

Pointing at the corner of the page, stained slightly with a tea color the letter was sent to the physician from Anonymous asked, *"How do I get a prescription for whiskey to ease chronic headaches and can I get denatured wine also?"*

The physician responded, "During the existing Prohibition, I am authorized to give you a prescription for whiskey, but you must have an examination first. Do not take denatured wine for any reason. Multiple poisonous additives added to grain alcohol as a result of a poisonous substitute. Please do not purchase it from anyone, you could die."

I asked, "Really Stephen, people drank poisonous drinks because they craved alcohol?"

"Dad loved to talk about Prohibition, almost as much as he talked about how he had the most outstanding Pinot Noir in the valley. Prohibition in Washington State started after World War I and ended in 1933. As the article states, there were opportunities to get liquor legally through a physician or the Catholic Church or a synagogue.

Bootleggers snuck liquor produced elsewhere over borders and supplied customers who could afford the expense."

"Most of the population could not afford whiskey or wine. They chose watered-down industrial alcohol, with a touch of color better known as the denatured alcohol that hired chemists used for coloring.

"Sadly, Clara, multiple formulas were created with poisonous additives from methyl alcohol to formaldehyde and these were added to denatured wine. Poisonous additives were not an act of the liquor syndicates attempting to beat the law but by the government. President Coolidge wanted bootlegging stopped. Hundreds of people died in the United States by ingesting poisonous wine."

"Because small amounts of wine and beer could be produced at home, an increase in the planting of concord grapes occurred in Washington. The home-grown vintners lacked knowledge of sugars and aging, resulting in wines with poor outcomes."

I dropped my pudding spoon on the tray, "Stephen, you are telling me our government poisoned people?"

A white-jacketed physician spinning his stethoscope in front of him like a steering wheel interrupted the conversation. "Prohibition, a conversation my grandfather lectured on every Thanksgiving after his third glass of whiskey."

Extending his hand with an introduction. "I am Dr. Jack and I have been part of the team caring for you since you arrived. I did not expect to hear the first words from your mouth to be about poisoned people but I must say I am pleased to hear you speak. You were a very ill woman with an infection that chose to take over your body with as a permanent lodging, but you are a fighter."

Patting Stephen on the shoulder, he said, "I think I know you and, Clara, you look very familiar to me, but I see this is your first hospital admission with us."

I smiled at the dark-haired version of Stephen, "I think you may have known my mother, Clarish, owner of the Long House Winery. Stephen and his father are my neighbors who own the Bennington winery in the valley."

"Yes, Clarish, I saw her several times in our emergency room. Ben; I remember him well. He often came with her. How are they doing? They were certainly a couple admired by our staff as symbols of love."

Stephen interjected quickly, "Clarish died months ago and my Dad died about three weeks ago. Clara and my father became acquainted when he visited her vineyard. We have become friends since my father died. Clara plans to return to her home in New Jersey, so I know she is seeking only good news from you."

Dr. Jack looked at Stephen resting his hand on mine, rubbing his fingers across the tiny blood draw scabs. I looked at Dr. Jack watching him move his lips without showing his teeth. "I see friendship is an unselfish gesture during times of death and sadness. You are both lucky to have found each other during this difficult time. To me, it looks as if Stephen is repaying your kindness by his attention to you."

Looking at my bedside computer he scratched his cheek that had a red, raised mark recently planted. "One of my patients admitted yesterday for hallucinations slapped me when I refused to take my clothes off and climb in bed with her. She was convinced I was her boyfriend who she had just seen on her birthday."

I wrapped my fingers on Stephen's hand squeezing tightly, "Dr. Jack was her name Susan? Stephen and I met her when she visited the winery with her boyfriend. Ben, his father, had an altercation with her boyfriend who possibly is the same man. Please say she is all right; I would love to see her if I could. She shared her sad life with me." We looked at each other speaking at the same time, "Did he have red hair?"

The physician looked surprised at our question, "Yes, I think he did and he had a service dog with him, a big hit with the staff. Do you know him?"

Stephen stood up, "Doc, I need to excuse myself while you talk with Clara and notify the sheriff. That man caused havoc in the valley and was responsible for the motorcyclists that came through the emergency room a few days ago. Nothing about him is honest and caring."

"Stephen, let me call the sheriff. I may have breached some confidence by sharing this story, and it would be better if it came from me. I will tell him of your concerns. Perhaps it would not be too late to catch him."

I began to cry, "No, Doctor Jack, this man has limousines, helicopters, and private planes. He could be anywhere now. I am afraid for Susan; please call the sheriff. Please, do not let anything happen to her."

My nurse came over to me, sponged my face with washcloths, and patted away my tears. Stephen knelt on the side of the bed whispering calming words to me. I sat straight up in bed and begged Dr. Jack. "Please do something now; her life may be in danger. She does not deserve to have anything else happen to her."

Dr. Jack nodded. "Yes, Clara, I will call right now. If the sheriff has any questions, I will be happy to answer them or ask my staff to be available. What were we thinking?

He left quickly, leaving his stethoscope lying on the end of my bed, like an uncoiled snake.

Bootlegging Grandmother Margaret

Stephen looked at the departing physician wishing to offer additional information, then quickly that I remained sitting up in bed needing attention. "I can quiz you on Prohibition, or we can finish reading the newspaper together, or I can just sit here and smile at you. Which do you choose?"

I laid my head on his shoulder, "Stephen, does this mean that as we go forward with our lives there will be no tragedy, no deaths, no bad people trying to destroy other people's lives? I feel as if I have lived a film festival of short movies over these past weeks. Features included life, death, happiness, sadness, abuse, high-school romance revisited, Native-American history, spirit sightings, and drinking parties. Are we through for now?"

Returning to the newspaper, he read. "Look at these advertisements, bottles of liquor, cigar-smoking men, a woman in a flapper dress and a gramophone. What does this mean?" 'Enjoy spirits within the confines of your local speakeasy. Entry only with your secret password, join us soon'.

"A speakeasy was an illegal salon where someone needed a password to get inside. I would find it unusual that your grandmother went to a speakeasy. It was long past women's suffrage but, unless she was a bootlegger, it's doubtful she was a regular. I am sure there was some amazing jazz played by African-American musicians; I would pay big money to listen to that quality of music today."

I nodded. "My grandmother was a victim of the Spanish flu, I do know that she survived but my mother said she had become so weak her work as the "innocent-looking but profitable bootlegger" ended. Originally, she delivered wine to physicians who wrote prescriptions for medicinal purposes, and to the churches. Who would have thought my sweet grandmother was a secret seller? The Depression ended her job at the local cannery. After Prohibition and the beginning of World War II, she found work sewing bandages to support our troops. She needed the money, or why else would she have taken a risky job?"

"I am not sure what she did or how long she could work, but Mother often said Grandmother never stopped helping others. She truly did not believe she was doing anything wrong by delivering wine during Prohibition. She felt everyone who needed the wine deserved to have it. Mother said Grandmother sipped wine during a Catholic service, her assurance that the angels were watching her."

"I wish I had known her while she was able to talk, to tell stories, to watch her, and Mother interact. Those memories are from only toddler moments. By the time I was in elementary school, she was not speaking. How can one person have so many sad memories?"

Stephen looked up from the newspaper, "Look here, the Walla Walla symphony had a performance at the college. The symphony is still performing and I must hear their Christmas performance this year. I dread the holidays without Dad, all of the traditions. Choral music filled our house, and he was quite a Santa to our team's families. Now that I think about it, I cannot imagine future holidays in our house without his off-key Christmas carols."

Stephen paused and I moved his face toward mine. "I will be lonely, too. Even with the glorious celebrations of New York City."

He became more solemn, "Tell me Clara what a New York Christmas visit would be for me? Would there be giant basketball ornaments on the trees in Rockefeller Center, would you wear a red wool jacket trimmed in white fur and pull me around the perimeter of the ice rink? Would we offer Santa a sip from our flasks as we each shared a seat on his red pant legs for a photograph?"

"Did your mother ever talk about romantic interests with your grandmother?"

I sighed knowingly. "Somehow men were never part of our conversations. I do not know who my father is; mother only said grandmother told stories of men she met but never specified any were her father. Does that mean we have one of a questionable history filled with loose women, uncommitted men, and fatherless children?"

He handed the newspaper article back to the petite food delivery woman. "Thank you for the condensed history newspaper. Clara wants to learn more about her family history. I will be happy to pass along any additional information you find."

Dr. Jack returned discussing my morning discharge with Stephen listening, knowing how frustrating it would for me. "Bed rest for one week. Her leg is to remain elevated on a pillow. She must return to see me after she has completed the antibiotic medications; any swelling or discoloration of her foot will require immediate admission and possible surgery."

"Doctor, will you be here in the morning before she is discharged? I think she needs to hear this from you plus I have a small thank you gift for you."

I heard Dr. Jack's voice whisper to Stephen, "She is beautiful. Take good care of her. I hope you convince her to stay and become part of this community forever. I will give you my private number. I cannot emphasize enough; a repeat bout of this infection could have consequences much more damaging. She could lose that foot."

"I am being as honest as I can, Stephen. This was a very serious situation. Wait until she hears she cannot wear heels, and she will have to see my colleague in New York weekly for six weeks. Do you know any of her friends in New Jersey?"

"No, I have overheard some random conversations mostly from her secretary. Clara is a very private woman. It would not be right to contact her secretary and ask her to align with us. Tomorrow you might ask one of the nurses to attempt to obtain an employer contact number. Someone besides Clara needs to know your number if you are needed in the weeks ahead."

Dr. Jack rested his hand on my leg, "I am on your side, Stephen. We need to surround her and gain her trust. I do not want to see her back."

I felt Stephens's finger on the wolf claw necklace and with a murmur, he said, "Spiritual wolves take care of her; do not let her get sick again. Send her white horse to watch over her. Tell me what I can do, please help us."
He kissed my forehead, nose. "I will see you in the morning. Sleep, my sweet Clara. Maria has washed your clothes, and we are all waiting to care for you. I love you, Clara."

The next morning was one filled with laughter and jazz music. My nurse had told me about the hospital volunteers' Sunday morning brunch and fashion show. I found myself clapping to the music when one of my nurses stood in front of me in a vintage dress. She had a leg on the end of my bed, a visible garter held her nylons, a brilliant emerald short dress rested above her knee in while she juggled a pack of candy cigarettes and a tube of lipstick. She put her feathered hat on my head, "Go on, Clara, try it on. If

I have to wear this dress all day to advertise the fashion show the least you can do is put the hat on."

I looked in the mirror, placed the hat on my head lopsided with the feather landing in the middle of my face like a beak. "Now the glasses, Clara, you must finish this look with the horn-rimmed glasses."

I placed the glasses over my feathered nose, "Do it again. Dance as they did when my grandmother was a girl."

Stephen walked into the room. "Is it my turn to sing?" He chirped an off-key bass operatic tone to the two of us, followed by a deep bow.

When I heard his voice, my laugh became pure excitement to see him. "Look, Stephen, my nurse is a model for the weekend fashion show. Do you think we could go and support the volunteer foundation? Costumes are optional but it might be fun to dress up a little."

"What would you like to wear from the Prohibition era? Maybe you can be a gambler or a bartender. Maybe you can carry a flask with our favorite wine. I could cut my hair short, and wear gaudy makeup."

He took the glasses from my face so he could look at my wide-eyed look. "We will need to follow the doctor's orders. If you are still on bed rest, I can certainly contribute in our names, or perhaps we should donate in your family's name."

I pouted, "Stephen, such fun we could have for one evening traveling back in time."

My nurse spoke, "I have to agree with Stephen, you need to stay off your feet. "

I tried to wiggle out of the covers, my patient gown falling off one of my shoulders, exposing the wolf-claw necklace. The nurse looked at the wolf-claw necklace and scooped it on the tips of her fingers, "I have seen this necklace before. Did you have a relative who was a patient here?"

I felt the tear blur my vision, covering my iris, toward the ends of my eyes attempting to blanket a memory, to protect me from the reality of Mother's mandated appointments that failed to offer hope, only facts that her disease continued to invade her body.

Stephen spoke up quickly, cupping my chin in his hands, salvaging the warmth of the drops in his human vessel of empathy. "Clara's mother came here for routine diagnostic tests but has died. Due to her illness these past few days, she did not realize she was in the same hospital where her mother died."

His lips perched on his hands, he whispered, "Clara, you have had a difficult recovery, but you made it through. Do not dwell on your mother's death, only focus on getting better. Today I heard your laughter for the first time in days."

"Stephen, my mother fought too. Why can't I hear her laughter?"

I rested my cheek on Stephen's hands; I rubbed his arms with lazy fingers that folded over each other at each movement. I laid my finger in the crease of his arm, moving against his skin like a pendulum lacking momentum. Slowly, I slid my hands up his arms, leaned forward, and laid my head on his chest. Stephen did not move. He knew he had become part of my emotional landscape, where I found comfort and acceptance.

I shared my drug-induced thoughts, "Over these past few days, I think I saw my mother and your dad, too. They were like a reflection in a mirror, gazing back at me. All I saw was their faces just watching me. Maybe they needed only to observe, to be assured I was going to get through my sickness, or maybe they were waiting for me to come to them."

I looked at my nurse, "I guess I was pretty sick. I remember so little, I just remember feeling as if I were in a swinging hammock; enough movement to keep me relaxed, and only when the hammock stopped did I wish to open my eyes. I cannot remember everything and everyone but I remember my Stephen."

The nurse balanced on the edge of the bed, her legs resting against Stephen, and spoke to me. "You were very sick, but I am confident you will not need to come back here as a hospital patient. If you would like to have any follow-up examinations at a different location, I will be happy to arrange that. I can have someone come to your home and you will not need to return here."

I looked at Stephen "I do not want to come back to the hospital. I want to leave because my heart is going to burst from the sadness of my mother's death. I cannot catch my breath, I feel like I need to lie down again. I just do not know how I feel, but I feel very sad."

I felt myself crumple in Stephen's arms, hearing the last of their conversation. He laid me gently on the pillow, looking up at the nurse.

"Stephen, she is fine. I just gave her a mild sedative before you came to prepare her for the ride home. She will wake shortly. I think she just needed to talk, cry, and remember. She is very lucky you are in her life, and you are lucky to have her."

"I recognized you when you came in, I have visited your winery. It's a popular place for the nurses around here. I am sure you will have fewer visitors once they learn Clara is part of your life."

A quiet rest, while a breeze rustles leaves

Stephen talked to Maria who was waiting outside the room and asked her to help me dress. He left to return to his car, leaning against the driver door, staring at the flagpole, the newspaper stands, and the latte bar, the barista leaning out of the window, the medical staff sitting on decorative cement stands, and he mumbled. "What am I thinking letting her go? Watching her leave, and maybe never returning?"

Stephen felt a nudge on his shoulder, Thomas One held a paper coffee cup. "Thought you might need this, Mr. Stephen. Let me know when you want me to unload the thank-you gifts for the staff."

Anticipating a hot coffee, Stephen smiled when his tongue felt the strong cherry and chocolate flavor of his own winery's Pinot Noir. Nodding at Thomas, he finished the cup quickly, and a sense of relaxation anchored itself in his tense body.

"I will lose her in a matter of days. I just have this feeling I may never see her again and I do not know what I will do without her. She may think she is strong and independent, but these last few days have shown how fragile and vulnerable she can be without someone to help her. I need to be that person, Thomas. How do I convince her she needs me?"

"Mr. Stephen, you cannot make her want you. Only she will feel how empty her insides will feel once she leaves the valley. I think you need to let her go, let her realize on her own why she needs you, the winery, and us. Can you let her go?"

Stephen walked away with his back to Thomas, and then turned angrily, "You are telling me to just forget her, forget every imprint she has made on my life, Dad's life, your life. I do not have the strength to let go again of something I love. With Dad, I had no choice; with her, it might be different. Who is going to take care of her in New Jersey? What doctor will she go to when she needs a follow-up visit? How will she know if her infection has returned? What if she has trouble walking or falls in her condominium and cannot reach her phone?"

They looked up, ducking when a pale-yellow Frisbee landed at their feet. A three-legged Border collie ran effortlessly toward them, its tongue hanging loosely from its black gums, his ears flattened against his black fur. "Belong to you?" Reaching down to pick it up, Stephen flipped the Frisbee like a fan in front of the dog's black moist nose. The dog sat bouncing his left paw in the air, staring at Stephen and twisting his head looking for his owner.

Licking the Frisbee, the dog brushed his tail back and forth, his mouth gripping the edge of the plastic scratched Frisbee edge, and he began to tug at the Frisbee while backing up slowly. Stephen held tight and pulled the Frisbee gently from the dog's mouth, avoiding the layer of thick mucus clinging to its edge.

"Not that easy. You need to run back to your owner and claim this Frisbee."

Stephen lifted his arm, bending it sharply with the Frisbee touching his chest, flinging it across the parking lot where it landed under a giant maple tree. Stephen waved at the dark-haired owner who patiently waited while his dog maneuvered across the cement, between the cars and finally dragged the Frisbee across the grass to him. He watched the owner who knelt next to the dog accepting a chin and ear rub. Standing, the owner and dog disappeared behind the tree under a cascade of maple leaves falling from the tree as if someone had shaken Nature's pillowcase.

He looked at Thomas. "Strange. What caused all of those leaves to shake down; there is not even a breeze."

Thomas smiled looking up at the sky. "Someone up there blew those leaves. Remember this moment, Mr. Stephen, and welcome the simple messages from the spirits that surround us. Listen for them, feel them, and know that your father is trying to be part of your life. Let him into your heart. He is here with you."

Costumed staff filed from the hospital to stand around the flagpole for a photograph. A pediatric patient in a wheelchair held the sign, "Volunteer Fashion Show this

Friday." Each model carried a sign that identified the historical character they were portraying. Another pediatric patient wearing an oversized green, operating room scrub outfit sat in a wheelchair. Holding a three-foot-long wooden spoon, he clanged a stainless steel bedpan painted in bright red colors, "Twentieth Century Woman's Fashion Show." The white hospital sheet covering his lap and hanging down his legs added additional details: Sunday afternoon in the hospital cafeteria. Proceeds from the ticket sales will help the foundation build a pediatric computer library.

Clara's nurse waved at Stephen motioning with her hands that Clara was still sleeping and lifted a gallon jug with a dangling sign, Prohibition. A tall, thin woman strained her neck like an inquisitive giraffe wearing a long, black dress with white cuffs and a white ruffled collar that spilled down the middle of her chest to her waist. Her hair, split in the middle of her head, was stretched taut over her ears. Occasionally, she pushed back the tiny glasses resting on her nose while balancing her sign, Susan B. Anthony for Women's Suffrage, under her arm.

A loud screech interrupted the procession, "Yee-Haw" a costumed cowgirl model slid sideways, jumping between the lines and hopping to the front. Balancing on a bright red hobbyhorse, she pulled the reins, shouted, "Whoa, boy" and stood near the child in the wheelchair who eagerly petted the horse, touching the felt nose. Waving her hat, her sign read, "Calamity Jane."

Wearing a striped, two-piece outfit, another model wore a chained license plate around her neck bouncing on her chest as she marched. Her sign read, "I called the Walla Walla prison my home."

The next model wore a black dress covered with a white apron. The hem of the dress dragged across the lawn, and when the model behind her accidentally stepped on it, the first model abruptly stopped and adjusted the lace doily resting on her head. Carrying a lantern with a battery-operated candle, she walked over to the pediatric patient and began to wrap his head in a white bandage. Giggling, he moved his eyes upward, while Calamity Jane's hobbyhorse nudged his cheek. He held her sign," Florence Nightingale," as she finished his gauze headdress.

Two models in military uniforms saluted each other, both wearing brown jackets with matching skirts. A baseball-shaped cap hid their eyebrows; their cards read, "World War I and World War II." An elderly man sitting near the procession applauded loudly, shouting, "I was there, young ladies; I was there." He stamped his feet on the ground, pumped his fist into the air.

One model wore a thin mesh cap covering all of her hair except her bangs; a leather apron covered her navy blue skirt and blouse. Balancing a hospital tray lined with tin cans labeled Walla Walla onions, her sign read, Cannery Worker.

The model wearing the white rabbit costume hopped on all fours on the ground over to the pediatric patient in a wheelchair. He took the carrot out of her mouth and began to beat the bedpan, her head, and his cheeks saying, "I know you. You are the bunny writer. My mother reads me your books before bedtime. "The rabbit stood up, pointing at her sign taped to the costume, "Beatrix Potter."

Following directly behind her was a model wearing a long plaid dress, carrying an armful of books with rulers sticking out from the pages. One book title printed in a large font on the book's binding read, "School Teacher." She tucked in three books next to the patient, pointed at the rabbit, and the little boy smiled holding up the books, each with illustrations of Peter Rabbit.

A model dressed in a rainbow-colored clown suit, a bright yellow vest, and deep-orange curly hair confused the observers who expected a laughing face. Instead, pale blue tears painted on her cheeks, her lips outlined in a white down-turned mouth, and she kept pulling out the empty pockets of her costume, shaking them, looking at the ground, and shaking her head. She pointed to the brim of her hat that read, "Great Depression."

Stephen stepped closer when the model appeared wearing a harnessed wine cask that started inches from her shoulders, and inches below her thighs. "I think I know her, Thomas. She looks familiar, maybe from my viticulture class?" He stopped when he recognized her as the student who had accused him of raping her at a fraternity party during his freshman year. Stephen remembered the police coming to the house and sitting in the living room answering multiple questions, accusations, and later meeting at the family attorney's office.

Thomas spoke, "It is her, the vintner's venomous daughter. I will never forget how her father attempted to ruin you and your father's reputation by creating a false scenario. You were confused because you had to admit that you had been drinking after celebrating your final class in the early morning. If I remember correctly, your first overindulging drinking experience resulted in you passed out in your dad's car. We found you at the end of the driveway, lying across the passenger seat. Fortunately, one of your friends had followed you home, and called us to let us know you may need some help getting into the house."

"Your dad's attorney knew exactly what facts were needed to establish innocence. A basic female examination showed that nothing had disrupted her virginity. "Thomas turned red as he continued to talk. "I thought your father would never get through the embarrassment of driving to court each day, sitting behind you in the courthouse, and listening to the lies from not only the vintner's daughter but also other winery owners determined to ruin his career. You know he always believed you, and never thought you were lying."

"Our local doctor looked straight at the daughter and told her that her story was not true. He told her he had delivered her as a baby, knew her mother and father, and did not understand how she could tell this false story to so many people. Harvest season came, the work buried the wineries, and eventually, everyone forgot. I think she left the valley for a while, returned to work in the family winery. I do not think she returned to finish her degree."

Stephen nudged Thomas when the model stepped out of the wine cask with a pregnant profile. Stephen smiled with his closed lips. Thomas turned around and laughed so hard he was afraid to face the model.

The pediatric patient began to beat the bedpan in a slow, rhythmic fashion when the next model walked out dressed in a leather Native-American dress. She wore a simple turquoise band around her hair braided in two long braids. Her sign read "MaMinny, Long House Winery." Stephen smiled, whistled and Thomas joined in shouting approval of the costume. She walked up to Stephen, "My grandmother knew Clara's great-grandmother. I honor her; I honor Clara who I understand leaves for home today. Call me if I can do anything for her once she goes home."

Thomas held his breath anticipating a card stuffed into Stephen's hand with a phone number, or shard of paper tucked in his shirt pocket, but she only nodded and stood at the end of the line.

The pediatric patients waved tickets above his head; the models dispersed after their group photograph and approached the families and visitors who had observed their parade of fashion. Clara's nurse came up to Stephen with her tickets laid out on her Prohibition sign. "I know you two cannot come, but if you would wish to support the computer library, it would be appreciated. "

Stephen placed a one-hundred-dollar bill on the sign, "Please give the tickets to a family that may not have the funds to attend. I would appreciate it if I could have a copy of that last photograph to send to Clara. I am happy to pay for the cost."

She placed the hundred-dollar bill and the donated tickets into the top of her dress, and left. "Clara should be ready to go if you want to return to her room."
"Thank you, I have one thing to finish and I will be up. Please do not let her leave the room until I come. I have another surprise for her and the staff."

Thomas disappeared and returned with a dolly holding two cases of wine. "Line them up and attach the balloons from the gift shop?"

Stephen watched as the pediatric patient attempted to wheel his chair over the grass. Stephen walked over to him, "Hey, I will make you a deal. I will push you back to the hospital if you will do me a favor and keep banging that bedpan for a special friend of mine when I wheel her away from her room."

The clown model was his nurse, who put her hand on the wheelchair handle. "Thank you. I can take him up to her floor, but he needs to get back to his room for his treatment, so it will be a short serenade."

Stephen looked at her, furrowing his eyebrows in a question. She continued, "Just a breathing treatment for his lungs to fight his cystic fibrosis that brought him here a few weeks ago. His breathing has improved and we think he will be going back to his foster mom at the end of the week. He is one of our frequent fliers and one of the stars of our hospital."

Winking at Stephen, she wheeled him to the hospital doors. Stephen chose to use the stairs to return to Clara. Visitors and models jammed the elevators and he did not want her to become impatient. When he arrived, Stephen saw Thomas working with the gift shop volunteer to attach thank-you balloons to the wine bottles that lined the walls from Clara's room to the elevator.

I was sitting in bed completely dressed when Stephen walked in. I stood and reached out to him, "Take me home. I want to be at your home, with your family and Pinot and Chardonnay."

I slid my hand into his. He smiled. "When was the last time I told you how beautiful you are? You look so relaxed."

Just as I took my first step, my nurse dressed in her costume appeared with a wheelchair. "Doctors ordered wheelchair only and that means to the car, in the house and outside for the next week." I began to protest, but the nurse put her hand up. "There is no discussion on this, no negotiating. If you are planning on flying back to New Jersey, you will follow these orders."

Stephen's arms scooped me up and put me in the wheelchair. Smiling I asked, "What do the doctor's orders say about being carried around by a handsome man?" The nurse opened the door, while Stephen pushed me through the doorway.

Rolling into the hallway, I heard the soft beating of the bedpan; saw the hallway lined with thank-you balloons floating from the wine bottles. We were both surprised to see the fashion show models holding a "Good Luck" sign in front of the elevator. "Stephen, how thoughtful of you to give them bottles of wine. What a perfect way to say thank you."

The nurses applauded and toasted me with empty wine glasses. I shook hands with each of them as I wheeled past. My lips began to tremble, "For all you have done for me and for what you did for my mother, I will always be grateful. Please stop by my winery someday; I would love to see all of you again."

Stephen questioned me, "Your winery. Will you be there to greet them?"

I ignored his question. After rolling me into the elevators, he turned the wheelchair and I faced the crowd of nurses blowing kisses at me as the elevator door closed. "Stephen," I looked at his reflection in the elevator door. "Stephen, I want to come back. I must go back to New Jersey now because that is my home, my friends are there, and my job is my only financial resource at the moment."

Stephen wheeled me to the car that Thomas had brought to the front door. Thomas looked at our faces. "Miss Clara, it is nice to see you. You look healthy and ready for some of Maria's home cooking. You have been missed by all of us."

Thomas held my wheelchair while I reluctantly put my arms around Stephen's neck as eased me out of the chair, turning me slowly into the backseat. Reaching over, he fastened the seatbelt, paused, and looked into my face.

"Clara, I understand. I am not the enemy."

"I am sorry Stephen, for being sick; sorry for having lived in a diva world, unprepared for the valley world" I didn't realize I was repeating my sorry mantra. "Sorry for accusing you of hiding my mother's mon…" I paused, knowing that Thomas had just slid into the driver's seat. "Sorry that I injured my foot, that I burnt the bread, sold Mildsgate wine, could not stop your father's death, help Susan or that my winery cannot self-sustain without your help."

I could say no more, my lips felt numb and I fell asleep. Stephen felt a tap on his shoulder and my nurse whispered, "It is the pain medication, and it's not her speaking. Be patient with her. I would recommend controlling her medication, slowly cut back on the dosage, and never leave the pills with her. She is very fragile for the moment and her body that was temporarily destroyed by infection is adding to her weak thoughts."

I felt the car start, and Stephen moves closer to me putting my head on his shoulder.

I heard the barking sounds and awoke to Pinot and Chardonnay waiting at the bottom of the driveway for the familiar car that brought Stephen home. I rolled down my window. Chardonnay put her paws on my hand, licking furiously. "Goodness, Stephen, even the dogs missed me, and I do not have a treat to give them."

Thomas leaned over the seat and handed me two dog biscuits. "I am always, prepared, Miss Clara. You'll learn to keep some in your pocket, purse, and even inside your boots in the wet weather."

I laughed as the dogs pulverized the biscuits into small pieces as the car moved toward the winery. "The valet at my condominium keeps an old fishbowl filled with dog and cat treats. I often contribute a bag; there are plenty of animals in my building. I do not have to worry about wolves; I just need to watch where I am walking for the occasional accident on the marble-tiled entrance. One of the owners slipped on poodle poop, broke her hip, and attempted to sue the building owners."

"The fine print on the contract stated no liability for property falls or injuries on the elevator, automatic lobby doors, parking garage, or city entry into the building. Based on the age of so many of the owners, the hospital might have gone bankrupt for all the times they caught their shopping bags in the elevator door or their scarf in the sliding lobby doors. The lobby staff keeps that marble floor dry during the snow season and constantly mops up the puddles from the melting snow, but someone always falls. I admit that I have slid a few times, but never became airborne. I guess I saved my falling for the Long House winery."

The crew stood outside, with Maria holding a "Welcome Home" sign. Everyone waved while Thomas Three played the accordion. The dogs had raced in front of the car and waited patiently for the car to stop, and the doors to open.

Thomas One took my wheelchair out of the car trunk, opened the door for me, and waited for Stephen to lift me out of the car. Seated in the wheelchair, I accepted the warm hug from Maria, and the crew's handshakes and greetings. Estavia was drinking a glass of wine in the living room waiting for me.

She greeted me firmly, "You may return to this living room as long as you promise to follow all of the doctor's orders. You must also permit me to visit you every day for the next week, and accept without any argument the help of Stephen, Maria, Thomas, and other family members." Smiling she said, "Raise your right hand."

I raised my right hand, "I promise; I promise. I need to get better so I can go back to my New Jersey home." Maria looked at Stephen, her family looked at each other, and Thomas broke the silence, "I promised Miss Clara your home cooking, Maria. Estavia, can Miss Clara have any wine?"

Estavia shook her head no, "Please, Clara not while you are on the pain medications. Let us give it a week or so and after you see your physician, you may be able to have a little wine. It is important over the next weeks that we give your body every opportunity to heal to ensure that infection does not return."

Stephen lifted me onto the couch and Maria immediately put pillows behind my back. Stephen lifted my legs, placing pillows under my knees and feet, and covered me with a blanket. "Supper on the couch tonight, Miss Clara, soon you will graduate to the dining room table."

Passage of Vines: Clara

The Bennington Winery Welcome

Everyone stood in the living room, eager to offer assistance. Chardonnay placed a toy on my lap and everyone smiled at the innocent, canine gesture. Stephen thanked everyone with a firm handshake, assuring them he would call if he needed help. He asked all to return to work.

Nodding at me, they tipped their worn hats and filed out through the dining room, avoiding the kitchen where Maria's dinner lined the counter. Some of the crew were her sons and they knew any attempt to pick a fresh corn tortilla would be considered impolite by their mother.

Stephen evolved into a temporary strong man, lifting me into the spa, bed, couch, patio chairs, and the wheelchair. He would stand guard over my healing foot, all medication dispensing, and listen to my unending emotional diatribe of the uncertain future, returning to New Jersey or staying in the valley.

Over the next week, Estavia's visits continued, excusing Stephen from my room during her exams of my legs, and pressing her fingers into arteries, checking pulses at my ankle, foot, groin, and behind my knee. She checked for any warmth or swelling of my skin, leg foot, thigh, and knee. She focused on my map of veins looking for red streaks or blisters.

Estavia gave Stephen positive updates and asked his assistance holding me while I walked the short distance from my bed to the door. Stephen clenched the buckled waistband she had placed over my skirt. He smiled when my hand slipped accidentally inside his jeans grabbing his boxers rather than his jeans. Giggling, I murmured, "Sorry, Stephen, wrong fabric to hold, although I do like the feel of silk."

Estavia coached me to shuffle with my healthy foot and pull my healing foot forward. I moved slowly on the tiled floor, sliding my feet across the tile wearing the new Alpaca socks Maria had knitted me as a welcome home gift. I reached to Estavia, "I am getting better. I want to do more. Can I walk to the living room? Can I stand on the patio to watch the sunset? Can I stand in the driveway and throw a ball for Chardonnay?"

She shook her head, "Tomorrow, Clara, you can walk from your bed to Ben's chair, twice. You cannot walk outside until I am sure there are no uneven surfaces that might cause you to lose your balance and fall."

Stephen responded in an insulted, arrogant tone, "Estavia, my winery is not our valley highway with potholes, uneven surfaces, and diminishing shoulders. That patio is as smooth as an ice skating rink. You are welcome to see for yourself." They left me sitting on my bed and walked out to the patio.

I could hear their argument, "Estavia, what was your point in there? Why would I ever put her in a position to fall or reinjure herself?"

She responded, "I just want to make sure that intentional or non-intentional mishaps do not occur. Keeping her here, wanting her to stay must not become an incident to assure she cannot return. Do you understand me, Stephen?"

"Estavia, we knew each other at a time when we were young. You know I have only praised your medical presence here in the valley. I will always be grateful for your help when Dad became ill. Why are you doing this?"

Her voice trembled, "I have not known your other women. I have heard through the years about your latest love, or as so many say in the valley, Stephen's conquest. I know Clara and we both feel that we could easily become friends outside of this injury. Do not hurt her, Stephen; do not find yourself in love with someone within moments of her departure."

"Clara is not one of us, not one of the clans who has lived here all their lives or moved here and calls this home. Clara has qualities that do not require her to have a man in her life; she has evolved into an independent woman who chooses who she invites someone into her life. Did you hear what I said, Stephen? People come into her life by invitation only. My question to you is have you received an invitation?"

Stephen's voice became more assertive, "I would like to ask you to leave. I do not know what to say to you and I fear I may say words I may regret. Please leave and I will tell Clara you will be back tomorrow."

I found out that Estavia had called Stephen and asked him to stay away from when she was with me. Stephen told me he did not understand her reasoning but made it clear to her that when I could walk down the path to the winery, I would become his temporary assistant finishing winery labels and finalizing the plans for the care of my vineyard when I am gone.

Maria greeted Estavia at the front door, inviting her into the living room where I sat in Ben's chair, petting Chardonnay and sipping a steaming mug of hot chocolate. I heard the patio door bang shut as Stephen walked out of the living room. I leaned forward to place the mug on the coffee table, gently pushing Chardonnay off my good foot, bracing my arms on the chair as I slowly lifted myself from the chair. "Good morning, Maria. Are we ready for our morning walk?"

Maria moved quickly to my side anticipating Estavia to scold her for her standing position but Estavia laughed and put her arms in front of her. "I am ready, Clara, walk to me nice and slow."

I slid my stocking feet across the tiled floor like a novice ice skater. Watching my feet, I responded to Estavia's request to lift my head and look directly at her, or the kitchen behind her, or the afternoon sun beaming over the winery.

I felt Maria's hand on my waist gripping the skirt's fabric, listened to her encouraging words, and within moments, I stood in front of Estavia. "Well, Clara, I would give you a sucker for your effort but our sucker jar at the clinic is looking pretty scant after the flu immunization clinic."

"Note to self, send suckers from New Jersey upon return to the office. Order them from Candy Heaven, rainbow suckers with cherry centers. I will set up an account for automatic shipments every month. Can I walk out the front door?"

Estavia held my hand and we walked the length of the hall. Maria stood behind me, tightening her grip on the belt as I took a small step from the house onto the pavement. "It smells so good; it smells like spring, but I know differently. I mean, I know that it is fall and I will be home for Christmas. Perhaps, I might even skate in New York under the magnificent Christmas tree."

I walked to the closest porch chair listening to her. "Clara, could you do me a favor and hold off on ice skating this year? You are healing, however, your muscles, tendons, and ligaments need time to become stronger. Before you leave, I need to make arrangements for physical therapy at a location close to your office or home."

I listened to the sounds of the highway, the distant barking of Chardonnay and Pinot, the Spanish conversations among the winery crew. "I missed all of this while I was in the hospital, and I know I will miss it more when I leave."

I patted her leg, touching mine, "My dear Estavia, where and who would have a physical therapy business in the middle of the city? Good luck finding someone. Please remember, I do not have a car, and spending money on a taxi may equal my plane ticket over the long-term."

She wrapped her fingers around my thumb, "I will not discharge you from care until arrangements are made for physical therapy, a physician, a pharmacy, and a practitioner familiar with your very serious infection."

I became silent, knowing how resentful I have been in the past of being controlled or told what to do. I understood Estavia was acting in her professional role to care for someone who left a hospital. I had no doubt the distance between unfamiliar medical doctors and the valley added to her concerns.

"I will give you the name of my family doctor who I have no doubt will cooperate with you. Will that satisfy you?"

I think Estavia sensed for the first time that I was not going to fight the inevitable rehabilitative care; however, my hesitancy from the beginning left her doubting my cooperation.

I twisted my fingers through my necklace and turned away from her, thinking I did not want to lie to her, but I know that I would not follow all of her directions.

I knew I had lied before, like faking the night in the hot tub years ago with my friend Lizzy and her boyfriend. I remembered how easy it was to lie and deny anything had happened after Lizzy left to use the bathroom.

I knew I had lied to clients over the years, promising I was the most qualified to evaluate their financial projections when I knew two other senior colleagues had the expertise I lacked.

I lied when I first applied for my position, stating on my resume I had an MBA in Business Administration before my thesis had been approved by my advisor.

Estavia nudged my shoulder, "Clara, this is not the time to pretend, or to make promises you cannot keep. I promise you whatever you choose to do when you return to New Jersey will not affect me. I would be lying if I said I did not care about you, but if I were you and if I were escaping this valley, I would say anything to assure I could leave. You do not owe me an apology, or your doctors, or the nurses who worked with you during your hospitalization. I ask only that you think about what could happen to that foot and leg. What would happen if you had another infection that would not respond to antibiotics? Please, think about perhaps losing an entire extremity, or spending your life in a wheelchair, or becoming dependent on someone to care for you. I know, Clara, you are not one to want a dependent lifestyle."

I pushed back, "Think we would have ever met if I ever came to the valley, or if Ben had not died, or if I had never injured my stupid foot?"

She turned my face toward hers, "I think we have met in some way, perhaps costumed in other people's roles. I feel I have known you for a long time." Holding my wolf claw, she continued, "Maybe we were wolf cubs, or two grape clusters hanging from a vine, or perhaps we were shopping at the same store in New York. I visited there a long time ago, loved the stores, food, Broadway shows, sidewalk vendors, but hated feeling like a human and easily crushed by the blindness of people scurrying, pushing, running down sidewalks, through subways, and across the streets."

I felt her scanning my body; my arms, bruised discolored maps where lab technicians stabbed needles into overworked veins, and intravenous lines flowed antibiotic fluids into my body immersed in a sea of infectious cells. When I looked at my face in the mirror before I left the hospital, it resembled sallow melted candle wax, cheeks and lips faded shades of pink.

I asked, "Do you hear the horse? I hear a horse. I would be so happy to see my horse."

Estavia followed my eyes as I scanned the winery grounds; first, the tasting room, followed by the winery, the patio, the teepee accommodations, and finally the vineyard. I wondered if she thought I heard imaginary sounds due to my medication, I was relieved when I saw Thomas One sitting on the carriage pulled by two draft horses.

Waving to me, he called, "Miss Clara, it is wonderful to see you outside. I have brought some of the barrels from your winery for us to watch for you during your visit home. Most of these will be ready for you to bottle when you return. I promise to take good care of them for you."

I remembered Thomas teaching me the history of the valley, finding Great-grandmother's grave with the lifeless baby chick, and his anger when I wrongly questioned his ability to speak English. After weeks of my hurtful, sarcastic, impatient question, we had slowly rebuilt our relationship. Slowly, I learned his quiet habits. Tipping his baseball hat when he called me Miss Clara, standing near to Maria in the house or hospital, touching her wrist with one finger, his chameleon eyes that reminded his sons frequently through one look the need to respect him, their mother and their employer, Stephen.

I dropped my hand that had eagerly waved back. "Estavia, no one, I mean no one, will accept the fact that I am not coming back, I mean not for a while, I mean, not until after Christmas, I mean, maybe by spring barrel tasting. Oh dear, Estavia, what do I mean?"

I put my head on her shoulder, accepting the protective hug. "Only you know what you mean, Clara. I think you need to go home, stay at home, and only then will you decide what you will do. You must go, Clara." She pointed at the spider web shimmering in a sun's ray. "You know, that spider began its journey looking for the perfect corners to connect the fragile strands, knowing that a forceful breeze, or a loud noise, or even a curious, sniffing dog would destroy its path. I have no doubt it hung on willingly to a fractured web, waiting, watching, until it once again could create its web. Weaving a memory of past webs, the spider anticipates a curious insect to devour, watching it struggle and die. Are you that spider filled with anticipation, Clara, or are you the curious insect who has chosen not to accept the invitation of the tangling web?"

I clenched her arm, "I know; I think I just needed to hear your words, "Clara you must go. I will, I promise, get a doctor, a physical therapist, a pharmacy, everything you said I must do. I will, Estavia." I kissed her cheek. "Thank you for being my friend."

"I will be visiting you until the end of the week, but then I am assigning one of the hospital nurses to continue with the visits. I am sorry, but the clinic needs me and I need to spend time with our community. I would like to talk to you each day, and I will get updates from the nurse."

"If all goes well, within another ten days you can start packing your bags. I think that by the end of the week you can start having conversations with your office. It would not be wise to talk with your assistant when you are feeling the effects of your pain medications. Perhaps you should start slowly, send a few emails."

I could not tell Estavia that in the past two days I had one conference call, reviewed a proposal for a new client seeking the company's services, and reviewed the firm's last-quarter bills. Estavia did not need to know that I was taking minimum medication and had started a list to pack.

"When can I go back to my winery?"

She shook her head, patting Chardonnay's head that had left a rubber ball wrapped in saliva at her feet. "Let's see how this week goes, how far you are walking by the end of the week, and what your pain level is. It will also mark the end of your antibiotics. Clara, perhaps your return to your winery to prepare for your trip home will become a celebration of healing."

I watched Stephen take the horse's bridle and walk slowly toward the winery. "Odd, Estavia, Stephen acted like he did not see me. It is unusual for him not to walk over here or congratulate me for sitting outside, especially after this morning."

She sighed as I continued, "He has been carrying me everywhere, and he is so strong. Have you seen his arms? I know that he does not go to the gym in town, I am sure his muscles are a result of all of the lifting he does. I have watched him move the casks, I have seen him stack the empty grape bins higher than his head, and I have noticed how effortlessly he puts boxes of wine in the truck for delivery."

"This morning he put me on the edge of the spa. While I was splashing the lavender-scented bubbles and sliding into the water, he tugged the towel away from my body. I was not completely submerged, I lay my head on the side of the tub with my legs floating. I know he got a good look at my bare breasts. I waited, no, I hoped he would touch me, but he did not. He looked at my face, tossed a handful of bubbles toward the top of my head, and said I will miss you so much."

"Clara, it is certainly none of my business but I assumed you and Stephen have been rolling in the sheets." I tossed Chardonnay's ball, dripping with saliva in the direction of Stephen who had unhitched the cart and was off loading the first cask with his team. "No, Estavia, we have only teased each other with our hands, kisses, I am still a winery virgin"

"Well, Clara, you qualified yourself as this property's virgin, but are you a New Jersey virgin?"

I watched Chardonnay follow Stephen with the ball in his mouth, waiting patiently for acknowledgment and another toss. "Estavia, these are questions you should have asked in my medical history, are you on birth control, have you ever had an STD, do you currently have a partner?" She waited.

"I have dated and slept safely with some amazing men in my life. The single scene is unending in New York, in the bars, social activities, building elevators, coffee shops, and shopping. I liked the men I have met, but none of them I loved. Stephen is different; between you and me as friends, I do have feelings for him. Leaving him will be the true test of my heart. If I miss him or feel, I need him, then I will return. If someone else walks into my life, things might be different."

"Tables turned Estavia; have you had any intimate relationships? Do you have someone in your life now?" Hesitating she swallowed. "I have loved, Clara, and I have lost love. I am not afraid to bring someone into my life again but somehow that person will need to embrace my commitment to this community's health. I do not need a medical person, although I changed my mind after I saw a few of the doctors who came into your room. Dr. Jack and I found the time to compare our medical backgrounds. I guess he decided to try out the hospital because he is the outdoors type, hiking, skiing, and the most important outdoor activity, wine tasting."

"I talked with him again after the hospital fashion show; maybe, if I am lucky, we will have an exotic date at the Boots Loose Tavern." She crossed her fingers.

I felt the warm blanket placed on my shoulders. I looked up expecting to see Stephen, but Maria stood over me. "The afternoon is becoming cooler. It smells almost like rain. I will be happy to walk behind you as your caboose while you return inside the house."

I stood and kissed Maria's cheek. "I will miss you the most. How could I have ever survived these past weeks without you? May I take the clothes you made for me home? I promise to bring them back when I return."

"Will you bring me back a pair of sexy high heels to wear for Thomas One?"

Estavia looked at the two of us trying to follow the conversation. "Not only will I bring you back sexy high heels, but I will bring you a beautiful negligee to go with the heels. If you would like them sooner than my return, I will send them to you."

"When will you be returning?" Maria continued to talk as she followed me through the doorway, past the empty dog bowls and over to the couch. Pillows were tilted on the armrest, a bright orange and green wool blanket hung over the back of the couch, and two dog toys rested on the cushions. I swatted the toys to the floor, eased onto the couch, moaning softly after elevating my legs onto the cushions.

"I do not know Maria, perhaps I should send them to you. I plan to send all the boys a gift in one box. Yours will be wrapped in beautiful scarlet paper with a silk bow."
I listened to Estavia's list of reminders to include taking antibiotic medications, soaking my foot in a warm bath of Epson salt before bed, walking only with assistance, and no alcohol.

I asked "Estavia, I need to have wine before I leave, don't I? I have missed tasting Ben's Pinot Noir, and Syrah, Cabernet."

Looking at Maria, Estavia spoke firmly, emphasizing each word loudly, "Nothing to drink until she is off the antibiotics and is only taking pain medication before she sleeps. Do not listen to her reasons for why she misses wine, or her promises that she will walk further, or that she will send more negligees. No bribes, understand, Maria?"
Maria winked at me while she began to walk toward the kitchen. "Yes, Estavia, and please do not forget you do not need to shout at me. I speak fluent English."

I laughed. "Last time I checked I was a grown-up woman, but something tells me I am being treated like a toddler whose hand is being held for my first steps. Estavia, I will listen to you, I will not bribe Maria, and I promise to be nice to the nurses who will be visiting."

Passage of Vines: Clara

Estavia hugged me, stepped over Chardonnay, leaned over the kitchen counter, and said something in Spanish to Maria that resulted in Maria throwing a towel at her and chasing her out the front door.

Independence

I closed my eyes, knowing another dinner would arrive shortly; another dinner I did not need to cook, clean up after, or even worry about shopping for the ingredients. I thought of how spoiled I had been, yet I could not wait to eat a hot pastrami sandwich, or a hotdog loaded with sauerkraut from one of New York's corner vendors.

I could almost see the maze of Christmas lights at Rockefeller Center. I pictured myself rushing down the stairs to the subway a block away from my New Jersey condominium, feeling the forceful shoves of everyone cramming into the subway train, the windows moist with heat, balancing, grasping the overhead bar, and avoiding the drunken stare from the dark-suited man who stood inches from me.

I had forgotten the subway rides, never able to sit, always standing holding my briefcase tightly against my chest filled with a laptop, wallet, cellphone, cosmetics, and work-related files that had consumed the prior evening. How was I going to run downstairs or stand on a subway train? I hope that my employer would still offer me car service; if not, what alternatives did I have to get to work?

I dozed, my chin covered by the couch blanket. Hearing Stephen's voice, I opened my eyes, ran my fingers through my hair, and wiped my lips with the back of my hand, waiting for him to approach me. Stephen, Maria, and Thomas Two were laughing and playing a riddle game all in Spanish. I realized again I could not understand. Stephen spoke Spanish and wondered why he did not speak to Estavia or his crew in Spanish when I was around him.

I sat up, watching him point at Thomas Two in charade-type motions demonstrating uncorking a bottle and hitting it over his head. Maria smiled widely after noticing me, "Mr. Stephen, I have not heard you laugh so loud for such a long time. It is wonderful to see you smile, and your laugh is like Mr. Ben. You must be relieved bottling is done; now you need to protect your grapes through the winter and babysit your barrels and the adopted barrels." Hugging him, she waved to me as I swung my legs onto the floor, stood, and holding onto the couch arm began to move slowly to the bathroom.

No one from the kitchen moved to help me, Stephen put his hand up to stop Maria from moving. Whispering, he said, "She is fine; give her the chance to try. She has plenty of shelves, furniture backs, and walls to hold on her way." I reached the bathroom doorframe, filled with exhilaration after my successful walk but overwhelmed by sadness, too. I was becoming independent from Stephen and closer to returning home but somehow felt wrong. Sitting on the toilet, I listened to the laughter from the kitchen. I thought please do not make comments about the way I walked, or how I sleep. Occasionally, I heard the word senorita.

I moved toward the bathtub spa, empty, the scent of lavender floating through the room. The wall hooks that had held my clothes when I first arrived at Stephen's house were empty, stark metal twisted shapes. A stack of bath towels rested on the carved, wooden table; face towels and washcloths rolled into tight newspaper shapes stood in a woven basket on the second shelf.

I pictured Maria sitting beside me the first time I bathed, talking softly, sharing stories, and telling me how beautiful I was. Maria had become my special friend; I absorbed her compliments into my uncertain heart. Twisting the wolf claw necklace on the tip of my finger, I whispered. "Mother, what should I do, what do you want me to do? You never told me about my father; did you ever fall in love with him? I know you loved Ben, but would you have married him if you were not ill? Did you tell him you loved him or did you just know without saying words of love? I have no one to ask now. I cannot dial you in Heaven, can I? I think I love Stephen, yes, I know I love Stephen. But Mother, how did you live in the valley all your life? I do not think I can."

"I know your winery; our winery needs a committed owner. I do not know if I can learn everything about wine. My teacher, Ben is with you now. How could I ever know what he had learned over years of trial and error?" Patting my pocket, I felt Ben's leather-bound book, his recipe book to successful wine-producing and winemaking deep in my pocket.

Leaning against the sink, I pulled the book out. I began to read the first page with bold black ink stating "Seasons." Each page was smooth, without frayed edges or wine-stained fingerprints. I imagined Ben taking the corner of each page between his thumb and forefinger, folding it over the previous page, sliding his fingernail across his written words, pausing to find a phrase requiring clarification and printing each word in perfect straight letters.

I read the bulleted words following the heading "Mid-November to December: Complete pressing, stack barrels, map, and top off barrels." Momentarily distracted, I looked at my fingernails, chipped, layered with the same purple nail polish left over from Ben's memorial. Patience, my dear nails, a manicure, and pedicure are weeks away. I avoided tugging a stray piece of cuticle skin with my teeth.

I continued to the next season: "January to February, pruning, racking, and blending". Talking to the page, "Ben, I am confused. I thought you stacked the barrels last season, so why are you racking? I will need to ask Stephen if racking and stacking are the same "

My cellphone rang, deep inside my skirt pocket. I exchanged the journal for my phone. The tiled bathroom echoed as I responded to the caller, "I asked you to transfer the money yesterday. I do not owe you an explanation. The money belongs to me. I will not argue with you, nor do I need to give you an explanation. Transfer the money and I will follow up as I requested. I can explain everything when I return. I need the money transferred so I can finish a project."

I paused, "Again, I understand we have known each other for a long time and I have appreciated your direction following my mother's death but this is my decision. Do you understand?"

I heard their laughter again and looked at myself in the mirror. My once flawless, the smooth face had acquired a few wrinkles under the eyes, my eyebrows were arched in a permanent, dissatisfied expression, and my lips were slightly cracked from not wearing any lip liner, substituting glycerin that lacked the scarlet color I ordered from the boutique near my condominium.

Forming a comb with my fingers, I brushed my hair. I saw Mother's image before she had lost her hair. She was walking quickly through the vineyard weaving in and out of the vines, tasting grapes, tossing dried leaves to the ground, and poking a finger into the soil beds to access the moisture. I thought of Jessica, the wig designer, who created the natural, thick, ink-colored wig for Mother. I watched Mother try on her wig, looking over her shoulder, shaking her head from side to side, and testing the stability of the shoulder-length wig.

I grabbed the thick ends of my hair and pushed them on top of my head. I said to my reflection, "There will no pigtails or braids in a few weeks: just my professional look, perfect, unshakable, and predictable as I will be in my daily performance."

After hearing the knock on the door I said, "I am coming; I would like to walk back to the couch on my own, please." Maria stood waiting, a tomato stain along the neckline of her white blouse, a hot pad in one hand, and a frosted glass filled with pink lemonade in the other.

"Maria, my special Maria, what will I do without you? You know I will miss you." Feeling Chardonnay nudge my hip, I relented by saying, "I will miss you and Chardonnay."

I shuffled back toward the couch that Stephen blocked, holding a folded blanket in his arms. "My lady, I have been hired by the household to provide warmth to you this evening. If you wish more than the blanket, I certainly have the means to offer other services."

I accepted the blanket. As he pulled me closer, he murmured, "You are the only one I am permitted to keep warm in this house." I touched his chin and sat on the couch. Maria placed the lemonade on the coffee table adjacent to two printed papers. I reached for the papers, both identified by a cover fax sheet.

"Where did these come from?"

Stephen responded in a stiff voice, "Looks like your friends know exactly how to reach you. One is from William who has been trying to set up a date at your favorite restaurant. Oh, and Christopher says he owes you an apology and wants to see you as soon as you return."

I read the fax from William, my childhood friend, now a successful architect who had prepared a portfolio of ideas, my secret gift to remodel the hospital waiting room outside the intensive care unit where Ben had died. He wrote in staggered, nonsensical prose not wanting to give away my farewell gift to Stephen. "For you, whom I adore and others adore more. A penciled castle awaits your eyes; I cannot wait to see your surprise."

I shrugged, acting like a child who had left muddy footprints not on a floor but Stephen's heart. "William is my wonderful William, a forever friend. He is just following up on one of the projects he and I were working on before I came here."

The second fax from Christopher I quickly crumped and threw across the room. Chardonnay pounced at the opportunity to play catch ran to pick up the paper ball and returned it obediently to my lap. "Christopher is the colleague who was with Mildsgate the day we were in town after you met your violin teacher, Miss Taylor. He must have seen me as we drove away. "

"He does not want to apologize for anything, he wants to connect, and he will be the wine conduit to Mildsgate. How did he know to fax me here? I am sorry, Stephen. I gave your fax number to my assistant requesting limited access for colleagues and clients."

Stephen sighed, placed a finger on my nose. "I guess boyfriends fell into the limited circle." He walked out the dining room door onto the patio; I heard him scrape a metal patio chair on the cement.

Maria walked over, "You have not told him that William has designed the new waiting room or that you are going to pay for the entire cost. Why do you not tell him, Miss Clara? He needs to know your amazing gift is not just for Mr. Ben but also for him. Tell him, Miss Clara."

"I planned on leaving the waiting room design with a check in a wrapped package when I leave. The call I just received was my accountant arguing with me about the amount. His job is not to tell me what to do. It is my job to tell him what to do. Without hinting at the transfer of my mother's money I added, "I have sufficient funds to honor Ben with the new waiting room. I just do not want to negotiate with Stephen right now about my contribution. I want to do this and all he needs to do is approve. My friend, William, has connections in Spokane for obtaining approval from the hospital administration and Stephen. It will be beautiful, Maria."

"The room will be painted in shades of purple, Bens' favorite color. Any possible way to create an image with purple will happen. Sunsets, purple grapes, and cars on the highway, bottles of grape soda, a purple cow, and most importantly a painted figure of Ben will be in the midst of rows of vines wearing his purple shirt."

"The idea is to create a scene as if someone were looking out a window at the valley, everything from the hills to downtown Walla Walla will unfold in little scenes. Now here is the best part, the window frame is a simple white three-dimensional illustration. The receptionist in the waiting room will have two-inch whiteboards where families can write hopeful thoughts or memories. The little boards will tuck into slats around the window frame. Isn't that beautiful?"

"I told William about the memorial statue for Ben that Stephen will be creating. He loved the idea of including the wine corks signed by the community in Ben's memorial. He asked me what it felt like sitting in the waiting room with Stephen and if I had remembered any conversations. I did tell him everyone spoke in subdued voices. Often, I heard families offer reassuring words, prayers, and they made repeated trips to the reception desk asking for new information about their family members. I tried to describe to him the sudden silence that occurred each time someone in hospital scrubs walked through the intensive care unit doors, seeking a family."

"A coffee bar with hot water for tea or packaged soup will be on the opposite wall in the waiting room. Part of the money I am donating will supply the coffee bar for five years. After that, I hope that a fund will be set up by the hospital. "

"Soft lights will hang from the ceiling, reading lights next to the chairs, and quiet violin music will be piped in. Only violin music because I do not doubt Ben and my mother hears the music, they will begin dancing in Heaven."

"I am still not sure about the furniture. I think there should be plenty of recliners, big pillows with removable covers for cleaning, and love seats for two or three people. I know that everyone needs to have an option of showering, especially after nights of sitting in the waiting room. I would like to add a shower but I think that may require a little political manipulation from Stephen. I know I could have used a shower just from the emotional stress."

"I must ask, Miss Clara, is William just a work friend, or is he...?"

I smiled, putting my hand on Maria's chin, "No, Maria, he is not a boyfriend, previous lover, former husband, or an associate in my firm. In truth, Maria, William likes me, and we have a loving friendship. He does not date girls, he prefers to date boys."

Maria's blushing face matched mine. "I understand, Miss Clara, I do understand. I promise you we have plenty of Williams in the valley but they are very secretive about who they are until they can trust that they will be accepted. We have two vintners who are Williams, and one of our crew is William."

I shook my head laughing, "Maria, use the right word, gay, they are not called Williams unless that is their name."

"I will practice a word that is not spoken in our family. Please, understand we do not judge, we just do not talk about it. It was just like when Thomas One's father became ill, confused, and spoke to people who did not exist. We have never talked about how ill he was; we just lived day by day. I think it is okay, to live day by day don't you, Miss Clara?"

"Maria, I think I understand what you are saying but I cannot agree with you. I cannot live day by day. My time with all of you is limited. I have decided I must return home and tomorrow or the next day will not change my mind. Please, do not be angry or disappointed in me. I must because that is the only way I will ever know if or how much I will miss all of you. I did have an important question to ask you."

Maria wiped her eyes quickly, widening them in anticipation. "Maria, tell me more about the pair of sexy heels I will buy for you. Tell me what color you want and I will make sure you receive them before Christmas."

She heaved a disappointing sigh. I know she was hoping that I would ask her advice one more time on staying or leaving the winery. Resolving to answer politely, she replied, "I would like something with sequins, sparkling, to catch the Christmas lights when I walk down the path to our home. You pick the color, Miss Clara." She kissed my cheek and walked over to the dining room window, and saw Stephen sitting with her husband, Thomas One. Although tempted to join them, Maria retreated to the kitchen and found solace in washing the pans, banging them against the tiled sink, and singing in Spanish.

I realized sparkling shoes would not substitute for our friendship. I stood, acknowledging the strength I had gained, walked slowly to the dining room reminding myself to walk heel to toe with one foot followed by the other foot. I opened the patio door, held onto the doorframe, and stepped slowly onto the paved tiles. I could hear activity coming from the winery as the crushers, vats, and de-stemmers were pushed outside after their final cleaning and preparation for winter hibernation. The crew's children chased each other down pruned vine rows appearing like stark skeletons. The parcel truck was loaded with boxes of wine sharing the space with stacks of apple crates.

As he re-secured the boxes, Stephen greeted him with a handshake and a bottle of wine. Both the driver and Stephen noticed me, and they waved simultaneously using the same parade wave with their left hands over their heads. I walked toward them, head held high.

<u>Christmas at Bennington Winery</u>

Stephen met me at the end of the path and faced the driver. "James, please meet the owner of the Long House Winery, Clara."

The driver removed his gloves and extended his hand, "A pleasure, and a real pleasure to meet the daughter of Clarish. I know I am not the first to say this but the resemblance to your mother is breathtaking. I feel she is standing in front of me." After shaking my hand, he stood, stared at me awkwardly, and fumbled with a question, "How are your vines?"

Stephen quickly observed James absorbing me like a dry sponge that had fallen into a bucket of water. "She has not been back to the winery for a couple of weeks; she has been a houseguest," emphasizing, "My houseguest."

Without taking his eyes off me, James smiled, "Yes, you have your mom's smile and your hair, thick, black just like hers. Well, I mean until she lost her hair during chemotherapy. I remember delivering a box to her house from New York that had a caricature on the return label of a stunning black woman tossing her hair in the wind; I assumed it was a wig."

I sighed, remembering helping Mother put on the wig. "You are very right James; Mother ordered it from a wig store not far from my office in New York. The caricature was the owner, Jessica, who is an extremely stunning person."

James furrowed his eyebrows, "I am a little confused, you own the Long House Winery and live in New York?" Stephen put his arm around me, claiming his temporary ownership for the short term. "I will be overseeing her winery when she returns to New York. Clara is deciding what her plans will be in the months ahead."

James grinned, pleased at the news. "Clara, I have family in New York, who I will be visiting over the holidays. I would love to have dinner with you and perhaps a skate at Rockefeller Center."

I pointed to my foot, "Probably no skating this year while I heal, but I am looking forward to the noise, lights, congestion, and sounds of honking cabs. I live in New Jersey; my office is in New York, three blocks from Rockefeller Center. I would appreciate your delivering any packages to Stephen once I leave, although I cannot imagine future deliveries to my winery. Stephen has my business card; just give my office a call when you come to town."

I watched Stephen who kept looking at James and at me to see if he was facing a potential suitor, someone who would serve as a threat to him. For me, I had to create a space between Stephen and me, an emotional airbag. James swung his cap from his head, sweeping it in front of his waist, and bowed. "Until we meet again, my lady, and I have no doubt we will meet again." He handed me his business card.

I curtsied, balancing on my good foot, knowing that I would like to see him in New York.

Stephen stood silently staring at the truck that disappeared in a cloud of dust. "Nice guy, Stephen. I assume you two are high school classmates like all of your other friends?"

He looked my face trying to glimpse a blush of approval. "No, he is a transplant just like you will be someday. He left his family to come to Eastern Washington. He struggled with the distance between here and New York. He is divorced, but he does not discuss his prior marriage. I do not ask, although many of the single women are curious." Raising his eyebrows, he released the words that had built up in his mouth, "He seemed to like Clarish's daughter"

I shrugged, offering a reassuring but lying response. "Clarish's daughter was only being polite. She is not interested in your transplant friend."

Stephen pressed me tightly against him, sealing our hearts in a silent path of commitment. We did not speak; our wordless dictionaries were drained from feelings since my arrival.

Thomas One interrupted us. "Mr. Stephen, tell me what to do with the Chardonnay bottles from Miss Clara's vineyard. Do you want them in the wine tasting room in the holiday display or would you wish to keep them boxed?" Stephen asked, "Clara what would you like to do with your Chardonnay?"

I tugged at his hand and walked to the wine tasting room, chortling loudly, "What will I do with my Chardonnay, oh what I will do today?" Chardonnay ran up to my side, hearing her name and kept stride as I walked with a slight limp to the winetasting room.

We heard the Christmas music, and just as our feet stepped on the wooden floor, Thomas hit the light switch and the walls, ceiling, posts, windows, tasting counter, and mirrors twinkled with multi-colored Christmas lights. The ceiling lights chased each other in gold, red, green, and blue synchronized lights, the lights on the posts twisted behind and down in a vine, the counter lights hung down like illuminated drapes, and window glass cast a red glow on the tasting room.

"Beautiful, absolutely beautiful," Clapping my hands together I slid my foot along the floor, leaned on the bar before sitting on the barstool. I cannot believe I will be missing this glorious season. Can you keep the lights up until I return?" Stephen slid onto the chair next to me. "And when will that be, Clara?"

I returned his look with a blank stare and walked to the wine bottle display stacked in a vine-twisted wine rack, with each wine bottle numbered like an Advent calendar from one to twenty-five. Grapevine topiary held strung corks named, Malbec, Cabernet Sauvignon, Merlot, Syrah, Cabernet Franc, Carmenere, and Chardonnay. Carved wood animal figures, squirrels, chipmunks, and raccoons, poked their heads out from between the leaves, wearing metallic tags around their necks, each with the name of a crewmember.

The topiary planted inside a large gold-sprayed pot was filled with pinecones sprinkled with artificial snow, topped with cranberries, and rolled corn tortillas stuck out at intervals appearing like fingers. I picked up the white, carved horse standing next to the mother coyote with two cubs. Holding the horse in my palm, I turned and looked at Stephen; kissing the horse, I placed it back next to the mother coyote. I will never forget the night at Stephen's winery when the mother had appeared with her babies.

I noticed my Chardonnay wine bottles next to the display table. Lifting two, I ran my fingers over the black threadlike sketch of the Long House Winery, my winery, my mother's winery, my grandmother's winery. Rubbing the label with the tips of my fingers, I wished the wine bottle was a magical lamp. I wanted resolution, to my dilemma of living in the valley or returning to New Jersey. I shook my head, thinking I saw a horse's tail move next to the mother coyote I whispered to the bottle's label, "Miss you, Mom."

I cushioned the topiary pot between each Chardonnay bottle, stepped back, and admired their placement. Taking two more bottles from the box, I nestled one deep into the pinecone topiary and placed the other near the wine Advent calendar. Stephen stood behind me, "I knew our display needed the touch of a woman, not any woman, a special woman." He kissed the back of my neck. We watched Thomas balance on the ladder hanging the pure white flags each with gold lettering outlined in iridescent red. The first flag read, "Super Tuscan Blends have several grapes, Cabernet Sauvignon, Cabernet Franc, Sangiovese, Syrah, and Petit Verdot."

The second flag read, "Bordeaux Blends grapes include, Cabernet Sauvignon, Merlot, Malbec, Petite Verdot, Carmenere, and Cabernet Franc." Another flag read "Vintage Wine Blends." The last flag read "Rhone wine regions: Côtes du Rhône grapes include Marsanne, Roussanne, Syrah, and Viognier."

Three long banners shaped like wine goblets hung side by side reading "Pinot Noir," the second "Chardonnay," and the final "Malbec." Stephen pointed. "Our stand-alone wines, one grape only."

Everyone in the room applauded after Thomas secured the last banner. Stephen added, "In every possible way we try to teach our guests. Often the banners are photographed, a visual primer for our guests who return home. I hope our guests will be curious and begin to read labels. Sometimes I forget that wine remains a mystery and learning about it can make people uneasy, especially in a tasting room. "

"Typically, my volunteer pourers repeat the same description of each wine as it is poured. Although we follow a pouring menu at our tastings, we often find our guests skipping whites and asking only for reds, or asking only for white wines. We are always flexible but we try to encourage every wine taster to try something they have not tried before."

"We always get the conversation that our wines cost more than stores. For many of us, our wines are sold only at our wineries, which influence the cost of wines. I have been lucky to have distribution channels in Seattle and Spokane. With your wine in New Jersey, you might open an entirely new route for our wine and yours."

I read each banner to remember which grape belonged in which blend. Pulling Ben's leather-bound book from Ben in my pocket, I found identical pages matching the banners with details of the blends. Shaking the book at Stephen, I said, "It looks like your dad knew everything. I will treasure the wisdom in his book. I might have to tuck it into my briefcase to be prepared for any unexpected questions from my colleagues. I heard my name called from outside the winery. "Clara, are you in there? It is time for me to check your foot dressing for one last time."

I watched a tall, blonde-haired woman nurse wearing a hospital name tag, approach with her unbuttoned lavender cardigan sweater exposing the edge of a deep purple lace bra under her uniform top. The scent of her perfume formed a trail as she walked by Thomas One and his family. She reached out her hand to shake hands with Stephen and me.

"This is my favorite winery in the valley during the holidays. I think the vintners need to create a holiday decorating contest with prizes for the best-looking vintner, I mean winery." She threw her head back laughing and slapped Stephen on the arm. Her appearance had temporarily mesmerized the crew who stopped what they were doing to listen and watch her.

She looked at me, "Off we go. Can you walk or do you need Stephen's help?"

The heated attraction between the nurse and Stephen was palpable; I looked remorsefully at Stephen, "My leg is feeling heavy from standing. Could I impose on you to carry me back to my room?"

Stephen scooped me up; I rubbed my fingers on the back of his neck, brushing the tattooed letters, S C. Stephen smiled when I blew into his ear, whispering "Thank you, I will see you at dinner, if not sooner. I think I may rest unless you need my help." Stephen brushed my lips with his. "Rest,

I will wake you for dinner." He pulled the window down, closed the shutters, and left the room.

My Goodbye

The nurse had made several comments about how well my foot looked, praising Estavia for her excellent care. Occasionally she would look back over her shoulder as if she were expecting someone. I fell into a deep sleep after she changed my dressing. I dreamt of Mother, Ben, my winery, quiet moments with Stephen, my hospitalization, awakened to a moist tongue on my cheek. "Stop it, Stephen," I murmured. Chardonnay whimpered, nuzzling her face into my neck.

I rubbed Chardonnay's nose saying, "You have been my best friend since the day Ben brought me here. Please do not forget me."

Chardonnay moved aside when I heard laughter outside on the patio. Opening the shutters, I saw Stephen and my nurse sitting on the patio with one empty wine bottle on the table and Stephen opening another cork with a swift pull. She laid her head on Stephen's shoulder and he took her hand. While she held the wine glasses, he held the wine bottle in the other hand, and they began to walk to the teepees.

I watched them as they disappeared inside one of the teepees. Shocked, filled with anger, slapped with the reality of the Stephen I thought I loved, I sat on the edge of the bed, ignoring the toy Chardonnay had placed in my lap.

Angrily I said loudly, "It is best I know you now, Stephen, now before I left and returned. I found out that you are a liar, that the only person you love is yourself. Thank you for allowing me to make a final decision. Thank you for sealing my indecisive self's future."

After I pulled out my suitcase, I talked quickly into the phone, "Just pull up by the garage, I will be there. Thank you. I owe you a New York dinner." I placed the brown envelope with William's drawings of the hospital waiting room under my pillow. Scrawling quickly, on the outside I wrote "A gift for Ben, not for his son, Stephen." I left Ben's book on top of the pillow.

Within fifteen minutes, I slipped out the kitchen door and stood outside the garage doors. Nervously, I stood on my tiptoes looking for the delivery truck to drive up the road. Within moments, he was there. I threw my suitcase into the truck, balanced on the runner, and climbed in. "Please, go quickly. Please."

The driver, my new friend, James, jerked the truck forward, leaving a cloud of smoke from the back tires. Chardonnay began to bark; Thomas walked out from the vineyard, looked at the front door, and, seeing no packages, returned to the vineyard.

I tried to imagine what was happening at the winery, when and who discovered I had left. I know he would see

Ben's leather-bound book on the bed I am sure Chardonnay was either sleeping in my room or on the bed as I had closed the door behind me when I left. He probably quizzed everyone. Maria most likely spun around my room like a little hurricane looking for any clue to my disappearance.

I pictured the nurse walking into the house looking startled at all of the commotion. I would love to hear Stephen defend himself; explain why she was still there and why I was not. I hope that Thomas and Maria gave him disgusted looks, and left him alone with his guilt.

I felt a sense of satisfaction knowing that his action and my departure confirmed that our relationship had ended. As James drove, I asked him, "Please, take me to the airport. I have booked a flight in two hours. I ask you please; do not tell anyone where you took me. I do not want you to be involved."

James began, "I do not know why you are leaving the most available bachelor in the valley so quickly. It is none of my business to comment but I must let you know his reputation with women is well-known, I should know. I get all of his leftovers, broken-hearts, and rejected loves who want a long-term relationship. I am that go-to person, the not-so-well-known, not so-good-looking one, but the one who embraces their sadness. I am guessing something has happened here, or you are anticipating that something may happen."

I held my hand up and said; "Not now, James, I can hear nothing more. I need to go home; I need to leave the valley. Would you please drive past the buildings in downtown Walla Walla, I need to tell them all good-bye." We drove down through the main street of Walla Walla, the streetlights flickering into a wide glow in the dusk. I looked out the window at the architects standing outside the bank pointing at the future site of Ben's memorial.

The architects were measuring, balancing on a ladder to determine its height, and forming an imaginary circle with their hands where the locked container would stand. I pressed my fingers against the passenger window and whispered, "Good-bye Ben. Thank you for all you have done for me. Tell Mom I love her."

He honked his horn when the woman with the walker stepped off the curb, onto the crosswalk, and waved to the bus driver who nodded while waiting for her. She stared at James, shook her head, and continued to slide her walker across the pavement toward the bus. I recognized Miss Taylor, Stephen's violin teacher, slowly pulling one leg, followed by the other leg, onto the curb and disappearing onto the bus. I could see her shadow as she moved slowly down the bus aisle.

"James, I met her a few weeks ago. She knew Stephen and his father. She is a beautiful woman. I am so sorry to see her struggle to walk. Stephen had promised to invite her for dinner to his winery; I hope he keeps his promise."

James nodded, made general statements like "I see, I understand, I know, I am sure you have your reasons." I spoke quickly and repeated a sentence or story for lack of knowing what to say to a man who had rescued me, agreed to drive me the four-hour distance to the airport, and just listened to me.

Arriving at the airport, he asked, "Are you sure you need to leave tonight? Is there anything you want me to tell Stephen? Will you please call me and let me know you have landed, although I am not sure I even know where you are going or when your flight leaves. Clara, please tell me if there is anything I can do for you before you leave."

I touched his face. "Thank you for not asking, thank you for being there for me. I prefer not to say anymore, except I will be safe. If Stephen gets angry with you, I am sorry. You have done nothing wrong except make a delivery to the airport. Thank you, James, I will be forever grateful."

Sliding the door of the truck open, I slid down to the ground, turned around for my luggage "Clara, can I call you if I visit my family in New York? Do we still have dinner and ice-skating date?"

Holding my luggage firmly in my hands, I said, "Please understand, I do not think I will be ready to see anyone from the valley. I need to have the time to build up my resistance to what I am leaving, and what I will be facing after I return. Understand it has nothing to do with you: however, it has everything to do with you living here. I have your number and I will call you. Hopefully, I can see you again."

James pounded his fist on the steering wheel, "You are so wrong, Clara, you are making a mistake by leaving this valley, by refusing to see anyone from the valley, by returning to a world that will not care for you as Stephen did, and like I wish I could."

I smiled through my teeth pulled my luggage behind me and walked through the glass sliding doors of the terminal. I turned and saw James truck moving slowly behind a taxi and a pickup truck.

My carry-on luggage bumped into a curly blond-haired gray-eyed toddler with arms wrapped around his mother's legs. His eyes widened as the bump caused him to tilt back slightly. Just as his mouth began to stretch into an ear-shuttering wail, he stopped, pointed down at my feet, and giggled, "Big duck, you a big duck." I followed his chubby fingers smashing two orange crackers and noticed I still had my yellow slippers on.

Offering him a quick "quack, quack", I tried to decide if I should change into my stilettos. I heard the echoing overhead page that my flight's first-class seating was boarding so I robotically shuffled my feet toward my gate. Approaching the gate, I dropped my phone, grabbed it as it slid under the ticket counter, chipping my nail, and scraping the surface of the phone. Nodding to the coach passengers who were queuing to board, I pushed it into my briefcase and hurried toward the airplane door.

The flight attendant's eyebrows furrowed when she saw my slippers. She whispered as she nodded toward my seat row. "I know there is a story behind the slippers, tell me later. I did want to ask you if an aisle seat would be acceptable as the passenger who is sharing your row can only use his right- hand for eating as his left side is paralyzed. He said he would happily move to coach if it is too much of an inconvenience for you, knowing it will be almost an eight-hour flight."

Just as I was about to protest, demand, expect, my assigned window seat I looked at the passenger, holding a glass of wine and staring out the airplane window. A lock of hair gray hair peppered with white threads of hair covered his right eye, and his attempt to shake it away without putting his glass down was unsuccessful. I took my phone from my briefcase. I pushed my briefcase into the overhead compartment between two boxes of wine labeled Bennington

Winery. I wondered who had bought the wine and asked, "Is there any other open compartment?" I pleaded to the flight attendant. Shaking her head no, I accepted the bookend boxes.

As soon as I sat down, I opened my seat tray. I gestured to his glass, nodding he put his empty glass down. He mumbled as if he had a wad of chewing gum in his mouth to the flight attendant. "One for me and one for my seatmate please." He took his napkin with his right hand capturing the string of mucous that hung loosely from his chin.

These were the moments I savored as a first-class passenger, boarding first, plush seats, a flight attendant standing guard to fulfill all wishes. I was tipping my phone from side to side trying to decipher the last phone call through the scratched surface when she appeared holding a bottle of white and a bottle of red wine. Our hands clashed, my phone flew backward toward the coach seating just as passengers began to board. I remember hearing a frail voice quivering, and apologetic. "Oh dear, I think I stepped on someone's phone. I am so very sorry. Will someone please pick it up for me; I cannot bend down with this oxygen tank strapped to my waist."

Our flight attendant, acting like a school crossing guard, stopped the oncoming passengers with a sweep of her hand, hurried down the aisle to obtain my phone while another flight attendant helped the passenger into her seat. I repeatedly heard her apologizing, offering to pay for it, and wanting to know who it belonged to so she could contact them. As if the airplane aisle had morphed into a highway, she returned with my phone flattened in her hand. "Here is your roadkill. I am afraid very dead and very unusable. Were you expecting a call before we departed, or did you need to make a call? I am happy to offer you my phone."

My face became flushed. As my eyes swelled with anticipated tears, I shook my head no. "Thank you. I sent the last text I need to send at the airport before I boarded." The flight attendant sensitive to my appearance returned with a bottle of white and a bottle of red wine. "More white, sir, or would you like to try the red?" He pointed at the white wine, she turned to me, "And you miss?"

I asked to read the label of the red wine. Running my fingernail down the print, I found myself thinking about all I have learned about wine, winemaking, wine tasting, and wine bottling. How I will miss the wine community that took care of me and took care of my mother. I wonder if Stephen will still take care of my winery, or if he will refuse to even walk onto my property. I will call Maria when I get home; I need to make a note to myself, as she will probably be the only person I might talk to. I have to ask her if she saw the blueprint under my pillow. I know that no matter what, there will be a new intensive care waiting room named Ben Bennington with or without Stephen Bennington.

The flight attendant removed the cork from a bottle of red wine, filling a glass and handing it to me. "Let me know what you think. This airline only serves wine from this valley when it departs from here. I have yet to have any passenger complain about the taste". I inhaled the wine, twirled it gently, lifted the glass to the ceiling lights admiring the color, and taking a sip. I smiled, "The taste of berries is strong, and I there is a hint of chocolate."

She added in a low tone, "So are you someone who knows something about wine? I am always intimidated when the coach passengers ask me questions about the wine. Typically, all I can say we have white or red."

"I just inherited my family's winery. I will be the fourth generation owner. My winery produces Cabernets, Merlots, Chardonnays, Syrah's, and Sauvignon Blancs. I would love to see them served on your airline." I turned my ticket over, wrote my number under Long House Winery, and handed it to her. "Let me know if we can work together. I should be back in the spring."

When the Captain asked the flight attendants to prepare for take-off, she buckled into her seat. I found myself rubbing my fingers on my wolf-claw necklace thinking about mother, rewinding the past few weeks in my mind as the plane slowly lifted. I asked my seatmate if I could lean toward his window as I watched the vineyards in the distance and rushing cars brush colors on the highway. I wondered if Stephen was in one of the cars if he had thought to look for me. Probably not I thought. I pictured him grabbing another bottle of wine and disappearing into his laboratory by himself.

The plane made a slight turn, the wing tipping slightly to the left slicing the evening dusk. I saw a white horse galloping down the boulders. It was dotted with lavender sunset drops as it ran to the edge of the road. Was it looking for me? Was it saying good-bye? Why was it just standing so close to the highway? Oh, please don't cross the road. There are too many cars. I am up here. I need you if I return.

As the plane lifted higher, I whispered goodbye to my white spirit horse. My seatmate laughed, "I realize I have not introduced myself. My friends call me Benny or Benjamin."

Once again, I clasped my necklace, "Hello Benny, my name is Clara. I knew a very special man by the name of Benjamin, so if you do not mind I might just say your name over and over."

Benny replied. "You may say my name as often as you wish in the next hours. Thank you for letting me sit by the window. Two years ago when I flew out here I had no problem walking, talking, using my arms, using my hands but things changed quickly after my accident."

I wanted to ask him more, I wanted to know all about this Benny but I decided this flight was my bridge from the winery to my life as a chief financial officer I just needed to think about nothing but myself. I was permitting myself to selfishly worry about me, only me. Reflecting for a brief moment, I remembered James driving me to the airport. Sending my last text to Stephen, as I was walking toward the boarding gate. A simple ending to our relationship *"I saw you walking into the teepee with the nurse."*

The flight attendant tucked a pillow behind my head, gave me a blanket, and asked, "Do you always wear yellow slippers when you go travel?"

"Yes, doesn't everyone? Good night." I closed my eyes and fell into a quick deep sleep unaware of what had happened 30,000 feet under me.

Stephen shrugged, turned the steering wheel sharply, and moved ahead of the buses, leaving the airport traffic in jerking acceleration, and approached the highway. He held his cell phone to the right of his head, read the text loudly, once, twice, and was unable to finish the third recital. He looked at his speedometer accelerating at ninety miles an hour.

When he saw the white horse approach the highway, he dropped his cellphone, grabbed the steering wheel only to swerve and slide under the bus driving north. The roof of his car pressed against the back of his head, flattened on the steering wheel, voices and sirens echoed mixed with the smell of gasoline, he gurgled, "My name is Stephen Bennington, and I am a vintner, my father Ben died. I am in love with Clara."

Stephen remembers: As I look back at that night, I remember so little. I cannot remember where I was, what my name is, and where I am. It smells clean, I cannot move, I can see blurred images of wavering figures, I cannot speak, there is something in my mouth pushing against my throat. They kept asking me to answer their questions by blinking my eyes. I tried to understand words mashed together, demanding my response. I could not blink when they asked me if I knew my name, or why I had been at the airport or the name of my winery.

When they asked if I knew a Clara, I blinked my eyes as many times as I could until my eyes filled with tears, my body trembled.

And I raise my glass to....

My editor Carol Treston, whose perfection in grammar and story content assured that the accuracy of the words in this book, flowing like bottle of wine into an awaiting goblet. I am grateful for her patience, and her friendship. To the vintners who guided and taught me, Bart Fawbush of Bartholomew Winery, Warren and Julie Moyles of La Toscana Winery, Eric Dunham of Dunham Cellars.

My valued resources

Wine Making

https://www.vinology.com/wine-terms/

https://www.winemag.com/2015/01/20/wine-for-beginners/

https://winemakermag.com/55-aging-gracefully

http://www.madehow.com/Volume-1/Wine.html

https://www.waterboards.ca.gov/waterrights/water_issues/programs/.../wr60.pdf

https://www.winemonthclub.com/the-wine-making-process.htm

http://www.cavetocellar.com/spotting-a-faulty-wine/

https://winemakermag.com/674-the-joys-of-blending Tim Patterson

https://www.huffingtonpost.com/ross-szabo/5-facts-about-blended-wine_b_1857193.html

http://www.coffaro.com/WannaBeWinemaker.html

http://www.washingtonwine.org/wine-1`01/perfect-classroom/

https://en.wikipedia.org/wiki/Winemaking

https://missouriwine.org/print/268 *(wine aromas)*

http://www.gallowebcentral.com/glossary.html

Wines

http://columbiacascadewines.com/wines

https://www.washingtonwine.org/wine/facts-and-stats/regions-and-avas

https://www.washingtonwine.org/wine/facts-and-stats/climate-and-seasons

http://www.greatnorthwestwine.com/2015/06/30washington-wine-grapes Andy Perdue

http://www.washingtonwine.org,/wine-101/wine-basics/

Finding a Niche 2012 Brian J. Cantwell Seattle Times NW Magazine

Wine Spirits 2015 Andy Perdue Seattle Times Pacific NW Magazine

Washington Wines and Wineries: The Essential Guide, Paul Gregutt

Walla Walla Wine Country

http://www.wwvchamber.com/list/ql/wine-tasting-26

www.winecouWntrywashington.org

http:/ Washington-wine-country-maps.php

http://planwashington.org/blog/archive/wine-industry-blossoms-in-washington-state/

http://www.wallawallawine.com/washington-ava/

https://www.theclorecenter.org/dr-walter-clore

http://www.wallawalla.org/wineries/

https://www.washingtonwine.org/wine/facts-and-stats/state-facts

http://www.wallawallawine.com/about-appellation/

http://www.union-bulletin.com/things_to_do/food_and_wine/this-year-s-celebrate-walla-walla-valley-wine-festival-features/article_2156906c-22fc-11e8-b21b-635ff7f2dcdc.html

https://www.washingtonwine.org/wine/facts-and-stats/climate-and-seasons

Washington State History

Washington Territory Robert E. Ficken

New Land, North of the Columbia Lorraine McConaghy

Historic Photographs of Washington State Dale E. Soden

The Wine Project. Washington State's Winemaking History Roald Irvine with Walter J. Clore

http://www.historylink.org/

http://www.historylink.org/File/9630

http://www.hbcheritage.ca/history/company-stories/a-brief-history-of-hbc

https://eh.net/encyclopedia/the-economic-history-of-the-fur-trade-1670-to-1870/

Walla Walla History

http://www.frenchtownwa.org/jane-boucher-1820-1905/

http://www.nationalregisterofhistoricplaces.com/wa/walla+walla/state.html

https://www.wallawallawa.gov/images/depts/Develpmentservices/Historic_Preservation.pdf

https://www.genealogytoday.com/articles/reader.mv?ID=422

http://smonahan48.blogspot.com/

https://wallawallaunionbulletin.newspaperarchive.com/

http://www.wallawalla.org/business/frenchtown-historic-site/

http://www.wallawalla.org/business/whitman-mission-national-historic-site/

http://www.wallawalla.org/wp-content/uploads/2015/06/Historic-Homes-Walking-Tour.pdf

https://www.wallawallawa.gov/depts/parksrecreation/parks

http://www.wallawalla.org/wp-content/uploads/2015/06/Walking-Tour-Brochure.pdf

http://www.washingtonhistory.org/research/columbia/

http://www.washingtonhistory.org/files/library/magnificent-gateway.pdf

http://courses.wcupa.edu/jones/his480/notes/deth-dic.htm

Lyman, William Denison. Lyman's history of old Walla Walla County: embracing Walla Walla, Columbia, Garfield and Asotin counties

Whitman Massacre

http://www.mman.us/whitmanmassacre.htm

https://www.loc.gov/item/today-in-history/february-16/

http://www.fortwiki.com/Whitman_Mission

www.nps.gov

https://www.nps.gov/whmi/index.htm

https://truewestmagazine.com/narcissa-whitman/http://www.womenhistoryblog.com/2012/08/narcissa-whitman.html

https://www.whitman.edu/newsroom/whitman-magazine/whitman-magazine-fall-2016/the-untold-stories-of-walla-wallas-frenchtown

Chief Joseph

https://www.loc.gov/item/today-in-history/october-05/ Chief Joseph

http://www.digitalhistory.uh.edu/disp_textbook.cfm?smtid=2&psid=3502

Nez Perce

http://www.nezperce.org/

https://www.warpaths2peacepipes.com/indian-tribes/nez-perce-tribe.htm

https://yellowstone.net/history/flight-of-the-nez-perce

https://serc.carleton.edu/research_education/nativelands/nezperce/index.html

http://www.native-languages.org/nez_culture.htm

http://www.native-languages.org/nez-legends.htm

https://www.accessgenealogy.com/native/nez-perce-tribe.htm

http://www.native-languages.org/legends-wolf.htm

http://www.everyculture.com/multi/Le-Pa/Nez-Perc.html

https://www.nps.gov/articles/hbcmarriages.htm

http://faculty.tcu.edu/jlovett/US_econ_hist/Paper/Sample-paper-5.pdf

The Spirit World (American Indians) Henry Woodhead

Woman's Movement

https://socialwelfare.library.vcu.edu/woman-suffrage/woman-suffrage-history/

http://history.house.gov/Exhibitions-and-Publications/WIC/Historical-Essays/No-Lady/Womens-Rights/

https://mymodernmet.com/womens-fashion-history/

Winery resources

- Tero Estates trwines.com

- Bartholomew Wines
  http://www.bartholomewwinery.com/

- Dunham Cellars https://www.dunhamcellars.com/

- La Toscana (retired)

Excerpt from second book in series

A super moon hovered over the Eastern Washington Mountains like a planet-size flashlight beam, glowing on a path of farmhouses, barns, staggering wood fences, and windmills. The highway, within the shadows of the moon, snaked along with reflector posts and warning signs that directed cars, semi-trucks, and homeward bound tractors to diminish speeds as they approached curves. Sirens echoed from the stone crags, reflecting crimson red flashes sweeping the jutted stone wall. Ambulances screeched, swerved, listening to the radio call, sports car, and bus crash at Milestone 171, the sports car is wedged under the bus and the driver is inside. It is unknown if the driver is alive.

I, Stephen Bennington, owner of Bennington Winery am confused; moments ago, the moon was so bright, I could dial my cellphone as if I were walking through the vineyards in the early afternoon. Now there is no light, and I feel like I am sitting inside of a wine barrel with the lid tightly restricting my ability to move. I feel my cellphone in my hand, yet I cannot move my fingers, or my hand, or my arm, or my head. My neck is wedged between two soft blocks, my right ear is pushed into the one block reminiscent of the mat during my wrestling days, and my left ear can feel a pulsing vibration.

What is happening? I have to try to remember, where I was and where I am. I know I have not been drinking, or did I sip our latest release of Pinot Noir? No, no that was earlier today before I returned to the house and, and. yes, I went back to the house and Clara was gone, my love, my soulmate, my future wife had left. I remember jumping in my car, driving to the airport. I knew that was the only escape route for her to take a plane back to her home in New Jersey.

I remember the baggage assistant pointing to the starlit sky saying the plane had just lifted from the tarmac, while the commuter bus driver belched coffee breath threats inches from my face and pointed his finger at his bus blocked by my car, yes, I remember.

I began counting the text messages I left for Clara, begging the Native American spirits of the valley to assure that she would see the message before she turned off her phone. I counted twenty texts, ten direct dials as I approached milestone 170, only ten more and I would pull up the driveway to my home, my winery. I saw a flash of white along the road, standing, unmoving, as still as a statue. After noticing my speed was over one hundred, I slowed to

eighty and saw a pure white horse, pawing the gravel
on the shoulder, bobbing its head as if it were
drinking water. I glanced one last time before I
turned the steering wheel sharply to the right of the
curve; I looked in my rearview mirror, the horse had
disappeared. Why can't I remember more?

(Spring 2021)Passage of Vines: Stephen